PENGUIN

PENGUIN POETS
GENERAL EDITOR: CHRISTOPHER RICKS

HORACE IN ENGLISH

QUINTUS HORATIUS FLACCUS was born in late 65 BC at Venusia in Apulia. His father, though once a slave, had made enough money as a revenue official to send his son to well-known teachers in Rome and subsequently to the university at Athens. There Horace joined Brutus's army and served on his staff until the defeat at Philippi in 42 BC. On returning to Rome, he found that his father was dead and his property had been confiscated, but he succeeded in obtaining a secretarial post in the treasury, which gave him enough to live on. The poetry he wrote in the next few years impressed Virgil, who introduced him to the great patron Maecenas in 37 BC. This event marked the beginning of a life-long friendship. From now on Horace was free from financial worries; he moved among the leading poets and statesmen of Rome. His work was admired by Augustus, and indeed after Virgil's death in 19 BC he was virtually Poet Laureate. Horace died in 8 BC, soon after Maecenas.

D. S. CARNE-ROSS was educated at Exeter College, Oxford. A long-time resident of the United States of America, he has taught at Texas University, Austin, and since 1971 has held the post of University Professor of Classics and Modern Languages at Boston University. By preference an essayist, his publications include *Instaurations* (1979) and *Pindar* (1985). Now partly retired, he meditates a short book on Ariosto.

KENNETH HAYNES is a Postdoctoral Fellow of the University Professors of Boston University. He has written on British Hellenism and is currently editing Swinburne.

HORACE IN ENGLISH

Edited by D. S. CARNE-ROSS *and* KENNETH HAYNES
With an Introduction by D. S. CARNE-ROSS

PENGUIN BOOKS

PENGUIN BOOKS

Published by the Penguin Group
Penguin Books Ltd, 27 Wrights Lane, London w8 5TZ, England
Penguin Books USA Inc., 375 Hudson Street, New York, New York 10014, USA
Penguin Books Australia Ltd, Ringwood, Victoria, Australia
Penguin Books Canada Ltd, 10 Alcorn Avenue, Toronto, Ontario, Canada M4V 3B2
Penguin Books (NZ) Ltd, 182–190 Wairau Road, Auckland 10, New Zealand

Penguin Books Ltd, Registered Offices: Harmondsworth, Middlesex, England

First published 1996
10 9 8 7 6 5 4 3 2 1

Copyright © D. S. Carne-Ross and Kenneth Haynes, 1996
Introduction copyright © D. S. Carne-Ross, 1996
The acknowledgements on pp. xi–xii constitute an extension of this copyright page
All rights reserved

The moral right of the editors has been asserted

Set in 10/12.5 pt Monotype Bembo
Typeset by Datix International Limited, Bungay, Suffolk
Printed in England by Clays Ltd, St Ives plc

Except in the United States of America, this book is sold subject
to the condition that it shall not, by way of trade or otherwise, be lent,
re-sold, hired out, or otherwise circulated without the publisher's
prior consent in any form of binding or cover other than that in
which it is published and without a similar condition including this
condition being imposed on the subsequent purchaser

CONTENTS

Acknowledgements xi
Preface xiii
Introduction 1
Further Reading 59
Table of Dates 60
'To the Translatour' Sir John Beaumont 63

TRANSLATIONS

Odes and *Carmen Saeculare*

Henry Howard, Earl of Surrey: II.10 67
Anonymous, in Tottel's *Miscellany*: II.10 (two versions),
    IV.7 68
Sir Philip Sidney: II.10 72
Anonymous: III.9 74
Ben Jonson: III.9, IV.1 75
Anonymous: II.3 77
Sir John Beaumont: III.29 78
Robert Herrick: III.9, after II.14 81
John Ashmore: II.16 85
Sir Thomas Hawkins: I.11, II.3 87
John Milton: I.5 88
Sir Richard Fanshawe: I.5, I.27, III.1, IV.7 89
Dr P. [Walter Pope?]: I.27 93
Richard Crashaw: II.13 94
Sir Edward Sherburne: I.9, IV.10 96
Abraham Cowley: I.5, III.1, III.16, IV.2 98

John Dryden: I.3, I.9, III.29   106
Wentworth Dillon, Earl of Roscommon: I.22 (two versions),
   III.6   114
Sir Charles Sedley: II.8   119
Aphra Behn: I.5   120
Thomas Otway: II.16   121
John Oldham: from I.31, II.14, III.9   123
Richard Duke: II.4   128
Thomas Creech: I.17, I.28, III.18, III.23   129
Francis Atterbury: IV.3   134
Richard Bentley: after III.2   135
George Stepney: III.7   137
Tom Brown: I.27, II.11   139
Jonathan Swift: from III.2   142
William Congreve: I.19   143
Joseph Addison: III.3   145
William Somerville: from IV.9   150
William Oldisworth: III.6, III.30   151
Allan Ramsay: I.1, I.4, I.5   154
Alexander Pope: IV.1, from IV.9   159
Thomas Tickell: I.15   161
Lady Mary Wortley Montagu: I.4, I.5   165
Christopher Pitt: I.22   168
James Thomson: from III.5   170
Samuel Boyse: I.38   171
Philip Francis: II.3, III.5, III.25, III.29, IV.2, IV.5, IV.9,
   IV.10   171
William Dunkin: III.15, III.26   186
Samuel Johnson: I.22, IV.7   188
Christopher Smart: II.4 (first version), III.30, I.3, I.5, I.8, II.4
   (second version), II.14, II.18, IV.13   190
Thomas Warton: III.13, III.18   200
Oliver Goldsmith: from II.15   202
William Cowper: I.9, I.38, II.10, II.16   202
Robert Fergusson: I.11   207
Richard Porson: I.27   208

Susanna Rowson: II.17   209
The Young Gentlemen of Mr Rule's Academy at Islington:
    I.25   211
John Quincy Adams: I.22   212
William Wordsworth: III.13   214
George Howard, Viscount Morpeth (later sixth Earl of
    Carlisle): I.35   215
James and Horatio Smith: I.9   217
Thomas Moore: I.22   219
Leigh Hunt: II.12   220
John Cam Hobhouse, Lord Broughton: II.6   222
George Gordon, Lord Byron: from III.3   223
Alexander Pushkin/Vladimir Nabokov: III.30   224
Edward Bulwer-Lytton, Lord Lytton: II.14   225
Alfred Tennyson: I.9   227
W. E. Gladstone: I.14, III.30   228
Sir Stephen de Vere: II.16   230
Patrick Branwell Brontë: I.16, I.21   232
Arthur Hugh Clough: I.3, III.7, from III.4   234
John Conington: II.9, II.11, III.12   237
C. S. Calverley: I.9, I.11, I.24   240
Austin Dobson: I.23, III.7   242
Gerard M. Hopkins: I.38, III.1   245
A. E. Housman: IV.7   248
G. M. and G. F. Whicher: I.27   249
Rudyard Kipling: III.9   251
Ezra Pound: I.11, I.31, III.30   252
Basil Bunting: II.14   254
J. V. Cunningham: I.9   256
C. H. Sisson: II.14, from II.15, *Carmen Saeculare*   257
Robert Lowell: II.7   262
Anthony Hecht: I.1   263
John Herington: I.11   264
David Ferry: I.1, I.4, I.10, I.11, I.15, II.3, II.7, III.5, III.6,
    III.22, IV.3, IV.11, IV.13   265
K. W. Gransden: I.34   282

Christopher Middleton: III.13   283
James Michie: I.20, II.11, II.15, III.4, III.10, *Carmen
    Saeculare*   284
Charles Tomlinson: I.37, II.20   293

Epodes

Ben Jonson: 2   299
Sir John Beaumont: 2   301
Sir Richard Fanshawe: 2   303
Thomas Creech: 13   306
John Dryden: 2   307
Thomas Yalden: 15   310
C. H. Sisson: 2   312

Satires

Ben Jonson: II.1   317
Sir John Beaumont: II.6   321
Abraham Cowley: I.1, from II.6   326
John Wilmot, Earl of Rochester: I.10   332
John Oldham: from I.9   336
Thomas Creech: from II.2   340
Jonathan Swift and Alexander Pope: II.6   342
Alexander Pope: II.1   349
George Ogle: from II.5   353
Philip Francis: from I.6   359
William Cowper: from I.5   363
Francis Howes: I.1, I.4, I.9, I.10, from II.3   368

Epistles

John Milton: from I.16   393
Abraham Cowley: I.10   393
Thomas Creech: I.6   396

Alexander Pope: I.1, I.6, II.1 (with Colin Macleod's translation *en face*)   399
Philip Francis: I.5, I.20   434
Anonymous: I.10   437
M. G. Lewis: I.20   439
Francis Howes: from I.2   442
John Conington: I.1, I.19   443
K. W. Gransden: I.4   450
Robert Pinsky: I.16   450
Colin Macleod: I.5   455
Ars Poetica: A composite version by Ben Jonson, the Earl of Roscommon, John Oldham, Thomas Creech, Philip Francis, Francis Howes, Lord Byron, John Conington, Roy Campbell, and C. H. Sisson   456

Coda: A Selection of Poems that would not have been written but for Horace

Giangiorgio Trissino: 'Amante e Donna'   479
Thomas Campion: The man of life upright   480
Sir Henry Wotton: 'The Character of a Happy Life'   482
Edward, Lord Herbert of Cherbury: 'To his Friend Ben. Johnson, of his Horace made English'   483
Thomas Carew: 'The Spring'   483
Casimire/G. Hils: Lines from the third Epode of Casimire Sarbiewski, translated   485
John Milton: 'Lawrence of vertuous Father vertuous Son'   487
    'Cyriack, whose Grandsire on the Royal Bench'   488
Sir Richard Fanshawe: 'An Ode upon occasion of His Majesties Proclamation in the yeare 1630'   488
Richard Lovelace: 'Advice to my Best Brother'   493
Andrew Marvell: 'An Horatian Ode upon Cromwel's Return from Ireland'   495
Henry Vaughan: 'The Praise of a Religious Life by Mathias Casimirus'   499
    'To my worthy friend Master T. Lewes'   503

CONTENTS

Allan Ramsay and William Hamilton: An Exchange of Verse Epistles 504
Matthew Prior: 'A Better Answer' 512
Alexander Pope: 'To a Lady. Of the Characters of Women' 574
   Lines from 'To Richard Temple, Viscount Cobham' 523
George Berkeley: 'Verses . . . on the prospect of Planting Arts and Learning in America' 523
Christopher Pitt: 'Invitation to a Friend at Court' 525
William Cowper: 'An Epistle to Joseph Hill, Esq.' 527
William Wordsworth: 'To M. H.' 529
Alfred Lord Tennyson: 'To the Rev. F. D. Maurice' 530
Constantine Cavafy: 'Horace in Athens' (translated by George Kalogeris) 532
Rudyard Kipling: 'Horace, Bk V, Ode 3. A Translation' 533
   'Horace, Ode 17, Bk V. To the Companions' 534
   'Horace, Ode 31, Bk V. The Last Ode' 535
Robert Frost: 'The Lesson for Today' 536
Ricardo Reis (Fernando Pessoa): 'To be great' 541
   'Already on my head' 542
   (translated by Alberto de Lacerda)
Donald Davie: 'Wombwell on Strike' 542

List of Editions 545
Table of Horace in Translation 552
Index of Translators 557

ACKNOWLEDGEMENTS

Grateful thanks are due to Faber & Faber Limited for permission to reprint 'Ischia' by W. H. Auden from COLLECTED POEMS, ed. Edward Mendelson (1976); to Oxford University Press Limited for 'Ode II.14' by Basil Bunting from COLLECTED POEMS (1978); to HarperCollins Publishers/Jonathan Ball Publishers (Pty) Limited for 'Ars Poetica' by Roy Campbell from COLLECTED WORKS (Francisco Campbell Custodio and Ad. Donker (Pty) Limited); to Jessie Cunningham for 'Ode I.9' by J. V. Cunningham from COLLECTED POEMS AND EPIGRAMS (1971); to Carcanet Press Limited for 'Wombwell on Strike' by Donald Davie from COLLECTED POEMS (1990); to Alberto de Lacerda for his translations of 'To be Great' and 'Already on My Head' by Ricardo Reis (Fernando Pessoa); to David Ferry for his translations of 'Odes'; to Random House UK Limited and Henry Holt & Co., Inc. for 'The Lesson for Today' by Robert Frost from THE POETRY OF ROBERT FROST, ed. Edward Connery Lathem (Jonathan Cape, 1971). Copyright 1942 by Robert Frost. Copyright © 1970 by Lesley Frost Ballantine. Copyright (1969) by Henry Holt & Co., Inc.; to K. W. Gransden for his translations (after 'Ode I.34' and 'Epistle I.4'); to Alfred A. Knopf, Inc. for 'Application for a Grant' by Anthony Hecht from COLLECTED EARLIER POEMS. Copyright © 1990 by Anthony E. Hecht; to John Herington for his translation of 'Ode I.11' from '*Arion*', Volume 9, Numbers 2–3, Summer/Autumn 1970; to Oxford University Press on behalf of the Society of Jesus for 'Ode I.38' and 'Ode III.1' by Gerard Manley Hopkins from THE POETICAL WORKS OF GERARD MANLEY HOPKINS, ed. Norman H. MacKenzie (1990); to George Kalogeris for his translation of

'Horace in Athens' by Constantine Cavafy; to Faber & Faber Limited for 'Going, Going' by Philip Larkin from HIGH WINDOWS; to Faber & Faber Limited and Farrar, Straus & Giroux, Inc. for 'Serving Under Brutus' by Robert Lowell from NEAR THE OCEAN. Copyright © 1967 by Robert Lowell; to James Michie for his translations of the 'Odes' and 'Carmen Saeculare'; to Christopher Middleton for his translation of 'Ode III.13'; to Brown University Library for 'Satire II.5' by George Ogle; to Princeton University Press for 'Epistle I.16' by Robert Pinsky from AN EXPLANATION OF AMERICA (1979). Copyright © 1979 by Princeton University Press; to Faber & Faber Limited and New Directions Publishing Corporation for 'Ode I.11' ('Ask Not Ungainly'), 'Ode I.31' ('By the Flat Cup') and 'Ode III.30' ('The Monument Will Outlast') by Ezra Pound from TRANSLATIONS. Copyright © 1954, 1963 by Ezra Pound; to Scottish Text Society for 'Ode I.5' by Allan Ramsay from THE WORKS OF ALLAN RAMSAY III (1961); to Carcanet Press Limited for translations by C. H. Sisson of 'Epode 2', 'Ode II.14' and 'Ode II.15', and 'Carmen Saeculare' from IN THE TROJAN DITCH (1974), and 'Ars Poetica'; to Charles Tomlinson for his translations of 'Ode I.37' and 'Ode II.20'; to Princeton University Press for 'Ode I.27' by G. M. and G. F. Whicher from ON THE TIBUR ROAD (1912). Copyright 1912, renewed, by Princeton University Press; to Cornell University Press for 'Blandusian Spring' by William Wordsworth from AN EVENING WALK, ed. James H. Averill (1984). Copyright © 1983 by Cornell University Press.

Every effort has been made to trace or contact all copyright holders. The publishers will be glad to make good any omissions brought to our attention in future editions.

PREFACE

The favourite poet of those who do not much like poetry but enjoy a well-turned commonplace. That is or was until yesterday one Horace. The other is the Horace whose lyrics have frustrated the best endeavours of criticism to account for their effortless endurance, the Horace who has ceaselessly tempted poets professional and occasional to translate him. It is this Horace who is to be found here seen through the medium of these translations, sometimes fairly close, often paraphrastic, sometimes taking the form of recreative imitation. This third kind, in which London, for instance, may be substituted for Horace's Rome, is easy to detect and is described as imitation. The distinction between the first two kinds is less easy to draw since a rendering that begins as a translation may shade off into a paraphrase, and is not always indicated except when the writer moves some distance away from the Latin, in which case his work is said to be 'adapted', or some such term, from the original. Those accustomed to the modern versions that professors call faithful (the translator can read Latin but cannot write English) may be startled by the liberties permitted and almost expected in the great ages of classical translation from the second half of the seventeenth century through the first half of the eighteenth. Where Horace, professing himself too old for a new love affair, bids Venus find a more suitable victim and offers her in his place a young Roman nobleman, Pope offers the goddess a young upper-class Englishman and obligingly provides her with his street address, as though she were a postal carrier: 'To Number five direct your Doves' (no. 5 King's Bench Walk). A pretty jest, Mr Pope, but you must not call it Horace? No. The closure of classic status that forbids such largesse had not yet been imposed on Latin poetry. Bentley would, however, have been right in claiming that Pope does not give us Horace. No translator does that; translation is never a substitute for the original but rather a parallel text that brings to the fore new aspects of a poem while playing down others. Judging how far a translator's enlargements, his liberties with and additions to his author's poem, are a wanton intrusion of his own substance, and how far (in Dryden's words) they are 'secretly in the poet, or may be fairly deduced from him', is a delicate business best decided case by case.

Certainly the liberties taken by translators in the vital periods of the art are considerable, for they enjoyed a relation to Horace and other Roman poets more intimate than we can now readily imagine, one so pliant that the marmoreal words soften into life, becoming permeable to new life and capable of countless transformations. A large part of the purpose of this anthology is to show, pleasurably, how open Horace has been to fresh readings, how wide a range of interests this poet of seemingly modest range has served, so that those who question his stature may come to recognize it, while the high-flyers and the low-sinkers who have always thought poorly of him may be led to wonder if the middle ground of experience, where his poetry takes its stand, is not a more commodious, a more rewarding, region than their own.

This book is addressed to those who may have no Latin or only a little and would like to know *why* Horace is a good poet, if he is a good poet, and what sorts of things he is good at. Professional Latinists too may be interested to see how one of their authors has fared in his passage into English. No one principle has governed the choice of translations. Instead the net has been cast as widely as possible, bringing in a variety of fish: the few great translations, the many more skilful than one has any right to expect, some perhaps not very remarkable in themselves but representative of their time or simply of the difficulty of Englishing Horace. Some have been included because they are funny – with the poet's permission, one feels, rather than at his expense. The first section is devoted to versions of the *Odes*, seventy to Horace's 103, some of the more famous in a number of different versions. Qualities missed by a translator in one period may be caught by his successor in another.

A glance at the 'Table of Horace in Translation' shows where other translations are to be found. A significantly different treatment of a poem is usually referred to in the headnote, so too, as a means of control, closer versions of a very free translation or imitation. The *Epodes*, which have never much appealed to translators or to readers for that matter, have only a token presence, though a number of different renderings of the very popular second Epode are given. Next come the hexameter poems, the *Satires* and *Epistles*. Unlike the *Odes*, they have not taken kindly to modern dress, but they went readily into seventeenth- or eighteenth-century dress and it is mainly in this guise that they are to be found here. Although they look easier to do than the *Odes*, they may well be no less difficult, hence the frequent recourse to imitation which often conveys Horace's tone more aptly than translation proper. The final section, 'Coda', offers a short selection of original poems that bear Horace's imprint and would not have been written without him.

Presented in chronological order by the author's birthdate,* the versions included in this anthology should provide what Pound called 'a fairly adequate graph of the development and changes of English verse style'. And also teach us something about that poetical wonder, the Horatian ode? Although professional classicists may balk at the claim, there is much to be learned from translations, from imitations, and from original poems influenced by Horace. From the duplicity and interaction of tones in Marvell or Larkin; from the placing of words in Milton; from the poetry of talk in Pope and the metres of Auden. Our poets and translators can reveal qualities in the Latin master that expert Latinists seem often to miss.

So deep is the imprint made by this poet on English poetry and English culture as a whole that H. A. Mason, a critic of wide and curious reading, once suggested that Horace should be treated as 'an integral part of English literary experience'. His poetry was

* Years given for individual translations indicate the date or probable date of first publication, in the form 'pub. 1704'. 'Writ. 1704' would indicate the date of composition, '1704' alone the date of the earliest version which the editors have seen. The date given sometimes precedes the date of the version chosen for this collection (for more information, see 'List of Editions').

laboriously thumbed by the young and read by everyone with a formal schooling until this century when well-intentioned changes in the educational system deprived many literate people of any knowledge of the central Western language. One might suppose that the loss of Latin signalled the end of Horace's long reign, but this has not happened. Bad translations continue to appear in something of the old reassuring abundance and, unexpectedly, some of the best ever written are quite recent. Against all the odds, Horace has made it into the twentieth century, and whatever happens to Classical Studies and whatever happens to our Latin it looks as though we are going to have to keep him on the books. We shall cease to need Horace only when we no longer need poetry.

For various help and advice, gratitude to Stephanie Corrigan, David Ferry, John Herington, Alberto de Lacerda, Christopher Ricks, Charles Tomlinson, Ann Vasaly, Rosanna Warren. And from Donald Carne-Ross to Teresa Iverson, *semper adiutrix consiliorum suorum*, a special mention.

Thanks are also due to the Bancroft Library and Gerard Wong of the University of California at Berkeley; the Burns Library and the microforms department of Boston College; Rhoda Bilansky and the interlibrary loan department of Boston University; the Special Collections of Bowdoin College; the Special Collections of Brown University; the Houghton Library and William J. Foster of Harvard University; Hiram College; the Historic New Orleans Collection Library; the Huntington Library; the Massachusetts Historical Society Library; the Special Collections of the Northeast Missouri State University; the Harry Ransom Humanities Research Center at Texas University at Austin; and the Special Collections at Wellesley College.

INTRODUCTION

When at the end of his most substantial volume of lyric poetry, the first three books of *Odes*, Horace claimed that he had achieved a monument more durable than bronze that would last as long as Rome itself, he could hardly have imagined that it would last a great deal longer. The immediate future he could foresee: classic status, read by the literati and used to teach children the rudiments. But beyond that? Barbarism moving in, the fall of eternal Rome . . . What hope had he of surviving through the shadowy interregnum stretching out on the far side of calamity? Yet survive he did; his book, unlike that of Catullus, never vanished but it suffered a partial eclipse. The Christian world could accept the *Satires* and *Epistles* for they were moral poetry, even though the morality was pagan. The *Ars Poetica* was useful, full of good tips for aspiring writers. The *Odes* were another kettle of fish, too sophisticated and too unlike any medieval lyric to be understood, let alone enjoyed. With the revival of classical studies in the eleventh and twelfth centuries Horace emerged a little further; his complete work was available, for those qualified to read it, in the better libraries, but some amiable lines of rhyming Latin (they can be Englished with no loss whatever) show that full acceptance was some way ahead:

> Horace is the next who comes, a wise discerning mind,
> Enemy of every vice, resolute and kind.
> Three in number are the main works this author wrote,
> And composed a couple more, though of lesser note,
> Epodes and a book of Odes. These, so people say,
> Are not highly valued by readers of today.

(The *Ars Poetica* was counted as the third of the main works.) It is in this diminished guise that Horace makes his brief but memorable appearance among the famous authors of antiquity in Dante's limbo. First comes Homer, 'sovran poet', sword in hand, and stepping out bravely behind him, *Orazio satiro*. Could our friend Quintus Horatius have seen himself in the pages of the great Christian epic, one may imagine him murmuring, 'What the devil am I doing in this *galère*?'

It is in the next literary generation, in the more congenial environment afforded him by Petrarch, that the lineaments of the Horace we know come together. In the *Rime* for the first time we find a poet doing what poets were to do until yesterday, working a Horatian phrase or line into the texture of their verse. Just as Milton will write 'fit audience find though few', confident that everyone will have in mind *contentus paucis lectoribus*, or Tennyson write 'our dark Queen-city, all her realm / Of sound and smoke', recalling words that Horace used of Rome in the great ode to Maecenas, so Petrarch in his introductory sonnet says with feigned dismay that his love poetry has made him a byword among people everywhere: 'al popol tutto / favola fui gran tempo', flattering instructed readers on their ability to supply from Epode 11 *heu me per Urbem . . . fabula quanta fui*. In Petrarch's prose, allusions to Horace are frequent and drawn from the whole range of his work. They are less so in the poems, often merely glancing though sometimes taking a more substantial form. Horace ends a playful ode by announcing that wherever he may be, he will always love sweetly laughing, sweetly speaking Lalage: *dulce ridentem Lalagen amabo, / dulce loquentem*. Turning Horace to very different purposes, Petrarch ends a sonnet to Laura on a note of rapt adoration: 'He does not know how Love heals and how Love kills, who knows not how sweetly she sighs, how sweetly speaks and sweetly laughs':

> non sa come Amor sana e come ancide,
>   chi non sa come dolce ella sospira,
> e come dolce parla e dolce ride.

Behind Petrarch's echo of Horace in his soft new Latin we can hear, though he could not, the voice of Sappho:

> καὶ πλάσιον ἆδυ φωνεί-
> σας ὑπακούει
> καὶ γελαίσας ἰμέροεν.*

The early notes of the full concert of European poetry are beginning to sound as the great dead speak again through living lips.

As usual Petrarch was ahead of the field, for it was over a century before the next important step in the recovery of Horace took place, again in his native Italy.† In the second and third decades of the sixteenth century Ariosto composed his seven *Satires*. Not predominantly satirical, though the tone is sometimes more acerb than Horace's, they are rather epistles, verse letters written in a *terza rima* as flexible and colloquial as the Horatian hexameter, with the easy confidential manner of friend speaking to friend about matters of mutual interest and giving us between the lines vivid pictures of the life of the time. Ariosto does not imitate let alone translate Horace; he uses him to write original poems of his own. His *Satires* mark a notable moment in the history of European poetry, putting back into circulation a sturdy, all-purpose genre, the *sermo* or *causerie*: what Reuben Brower calls the poetry of talk.

The *Odes* proved more difficult to domesticate, though here too efforts were under way in Italy. The sonnet in the Latinized form introduced by Pietro Bembo in the early sixteenth century was seen as the vernacular equivalent of the ode or epistle, and although not much was done that we can confidently call Horatian, Milton took over the Italian experiments a century later and wrote sonnets to great public figures like Cromwell or Sir Henry Vane as Horace had written odes to the eminent men of his day, and issued an invitation to dinner in the sonnet to Lawrence with its beautiful sestet, Horace's plainer manner transposed to fastidious Miltonic. The first translation or rather imitation of any quality seems to be

---

* 'And close by hears your sweet speech and lovely laughter.'
† There is no good reason, certainly no necessity, to believe that Chaucer's 'Envoi a Scogan' shows the influence of the Horatian epistle. The *Ars Poetica* he may well have seen, for it was common property; other allusions that have been detected or suspected are likely to derive from florilegia, collections of classical sayings.

the version of the love duet, Ode III.9, of 1519 or thereabouts by Giangiorgio Trissino. Writing an elegant Petrarchan, Trissino captures the light, graceful movement of the original more successfully than Jonson or Herrick were to do a century later, and to find anything as accomplished we must move forward to the version by John Oldham in the Restoration period.

Spain and France were quick to follow the Italian lead. The Augustinian friar Luis de León translated twenty-three or twenty-four odes, using the five- or six-line stanza of seven and eleven syllables which Spaniards call the *lira*, the first of the many forms devised for Horace's strophes. This is early work, not of great interest in itself, and Spanish critics judge his versions to be more truly Horatian when he imitates Horace, as he does very freely in his celebrated poem 'Vida retirada' inspired by the second epode, *Beatus ille*. The contribution of France is more notable as Ronsard turns to Horace and makes the *Odes* part of French literature as English poets were soon to do for their own literature. Native students of Ronsard distinguish an initial Pindaric phase followed by an Anacreontic phase where the influence of Horace makes itself felt, but in reality Horace was there from the start and was far closer to him and left a profounder mark on his lyric poetry. There are virtual translations like 'A la fontaine Bellerie', modelled closely on Horace's ode to the Bandusian fountain where Ronsard risks the introduction of Latin syntax into French: 'moi çelebrant le conduit / Du rocher persé' (*me dicente cavis impostam ilicem / saxis*). There are imitations like 'A sa Muse' beginning 'Plus dur que fer, j'ai fini mon ouvrage' (*Exegi monumentum aere perennius*), or festive poems like 'Du retour de Maclou de la Haye' with its charming recall of Ode II.11 where a servant is told to summon Lyde, *in comptum Lacaenae / more comas religata nodum* ('her hair bound back neatly in the manner of a Spartan girl'):

> Et di à Cassandre qu'el' vienne
> Les cheveus tors à la façon
> D'une follatre Italienne.

There is nothing pedantic in these classical allusions; they are all for our delight, bidding us drink our fill from this fresh poetic source that has just opened up, yielding verse more delicious than France was to know again. Yet graver purposes were at work here too, for Ronsard and his colleagues of the Pléiade were seeking to fulfil the ambitions set out by du Bellay in his *Deffence et Illustration de la Langue Françoyse* and raise French poetry to the level of Greek and Latin, introducing new forms like the ode and the epistle (elegy, to use his term).

England was slower off the mark. Surrey at some time during his brief life translated Ode II.10, aiming no doubt at an English equivalent of the compression of the Latin, but the ease he sometimes achieved in his handling of Virgil escaped him. Diction, syntax and metre are clumsy, and the sentence beginning 'Once Phoebus to lowre' is scarcely comprehensible without reference to the original. Compared, however, with the first of the two anonymous translations in Tottel's *Miscellany* (first edition 1557), Surrey's must be counted an accomplished rendering. Tottel's author is like someone doggedly hacking his way through a thicket of brambles, not seeing where he is going nor why he is going, except that somewhere in this tangle of words which he seems hardly to understand he believes that Horace is to be found. It was left to Sidney two decades or so later to find him with a translation of the same ode that can claim the honour of being the first that can stand in its own right as a fine English poem. Where Horace's fluid movement runs the sense on from line to line and in one case beyond the stanza, Sidney's less flexible syntax and rhythmically end-stopped lines make the poem seem to consist of a series of gnomic statements ('The golden meane who loves, lives safely free', 'The wynde most oft the hugest Pine-tree greeves'). In itself unhoratian and too overtly didactic, this gives the writing a sturdy moral note too often missed or misrepresented by later translators. Despite Sidney's breakthrough, the Horatian ode was still well out of reach, and if a poet of Surrey's calibre had difficulty with it, routine versifiers were completely at a loss, not so much failing to capture the sophistication of the style as failing even to recognize it. What they did recognize or thought they recognized was the moral note, but they got the moralism wrong. Tottel included an anonymous version of Ode IV.7 which reveals by its very title, 'All worldly pleasures fade', the homiletic Christian tone that the author felt bound to impose on Horace's sombre pagan melancholy. It begins:

> The winter with his griesly stormes no lenger dare abyde.

Horace does it in two words, *Diffugere nives*. The rapid succession of the seasons in lines 9–12 (*frigora mitescunt Zephyris . . .*) is admittedly hard to manage with anything like the Latin concision. Centuries later Housman was to do it superbly; Tottel's man wambles through eight lumbering fourteeners ('For Zepharus doth mollifye . . .').

An age which judged this to be the right measure for a Horatian ode was inevitably going to use it for his hexameter poems. Thomas Drant did so in his 1566 version of the *Satires* (*A Medicinable Morall*, he called his book) and, in the following year, of the *Epistles* and *Ars Poetica*. He too was a Christian moralist and found that his theological preoccupations got in the way (should a reformed Christian spend time on a heathen poet?) no less than his dray-horse metre. He begins the *Ars Poetica* like this:

> A Paynter if he shoulde adjoyne
>   unto a womans heade
> A longe maires necke, and overspred
>   the corps in every steade
> With sondry feathers of straunge huie,
>   the whole proportioned so
> Without all good congruitye:
>   the nether partes do goe
> Into a fishe, on hye a freshe
>   welfavored womans face:
> My frinds let in to see this sighte
>   could you but laugh a pace?

Apparently this was felt to be the right way about it, for no less a personage than Queen Elizabeth began her partial translation of the poem in the same metre two decades later.

But if the English were slow to make themselves at home with

Horace, they soon caught up with him in the new century. The decisive figure is Ben Jonson, the decisive event *The Poetaster* (1601) in which, he tells us, he chose

> ... Augustus Caesars times,
> When wit, and artes were at their height in Rome,
> To shew that Virgil, Horace, and the rest
> Of those great master-spirits did not want
> Detractors, then, or practisers against them.

In similar fashion Jonson saw himself subject to the envious slanders of rival poets, Marston and Dekker. Even if a cast composed of so many glittering figures, some of them, like Maecenas, having little more to do than pass an occasional remark, may sometimes remind us of Beerbohm's *'Savonarola' Brown*, the effect of putting Horace and the other leading Roman poets of the day on the stage was to make them more accessible. Naturalizing Horace was the necessary prelude to translating him. Jonson himself made only one translation that can be called successful, of Ode IV.1, but he prepared the way for other translators. And he taught the members of his tribe to strengthen their own original poetry by drawing on Horace at need, sometimes using the *Odes* as so much materia poetica. Herrick adopted this procedure in 'His age, Dedicated to his peculiar friend, M. John Wickes, under the name of Posthumus', studded so thickly with Horatian allusions that the poem is almost a cento, though the voice remains his own. He begins with a direct translation of the Postumus Ode (II.14), 'Ah, Posthumus! Our yeares hence flye', introduces a detail of his own, then turns back to Horace: 'The pleasing wife, the house, the ground,/Must all be left' (II.14 again), but by the end of the stanza cheerfulness breaks in: 'Let's live, my Wickes, then, while we may, / And here enjoy our holiday.' The third stanza distantly recalls Ode IV.7, the fourth returns to the Postumus Ode: 'But on we must, and thither tend, / Where Anchus and rich Tullus blend.' And so forth. 'Crown we our Heads with Roses then, / And 'noint with Tirian Balme' is generalized Horace, 'no roofs of Cedar' is from II.18, the 'shining Salt-seller' from II.16. Other poets of Jonson's school used Horace more subtly by taking a single ode and assimilating it into the substance of a poem of their own, as Carew did in 'The Spring' or Lovelace in 'Advice to my Best Brother'. In so doing, as Joanna Martindale writes in her paper 'The Horace of Ben Jonson and his heirs', they achieve 'a translation of Horace into contemporary idiom and style'.*

Translation proper was by this time well under way, if with less success. By mid-century three complete translations of the *Odes* had appeared and several volumes of selections.† With one exception, these attempts show how hard it was to capture anything of Horace's style. Prudently concealing his identity, 'Unknown Muse', translating the little poem (II.4) in which a man who has fallen in love with his servant is told not to be ashamed since the heroes of old suffered the same fate, writes 'servant Briseis mov'd / Achilles, though in Venus rude, / With pulchritude,' trying for the snap of a neat rhyme with reckless disregard for diction. More pleasingly, some translators sought to feel Horace into contemporary English by introducing touches of local colour as John Ashmore did in his rendering of I.13, giving us a fine tang of Jacobean London with 'jarre-breeding war / Caus'd roaring Boyes to wrong thy shoulders faire'. The dialogue between 'Horace' and Lydia, III.9, the most popular ode of the century with some twenty or more versions known to have been written between 1608 and 1684, lent itself readily to this treatment. Francis Davison, in his collection called *A Poetical Rhapsody* (1602–21), has the lady telling her former lover of the talents of the present incumbent:

> Though Crispus cannot sing my praise in verse,
> I love him so for skill in Tilting showne,
> And graceful managing of Coursiers fierce:
> That his deare life to save, ile lose mine owne.

---

* *Horace Made New*, p. 72.
† Henry Ryder (1638), John Smith (1649) and 'Unknown Muse' (formerly confused with Barton Holyday, 1653) all translated the complete Horace, and John Ashmore (1621), Thomas Hawkins (1625) and Sir Richard Fanshawe (1652) translated selected works. In 1666 Alexander Brome edited an anthology of translations by different hands.

With less metrical address Ashmore in the first and best of his three translations of the poem shows the gentleman returning the ball:

> Now Thracian Chlo' has my heart sure,
> That Sweetly bears a part in prick-song, and can play:
> For whom I would deaths paine indure,
> If so the Dest'nies would put off her dying day.

Taking a loftier line, the author of an anonymous version found among the papers of Sir Henry Wotton transmogrifies the ode into a dialogue between God and the soul.

The one exception is Sir Richard Fanshawe, a translator of real accomplishment. Metrically enterprising, instead of sticking to rhyming couplets as many of his predecessors had done, he tries to suggest Horace's metrical variety by using different English stanza forms – the 8/6 syllable quatrain, for instance, which Marvell was to use in his 'Horatian Ode':

> Shut to thy gate before it darken,
> Nor to his whining Musick hearken:
> And though he still complain
> Tho'rt hard, still hard remain.   (III.7)

His version of IV.7 is the best we have of this great poem before Housman:

> But the decays of time, Time doth repair:
> When once we plunged are
> Where good Aeneas, with rich Ancus wades,
> Ashes we are, and shades.

'Wades' is unhappy since Charon provided dry conveyance across the infernal rivers, but the verb allows Fanshawe to find a better equivalent for the slow thunder of *pulvis et umbra sumus* than Housman's 'we are dust and dreams'. He gives a vigorous account of III.1, the first of the Roman Odes, which translators have found difficult to bring across. And he at least makes something of I.27, a story-poem of a kind we seem hardly to have in English, where the story has to be read between the lines. One may perhaps prefer the very free rendering by Dr P. which follows Fanshawe's translation in Brome's collection, an imitation that, if it quite fails to reflect the subtlety and different stylistic levels of the original, does, while bringing it down, bring it to life – *The Marriage of Figaro*, as it were, transposed into rousing Jacobean ragtime. Fanshawe has a shot at the Ode to Pyrrha (I.5), far from the worst attempt at this famously untranslatable poem, even if it is disconcerting to find the inexperienced and soon-to-be-jilted lover turned into 'the poor cuckold', an example of the hearty grossness that often marks or mars translation of this period (as when Fairfax in his *Jerusalem Delivered* writes 'He sided with a lusty lovely lass, / And with some courtly terms the wench he boards', light-years distant from Tasso's high, nervous manner). Standing utterly aloof from this juicy, coarse-fibred work is Milton's version of the Pyrrha Ode. Something more will be said later of this poem, sometimes highly praised, often severely censured.

Not of the school of Jonson and too original a poet to fit neatly into any category, Andrew Marvell contributes centrally to the process of domestication which makes it possible to describe Horace's poetry as an integral part of English literary experience. To speak of adaptation here would be inadequate, still more so to speak of imitation unless in the Renaissance sense of *superare imitando*, for 'To his Coy Mistress' may well be superior to any of Horace's love poems, and 'An Horatian Ode' is more searching in its implications and engages the mind more deeply than the only work of Horace to which it can be directly compared, the Cleopatra Ode (I.37). The greatness of Marvell's ode, most readers have believed, is the way it holds in balance two seemingly or truly irreconcilable claims: the claim for Cromwell, 'Much to the Man is due . . .', and the King's claim not only for our sympathy but also to our allegiance: 'He nothing common did or mean', and the incomparable lines that follow. The two opponents in Horace's briefer work (thirty-two lines against 120) are set against each other more by the poetic structure than by any complex issue. Horace first presents Cleopatra in the terms of Roman propaganda as a half-crazed

Oriental who dared to try to bring down Rome in ruin and is effortlessly repulsed by the heroic Octavian. To see through this vulgar stuff required no great breadth of mind, and in the second half of the poem Horace turns, very skilfully, on a relative pronoun and presents the queen in a light we cannot but see as noble, scorning flight, bravely contemplating her fallen palace, and dying by her own hand rather than allowing herself to be led in triumph through the streets of Rome. The poem ends with Cleopatra as 'no common woman', the phrase set between two words officially applied to Octavius' victory, *superbo* non humilis mulier *triumpho*, which in effect hands over the triumph to Cleopatra. For Horace's great achievement in the poetry we call public or political we need to look elsewhere, to the Roman Odes at the start of Book III, above all to the fourth which sees the order of the Roman state as an analogue to the order of the heavens, both always potentially threatened, one by cosmic, the other by political disorder. No translation that rises to the height of this great poem exists because we have nothing comparable in English. Translation aiming at more than an efficient transfer of content requires that there be something in the soul of the translator and in his cultural tradition akin to the original. English poets have often taken pride in their country and sometimes criticized its failings, but we have nothing resembling what Gordon Williams calls the Roman 'poetry of institutions'. Nothing in our poetry and perhaps in any poetry can stand beside the lines with which Virgil concludes the story of Nisus and Euryalus in Book IX of the *Aeneid* (446–9):

>   fortunati ambo! si quid mea carmina possunt,
>   nulla dies umquam memori vos eximet aevo,
>   dum domus Aeneae Capitoli immobile saxum
>   accolet imperiumque pater Romanus habebit.

Dryden's translation is mere chaff beside them:

>   O happy Friends! for if my Verse can give
>   Immortal Life, your Fame shall ever live:
>   Fix'd as the Capitol's Foundation lies;
>   And spread, where e're the Roman Eagle flies!

Horace cannot rise to these Virgilian heights, but he too has the sense of Rome as not simply a state or empire but a necessary, eternal idea in a labile world.

Meanwhile the ground was being prepared for the reception of the *Satires* and *Epistles*, poems that in a familiar style touch on some feature of contemporary life, tell a story, address a friend, and so forth. Horace is not the only model here, but he is the most important one. The third epistle of his first book begins:

> Julius, I long to know in what part of the world
> Augustus' stepson Claudius is now serving.

Ariosto, opening up the field, begins his first satire:

> I want the pair of you to tell me, please,
> Alex my brother and you too, friend Bagno,
> If people still remember me in court.

Wyatt, the first in the English field, drawing not on Ariosto but on the less rewarding Luigi Alamanni, begins an epistolary satire:

> Myne owne John Poyntz, sins ye delight to know
> The Cawse why that homeward I me draw –

And the explanation follows. Although Wyatt's diction is still Chaucerian, nevertheless, as K. W. Gransden writes, his three satires 'offer a new *idea*, based on classical models, of what a verse-satire ought to be like in spirit and structure. He successfully sustains . . . the Horatian convention of a man talking in private to a friend, rather than shouting indignantly in public.'* During the sixteenth century poets minor and sometimes major (Spenser, Donne) worked in the new form, but it was left to the magistral hand of Jonson to establish the Horatian *sermo* as a *useful* genre, a verse conversation pitched at the appropriate stylistic level, grand and ceremonious in the superb lines to Camden ('Camden, most reverend head'), courtly ('To Mary, Lady Wroth'), more colloquial in 'An Epistle answering

---

* *Tudor Verse Satire* (1970), p. 16.

to One that Asked to be Sealed in the Tribe of Ben' where he speaks out bluntly on the behaviour of the literati, '... those that merely talk, and never think, / That live in the wild anarchy of drink'. The verse invitation belongs here too ('Inviting a Friend to Supper') and at a slight remove the country-house poem where Jonson scores again with 'To Penshurst'.

The *Odes*, repeatedly Englished though they have been, are often so complete in their perfection as to be intimidating. The *Satires* and, in their more formal but still conversational manner, the *Epistles*, left poets a more tractable bequest, providing them with a medium in which to move at their ease within the accommodating constraints of metrical form without which ease can become sloven, and keeping poetry close to the ordinary ways of life, checking its tendency to put on airs and become too big for its boots. Yet these poems were to prove resistant to translation in the strict sense. The larger freedom of imitation was often a better medium, allowing poets to come nearer to Horace's manner and, at some removes, his matter, and nearer still in original poems in the Horatian mode. These pleasantly relaxed verses of Drayton, for instance:

> My dearely loved friend how oft have we,
> In winter evenings (meaning to be free,)
> To some well chosen place us'd to retire;
> And there with moderate meate, and wine, and fire,
> Have past the howres contentedly with chat,
> Now talk'd of this, and then discours'd of that ...

A century and a half later Cowper, again in an original poem, his 'Epistle to Joseph Hill, Esq.', writes what one may think the most perfect Horatian verse letter in the language:

> Dear Joseph – five and twenty years ago –
> Alas, how time escapes! – 'tis even so –
> With frequent intercourse, and always sweet,
> And always friendly, we were wont to cheat
> A tedious hour – and now we never meet!

If translators found it difficult to pitch the tone right for the hexameter poems, the explanation may be that the form that was increasingly to be adopted, the end-stopped couplet, is not really appropriate, despite the marvellous uses it was put to, above all by Pope. It is too neatly shaped, too balanced, inclining too readily to epigrammatic point, too resounding often (think of Dryden's epistle to his cousin John Driden), to represent the satiric or epistolary hexameter which is an agile, flexible medium, rhythmically inconstant and allowing much variation of pause. The couplet, as Cowper uses it here, can serve, but an apter medium, if one could forget the tone of voice and think only of the metre and sentence structure, might well be the blank verse of Browning's 'Bishop Blougram's Apology'.

With the second half of the seventeenth century a new Horace comes on the scene, shorn of moral weight while gaining in wit and urbanity. It was moral Horace who had most impressed previous translators; they were not much drawn to the love poems. A witty Horace interested in affairs of the heart now appears and calls for a new treatment. Fanshawe's handling of Ode II.8, a poem about a young woman whose deplorable conduct does nothing to diminish her attractions, is decent enough:

> If any punishment did follow
> Thy perjuries, if but a hollow
> Tooth, or a speckled nail, thy vow
>   Should pass. But though –

and an account of her iniquities follows. But how much better is Sir Charles Sedley some fifty years later:

> Did any Punishment attend
>   Thy former Perjuries,
> I should believe a second time,
>   Thy charming Flatteries:
> Did but one Wrinkle mark this face,
> Or hadst thou lost one single Grace.

Sedley's lines have a dash, an easy well-bred polish that marks a new stage in the Englishing of Horace. 'The best master of wisdom and virtue', as Jonson had seen him, is now a thoroughly likeable fellow, one of the wits of Restoration London. 'The most distinguishing mark of all his character,' Dryden said, 'seems to me to be his briskness, his jollity and good humour.' The Stoic sage has become an Epicurean, a bon vivant, sometimes even a libertine; a Horace grossly reduced by Otway to the poet of 'A generous bottle and a lovesome she', reduced very amiably by Prior to a companion on a gallant occasion: 'In a little Dutch chaise on a Saturday night, / On my left hand my Horace, a Nymph on my right.' In a free and easy version of the Soracte Ode (I.9) doubtfully attributed to Tom Brown, *permitte divis cetera* becomes 'We'll have no more business; but, friend, as you love us, / Leave it all to the care of the good folks above us', a nonchalance about divinity which Horace, hardly *pratiquant* yet always conscious (in the words of a great latter-day Horatian) 'of what the unaltering gods require', would surely have found unseemly.

With Pope Horace becomes a moralist again, but a moralist of a different, a more amenable kind:

> Horace still charms with graceful Negligence,
> And without Method talks us into Sense,
> Will like a Friend familiarly convey
> The truest Notions in the easiest way.

Though we may feel some reduction of stature here, this hits off essential qualities of the *Epistles* very nicely (the *Epistles* rather than the *Satires*), the conversational tone of a friend speaking to friend about everyday matters, passing every so often to serious moral issues but without presuming to lecture. This is a new Horace reflecting a change in English poetry and in English civilization. The Rome of the Renaissance – Mantegna's monumental figures inhabiting a distant, nobler world, the world which provided Shakespeare's heroes with the pattern for great actions performed in 'the high Roman fashion' – has given way to a more approachable Rome, one that, as we move into the world we still call

Augustan, was felt to be very like contemporary England. 'For the eighteenth-century gentleman,' Reuben Brower writes, 'the world of Horace's *Satires* and *Epistles* offered striking parallels to his own ... Whatever may have been the actualities of English life in the reign of Anne, it was quite easy for a citizen of that world to see himself and his fellows through Horace's eyes.'* And this new relation called for a new way of translating Roman poetry, the way of imitation.

It is in Pope's imitations of Horace that the genre comes to full flower, but both the theory and the practice of this form of translation were well established in the previous century. In the 1680 preface to *Ovid's Epistles Translated*, Dryden wrote that the growing distaste for literal, word-for-word renderings led 'two of our famous Wits, Sir John Denham and Mr Cowley, to contrive another way of turning Authors into our Tongue, called by the latter of them, *Imitation*.' He was referring to Denham's imitation of Virgil in *The Destruction of Troy* (a version of the *Aeneid*, Book II) and Cowley's of Pindar, both published in 1656. With his usual clarity Dryden provided the classic definition: 'I take Imitation of an Author in their sense to be an Endeavour of a later Poet to write like one who has written before him, on the same subject: that is, not to Translate his words, or be confined to his Sense, but only to set him as a Patern, and to write, as he supposes, that author would have done, had he lived in our Age, and in our Country.' Rochester ten or eleven years later led the field of Horatian imitation with his version of the tenth satire of the first book, a swingeing attack on Dryden, and handled the new genre with great brio in his 'Timon', an imitation not of Horace but of his French disciple, Boileau. Oldham followed with his 1681 imitation of the *Ars Poetica* and described his intentions much as Dryden had done: putting Horace 'into a more modern dress ... I conceiv'd would give a kind of new Air to the Poem, and render it more agreeable to the present Age.'

* *Alexander Pope: The Poetry of Allusion* (1959), p. 164.

INTRODUCTION

With this we can pass directly to Pope's imitations which bring two great poets together in a relation that is perhaps without parallel. Of Pope's version of Satire II.1 Frank Stack writes in a fine study: 'It is impossible to describe this adaptation of Horace in simple terms, that it is either "like" or "unlike" Horace. Every point in Pope has been inspired by Horace, and yet every point is different. And it is this lively, endlessly open, play between the texts which makes reading the poem as an Imitation so invigorating. Each poem seems to open up the other and give it new vitality. What we are aware of is the endless play of similarity and disparity, re-creation and transgression.'* Still more impossible in a broad survey of this kind to give an adequate account of the various strategems of re-creation which Pope employs, and all that can be done is to prepare readers unfamiliar with this eighteenth-century genre for what to expect. Take these lines from Epistle I.1 where Horace is talking about human inconstancy. To make his point he tells a little story:

> 'There's not a beach in the world to outshine Baiae,'
> says the rich man, and his waters feel the lust
> of the impatient magnate; but if some morbid whim
> has lent its sanction, it's 'Off with your tools tomorrow
> to Teanum, workmen!'

Though the harmony of the numbers has gone, Colin Macleod's straight rendering gives a fair account of the sense of the original. Turn now to Pope's imitation:

> Sir Job sail'd forth, the evening bright and still,
> 'No place on earth (he cry'd) like Greenwich hill!'
> Up starts a Palace, lo! th' obedient base
> Slopes at its foot, the woods its sides embrace,
> The silver Thames reflects its marble face.
> Now let some whimzy, or that Dev'l within

---

* *Pope and Horace: Studies in Imitation* (1985), p. 33.

> Which guides all those who know not what they mean
> But give the Knight (or give his Lady) spleen;
> 'Away, away! take all your scaffolds down,
> For Snug's the word: My Dear! we'll live in Town.'

Put case the original had been lost, we could scarcely use Pope to reconstruct it. Horace's anonymous rich man has acquired a name, his projected mansion that in due course will push its foundations into a lake or the sea has provided Pope with the water of the Thames reflecting the marble face of the completed building which, lo! rises miraculously before us like an exhalation, and prompts Sir Job, now with his own style of speech and a wife to boot, to reveal his weathercock propensities. A superb performance, for which Horace has done little more than provide Pope with his cue. More often, though, he reaches deep into Horace and writes something that is neither simply Pope nor simply Horace but something new, an amalgam created by what Gadamer calls the fusing of horizons. We find this amalgam at its richest in the imitation of the epistle to Augustus (II.1) where Horace writes of the way Rome's cultural inferiority to Greece is counterpoised by the native energies of the Roman spirit: *Graecia capta ferum victorem cepit* – but let Macleod again stand in modestly for Horace:

> The capture of Greece took her brutish victor captive
> and civilized rustic Latium. Thus the crude
> Saturnian verse ran out, good taste expelled
> the smell of muck; and yet for years the traces
> of rusticity remained, and still remain.
> For it was late when they trained their minds on Greek:
> at peace after the Punic wars, they started
> to see what the tragedians could teach them.
> They tried their hand at composing too, and well,
> in their own eyes; to soar came naturally,
> they had inspiration and a happy boldness –
> but also a foolish horror of crossing out.

Pope:

> We conquer'd France, but felt our captive's charms;
> Her Arts victorious triumph'd o'er our Arms:
> Britain to soft refinements less a foe,
> Wit grew polite, and Numbers learn'd to flow.
> Waller was smooth; but Dryden taught to join
> The varying verse, the full resounding line,
> The long majestic march, and energy divine.
> Tho' still some traces of our rustic vein
> And splay-foot verse, remain'd, and will remain.
> Late, very late, correctness grew our care,
> When the tir'd nation breath'd from civil war.
> Exact Racine, and Corneille's noble fire
> Show'd us that France had something to admire.
> Not but the Tragic spirit was our own,
> And full in Shakespear, fair in Otway shone:
> But Otway fail'd to polish or refine,
> And fluent Shakespear scarce effac'd a line.
> Ev'n copious Dryden, wanted, or forgot,
> The last and greatest Art, the Art to blot.

With appropriate additions and not too much forcing, Horace's account of Roman literary culture becomes England's. English poetry has much to offer, and yet:

> Late, very late, correctness grew our care.

The gravity of the cadence tells us that correctness, to our loose ears a limited, cramping thing, means a great deal more to Pope than observing the rules, means at full stretch as much as he meant when he told Bolingbroke: 'To write well, lastingly well, Immortally well, must one not leave Father and Mother and cleave unto the Muse?' In these high words Pope is asserting the concept which lies at the heart of humanism and the art of letters first articulated by Isocrates in the fourth century BC. Correctness, yes, and all that it implies, and yet there is something else, the 'energy divine' of Dryden, the 'noble fire' of French Corneille that shone even more fully in English Shakespeare. And yet, again, as Pope doubles back on himself, there is something else, 'The last and greatest Art, the Art to blot' that English poets forget too easily.

Is Pope's passage richer than Horace's? A bad question: there is no comparison here but rather an enriching collaboration. If, after Pope, we find more in Horace's lines than we did before, this may be because he read Horace better than we do and was closer to him, bound by the dream that for a generation or so seemed possible of building on England's green and pleasant land not Jerusalem but Rome.

Imitation at this level was not to be written again except by Johnson with his grand version of Juvenal's tenth satire, 'The Vanity of Human Wishes', but the Horatian *furor imitandi* was at its height; Stack counted thirty-eight imitations in a single decade, the 1730s. Horace was felt to be endlessly adaptable and could always be made to speak to the interests of the day. He has, for instance, by now read Newton and become something of a scientist. 'The eighteenth-century translator,' Maren-Sofie Røstvig writes, 'often felt compelled to enrich Horace's Sabine farm with telescopes, microscopes, and similar incongruous equipment. This Newtonian invasion of the quiet precincts of cows and buttercups seemed logical enough to the age.'* In Christopher Pitt's epistle, 'Invitation to a Friend at Court', an original poem as Horatian in tone as his imitations of Horace, we find the *beatus vir* of the second epode busy with his telescope:

> Thro' the long levell'd tube our strengthen'd sight
> Shall mark distinct the spangles of the night;
> From world to world shall dart the boundless eye,
> And stretch from star to star, from sky to sky.

'In the summer [Røstvig again] the telescope will be exchanged for the microscope:'

---

* *The Happy Man*, Vol. II (1958), p. 127.

> Thro' whose small convex a new world we spy,
> Ne'er seen before, but by a Seraph's eye!
> So long in darkness shut from human kind
> Lay half God's wonders to a point confin'd.

Like his Roman persona this eighteenth-century English Horace also keeps a close eye on the political scene, but unlike his Roman persona he sometimes supports and sometimes opposes constituted authority. During the two Jacobite rebellions he can be found on either side of the fence. A few decades later, now decidedly subversive, we see him in the unappetizing company of John Hall-Stevenson who introduces a group of Horatian imitations, beginning with one of Ode III.3 dedicated to the radical John Wilkes, by protesting against the way 'the nobility and opulent gentry of this land ... have enjoyed, time out of mind, an exclusive right to all imitations of the odes of Horace ... No one, say they, that is not saturated with claret and champaigne should presume to imitate his odes.' Some truth in this, no doubt, but truth and Hall-Stevenson have little to say to each other. With the next big political excitement, the turmoil across the Channel, Horace is back on the other side of the ideological fence. Lord Morpeth, Eton and Christ Church, uncovers in the Ode to Fortune, I.35, an 'Ode to Anarchy' put in the mouth of a fervent spokesman for the French Revolution:

> Goddess, whose dire terrific power
> Spreads, from thy much-loved Gallia's plains,
> Where'er her blood-stain'd ensigns lower
> Where'er fell Rapine stalks, or barb'rous Discord reigns!

Whatever is happening, Horace with a little help can always be trusted to provide the timely words.

Although imitation was all the vogue, translations continued to be called for. Then as now, it was interesting to see how far Horace could go directly into English verse, and even in a Latinate age there were the unfortunate souls who did not read Latin. (George Ogle quotes some lines from Juvenal and then gives them, 'English'd for the Benefit of the Ladies', in translation.) As we have seen, several complete Horaces were published in the course of the seventeenth century, but none showed any staying-power until the appearance in 1684 of *The Odes, Satyrs, and Epistles of Horace. Done into English by Thomas Creech*. His rendering of Lucretius had been published two years before, a work good enough for Dryden to steal from, but his Horace seems never to have enjoyed the same favour. No doubt an age that was demanding polish found Creech too homespun. So far as posterity is concerned, if his name survives at all it is because Pope began his imitation of the sixth epistle of the first book by quoting or rather misquoting him:

> 'Not to Admire, is all the Art I know,
> To make men happy, and to keep them so.'
> (Plain Truth, dear Murray, needs no flow'rs of speech,
> So take it in the very words of Creech.)

But these are not Creech's very words and Pope is not playing fair. Creech wrote 'It is the only method that I know' – 'all the Art I know' is Pope's gift, and he makes Creech sound slightly ridiculous by changing 'To make Men happy, and to keep 'em so' to 'keep them so', insisting with a fussy precision on the pronoun as though there could be some doubt about its antecedent. Pope's malice goes astray here, for he apparently did not see that Creech's line is modelled on *Paradise Regained* IV.362, 'What makes a Nation happy and keeps it so'. Quite legitimately Creech is drawing on the plain style of Milton's poem to render the didactic manner of Horace's epistle.

By Pope's standards Creech's versification may be splay-foot, but his Horace has its sturdy virtues and held its ground from the time of the first edition to that of the last in 1743 or thereabouts. He did not, it must be granted, have a reliable ear, and in the *Odes* often simply jogs along, content if he has supplied the required number of iambs. ('Yet, faith, if vext, my Rage will rise,/ And when these hated Chains are broke,/I'll leave these dull Complaints, be wise,/ And scorn to take another Yoke.') Yet he can sometimes write with lyrical ease:

> Thee, Thee for Troy the Gods design
> > Where Simois Streams do play,
> Scamander's thro the Vallies twine
> And softly eat their easy way.

He can rise a little when the occasion calls for it and bring off a Drydenesque swagger ('Than all the Spices of the Eastern King'), and achieve a sufficiently dignified level in some of the graver odes, but it is in the homely style — what Pope superciliously calls 'our rustic vein' — that he is at his best, as in the happy little poem about a rural *festa*: 'The Ditcher, with his Country Jugg/Then smiles to Dance where once he dug' (III.18). He performs well enough with the hexameter poems, particularly the *Satires*, for there, although Horace's satirical hexameter is a more finely tempered instrument than Creech commands, the impression Horace wants to convey is of everyday speech, a casual, seemingly offhand manner. Horace created this style through conscious artistry; to Creech it came naturally. If he avoided the flowers of speech which Pope bestowed on Horace, he did not do so because he judged them to be out of place; they did not grow in his garden. Students of translation looking for a forgotten master of the art will not find one in Creech's Horace. He is not a great translator but he is a good one, an honest one, better certainly than those who know of him only through Pope's maltreatment have been led to suppose.

The final edition of Creech's Horace appeared at about the same time as the first edition of the translation by Philip Francis which was to replace it. Francis ranks as the Horatian translator-general of the second half of the eighteenth century and the first half of the nineteenth, with new editions constantly called for. Though now hardly more than a name even to connoisseurs of English poetry, he has good claims to be considered the best translator of Horace, certainly of the *Odes*, to date, and Johnson's praise is just: 'Francis has done it best; I'll take his, five out of six, against them all.' He had the luck to be born just at the right moment. Horace had by now been thoroughly domesticated and Pope's description of Ciceronian prose, 'So Latin, yet so English all the while', was felt to apply no less to Horatian verse. Moreover Francis was writing at a time when the art of versification had reached a very high standard. As eighteenth-century memorial poems in English parish churches show, many educated people could do some very decent versing when the occasion called for it, and the more professional poets, whose names have sunk to the footnotes of literary history, handled the style of the period with a more practised skill. 'Who now reads Cowley?' Pope asked. Cowley some people still do read, but who now reads Richard Duke, George Stepney, William Walsh, William Somerville, Christopher Pitt, Samuel Boyse? Yet these men wrote well, and are still worth reading. Not perhaps having a great deal to say, they translated or for preference imitated, turning repeatedly to Horace, the presiding poet of the day. It is in this good company that Francis belongs, translating, not imitating, Horace, and tackling the whole oeuvre rather than picking on a handful of continually Englished odes. Open his book almost anywhere (if you can find a copy – it is practically unobtainable) and you are likely to come across something as sound as this (from Ode II.12):

> You in historic Prose shall tell
> >   The mighty Power of Caesar's War;
> How Kings beneath his Battle fell,
> >   Or dragg'd indignant his triumphal Car.
>
> Licymnia's Voice, Licymnia's Eye,
> >   Bright-darting its resplendent Ray,
> Her Breast, where Love and Friendship lie,
> >   The Muse commands me sing in softer Lay;
>
> In Raillery the sportive Jest,
> >   Graceful her Step in dancing charms,
> When playful at Diana's Feast
> >   To the bright Virgin Choir she winds her Arms.
>
> Say, shall the Wealth by Kings possest,
> >   Or the rich Diadems They wear,
> Or all the Treasures of the East,
> >   Purchase one Lock of my Licymnia's Hair?

Francis can write like a poet but, not being a poet himself, does not have to clear the ground of his own poetry to make way for Horace's. His achievement is to have made himself at home in the *Odes* more completely than any other translator had done. He does not give us everything. He is less witty than Horace can sometimes be, the weight of mortality does not press so hard upon him, he lacks Horace's quiet, unsentimental feeling for nature, for the still heat of Mediterranean noon and the movement of water in rivers. He does not give us everything, but he gives us as much as a translator can be expected to do. What he gives us, it is true, is an eighteenth-century Horace, but if we feel the need to add, 'Not *merely* an eighteenth-century Horace', it is because so much in the culture of the age could then be seen, and in a measure still can, as genuinely Horatian. Johnson's judgement stands: Francis has done it best.

On one occasion he wrote something that leaves us perplexed. He begins his translation of the Ode to Maecenas, III.29, in this way:

> Descended from an antient Line,
>   That once the Tuscan Sceptre sway'd,
> Haste thee to meet the generous Wine,
>   Whose piercing is for Thee delay'd.

But this is Dryden, not Francis? No, not exactly. Dryden has '*of* an ancient Line', not 'from', 'that *long*' not 'once', not 'Haste thee' but 'Make haste'. The fourth line is left unchanged. From this point on, apart from a few echoes, Francis leaves Dryden and turns directly to Horace, translating where Dryden paraphrases and replacing his Pindarique stanza, irregular in line- and syllable-length, with a regular six-line stanza. Whatever his intentions, by beginning as he does (a note by a later hand tells us that 'the first four lines of his translation are taken from Dryden's translation of this ode'), Francis implicitly invites us to compare the two approaches, translation and paraphrase. There are probably readers today, particularly those of the academic persuasion, who would vote for Francis. Dryden (a great translator who did not feel the need to clear the ground of his own poetry before he translated another man's) is splendid, but does he not often lose sight of the original and strike out on his own whereas Francis keeps faith with the original? It is true that where Dryden is great, as in the lines beginning 'Happy the Man, and happy he alone', Francis is no more than good. Further than that he cannot go. But is this far enough? The ode is after all agreed to be one of the finest things Horace ever wrote. Is Francis' good good enough? His performance raises troubling theoretical questions that cannot be pursued here but cannot simply be passed over. It is often said that only a poet can translate poetry. If we mean that only a poet of Dryden's stature can do what he did here, write a great English poem inspired by a great Latin poem, then plainly the assertion is correct. But if we mean that no poetry can be translated except by someone who has written fine original poetry of his own, then very little poetry has ever been or ever will be translated, and Horace has hardly been translated at all. The world, however, continues to demand translation – without it, George Steiner powerfully observes, 'we would live in arrogant parishes bordered by silence' – and in all sanity we must lower our sights sufficiently to grant the name of translation to good verse that stands in a responsible relation (vague enough term, heaven knows) to its original, and also recognize that a good verse-man can sometimes, lifted above his normal level by what he is translating, write what we need not hesitate to call poetry. (Is Francis' limpid version of IV.10 not a poem?)

Still, it is the poet-translators who matter most, for although they may not rise to Dryden's heights, they can do something that the ordinary good translator cannot. They may break fresh ground and (like Milton's Death) snuff the smell of change on earth. Of the two poet-translators who next claim attention, Christopher Smart and William Cowper, this is true primarily of Cowper, in whose translations we sense new forces stirring, the initial tremors of the vast movement that was to dislodge Horace from the pre-eminent position he had enjoyed since the Renaissance and bring him into a world he never made. Put it that he is now keeping strange company. He would have been surprised had he been able to read some of the poems these two men wrote when they were not translating him. 'A Song to David', for example. Longinus found something to admire in Moses ('no common man'); Horace would surely have been perplexed to learn that as 'the Heathen Psalmist' he shared with the Judaic the place he occupied in Smart's esteem, and more than perplexed by Cowper's 'The Castaway' or the poem beginning 'Hatred and vengeance, my eternal portion'. That the gods could be cruel he knew; deity of this insane malignity would have been beyond his comprehension.

Smart, in his translation of Horace, belongs to the eighteenth (the earlier eighteenth) century in a way that Cowper does not. He is, however, at his more rewarding, or anyway more pleasing to modern taste, when he writes not in the resounding manner we think characteristic of the period, affecting its mannerisms (the finny race and so forth), but comes down several pegs and adopts a colloquial style. Writing in the conventional neoclassical way he can be dull:

> The slave Tecmessa at her feet
> Saw her lord Ajax – Atreus' son
> Lov'd his fair captive in the heat
>   Of conquest, that he won.

(The last three words tacked on for the rhyme.) But in his earlier imitation of this sprightly poem he writes with the neat point and wit of Prior:

> The thundr'ing Ajax Venus lays
> In love's inextricable maze.
> His slave Tecmessa makes him yield,
> Now mistress of the seven-fold shield.
> Atrides with his captive play'd,
> Who always shar'd the bed she made.

Cutting through the classical cackle he can see a Roman soldier, object or victim of a lady's affection, as 'the dear enamour'd boy ... dress'd in his regimentals' (I.8), a lively young fellow from the pages of Fielding. He can bring into sharp focus the famous Pyrrha of Ode I.5 'whose plainness is the pink of taste'. This may not have worn well, but it is good eighteenth-century usage, in its day pleasantly *à la page*, and at least makes something of the untranslatable *simplex munditiis*.* Sometimes he is waggish. In his version of IV.13, an old woman who still aspires to the honours of youth is told 'You would be beauteous with a beard', that is, you want to look beautiful even though you now have a beard, but in vain, for you are no longer of interest to Cupid, 'a sauce-box' who 'scorns dry chips'. Now and then we meet Smart the Latinist, as when he risks an internal accusative for the benefit of the fugitive Chloe of I.23 who 'trembles knees and heart'. He can be charming, finding agreeable young persons he calls 'Damsels of condition' in *honestae clientae* (well-born female dependants?). We hear Smart the poet in his version of the Ode to Leuconoe, turning Horace's beautiful choriambics into a graceful English lyric, or when in I.3 he speaks of 'the sweet star-light smile' of Helen's enskied brothers the Dioscuri, giving the Latin *lucida sidera* more poetry than it deserves. His treatment of the *Odes* is uneven but very often rewarding, sometimes a good deal more, and quite unlike anyone else's. It deserves far better than the neglect into which it has fallen, with no new edition after its first appearance in 1767 until the recent academic publication of 1979.†

John Conington, speaking of Cowper's translation of a couple of *Satires*, remarked, as others have done, that 'in his original poems [he is] perhaps the greatest master of the Horatian style.' An interesting judgement, especially if we apply it to his all-too-few translations of the *Odes* which uncover something in the famous style which previous translators had missed, something plainer, more heartfelt, the neoclassical patina scraped off to reach through to the human reality beneath the cunning words. Coleridge praised him for the way he 'combines natural thoughts with natural diction',

---

* The best rendering to date is by Anthony Hecht: 'For whom do you / Slip into something simple by, say, Gucci?', 'An Old Malediction', *The Venetian Vespers* (1979).
† *Christopher Smart's Verse Translation of Horace's Odes* (1979), edited by Arthur Sherbo who contributes a useful introduction.

and in a letter Cowper wrote of the art of making verse 'speak the language of prose without sounding prosaic'. We can measure his success in bringing this new more natural diction to Horace by comparing his version of II.16 with that of Francis. It is a poem about the human longing for *otium*, peace of mind and heart, 'A Blessing never to be sold,' Francis wrote,

> For Gems, for Purple, or for Gold.
> For neither Wealth, nor Power controul
> The sickly Tumults of the Soul,
> Or bid the Cares to stand aloof,
> That hover round the vaulted Roof.
>
> Happy the Man, whose frugal Board
> His Father's Plenty can afford . . .

The verse is external to the feelings it purports to present, the even beat of the iambics does nothing to bring them home to us. Cowper writes:

> For Neither Gold can Lull to Rest,
>   Nor all a Consul's Guard beat off,
> The Tumults of a troubled Breast,
>   The Cares that Haunt a Gilded Roof.

Specifying where Francis generalizes, he continues:

> Happy the Man whose Table shews
>   A few clean Ounces of Old Plate . . .

This is a direction that the translator of the *Odes* can profitably take. Many have tried in different ways to reproduce the manner, the *curiosa felicitas*, and failed. They might have done better to follow Cowper and try for the matter, the broad middle range of human experience, the good sense and, yes, the wisdom that have made Horace dear to so many readers.

New in a different way is the religious 'Reflection' which Cowper appends to his translation of II.10, an ethical poem previously translated by Surrey and Sidney and many others:

> Sweet moralist! afloat on life's rough sea
> The christian has an art unknown to thee.

Or, if not new, Cowper's addition raises an issue that seems not to have been troubling since the earlier seventeenth century. Christians had always been aware that on the gravest questions facing humankind the classical authors they revered were either quite simply wrong or possessed of only a partial truth, but the hard-won, uneasy concordat between Rome (and Athens) and Jerusalem allowed them to inhabit both realms. Samuel Johnson, a profoundly devout man, in the month before his death translated Horace's great poem of pagan melancholy, IV.7. The seasons follow their eternal round:

> But wretched man, when once he lies
> Where Priam and his sons are laid,
> Is naught but ashes and a shade.

As a Christian Johnson knew that after death man is very much more than ashes and a shade, and yet, with the great assize only just ahead of him, he could still turn to Horace with no apparent sense of conflict. Yet conflict there always potentially was, and various attempts to solve it had been made. Although the ancients could not themselves be converted, nothing prevented the translator from converting their works. Thomas Randolph in the early seventeenth century translated the second epode which unexpectedly ends by revealing that the wise and happy countryman is really a usurer who, having chosen a life on the land, 'calls his Money in, / But ere the Moon was in her Wane, / The Wretch had put it out to Use again.' (Francis.) Randolph provides a more charitable ending: 'Lord, grant me but enough; I ask no more / Than will serve mine, and helpe the poore.' This is no more than a local improvement. Wholesale baptism was undertaken by the Polish Latinist Casimire Sarbiewski who in the 1620s brought out four books of odes, and a fifth of epodes in which Horace – *Horatius redivivus*, a title often given to Casimire himself – writes as a Christian. Concentrating on the Stoic elements in Horace, Casimire combined 'Horatian elegance and Horatian motifs with a partly mystic Christian piety [which] gained instant popularity with the public'* and influenced a number of English poets of the period. William Habington, in an epistle on the Horatian theme of country versus town, advocated retirement 'To the pure innocence oth' Country ayre':

> There might not we
> Arme against passion with Philosophie?

A sound Stoic procedure that Horace too commends. Habington continues, however:

> And by the aide of leisure, so controule
> What-ere is earth in us, to grow all soule.

An aspiration that would have gravelled the Roman moralist.

Cowper did not feel able, as Johnson did, to inhabit both realms, nor did he adopt the extreme measures taken by Casimire. Instead he faithfully translated the heathen poet while adding his gentle 'Reflection' telling him that 'The christian has an art unknown to thee.' In its small way this eight-line postscriptum signals a momentous change in Horace's fortunes, a distancing that was also a diminution, coming from several quarters. Those affected by the persuasions of the Evangelical movement could not find the solace they craved in the *Odes*. They looked to very different sources:

> There is a fountain fill'd with blood
> Drawn from EMMANUEL'S veins;
> And sinners, plung'd beneath that flood,
> Lose all their guilty stains.

Horace's fountains were not of this kind. Cowper himself, the author of the Olney Hymns, remained, and we may wonder at the fact, a lover of Horace, but even for him Horace could no longer be what he had once been, the best master of virtue and wisdom. Diminution on another front he faced from the growing

---

* Maren-Sofie Røstvig, 'Casimire Sarbiewski and the English Ode', *Studies in Philology* (51) 1954, pp. 443–4.

professionalism of classical scholarship, leading in the nineteenth century to the German 'science' of antiquity, *Altertumswissenschaft*, which discouraged that easy, slippered commerce with Greek and Latin writers which Goethe agreeably called *Hausgebrauch*. Tully's *Offices* shrank into Cicero's *De Officiis*, Horace was left not much more than a stylist, a master of the Latin language, the truth of what he had to say and its bearing on human life all but irrelevant. And if this were not enough he was confronted by the great changes in poetic taste and sensibility which made the qualities for which he had always been admired look more like limitations.

Before we follow Horace into the Romantic world, however, he must first be transported to the New World across the Atlantic. His earlier experiences there are reassuring; he seems to survive the passage very well:

> And now the Fields, in native Beauty drest,
> Are by the Arms of Frost no more carest;
> The Cytherean Goddess graceful moves,
> Encircl'd with a Crowd of blooming Loves;
> Whose nimble Steps fly o'er the verdant Meads,
> While the gay Morn her Silver Lustre sheds.   [*Moon?*]
> The Graces, who with heavenly Features glow,
> And comely Nymphs, whose Eyes Destruction throw
> O'er the soft Grass lead up a bright and solemn Show.   (from I.4)

Charming verses, that give no indication of their provenance. The author is the Reverend John Adams, the place of publication Boston, the date 1745. No less English is the volume by Phillis Wheatley (1773), described on the title page as 'Negro Servant of Mr John Wheatley of Boston, in New England'. A drawing shows the young author in her mob-cap, quill in hand, waiting for the muse to descend. She writes accomplished eighteenth-century verse, but unfortunately does not fall within our purview, for although her first poem is addressed 'To Maecenas', she was drawn not to Horace but to Terence, 'an *African* by birth', she reminds us. No less English in tone though published several decades later, in Boston in

1804, are some translations by Susanna Rowson, the daughter of an English naval officer, the best a version of an ode to Maecenas (II.17) which plain persons may persist in being moved by even though authority warns us not to take it too seriously – an instance of translation's power to save a poem's life from the academy's under-reading.

By this time, however, the new country is making its voice heard and a new Horace is emerging, not always, it must be said, a very happy one. A decidedly American note is sounded by Philip Freneau, 'Poet of the American Revolution', in a spirited adaptation of the tenth epode launched against the turncoat General Arnold on his departure for England after the capitulation at Yorktown in 1781:

> With evil omens from the harbour sails
> > The ill-fated barque that worthless Arnold bears, –
> God of the southern winds, call up the gales,
> > And whistle in rude fury round his ears.

In the same decade, from the Coffee-House at Philadelphia, comes *The Lyric Works of Horace translated into English verse . . . by a Native of America*. The first poem, an imitation of I.12, composed by this native, whose name was John Parke, is addressed to 'The Illustrious Order of the Cincinnati':

> What deity employs the Muse's lore?
> > What man or hero fills this ample round?
> What name shall sportive echo's voice resound
> Along the Delaware's loud-sounding shore?
> > Or to the banks of Mississippi's shore? [*flood?*]
> Or desart Allegany's hostile wave;
> Or, where St Lawrence's lake-swoln torrents lave,
> > The earth yet crimson'd with Columbia's blood.
> 'Twas there, trepan'd by British arts,
> Montgom'ry drew his latest breath;
> > 'Twas there, transfix'd, – a thousand hearts,
> The sons of freedom bow'd to naught, but death.

This is Horace writing as he would (perhaps) have done 'had he lived in our Age, and in our Country', only now the country is America. Horace's lighter manner proved still more difficult of capture. From Virginia in 1806, in sapphics, comes this distant recall of I.22 by Royall Tyler. The faithful lover has now ceded his place at the centre of the action to the lady, a Southern belle:

> Such a smart tippy fashionable England
> Ne'er could produce through all her realms of Bond-Street,
> Nor dressy France, that nursery of fashion,
>   Land of petit-maîtres.
> Place her where never lemonade or silk fan . . .

(*pone me pigris ubi nulla campis* . . .) and so forth. On a very different level is the unexpectedly witty treatment of the same ode by America's sixth president, John Quincy Adams, in whom the light of the eighteenth century still shone. Scoring a first for his country, Adams urbanely leads the lover into regions where he had not previously ventured, Zara's burning desert, Popacatapetl and Chimborazo. But the light soon guttered and had gone out completely by the time another servant of the state, John D. Long, governor of Massachusetts in 1880 and later secretary of the navy, had a go at *Persicos odi*, as graceful an odelette as Horace ever made:

> I hate this Persian gingerbread,
> These fixin's round a feller's head;
> The lingering roses from their bed
>   Cut not asunder.

One should, however, put in a word for poor James Garfield, assassinated a few months after becoming President. Though he came of unlettered stock, he was an eager student of antiquity and, as his correspondence shows, a devoted Horatian. He made a translation of Ode I.3 in blank verse, but unfortunately this seems not to have survived.

To follow Horace in nineteenth-century America is unrewarding. It was not his country nor was it his century, there or elsewhere, and what leads could be discovered were frustrated. Longfellow, during his senior year at Bowdoin College in Maine, translated an ode so successfully, it was judged, that he was subsequently appointed to the chair of Romance Languages, an adventurous choice since he scarcely knew even French at that time. Regrettably, this translation too seems to have vanished without trace. The report that 'the greatest Latin scholar of Louisiana' translated Horace sounded worth following up, but this gifted person, by name Constant Lepouzé, turned out to be a Frenchman. Having lived in Louisiana for over twenty years, he felt that he had the right to consider himself a native, hence, he claimed, 'the volume that I offer to the public belongs to the literature of Louisiana.' Perhaps so, but although it was published in New Orleans (in 1838), France has a stronger claim on it, and Pyrrha's young man preserves a distinctly Gallic air:

> Pyrrha, dis-moi, quel est ce tendre adolescent,
> Aux cheveux parfumés, à la taille élégante.

So Horace had best be returned to Europe, until such time as America is ready for him, to make his reluctant entry into the Romantic age. In most great classical poets there is something that if we wish we may term Romantic. It is not common in Horace, but it is there. It is there very strongly in III.25, an ode that readers have found difficult because of the way it combines a theme of the kind we call political with a vision at the furthest remove from the public realm of politics. Horace describes himself as inspired by the god Bacchus (it may help to call him Greek Dionysus), driven by a power greater than himself to undertake a subject never treated before, 'nothing trivial or of humble scale, nothing of mortal utterance': he is to praise Augustus and set his immortal glory among the stars. As an analogue to the exalted emotion that has taken possession of him, he tells how a ministrant of the god, a Bacchanal, standing on a mountain ridge at night, gazes in wonder at a strange remote world, trodden only by wild, barbarian feet. Critics disagree about his success in blending elements seemingly so discordant. Novalis, that most Romantic of German poets of the period, responding to the visionary quality of the writing, took hold of the ode with both hands and translated it as Horace had never been translated before:

> Wohin ziehst du mich,
> Fülle meines Herzens,
> Gott des Rausches,
> Welche Wälder, welche Klüfte
> Durchstreif ich mit fremdem Mut.
> Welche Höhlen
> Horen in den Sternenkranz
> Caesars ewigen Glanz mich flechten
> Und den Göttern ihn zugesellen.
> Unerhörte, gewaltige
> Keinen sterblichen Lippen entfallene
> Dinge will ich sagen.
> Wie die glühende Nachtwandlerin,
> Die bacchische Jungfrau
> Am Hebrus staunt
> Und im thrazischen Schnee
> Und in Rhodope, im Lande der Wilden,
> So dünkt mir seltsam und fremd
> Der Flüsse Gewässer,
> Der einsame Wald

(*Where are you drawing me, fullness of my heart, god of drunken ecstasy, what woods, what chasms am I roaming through with strange courage. What caves hear me weave Caesar's eternal splendour into the garland of stars and rank him with the gods. Enormous, mighty words fallen from no mortal lips I want to say. As she the passionate night-wanderer, the Bacchic maid, marvels at the Hebrus and in the Thracian snow and in Rhodope, land of savages, so to me seem strange and alien the waters of the river, the lonely wood*). Intensified to some extent by Novalis yet undeniably present in the Latin is something quite outside Horace's normal range, a vision of nature seen not *sub specie humanitatis*, a spectacle affording urban man a serenity of spirit denied him by the city, but existing in its own strange non-human being.

There is nothing else like this in the *Odes*, but some lines in IV.3 may also suggest an 'unclassical' response to the natural world, not a sense of 'unknown modes of being', but rather a more than usually intimate relation between human and natural. Ode IV.3 is a song of thanksgiving to the muse who has given the poet (will give him, by the poem's fiction) his gift. It will not be athletic or military achievements that bring fame to the man she has once looked on –

> sed quae Tibur aquae fertile praefluunt
> et spissae nemorum comae
> fingent Aeolio carmine nobilem

'but rather the waters that flow past fertile Tibur and the thickly-leaved groves will make him famous for Aeolian song.' The last line is regularly translated in this way, but the verb *fingere* properly means to fashion or form, not make, and it may be that what Horace means is that the beauty of the natural scene will form him, pass into him and make him what he is – a poet famous for Aeolian song. The young Hölderlin translated the poem in 1798 and his rendering of the last line, with *fingere* given its full meaning, suggests that he understood the Latin in this way: 'Werden ihn trefflich bilden zum äolischen Liede', 'will form him wonderfully for Aeolian song'. It looks as though he found in Horace, that pillar of the classical establishment, something akin to 'And beauty born of murmuring sound / Shall pass into her face.'*

In the same decade Wordsworth translated the famous ode for the fountain of Bandusia. Still largely neoclassical in style, it is not a notable performance. It matters because the ode left its mark on his work, overtly in the first of the sonnets for the river Duddon ('that crystal Spring, / Bandusia, prattling as when long ago / The Sabine Bard was moved her praise to sing') and again in 'Liberty' ('Or when the prattle of Bandusia's spring / Haunted his ear'). More interesting than these clear allusions is the fifth of the *Poems on the Naming of Places*, 'To M.H.'. Although there is nothing here that

---

* L. P. Wilkinson, *Horace and his Lyric Poetry* (1945), p. 57, caught the Wordsworthian note.

directly recalls Horace's ode, we sense its informing presence in the description of 'the small bed of water in the woods' round which cattle can drink sheltered from sun and wind, a veiled classical echo that also describes a known place near where Wordsworth and his sister chose a home. 'The scene comes from Horace, and also from life,' David Ferry writes. Ronsard in 'A la fontaine Bellerie' had imitated Horace's ode and at the same time celebrated a spring near his own birthplace, but with Wordsworth the relation between poem and place is more intimate, the imprint of the ode more lasting.

Wordsworth's feeling for Horace – 'he is my great favourite,' he wrote in a letter; 'I love him dearly' – is by this time somewhat unusual. The great tidal changes in taste and sensibility did not leave Horace high and dry, but they left him a diminished figure. Like other Latin poets he suffered from nineteenth-century *Gräkomanie* – 'we are all Greeks,' Shelley said enthusiastically. And within the Latin field he faced stiff competition from Catullus who was passionate and sincere whereas he withdrew defensively into irony to distance himself from his tepid emotions. 'No passion here,' Landor complained of an ode for the death of a friend, a charge that was to continue to be levelled against him in the present century. 'Against the granite acridity of Catullus' passion,' Pound wrote, 'Horace has but the clubman's poise.' Eliot, quoting some lines from Marvell's 'Coy Mistress', observed the presence of Horace there, adding 'And not only Horace but Catullus himself.' *Himself* – we move on to a higher plane.

Virtues for which he had always been admired – Horace the great artificer, the cunningest maker we have ever had – begin to look more like defects. He is seen as a technician, skilfully manipulating Latin words into complicated Greek metrical forms. His verbal artistry and *curiosa felicitas*? Why yes, a gift for the well-turned phrase, for the well-rubbed tags that come pat to their occasion. A clever, entertaining poet certainly, but perhaps not a sufficiently serious one? Arnold, sounding more like Beerbohm's earnest little girl in pigtails than his own distinguished self, addressed the question frontally, not to say ponderously, in his 1857 inaugural address as Professor of Poetry at Oxford:

... Horace wants seriousness ... the men of taste, the men of cultivation, the men of the world, are enchanted with him; he has not a prejudice, not an illusion, not a blunder. True! yet the best men in the best ages have never been thoroughly satisfied with Horace. If human life were complete without faith, without enthusiasm, without energy, Horace ... would be the perfect interpreter of human life: but it is not ... Horace warms himself before the transient fire of human animation and human pleasure while he can, and is only serious when he reflects that the fire must soon go out: –

> 'Damna tamen celeres reparant coelestia lunae:
> Nos, ubi decidimus –'

'For nature there is renovation, but for man there is none' – it is exquisite, but it is not interpretative and fortifying.*

Others were less polite. For Meredith, Horace was 'the versifier of the enthroned enemy: poet of the conforming unbeliever ... for old men who have given up thinking and young men who never had feeling'. Victorian reservations about Horace's poetry do not mean that he was less read or less well known. He was all too well known, that was part of the trouble. Everyone with a formal education had read him at school, and they often disliked what they read. 'Then farewell, Horace, whom I hated so,' Byron sang in *Childe Harold*, recalling 'The drill'd dull lesson, forc'd down word for word.' Swinburne wrote to a friend expressing his regret that 'you are spending any part of your valuable time on Horace ... My dislike of him – dating from my schooldays – is one of the very few points on which I find myself in sympathy with Byron.' Kipling wrote in his autobiography that his classics master 'taught me to loathe Horace for two years; to forget him for twenty, and then to love him for the rest of my days and through many sleepless nights.'† In his story 'Regulus' he gives a vivid picture of the classroom grind, the boys struggling to come up with a construe accurate enough to pass muster, the poem itself meaning nothing to

---

* Matthew Arnold on the Classical Tradition, ed. R. H. Super (1960), p. 36.
† *Something of Myself* (1937), p. 37.

them. Tennyson suffered in the same way in his youth, but his mature work shows that he too came to love Horace and did him splendid service with his invitation poem 'To the Rev. F. D. Maurice', bringing the genre back to life at a level that can stand beside the best seventeenth-century work.

If translation of Horace does not show to advantage in the Victorian age, this is hardly surprising; it was not a period when the art flourished. Early in the century there is Shelley, still insufficiently recognized as one of our major poet-translators, but in the years that follow little is worth reading apart from FitzGerald's *Rubáiyát*, Rossetti's delicate versions from early Italian lyric, and Swinburne's Villon and the superb chorus from Aristophanes' *Birds*. The best Horace is the not quite complete translation of the first of the Roman Odes which Hopkins wrote in his twenties, ballasting his lines – with an English not a Latin weight – in a way that may distantly remind us of Jonson:

> One better backed comes crowding by: –
> That level power whose word is Must
> Dances the balls for low or high:
> Her urn takes all, her deal is just.

But the Horace who went so well into Jacobean or Augustan dress does not readily pass disguised as a Victorian. One of the very few translators who managed to make him do so is Sir Stephen de Vere in his version of Ode II.16:

> When the pale moon is wrapt in cloud,
> And mists the guiding stars enshroud;
> When on the dark Aegean shore
> The bursting surges flash and roar;
> The mariner with toil opprest
> Sighs for his home, and prays for rest.

The blurred, evocative effect (evoking what? Perhaps, though hardly to the purpose, Shelley's waning moon, 'like a dying lady, lean and pale / Who totters forth, wrapt in a gauzy veil') is attractive in its way, but how anaemic it feels beside Horace's Latin or beside Cowper's sturdy verse:

> Ease, is the weary Merchant's Pray'r,
>   Who Ploughs by Night th' Aegean Flood,
> When neither Moon nor Stars appear,
>   Or Glimmer faintly thro' the Cloud.

'Why hope that foreign suns can dry our tears?' de Vere writes, but Horace, who wrote *quid terras alio calentis / sole mutamus?*, does not break up his lines to weep. There is iron in the *Odes* as in all the best poetry and it must not be softened.

John Conington, the Horatian translator-general of the nineteenth century as Francis had been of the eighteenth, cannot be accused of writing in the style of the day, and indeed laid it down that 'the chief danger which a translator has to avoid is that of subjection to the influences of his own period.' In avoiding this danger, however, the translator runs into another, that of writing in the style of no period, writing of actions and emotions that take place nowhere:

> What, fight with cups that should give joy?
>   'Tis barbarous; leave such savage ways
> To Thracians. Bacchus, shamefaced boy,
>   Is blushing at your bloody frays.
> The Median sabre! lights and wine!
>   Was stranger contrast ever seen?
> Cease, cease this brawling, comrades mine,
>   And still upon your elbows lean.   (from I.27)

But no one is brawling here and the scene takes place nowhere except in a limbo marked Classical Roman. It is refreshing to turn back to Dr P.'s hearty Jacobean rumpus. Vigorous but, a reader may object, the good doctor doesn't give you Horace. Nor does Conington, even though his words match Horace's as closely as a rhyming version can, for he was a distinguished classical scholar, Corpus Professor of Latin at Oxford. It is a curious performance, this long labour of – what? Hardly of love, for of the *Odes* at least he seemed to have thought rather poorly, finding them full of 'lyrical commonplace' made tolerable only by the attractive Latin.

It is easy to be unjust to Conington. His accomplishment is of a kind that now gives the least pleasure, and if he leaves us with no sense of intimacy with Horace, that sense was no part of his purpose. The Horace whom Francis could describe as a poet 'who was by no means an enemy to a glass of good wine' has become a classic; one doesn't have to like him, merely know all about him. If Conington's verse is chilly and unloving – so that one is pulled up short by the sudden adventitious warmth of an ode beginning 'The rain, it rains not every day' – it is very efficient and metrically dexterous. Here the *Odes* all are, Latin on the left page, English on the right, except when a minatory note informs us that 'this ode is not included in Professor Conington's translation.' His handling of the *Satires* and *Epistles* is no less competent and on the whole more satisfying. Writing in heroic couplets, he aimed at a generally eighteenth-century style in the manner of Cowper, but if you use eighteenth-century couplets you risk coming fatally close to the master of the couplet. ('With sword and shield the commonwealth protect, / With morals grace it and with laws correct.') Conington was praised in his day because readers with good Latin admired his skill in packing so much of the literal sense of the original into neat rhyming lines; but until such time as living poets are moved to try their hand at the hexameter poems, those wishing to enjoy this substantial part of Horace's oeuvre had best remount the stream and turn to plain, honest Creech, to the accomplished Francis and the many eighteenth-century gentlemen who wrote with ease, or – the best course – to their final successor, the now quite forgotten Francis Howes. Although not published until 1848, his translation of the *Satires* and *Epistles* (he did not tackle the *Odes*) seems to have been written early in the century and still has the old confidence and style.

It is a relief to pass from Conington to C. S. Calverley whose translation of fifteen odes and of Epode II appeared in the same period, the 1860s. He too keeps close to the Latin and uses a standard poetic koiné bearing no special mark of the time, but he is a writer in a sense that Conington isn't. He has a finer ear, his diction is superior, and at his best he leaves one wondering whether to speak of a genuine poetic gift or of a knack so clever that it looks like the real thing. The product of a cultivated Victorian amateur, Calverley's poems were popular and reprinted a number of times, the last in 1913. They include translations of Greek and Latin poems into English and of English poems into Latin, with Horace's alcaics done in the *In Memoriam* quatrain, Tennyson's quatrains in Horatian alcaics. There are original poems sometimes in English – an 'Ode to Tobacco', for instance, where Horace's Black Care seated behind the rider finds a place in the first of the deft little stanzas – and sometimes in Latin, like *Carmen Saeculare*, full of august Virgilian phrases introduced for light purposes, and contemporary references duly explained in Latin footnotes (*'bacciferas tabernas*: id quod nostri vocant "tobacco shops"'). All hopelessly dated? No doubt, yet those who find themselves ill at ease in the cultural climate of our own happy day (Mr Sisson's phrase) can still read Calverley with pleasure, pleasure that hindsight turns to melancholy at the thought that these are late autumnal graces hanging at the edge of winter: 1913, Armageddon one year away. The sense of an ending, of *tout ce qui se resume dans ce mot: chute*, is still stronger if we turn from Calverley to the Horatian versions by Austin Dobson, the strong Roman stanzas miniatured into dainty late-medieval French forms, rondeaux, rondelles, villanelles. Armageddon just round the corner, the loss of a whole generation of the best-educated in the trenches in France, virtues slowly built up over the centuries blown to nothing in four terrible years, the Russian revolution, new styles in the arts challenging and threatening to destroy everything that had gone before, the profound social and educational changes that were to dislodge classical culture from its place at the centre and leave most literary people less handy with Latin than their forerunners had been in the dark ages. We might imagine Horace saying to himself as he looked down from Olympus, 'So this is the end of me, and the end of a lot more too. Well, I've had a pretty good run for my money!' As indeed he had, outlasting eternal Rome by fifteen hundred years.

History had a different turn of events in mind. Much was to be lost irreparably, but in all forms of artistic and intellectual life there was also renewal, not least in literature, a recovery of forgotten resources in which two Americans led the way. Eliot, after establishing relations with recent French work, reached back to the metaphysicals and to Jacobean drama, and further still to the great strength of Dante and to antiquity. The lines in *The Waste Land* beginning 'Phlebas the Phoenician' are more *classical* than anything written in the nineteenth century. Pound sought for nothing less than the renewal of the whole tradition of Western literature while making a profitable long arm to ancient China, and regained for translation a position it had not enjoyed since Dryden.

These recoveries did not immediately benefit Horace, but they prepared the way for his recovery later in the century, and here too Eliot and Pound played important roles, even though Eliot seems never to have cared for Horace, and Pound turned to him seriously only towards the end of his creative life. Yet he always knew that Horace was there. In a letter of 1917 to Joyce he included a rather poor version of part of Ode IV.10 in 'mellifluous archaism' ('I am reduced to translating Horace'), and in the curmudgeonly article on Horace published in *The Criterion* of 1930 he quoted the first line of I.4 (*Solvitur acris hiems grata vice veris et Favoni*), remarking that it 'has a week's work in it for any self-respecting translator'. Eliot, in his essay on Marvell, seeking to define the kind of wit found in the seventeenth-century lyric, spoke of 'a tough reasonableness beneath the slight lyric grace'. Omit the word 'slight' and from the same essay add 'this alliance of levity and seriousness (by which the seriousness is intensified)', and you might think that Eliot was speaking of the *Odes*. The importance of this essay for our present purposes is that it established a critical climate, critical expectations and standards, more hospitable to Horace than those of the previous century. Eliot's essay dates from 1921. Four years earlier Pound had completed *Homage to Sextus Propertius*, a 'regrounding of the original in a contemporary sensibility'* which discovered in another Augustan poet the alliance which Eliot spoke of.

Horace was none the less to remain on the sidelines for some years yet. Poets seldom worked Horatian allusions into their verse; the New Critics, so concerned with irony and wit, could have found a good deal in the *Odes* that was grist to their mill, had they thought of looking into them. I. A. Richards ignored him; Empson too, who might have pointed to much that in our dullness we have missed, passed him by. Among the poets, however, there were those who did not forget Horace. In Portugal we have the strange phenomenon of Pessoa's Horatian heteronym Ricardo Reis writing the brief lyrics that in translation may seem no more than clever echoes of antiquity but rather are 'subtle and original modulations on the Horatian stance' (Alberto de Lacerda). In England there is Kipling who saw in Horace a virtuoso close to his heart and made creative use of him as few have done. His story 'Regulus' (1917) ends with a poem called 'A Translation. Horace, Book V, Ode 3', a part of the oeuvre that is of course not easy to lay one's hands on. Nor is this a translation; it is on the face of it a parody of a schoolboy's construe that, as Charles Martindale remarks, reveals 'an alert understanding of the nuts and bolts of Horace's style',† and ends with the memorable picture of the poet 'sunk in thought profound / Of what the unaltering Gods require', a more serious Horace than had been glimpsed for a long time. Kipling was to go on to write several more odes from 'Book V', the finest placed at the end of 'The Eye of Allah' (1926), Kipling at his gravest speaking with the grave voice of Horace reincarnate. But the literati were ignoring Kipling just as they were ignoring Horace, and few paid any attention to these masterly poems.

It was not until the middle of the century that Horace began to make himself felt again. He had to contend with the general lack of Latin, but this was less of a disaster than one might have expected, for it meant that he was no longer dogged by memories of

---

* J. P. Sullivan, *Ezra Pound and Sextus Propertius* (1964), p. 20.
† *Horace Made New*, p. 4.

classroom drudgery, no longer was he all-too-familiar boring old Horace, great-uncle's favourite bard. Having lain idle for fifty years, the soil was ready to be turned again, his poetry once again virgin territory that it might be fun to inspect. The title of Lawrence Durrell's poem 'On First Looking into Loeb's Horace' probably reflects the experience of a certain number of people, poets on a day when the fish were not biting and literary types here and there who, stumbling on a promising phrase in the stilted Loeb translation, might try to elicit it from the facing original, acquiring a smidgen of Latin in the process and picking up a bit more later.

The first important indication of a real return comes with Auden, who in 'Thanksgiving', written in the last months of his life, named Horace, 'adroitest of makers', as one of the poets without whom 'I couldn't have managed / even my weakest of lines.' There may be some suggestion of Horace in the formal, rather stiff stanzas of his 1939 'In Memory of Sigmund Freud', but the Horatian presence only comes clear in a poem like 'Ischia' (1948) where the ear attuned to these pleasures can hear, in lines that move to the natural rhythms of speech, English approximations to classical metrical units, choriambs, bacchiacs, iambs, trochees, cretics, like cut Roman bricks strengthening the walls of a laxer age:

> Deàrèst tŏ eách hĭs bírthpláce; bùt tŏ rĕcáll ă green
> vállĕy whĕre múshroŏms fáttèn ĭn thĕ súmmĕr níghts
>   ănd sílvèred wíllŏws cópў
>   thĕ círcŭmfleĭctiòns ŏf thĕ stréam.

(An acute in this rough and ready notation marks a stressed syllable, a grave a syllable carrying a lighter stress (nònplússed), ˘ a syllable with no or minimal stress.) The single lines in this poem have their place in sentences that overrun the stanzas (indented in a manner resembling the Horatian alcaic stanza), sometimes in ways as syntactically complex as this:

> Always with some cool space or shaded surface, too,
>   you offer a reason to sit down; tasting what bees
>   offer from the blossoming chestnut
>   or short but shapely dark-haired men

> from the aragonian grape distil, your amber wine,
> your coffee-coloured honey . . .

The construction is chiastic:

> tasting what bees from the chestnut   or men from the grape distil
>
> your amber wine   your coffee-coloured honey

This is more Latin than English, certainly than modern English, and it seems likely that Auden, feeling his way into the role of a latter-day Horatian, was led to try his hand at complicated constructions of this sort because he had found similar things in the *Odes* – the intricate architecture of the final stanzas of the Cleopatra Ode, for example, to which Fraenkel drew attention:*

> . . . quae generosius
> perire quaerens nec muliebriter
>   expavit ensem nec latentis
>   classe cita reparavit oras;
>
> ausa et iacentem visere regiam
> vultu sereno, fortis et asperas
>   tractare serpentis, ut atrum
>   corpore combiberet venenum,
>
> deliberata morte ferocior,
> saevis Liburnis scilicet invidens
>   privata deduci superbo
>   non humilis mulier triumpho.

(*But she, seeking to die more nobly, neither in woman's fashion feared the sword, nor tried to reach some secret shore with her swift fleet. She brought herself to look with serene face on her fallen capitol, brave enough to handle the poisonous asps, that she might draw the black venom into her body, fiercer now that she had resolved on death; grudging the cruel Liburnian galleys her passage to Rome, a queen no longer, for a haughty*

---

* *Horace* (1957), p. 160.

triumph – no common woman this!) Enclosed within the two participial clauses (*quaerens, invidens*) are two *nec* clauses followed by two *et* clauses, the second opening out with *ut* into a final clause. A diagram may show the pattern more clearly:

>   quaerens   nec muliebriter
>   nec latentis
>
>   ausa et iacentem
>   fortis et aspera ... ut ...
>   invidens ...

Auden knew Latin and read Horace in the original. We may however find qualities that seem genuinely Horatian – the tough reasonableness beneath the lyric grace, the alliance of levity and seriousness by which the seriousness is intensified – in poets who show no interest in Horace and may not even have had any Latin. These qualities we can expect to find in poets at home in English poetry and hence influenced, consciously or not, by the pervasive presence of Horace. Poets in full command of their medium, capable of moving up and down the tonal scale and unaffected by 'the rumour that verse has been liberated' (Eliot's impeccable words). Philip Larkin suggests himself as a poet who meets these conditions, 'Lines on a Young Lady's Photograph Album' as a poem that might be worth looking at in the light of an ode like I.19. Let admirers of Larkin who prize his stern insularity not be affronted by the relation to Horace proposed here. Let them, if they wish, insist that no such relation ever entered Larkin's mind, and attend rather to what his poem, one written in our own day in our own idiom, may have to tell us about Horace's poem, written in Latin two thousand years ago.

Both poems start from a particular occasion, Larkin's from the album which the girl has let him look at, Horace's (after a flourish of mythology which can be left to look after itself) from a party he has just left, very excited by someone he met there.* Larkin's

---

* To speak in this way is to disregard the warning in the latest commentary that 'needless to say the ode has no bearing on real life.' Classical scholars have a touching faith in their ability to decide what constitutes the real life of a poem.

snapshots show different aspects of the girl, Horace provides several descriptions. The first is quite conventional: her beauty shines like Parian marble (famous for its dazzling whiteness). He is not so deeply involved after all. Larkin's way of misdirecting us is by his tone or pose of amused detachment: 'Too much confectionery, too rich: / I choke on such nutritious images.' Horace now becomes more specific, recalling the girl's *grata protervitas* – she is attractive in a provocative way; so perhaps he is a little involved. Larkin looks at a shot of the girl wearing a trilby hat: 'faintly disturbing, that, in several ways', putting the line in brackets – only *faintly* disturbing, you understand. Then, abruptly, no longer detached, his carefully maintained balance shaken, he speaks out: 'From every side you strike at my control.' Horace too is jolted and uses a word that in this context is startling: her face is *lubricus*, 'slippery' ('slippery looks that balk the lover's gaze'. Smart translated). Then he too speaks not out but up, very far up: *in me tota ruens Venus*, 'Venus rushing on me in full force.' Editors speak of 'the high tragic tone'. Roman readers would recall a powerful line from Greek tragedy, we are likely to recall Racine's version of the Greek line, 'C'est Vénus tout entière à sa proie attachée.' Both poets then go their different ways.

The English and the Roman poems interact, helping each other and helping us to read them better, or could do so if we let them. By negotiating Larkin's shifts of tone and perspective we respond more sensitively to similar manoeuvres in Horace. And responding to Horace's ability suddenly to rise to a higher stylistic level (or to similar effects in a great English Horatian like Pope) allows us, since this is a resource less readily available to modern poets, to bring an extra edge of admiration to the way that Larkin, after the beautifully modulated banter of 'Not quite your class, I'd say, dear, on the whole', invokes photography, of all things, in the formal eighteenth-century manner: 'But o, photography!' Not 'O', that would be too period, and not of course 'oh'.

The time had come to start translating Horace again, and three poets set to: C. H. Sisson, Basil Bunting and Pound. Sisson and Bunting both translated the same poem, II.14, the Postumus Ode, and their versions reveal a range of options open to the translator today. Sisson, trusting to the traditional resources of English poetry, has given us the gravest account of this great poem that we have:

> The years go by, the years go by you, nameless,
> I cannot help it nor does virtue help.
>   Wrinkles are there, old age is at your elbow,
>   Death on the way, it is indomitable.

This does everything that translators in the past have been expected to do; taking the permissible liberties, it matches Horace's powerful Latin with hardly less powerful English. What it does not do and does not try to do is directly convey the 'feel' of the original, the weight, the slow implacable thud, of the Latin syllables:

> Eheu fugaces, Postume, Postume,   ––∪–– –∪∪–∪∪
> labuntur anni, nec pietas moram   ––∪–– –∪∪–∪–
>   rugis et instanti senectae   ––∪–––∪––
>   adferet indomitaeque morti.   –∪∪–∪∪–∪––

(Alas, rapid, Postumus, Postumus,
glide by, years, nor will piety a barrier
against wrinkles and forward-pressing age
bring and, unconquerable, death.)

The first naked encounter with Horace's words lies some way behind Sisson's version; they have been absorbed, transmuted, and an English poem has taken the place of the Latin poem. Bunting, by contrast, has tried to make his English words enact the physical impact of Horace's Latin:

> You can't grip years, Postume
> that ripple away nor hold back
> wrinkles and, soon now, age,
> nor can you tame death . . .

Allowing for the fact that English words are usually shorter than Latin, this moves at about the same slow pace as the original, some fifteen seconds to Horace's twenty, and has some of the Latin weight. Bunting believed, like Pound, that quantity plays an important role in English verse, not quite Latin syllabic length but weight enforcing our native stress accent, and his lines must be scanned in something of the way that we scan the Latin lines. 'You cán't gríp yeárs, Póstŭmĕ', three weighted syllables (a molossus, if one wants classical terms) followed by a dactyl, followed in the next line by a choriamb, 'that rípplĕ ăwáy', followed by another molossus, 'nór hóld báck', still another in the next line, 'soón nów, áge', with the stanza coming to an end with a spondee and with 'death' the final word, as in Horace though not in Sisson.

Where Sisson's allegiances are to the English tradition, Bunting tries to move on English ground as though it were Roman. Readers will have their own views about the method and merits of the two translations. What can be said against Bunting's verse form is that it requires the translator to keep at it all the time; he can never relax and let his form work for him. Bunting picks the wrong place to relax when he comes to *linquenda tellus et domus et placens / uxor*. This calls for poetry at the level of 'Men must endure / Their going hence, even as their coming hither.' Beyond any translator's reach; but something better is needed than Bunting's casual 'We must let earth go and home, / wives too.' Sisson scores here, using words as simple as Horace's set within our traditional metric which has carried some of the greatest poetry ever written: 'Your house, your wife, and the familiar earth, / All will recede.' This has something of what is required, what Christopher Ricks, speaking of another poet, calls 'a flat fidelity' with 'no sense of grievance or of being victimized'.[*]

Remarkable too is Sisson's treatment of the *Carmen Saeculare* or Centennial Hymn, an imitation in the full eighteenth-century manner (as Lowell's for the most part are not, being very free paraphrases), with Rome and Roman circumstance replaced by England and English circumstance. Not often translated and not much admired, the Hymn is a religious, patriotic ode commissioned by Augustus, a prayer for the prosperity of Rome designed to support the moral reforms which the princeps was calling for, and in

---

[*] *The Force of Poetry* (1987), p. 279.

particular to endorse his proposed marriage laws. A difficult assignment, since Horace felt himself called on to assert that the traditional Roman virtues were now truly returning, a claim that many must have treated with scepticism. A far more difficult poem, one would imagine, for Sisson to English in the decade after the swinging, miniskirted sixties. What he does is pick his way through the original, abandoning whatever is beyond his reach, imitating when he can (where Horace speaks of Aeneas bringing the survivors of ruined Troy to Italy, Sisson describes the legendary founding of England by Brutus), and replacing affirmation by questions about the all but impossible possibility of recovering the old English virtues. When Horace affirms (in Michie's close translation)

> Now Faith and Peace and Honour and old-fashioned
> Conscience and unremembered Virtue venture
> To walk again –

Sisson asks

> Might you not even remember the old worship?
> Can you remember the expression 'Honour'?
> There was, at one time, even Modesty.
> Nothing is so dead it does not come back.

Having gone, questioning, as far as he can, Sisson, a man of the old covenant, a Christian, a patriot, a monarchist, finally comes down plump on affirmation:

> There is God. There are no Muses without him . . .
>
> It is he who holds London from Wapping to Richmond . . .
>
> Have you heard the phrase: 'the only ruler of princes'?
> Along the Thames, in the Tower, there is the crown.
> I only wish God may hear my children's prayers.
>
> He bends now over Trafalgar Square.
> If there should be a whisper he would hear it.
> Are not these drifting figures the chorus?

If these drifting figures are closer to Eliot's hapless crowd flowing over London Bridge than to the comely Roman children who sang Horace's hymn on a June day in 17 BC, so be it. Sisson will not, as Horace felt himself compelled to do, affirm more than he himself can believe. His imitation is a finer, truer poem than the stately original.

Pound, recognizing virtues he had missed before, eventually, inevitably, turned to Horace, perhaps in the 1950s. The three translations he made may be taken as the final testament of *le grant translateur*. Ode I.31, notable if only though not only for two lines as beautiful as those of Horace, with the gentle felicity of cadence he achieved in his final phase:

> Land where Liris crumbles her bank in silence
> Though the water seems not to move.

(*Non rura quae Liris quieta* / *mordet aqua taciturnus amnis*). Ode III.30, *Exegi monumentum*, which makes for Horace the proud claim for work done and achieved that in his sad old age Pound felt unable to make for his own. And I.11, probably the most closely thought-through translation of Horace that we have. The burden of long familiarity lifted, the *Odes* are now open at every point to fresh reading; they must be re-explored, reimagined, all over again with nothing taken for granted. Fully to read this uncommonly dense piece of writing is not possible here, so a couple of passages must suffice. Horace writes:

>   ut melius, quidquid erit, pati,
>   seu pluris hiemes seu tribuit Iuppiter ultimam,
>   quae nunc oppositis debilitat pumicibus mare
>   Tyrrhenum.

(*How much better to take what comes, whether Jupiter has granted many* hiemes, *or whether this is the last which now wears down the Tuscan sea against the opposing rocks.*) *Hiemes* are winters or winter storms, also by convention years, the years of our life. Horace calls the rocks *pumices*, pumice, volcanic rock eaten into holes by the sea (the sea that is worn down, Horace says, by the rocks against which it is driven; like most translators, Pound turns the sea from patient to agent). The sea's action against the rocks yields Pound's 'gnawing', a more aggressive verb than *debilitat*, which gives him 'tooth' which in turn uncovers the ancient figure of the tooth of time, Ovid's *tempus edax rerum*, Shakespeare's 'devouring time'. For Pound's poem, as Horace's is not, is a poem of old age, still resilient, facing and fighting against the winter of our days: 'winter is winter.'

Pound opens up a new stanza for his counter-attack, unlike Horace who continues without a break:

> . . . spatio brevi
> spem longam reseces. dum loquimur, fugerit invida
> aetas: carpe diem, quam minimum credula postero.

(*In the brief space [allotted us], cut back long hope. While we are speaking, envious time will have run on. Pluck [the flower of] today, believing as little as possible in tomorrow.*) *Reseco* means cut back, a metaphor from pruning vines. (*Vina liques*, Horace has just written.) Pound takes the verb in another way which the Latin permits: cut back so as to loosen or remove. Hope is like a trailer that impedes our movement, preventing us from living fully in the moment, our only true possession. Hence, since life is short, we should cut off long hope for a time that is denied us, that we can't count on. While we talk, time will have run on, so: *carpe diem*. This famous injunction has become hardly more than a cracker-motto; it must be rethought and worked back into the poem by another route. Horace bids us take hold of the brief essence of our day and relish it. Pound provides a stronger defence by turning the tables on time and making it serve us. Time is itself to hold our day, holding it and so making us hold it – in unbelief, the wise unbelief that saves us from the folly of thinking that we have a long span ahead of us. 'Trusting as little as possible in tomorrow', Horace ends. Pound's final line has a braver ring, for the old poet has a more urgent enemy to fight against: 'Holding our day more firm in unbelief.'

There is always something missing in the poetry of an age when Horace is missing, and if there is any charge that can be levelled against even the best nineteenth-century poetry it is that – for the first time since the later days of Elizabeth – his steadying hand is felt so seldom there. To some extent we are better off today and it is heartening to be able to report that a true Horatian poet is now writing in Cambridge, Massachusetts, David Ferry. The translation of the past, however much we may cherish it, cannot keep a poet alive; he must be re-embodied in the speech of each new day.

The translations of Pound and still more of Bunting reveal the difficulty of this re-embodiment. They acknowledge a rift that has opened up between Horace and ourselves even while seeking with much virtuosity to overcome it. Ferry by contrast has found an English into which Horace's lyrics will pass with no apparent strain; the gravely beautiful language he made for his own poetry will, he has discovered, accommodate Horace's with very little waste. Odes of which one could say that the best translation was made at such and such a date – Bishop Atterbury's late seventeenth-century version of IV.3, for instance, the poet's homage to the muse who gave him his gift – have now a fresh, no less satisfying incarnation. Odes hitherto imperfectly rendered are coming alive for the first time. The opening ode of the first book we can now see as more than a rather trite comparison of men's various pursuits to the poet's calling; Ferry has uncovered a real poem there. The high Roman stance of a patriotic poem like III.6, too high for our humbler day, has been chastened and given at least a chance of addressing us. Ode IV.13, on the face of it one of Horace's unpleasantly Gilbertian pieces about amorous old women, turns out to be a moving poem. If time has brought once beautiful Lyce down, it has dealt no more kindly with her former lover who has seemed to be mocking her. There is no mockery in Ferry's final line, 'Old crow, old torch burned out, fallen away to ashes', rather a deeply pathetic even tragic sense of loss. The *Odes* are coming steadily to David Ferry's hand, over seventy by now, with the prospect of the whole four books plainly in sight.

Thirty years before in England James Michie had brought off this feat at a consistently readable level. If we may not often feel required to speak here of poetry, we can count ourselves lucky in getting that very honourable and now very rare thing, good verse with no pretensions to be anything more than that. Horace has been the recipient of too much failed poetry from people known as 'poets in their own right', for the most part poor poets and even poorer translators. Michie is an accomplished verse-man who can shape a stanza, catch the tone, especially of the lighter poems, very happily, and is skilful at devising English equivalents for Horace's Greek metres. And he has given us credible versions of some of the public, political poems (notably of the Centennial Hymn or *Carmen Saeculare*) which poet-translators shy away from, finding them to be outside our present cultural range. Perhaps they are, but we still want to have them in English if we can get them.

The *Satires* and *Epistles* have fared less well than the *Odes* and still await their modern re-embodiment. A poem like Frost's 'The Lesson for Today' shows however that what Reuben Brower calls the Horatian poetry of talk can still be written, and very recently there is Thom Gunn's superb 'An Invitation' modelled on Jonson's 'Inviting a Friend to Supper', strong Jonsonian coin that rings as true as when the master coined it. We must hope that poet-translators will take the *sermones*, the hexameter poems, in hand too, for this is a useful, all-purpose form generically impure enough to welcome the small change of life, open also to graver issues approached in a seemingly offhand manner, yet written in formal verse submissive to the proper metrical discipline.

Looking back over the long venture of Horatian translation, one may ask how successfully has Horace been Englished. One answer is: rather more so than one might have expected. Another is: all too successfully, for if there is any charge that can be levelled against even the best translations of Horace over the last four centuries it is that they have made him sound far too English. The fact is that the *Odes* are very unlike any English poems, and unlike other Latin poems. When they first appeared, Charles Martindale remarks, Roman readers may have found them 'weirdly experimental. In them we meet a style which combines the arty and the prosaic, along with a highly artificial, mannered word order and a structural wilfulness which can require a reader to strain in the attempt, taxing or vain, to apprehend.' (*Horace Made New*, p. 3.) The contortions of Kipling's parody ('There are whose study is of smells') are closer to the way that Horace actually writes than any translation. To bring Horace over into English and make an English poet of him is certainly a great achievement, but for which he would not have left so lasting a mark on our poetry and our national culture, yet it is open to the accusation which George Steiner makes when he claims that the translator who takes this course 'only appropriates what is concordant with his own sensibility and the prevailing climate. He does not enforce new, perhaps recalcitrant sources of experience on our consciousness. And he does not preserve the autonomous genius of the original, its powers of "strangeness".'* We may regret that translators did not on occasion go this way about it and force English into Horace's Latin mould. This, Goethe held, is the highest form of translation, the third and chronologically last in the tripartite scheme he proposed. Here the translator more or less abandons the genius of his own language and seeks to create something new, an amalgam of the foreign or alien and the native. Translations of this kind are very rare in English and indeed there is only one example that can be considered successful, Milton's version of the Ode to Pyrrha. One must speak cautiously here since much depends on when it was written. If early, perhaps in his later teens, then it may be that he was doing simply what he described himself as doing with no theoretical purpose in mind, rendering the original 'almost word for word without Rhyme according to the Latin Measure, as near as the Language will permit'. If, however, this translation was written in his full maturity after he had studied the linguistic innovations carried out in early sixteenth-century Italy – which aimed at what amounts almost to a new language, Italian with Latin diction and syntax imposed on the native stock – then the Pyrrha Ode may be more ambitious than either its admirers or detractors have seen. We find Milton inventing a new form, a stanza that was

---

* *After Babel* (1975), p. 259

to have great influence on original poetry (between 1700 and 1837, it has been reckoned, at least eighty-three poems were written in Milton's stanza, most notably Collins' 'Ode to Evening'), but not, curiously enough, on Horatian translation. The only instances seem to be the two renderings 'after the Manner of Milton' by Thomas Warton. Like Horace, Milton runs the sense on from stanza to stanza, and he does not rhyme. For all *les bienfaits de la rime* (it gave Milton the lovely Bellini blue at the end of 'Lycidas'), there is a good case to be made against turning Horace into a rhymer. Quiller-Couch made it, rather too strongly, when he argued that 'the nuisance of rhyme [is that] it can hardly help suggesting the epigram, the clinch, the verse "brought off" with a little note of triumph.'* Milton's avoidance of rhyme has not caused displeasure, but his Latinisms have. Seen, however, in this experimental light they no longer look like pedantry. It is beside the point to complain that a line like 'Who now enjoyes thee credulous, all Gold' is more Latin than English. It is meant to be. To say that it is not comprehensible without the Latin is simply not true; it is perfectly clear in the context that 'credulous' applies to the observer, 'all Gold' to the person observed. More important, this is convincing poetic speech – of a new kind.† A kind that, we must hope, translators in the days to come will learn to write, in the process giving us, sometimes (the word should be stressed), not English Horace but difficult, foreign, *Latin* Horace through whose intricate stanzas we make our careful way as we do with the originals.

---

* 'The Horatian Model in English Verse', *Studies in Literature*: First Series (1930), p. 66.
† Clough tried his hand at translation of this sort, juggling *qui fragilem truci / commisit pelago ratem* (Ode I.3) into 'who, frail to fierce, / committed bark to billow', but he lacked the strength effectively to force English into the Latin mould.

FURTHER READING

Reuben Brower, *Alexander Pope: The Poetry of Allusion*, Oxford, Clarendon Press, 1959.
Steele Commager, *The Odes of Horace: A Critical Study*, Yale University Press, 1962.
Eduard Fraenkel, *Horace*, Oxford, Clarendon Press, 1957.
J. B. Leishman, *Translating Horace*, Oxford, Bruno Cassirer, 1956.
Horace Made New, ed. Charles Martindale and David Hopkins, Cambridge University Press, 1993.
Maren-Sofie Røstvig, *The Happy Man*, second edition, Norwegian University Press, 1962.
George Steiner, Introduction to *The Penguin Book of Modern Verse Translation*, London, 1966.
Gordon Williams, *Tradition and Originality in Roman Poetry*, Oxford, Clarendon Press, 1968.

TABLE OF DATES

65 BC — Birth of Quintus Horatius Flaccus at Venusia (modern Venosa) in Apulia. His father, born a slave, won his freedom and held the post of tax-collector.

— — Accompanied by his father, Horace goes to Rome for his schooling.

c.46 — Goes to Athens for the equivalent of a university education.

44 — Assassination of Julius Caesar. Brutus arrives in Athens and raises the Republican standard. Like many young Romans, Horace rallies to the cause, and despite lack of military training is appointed to the post of *tribunus militum*, staff officer attached to a legion.

42 — Republican defeat at Philippi. Horace's experiences in the rout obliquely described in Odes II.7.

41 — Returns to Rome to find his father's property confiscated. Supports himself by procuring a clerkship in the Treasury. Begins to write verse, probably the *Epodes*.

39/8 — On friendly terms with Virgil, who introduces him to Maecenas. Joins his circle in the next year.

c.35 — First book of *Satires*.

c.34 — Maecenas presents Horace with his Sabine 'farm', an estate about thirty miles north-east of Rome with five attached farms, a bailiff and eight slaves.

30 — Second book of *Satires*.

23 — Books I–III of the *Odes*.

? — Introduced to Augustus and comes to be on close enough terms with him to receive humorous personal letters. Invited to become his private secretary, but tactfully declines, alleging poor health.

20   *Epistles*, Book I.
17   Commissioned by Augustus to compose the *Carmen Saeculare*, a prayer for the prosperity of Rome designed for public performance.
18–14 Book II of the *Epistles* (including the *Ars Poetica*)
13   Book IV of the *Odes*
8   Death of Maecenas. Horace dies two months later.

To the Translatour

What shal I first commend? your happy choice
Of this most usefull Poet? or your skill,
To make the Eccho equall with the voice,
And trace the Lines drawne by the Authors quill?
The Latine Writers by unlearned hands,
In forraine Robes unwillingly are drest,
But thus invited into other Lands,
Are glad to change their tongue at such request.
The good, which in our minds their labours breed,
Layes open to their Fame a larger way.
These strangers England with rich plentie feed,
Which with our Countreys freedome we repay:
   When sitting in pure Language like a Throne,
   They prove as great with us, as with their owne.

Sir John Beaumont

(Prefixed to Sir Thomas Hawkins' *Odes of Horace*, 1625)

ODES

HENRY HOWARD, EARL OF SURREY (1517?–1547)

Courtier and soldier, executed for treason on a trumped-up charge. Described by Thomas Warton in his *History of English Poetry* (1781) as 'the first English classical poet'. Notable for his pioneer use of blank verse in his translation of Books II and IV of the *Aeneid*, and for introducing (with Wyatt) the sonnet into English.

Ode II.10

Of thy lyfe, Thomas, this compasse well mark:
Not aye with full sayles the hye seas to beat,
Ne by coward dred, in shonning stormes dark,
On shalow shores thy keel in perill freat.
Who so gladly halseth the golden meane
Voyde of dangers advisdly hath his home:
Not with lothsom muck, as a den uncleane,
Nor palacelyke wherat disdayn may glome.
The lofty pyne the great winde often rives;
10 With violenter swey falne turrets stepe;
Lightninges assault the hye mountains and clives.

---

5 *halseth* embraces

A hart well stayd, in overthwartes depe
Hopeth amendes; in swete doth feare the sowre.
God that sendeth withdrawth winter sharp.
Now ill, not aye thus. Once Phebus to lowre
With bow unbent shall cease, and frame to harp
His voyce. In straite estate appere thou stout;
And so wisely, when lucky gale of winde
All thy puft sailes shall fil, loke well about,
20   Take in a ryft. Hast is wast, profe doth finde.   (pub. 1557)

ANON.

Ode II.10

From Tottel's *Miscellany* (1557).

Of the golden meane

The wisest way, thy bote, in wave and winde to guie,
Is neither still the trade of middle streame to trie:
Ne (warely shunnyng wrecke by wether) aye to nie,
    To presse upon the perillous shore.
Both clenely flees he filthe: ne wonnes a wretched wight,
In carlish coate: and carefull court aie thrall to spite,
With port of proud astate he leves: who doth delight,
    Of golden meane to hold the lore.
Stormes rifest rende the sturdy stout pineapple tre.
10 Of lofty rising towers the fals the feller be.
Most fers doth lightenyng light, where furthest we do se.
    The hilles the valey to forsake.

---

12 *overthwartes* difficulties
20 *ryft* reef (part of a sail)
9 *pineapple* pine cone

Well furnisht brest to bide eche chanses changing chear.
In woe hath chearfull hope, in weal hath warefull fear,
One self Jove winter makes with lothfull lokes appear,
    That can by course the same aslake.
What if into mishap thy case now casten be?
It forceth not such forme of luck to last to thee.
Not alway bent is Phebus bow: his harpe and he,
20   Ceast silver sound sometime doth raise.
In hardest hap use helpe of hardy hopefull hart.
Seme bold to beare the brunt of fortune overthwart.
Eke wisely when forewinde to full breathes on thy part,
    Swage swellyng saile, and doubt decayes.   (pub. 1557)

ANON.

Ode II.10

From Tottel's *Miscellany*.

The meane estate is to be accompted the best

Who craftly castes to stere his boate
    and safely skoures the flattering flood:
He cutteth not the greatest waves
    for why that way were nothing good.
Ne fleteth on the crocked shore
    lest harme him happe awayting lest.
But wines away betwene them both,

---

15 *One self* One and the same
22 *overthwart* adverse
24 *doubt decayes* fear ruin
2 *flattering* delusively promising
6 *awayting lest* expecting it least

as who would say the meane is best.
Who waiteth on the golden meane,
   he put in point of sickernes:
Hides not his head in sluttishe coates,
   ne shroudes himself in filthines.
Ne sittes aloft in hye estate,
   where hatefull hartes envie his chance:
But wisely walkes betwixt them twaine,
   ne proudly doth himself avance.
The highest tree in all the woode
   is rifest rent with blustring windes:
The higher hall the greater fall
   such chance have proude and lofty mindes,
When Jupiter from hie doth threat
   with mortall mace and dint of thunder,
The highest hilles ben batrid eft
   when they stand still that stoden under.
The man whose head with wit is fraught
   in welth will feare a worser tide,
When fortune failes dispaireth nought
   but constantly doth stil abide.
For he that sendith grisely stormes
   with whisking windes and bitter blastes
And fowlth with haile the winter's face
   and frotes the soile with hory frostes,
Even he adawth the force of colde,
   the spring in sendes with somer hote.
The same full oft to stormy hartes
   is cause of bale: of joye the roote.
Not always il though so be now
   when cloudes ben driven then rides the racke.
Phebus the fresh ne shoteth still
   sometime he harpes his muse to wake.

---

10 *put* is put; *sickernes* security
32 *frotes* chafes
33 *adawth* subdues

Stand stif therfore pluck up thy hart
    lose not thy port though fortune faile.
Againe whan wind doth serve at will,
    take hede to hye to hoyse thy saile.   (pub. 1557)

ANON.

Ode IV.7

From Tottel's *Miscellany*.

All worldly pleasures fade

The winter with his griesly stormes no lenger dare abyde,
The plesant grasse, with lusty grene, the earth hath newly dyde.
The trees have leves, the bowes don spred, new changed is
    the yere.
The water brokes are cleane sonke down, the pleasant bankes
    apere.
The spring is come, the goodly nimphes now daunce in
    every place.
Thus hath the yere most plesantly of late ychangde his face.
Hope for no immortalitie, for welth will weare away,
As we may learne by every yere, yea howres of every day.
For Zepharus doth mollifye the colde and blustering windes:
10 The somer's drought doth take away the spryng out of our
    minds.
And yet the somer cannot last, but once must step asyde,
Then Autumn thinkes to kepe hys place, but Autumn cannot
    bide.
For when he hath brought furth his fruits and stuft the barns
    with corn,
The winter eates and empties all, and thus is Autumn worne.

Then hory frostes possesse the place, then tempestes work much harm,
Then rage of stormes done make al colde whiche somer had made so warm,
Wherfore let no man put his trust in that, that will decay,
For slipper welth will not cuntinue, plesure will weare away.
For when that we have lost our lyfe, and lye under a stone,
20 What are we then, we are but earth, then is our pleasure gon.
No man can tell what god almight of every wight doth cast,
No man can say to day I live, till morne my lyfe shall last.
For when thou shalt before thy judge stand to receive thy dome,
What sentence Minos dothe pronounce that must of thee become.
Then shall not noble stock and blud redeme the from his handes,
Nor sugred talke with eloquence shal lowse thee from his bandes.
Nor yet thy lyfe uprightly lead, can help thee out of hell,
For who descendeth downe so depe, must there abyde and dwell.
Diana could not thence deliver chaste Hypolitus,
30 Nor Theseus could not call to life his frende Periothous.

(pub. 1557)

SIR PHILIP SIDNEY (1554–1586)

Born at Penshurst, attended Christ Church, Oxford. Travelled in Europe between 1572 and 1577, fought in the Low Countries against the Spaniards and died of a wound received in a skirmish near Zutphen. His work – the two versions of *Arcadia*, the sonnet sequence *Astrophil and Stella* and *The Defence of Poesie* – and the romantic character of his personal history won him an almost ideal fame.

Ode II.10

You better sure shall live, not evermore
   Trying high seas, nor while Sea rage you flee,
   Pressing too much upon ill harbourd shore.

The golden meane who loves, lives safely free
   From filth of foreworne house, and quiet lives,
   Releast from Court, where envie needes must be.

The wynde most oft the hugest Pine-tree greeves:
   The stately towers come downe with greater fall:
   The highest hills the bolt of thunder cleeves:

10 Evill happes do fill with hope, good happes appall
   With feare of change, the courage well preparde:
   Fowle Winters as they come, away they shall.

Though present times and past with evils be snarde,
   They shall not last: with Citherne silent muse
   Apollo wakes, and bow hath sometime sparde.

In hard estate with stowt shew valor use,
   The same man still in whom wysdome prevailes,
   In too full winde draw in thy swelling sailes.   (pub. 1598)

ANON.

Ode III.9 An imitation, found among the papers of Sir Henry Wotton

A Dialogue betwixt God and the soul

Soul.   Whilst my Souls eye beheld no light
        But what stream'd from thy gracious sight
        To me the worlds greatest King,
        Seem'd but some little vulgar thing.

God.   Whilst thou prov'dst pure; and that in thee
        I could glass all my Deity:
        How glad did I from Heaven depart,
        To find a lodging in thy heart!

Soul.   Now Fame and Greatness bear the sway,
10   ('Tis they that hold my prisons Key:)
        For whom my soul would die, might she
        Leave them her Immortalitie.

God.   I, and some few pure Souls conspire,
        And burn both in a mutual fire,
        For whom I'ld die once more, ere they
        Should miss of Heavens eternal day.

Soul.   But Lord! what if I turn again,
        And with an adamantine chain,
        Lock me to thee? What if I chase
20   The world away to give thee place?

> *God.* Then though these souls in whom I joy
> Are Seraphins, Thou but a toy,
> A foolish toy, yet once more I
> Would with thee live, and for thee die. (1651)

BEN JONSON (1572–1637)

Educated at Westminster School under the antiquarian William Camden, worked briefly as a bricklayer's apprentice, saw military service in Flanders, and then joined Henslowe's company as player and playwright, his first play *Every Man in his Humour* coming four years later in 1598. Dramatist, poet, masque-writer, scholar, one of the greatest figures of the 'Giant Race before the Flood'.

Ode III.9

Dialogue of Horace, and Lydia

> *Hor.* Whilst, Lydia, I was lov'd of thee,
> And ('bout thy Ivory neck,) no youth did fling
> His armes more acceptable free,
> I thought me richer then the Persian King.
> *Lyd.* Whilst Horace lov'd no Mistres more,
> Nor after Chloë did his Lydia sound;
> In name, I went all names before,
> The Roman Ilia was not more renown'd.
> *Hor.* 'Tis true, I'am Thracian Chloës, I,
> Who sings so sweet, and with such cunning plaies,
> As, for her, I'ld not feare to die,
> So Fate would give her life, and longer daies.
> *Lyd.* And I, am mutually on fire
> With gentle Calais, Thurine Orniths Sonne;
> For whom I doubly would expire,

        So Fates would let the Boy a long thred run.
Hor.   But, say old Love returne should make,
        And us dis-joyn'd force to her brazen yoke,
           That I bright Chloë off should shake;
20   And to left-Lydia, now the gate stood ope.
Lyd.   Though he be fairer then a Starre;
        Thou lighter then the barke of any tree,
           And then rough Adria, angrier, farre;
        Yet would I wish to love, live, die with thee. (pub. 1640)

Ode IV.1

Venus, againe thou mov'st a warre
Long intermitted, pray thee, pray thee spare:
   I am not such, as in the Reigne
Of the good Cynara I was: Refraine,
   Sower Mother of Sweet Loves, forbeare
To bend a man, now at his fiftieth yeare
   Too stubborne for Commands so slack:
Goe where Youths soft intreaties call thee back.
   More timely hie thee to the house,
10 With thy bright Swans, of Paulus Maximus:
   There jest, and feast, make him thine host,
If a fit livor thou dost seeke to toast;
   For he's both noble, lovely, young,
And for the troubled Clyent fyl's his tongue,
   Child of a hundred Arts, and farre
Will he display the Ensignes of thy warre.
   And when he smiling finds his Grace
With thee 'bove all his Rivals gifts take place,
   He'll thee a Marble Statue make
20 Beneath a Sweet-wood Roofe, neere Alba Lake:
   There shall thy dainty Nostrill take
In many a Gumme, and for thy soft eares sake
   Shall Verse be set to Harpe and Lute,

      And Phrygian Hau'boy, not without the Flute.
         There twice a day in sacred Laies,
      The Youths and tender Maids shall sing thy praise:
         And in the Salian manner meet
      Thrice 'bout thy Altar with their Ivory feet.
         Me now, nor Wench, nor wanton Boy,
30   Delights, nor credulous hope of mutuall Joy,
         Nor care I now healths to propound;
      Or with fresh flowers to girt my temple round.
         But, why, oh why, my Ligurine,
      Flow my thin teares, downe these pale cheeks of mine?
         Or why, my well-grac'd words among,
      With an uncomely silence failes my tongue?
         Hard-hearted, I dreame every Night
      I hold thee fast! but fled hence, with the Light,
         Whether in Mars his field thou bee,
40   Or Tybers winding streames, I follow thee.   (pub. 1640)

ANON.

Ode II.3

Attributed to Ben Jonson in John Ashmore's *Certain Selected Odes of Horace* (1621). The style and the paraphrastic treatment of the original make the attribution improbable.

      Remember, when blinde Fortune knits her brow,
    Thy minde be not dejected over-lowe:
    Nor let thy thoughts too insolently swell,
    Though all thy hopes doe prosper ne'r so well.
    For, drink thy teares, with sorrow still opprest,
    Or taste pure vine, secure and ever blest,
    In those remote and pleasant shady fields

Where stately Pine and Poplar shadow yeelds,
Or circling streames that warble, passing by;
10 All will not help, sweet friend: For, thou must die.
   The house, thou hast, thou once must leave behind thee,
And those sweet babes thou often kissest kindly:
And when th'hast gotten all the wealth thou can,
Thy paines is taken for another man.
   Alas! what poor advantage doth it bring,
To boaste thy selfe descended of a King!
When those, that have no house to hide their heads,
Finde in their grave as warm and easie beds.   (pub. 1621)

SIR JOHN BEAUMONT
(1583?–1627)

Author of narrative and religious poetry (*Bosworth-field*, *Crowne of Thornes*), one of those who helped to develop the heroic couplet towards its classical form, and brother of the dramatist Francis Beaumont. His translation of this ode is remarkably accomplished for the period.

Ode III.29

Mecaenas, (sprung from Tuscan Kings) for thee
Milde Wine in vessels never toucht I keepe,
   Here Roses, and sweete Odours be,
      Whose dew thy haire shall steepe:

O stay not, let moyst Tibur be disdain'd,
And Aesulaes declining fields, and hills,
   Where once Telegonus remain'd,
      Whose hand his father kills;

ODE III.29 · SIR JOHN BEAUMONT

    Forsake that height where lothsome plenty cloyes,
10 And towres, which to the lofty clouds aspire,
      The smoke of Rome her wealth and noyse
        Thou wilt not here admire.

    In pleasing change, the rich man takes delight,
    And frugall meales in homely seates allowes,
      Where hangings want, and purple bright
        He cleares his carefull browes.

    Now Cepheus plainely shewes his hidden fire,
    The Dog-starre now his furious heate displayes,
      The Lion spreads his raging ire,
20   The Sunne brings parching dayes.

    The Shepheard now his sickly flocke restores,
    With shades, and Rivers, and the Thickets finds
      Of rough Silvanus, silent shores
        Are free from playing winds.

    To keepe the State in order is thy care,
    Sollicitous for Rome, thou fear'st the warres,
      Which barbrous Easterne troopes prepare,
        And Tanais us'd to jarres.

    The wise Creator from our knowledge hides
30 The end of future times in darksome night;
      False thoughts of mortals he derides,
        When them vaine toyes affright.

    With mindfull temper present houres compose,
    The rest are like a River, which with ease,
      Sometimes within his channell flowes,
        Into Etrurian Seas.

Oft stones, trees, flocks, and houses it devoures,
With Echoes from the hills, and neighb'ring woods,
   When some fierce deluge, rais'd by showres,
40   Turnes quiet Brookes to Floods.

He master of himselfe, in mirth may live,
Who saith, I rest well pleas'd with former dayes,
   Let God from heav'n to morrow give
      Blacke clouds, or Sunny rayes.

No force can make that voide, which once is past,
Those things are never alter'd, or undone,
   Which from the instant rolling fast,
      With flying moments run.

Proud Fortune joyfull sad affaires to finde,
50 Insulting in her sport, delights to change
   Uncertaine honours: quickly kinde,
      And straight againe as strange.

I prayse her stay, but if she stirre her wings,
Her gifts I leave, and to my selfe retire,
   Wrapt in my vertue: honest things
      In want no dowre require.

When Lybian stormes, the mast in pieces shake,
I never God with pray'rs, and vowes implore,
   Lest precious wares addition make
60   To greedy Neptunes store.

Then I contented, with a little bote,
Am through Aegean waves, by winds convay'd,
   Where Pollux makes me safely flote,
      And Castors friendly aide.   (pub. 1629)

ROBERT HERRICK (1591–1674)

Born in London, apprenticed for ten years to his uncle, a goldsmith, after which he attended St John's College, Cambridge. Ordained, he spent nearly twenty years as a parish priest at Dean Prior in Devonshire, 'this dull Devon-shire', he calls it, though he tells us that he wrote some of his best verse there. He only once translated Horace, but his work is full of Horatian echoes and no less of Martial and the *Anacreontea*.

Ode III.9

A Dialogue betwixt Horace and Lydia

Hor. While, Lydia, I was lov'd of thee,
　　　　Nor any was preferr'd 'fore me
　　　　To hug thy whitest neck: Then I,
　　　　The Persian King liv'd not more happily.

Lyd. While thou no other didst affect,
　　　　Nor Cloe was of more respect;
　　　　Then Lydia, far-fam'd Lydia,
　　　　I flourish't more then Roman Ilia.

Hor. Now Thracian Cloe governs me,
　　　　Skilfull i' th' Harpe, and Melodie:
　　　　For whose affection, Lydia, I
　　　　(So Fate spares her) am well content to die.

Lyd. My heart now set on fire is
　　　　By Ornithes sonne, young Calais;
　　　　For whose commutuall flames here I
　　　　(To save his life) twice am content to die.

Hor. Say our first loves we sho'd revoke,
And sever'd, joyne in brazen yoke:
Admit I Cloe put away,
20 And love againe love-cast-off Lydia?

Lyd. Though mine be brighter then the Star;
Thou lighter then the Cork by far:
Rough as th' Adratick sea, yet I
Will live with thee, or else for thee will die.   (pub. 1648)

After Ode II.14 and other odes. Here abridged.
(For the allusions, see Introduction, p. 7.)

*His age, Dedicated to his peculiar friend, M. John Wickes,
under the name of Posthumus*

Ah Posthumus! Our yeares hence flye,
And leave no sound; nor piety,
    Or prayers, or vow
Can keepe the wrinkle from the brow:
    But we must on,
As Fate do's lead or draw us; none,
None, Posthumus, co'd ere decline
The doome of cruell Proserpine.

The pleasing wife, the house, the ground
10 Must all be left, no one plant found
    To follow thee,
Save only the Curst-Cipresse tree:
    A merry mind
Looks forward, scornes what's left behind:
Let's live, my Wickes, then, while we may,
And here enjoy our Holiday.

W'ave seen the past-best Times, and these
Will nere return, we see the Seas,
  And Moons to wain;
20 But they fill up their Ebbs again:
   But vanisht man,
Like to a Lilly-lost, nere can,
Nere can repullulate, or bring
His dayes to see a second Spring.

But on we must, and thither tend,
Where Anchus and rich Tullus blend
  Their sacred seed:
Thus has Infernall Jove decreed;
   We must be made,
30 Ere long, a song, ere long, a shade.
Why then, since life to us is short,
Lets make it full up, by our sport.

Crown we our Heads with Roses then,
And 'noint with Tirian Balme; for when
  We two are dead,
The world with us is buried.
   Then live we free,
As is the Air, and let us be
Our own fair wind, and mark each one
40 Day with the white and Luckie stone.

We are not poore; although we have
No roofs of Cedar, nor our brave
  Baiae, nor keep
Account of such a flock of sheep;

> Nor Bullocks fed
> To lard the shambles: Barbels bred
> To kisse our hands, nor do we wish
> For Pollio's Lampries in our dish.
>
> If we can meet, and so conferre,
50 Both by a shining Salt-seller;
> And have our Roofe,
> Although not archt, yet weather proofe,
> And seeling free,
> From that cheape Candle baudery:
> We'le eate our Beane with that full mirth,
> As we were Lords of all the earth.
>
> Well then, on what Seas we are tost,
> Our comfort is, we can't be lost.
> Let the winds drive
60 Our Barke; yet she will keepe alive
> Amidst the deepes;
> 'Tis constancy (my Wickes) which keepes
> The Pinnace up; which though she erres
> I' th' Seas, she saves her passengers.
>
> Say, we must part (sweet mercy blesse
> Us both i' th' Sea, Camp, Wildernesse)
> Can we so farre
> Stray, to become lesse circular,

---

46 *shambles* slaughter-house; *Barbels* fish
48 *Pollio's Lampries* Pollio punished a slave by throwing him to his lampreys.
50 refers to the English custom of dividing the honoured guests who sat 'above the salt' (a large salt-cellar was placed in the middle of the table) from less honoured guests who sat 'beneath the salt'. Also alludes to Ode II.16.
54 *baudery* dirt
68 *circular* complete, perfect

                    Then we are now?
70   No, no, that selfe same heart, that vow,
        Which made us one, shall ne'r undoe;
        Or ravell so, to make us two ...   (pub. 1648)

JOHN ASHMORE (*fl.* 1621)

Probably a native of Ripon in Yorkshire, the first translator to produce a whole book of odes. His *Certain Selected Odes of Horace* was published in 1621.

Ode II.16

No outward thing thee well can bring
  Unto a quiet minde.
Within it is, that brings this bliss:
  There helpe we best may finde.

The Marchant toyl'd in the Egëan Sea,
  When Phoebe's face is vail'd with a dark cloud,
And the known stars from sight are fled away,
  For ease unto the gods doth cry aloud.

For Ease, the Thracians (terrible in warre)
  For ease, the Medes (with comely quivers bold)
O Grosphus, to the gods still suters are,
  Bought with no gems, with purple, or with gold.

No treasure, neither Sergeant can arrest
10   The wretched hurly-burlies of the minde,
And cares with rest-less wings that beat the breast,
  And in faire-fretted roofes still harbour finde.

He lives well with a little, that doth keep
　　His late Sires table furnisht with meane fare;
That is not robd of rest, nor scar'd from sleep
　　With hide-bound Avarice, or heart-scorching Care.

Why doe we, short-liv'd things, on tentars set
　　Our greedy thoughts with vaine desire of pelf?
In climats furthest off, What would we get?
　　Who, from his Countrey exil'd, flees from himselfe?

Care, vice-borne, climbs into the brass-stemd ships:
　　In warlike troupes her selfe she slily shrowds:
Swifter then Stags, swifter then windes she skips,
　　That do disperse, and drive away the clowds.

Be Joviall while time serves (Time will not stay.)
　　Hate curiously t' enquire what will betide:
Sowr discontentments with sweet mirth allay.
　　Entirely good, nothing doth still abide.

Untimely death did stout Achilles slay:
　　Old age Tithonus did Epitomize:
And my birth-star perhaps grants me a day
　　To date my life; which thine to thee denies.

Faire flocks of sheep, fat heards of cattell low
　　About thee, and thy lustfull Mare with pride
Neighs out, now for the Chariot fit: and thou
　　Wearst purple, twice in Tyrian liquors dy'd.

The Dest'nie, ne'r deceiv'd, on me bestowes
　　A little ground, and veine of Poësie
Which from the plesant Greekish fountains flowes,
　　And th' un-taught Vulgar wils me to defie.　　(pub. 1621)

SIR THOMAS HAWKINS (d. 1640)

A Catholic recusant, with family estates at Nash Court, Kent. His *Odes of Horace The Best of Lyrick Poets, Contayning much morallity, and sweetnesse* was published in 1625, with further editions in 1631, 1635 and 1638.

Ode I.11

Strive not (Leuconoe) to know what end
The Gods above to thee or me will send:
Nor with Astrologers consult at all,
That thou may'st better know what can befall.
Whether, thou liv'st more winters, or thy last
Be this, which Tyrrhen waves 'gainst rocks do cast;
Be wise, drink free, and in so short a space,
Do not protracted hopes of life embrace.
Whilest we are talking, envious time doth slide:
10 This day's thine own, the next may be deny'd. (1666)

Ode II.3

In adverse chance, an equall mind retaine,
As in best fortunes temp'red, free from vaine
Of mirth profuse: For (Delius) thou must dy,
Though with sad thoughts oppress'd, thou silently;
Or, on Feast dayes retyr'd to grassie shade,
Thou with choyce Falerne wine art happy made:
Where the white Poplar, and the lofty Pine,
In friendly shade their mutuall branches twine:
And Rivers swiftly gliding strive, apace
10 'Bout crooked bankes, their trembling streames to chase.

Bring hither Wine, and od'rous Unguents. Bring
The dainty Rose, a faire, but fading thing.
While Fortune, age, and wealth yeeld seasons fit,
And the three Sisters sable loomes permit:
Thou from thy house must part, and purchas'd woods,
From village lav'd, with yellow Tybers floods,
And thy vast hoarded heaps of wealths excesse,
An Heire (perhaps) ungratefull shall possesse.
No matter 'tis, whither thou rich art borne,
20   Of Argive Kings; or low, expos'd to scorne,
Sprung from poore Parents, liv'st in open fields;
Thou art Death's sacrifice, (who never yeelds.)
Wee all are thither brought, 'tis hee that turnes,
And winds our mortall life's uncertaine Urnes.
Sooner or later each man hath his lot,
And hence exil'd, embarques in Charon's Boat.   (pub. 1625)

JOHN MILTON (1608–1674)

Ode I.5 'Rendred almost word for word without Rhyme according to the Latin Measure, as near as the Language will permit.'

For the date of this translation and a discussion of Milton's intentions, see Introduction, pp. 57–8. The frequent complaint that 'plain in thy neatness' (*simplex munditiis*) is 'too Puritan' is unfounded. 'Neat' in seventeenth-century usage ('finely or elegantly dressed; trim or smart in apparel', *OED*) is a close equivalent of Latin *mundus*, elegant or refined in appearance.

What slender Youth bedew'd with liquid odours
Courts thee on Roses in some pleasant Cave,
    Pyrrha for whom bindst thou

In wreaths thy golden Hair,
Plain in thy neatness; O how oft shall he
On Faith and changèd Gods complain: and Seas
    Rough with black winds and storms
    Unwonted shall admire:
Who now enjoys thee credulous, all Gold,
10 Who always vacant alwayes amiable
    Hopes thee; of flattering gales
    Unmindfull. Hapless they
To whom thou untry'd seem'st fair. Me in my vow'd
Picture the sacred wall declares t' have hung
    My dank and dropping weeds
    To the stern God of Sea.   (pub. 1673)

SIR RICHARD FANSHAWE
(1608–1664)

The first of the major translators of Horace, educated at Jesus College, Cambridge. Fought on the Royalist side in the Civil War; with the Restoration, knighted for his services and appointed ambassador to Portugal and Spain. In addition to *Selected Parts of Horace, Prince of Lyricks* (1652), translated Guarini's *Il Pastor Fido*, the *Lusiads* of Camoëns and, in Spenserian stanzas, the fourth book of the *Aeneid*. J. W. Mackail's *Studies of English Poets* (1926) includes an essay on Fanshawe.

Ode I.5

What Stripling now thee discomposes,
In Woodbine Rooms, on Beds of Roses,
    For whom thy Auburn hair
    Is spread, unpainted fair?

How will he one day curse thy Oaths,
And Heav'n that witness'd your Betrothals!
  How will the poor Cuckold,
  That deems thee perfect Gold,
Bearing no stamp but his, be maz'd
10 To see a suddain Tempest rais'd!
  He dreams not of the Windes,
  And thinks all Gold that shines.
For me my Votive Tablet showes
That I have hung up my wet Clothes
  Upon the Temple Wall
  Of Seas great Admirall.   (pub. 1652)

Ode I.27

No really satisfactory translation has yet been made of this, the cleverest of Horace's story-poems. For a good reading, see Eduard Fraenkel, *Horace*, pp. 179–83.

With Goblets made for Mirth, to fight,
'Tis barbarous: leave that Thracian rite,
  Nor mix the bashful blushing God
  Of Wine, with quarrels and with blood.
A Cand-stick, and Quart-pot, how far,
They differ from the Cymitar?
  Your wicked noise Companions cease,
  And on your Elbows lean in peace.
Would you have me to share th'austere
10 Falernian liquor: Let me hear
  Megella's brother, by what eyes,
  Of what blest wound and shaft he dies.
No! then will I not drink: whatever
Venus tames thee, she toasts thy Liver
  With fires thou hast no cause to cover,
  Still sinning an ingenuous lover.

Come, thou may'st lay it whatsoere
It is, securely in my Ear.
 Ah wretch! in what a Whirl-pool tane?
20 Boy worthy of a better flame,
What Witch with her Thessalian Rod
Can loose thee from those charmes? What God?
 Scarce Pegasus himself can thee
From this three-shap'd Chimera free.   (pub. 1652)

Ode III.1

I hate lay-Vulgar: make no noise,
Room for a Priest of Helicon:
I sing to noble Girls and Boyes
Such verses as were never known.
 Fear'd Kings command on their own Ground;
The King commanding Kings is Jove:
Whose Arme the Giants did confound,
Whose aweful brow doth all things move.
 One man may be a greater Lord
10 Of land than other: this may show
A nobler Pedegree: a third
In parts and fame may both out-go:
 A fourth in Clients out-vie all.
Necessity in a vast Pot
Shuffling the names of great and small,
Draws every one's impartial lot.
 Over whose head hangs a drawn sword,
Him cannot please a Royal feast:
Nor melody of lute or bird,
20 Give to his eyes their wonted rest.
 Sleep, gentle sleep, scorns not the poor
Abiding of the Plough-man: loves
By sides of Rivers shades obscure:
And rockt with West-windes, Tempe Groves.

That man to whom enough's enough,
Nor raging seas trouble his head,
Nor fell Arcturus setting rough,
Nor fury of the rising Kid:
   Not hail-smit Vines and years of Dearth;
30 Sometimes the too much wet is fault,
Sometimes the stars that broil the earth,
Sometimes the Winter that was nought.
   The Fish fear stifling in the sea,
Damm'd up. The Master-builder and
His men, the Land-sick Lord too, he
Throws rubbish in with his own hand.
   But fear and dangers haunt the Lord
Into all places: and black Care
Behind him rides: or, if on board
40 A ship, 'tis his companion there.
   If Marble keep not Feavers out,
Nor purple rayment help the blind,
Nor Persian Oyntments cure the gout,
Nor Massick Wines a troubled mind,
   With envied posts in fashion strange
Why should I raise a stately pile?
My Sabine vale why should I change
For wealth accompani'd with toyl?   (pub. 1652)

Ode IV.7

The snows are thaw'd, now grass new cloaths the earth,
   And trees new hair thrust forth.
The season's chang'd, and brooks late swoln with rain,
   Their proper banks contain.
Nymphs with the Graces linkt dare dance around
   Naked upon the ground.
That thou must die, the year and howers say
   Which draw the winged day.

First Spring, then Summer, that away doth chase,
    And must it self give place
To Apple-bearing Autumn, and that past,
    Dull Winter comes at last.
But the decays of time, Time doth repair:
    When we once plunged are
Where good Aeneas, with rich Ancus wades,
    Ashes we are, and shades.
Who knows if Jove unto thy life's past score
    Will adde one morning more?
When thou art dead, and Rhadamanthus just
    Sentence hath spoke thee dust,
Thy blood, nor eloquence can ransome thee,
    No nor thy piety.
For chast Hippolytus in Stygian night
    Diana cannot light:
Nor Theseus break with all his vertuous pains,
    His dear Perithous chains.   (pub. 1652)

Dr P.

Ode I.27 A paraphrase

Follows Fanshawe's version of the ode in Alexander Brome's *Poems of Horace . . . Rendred in English Verse by Several Persons* (1666). The author has been tentatively identified as the astronomer Walter Pope (d. 1714).

What? Quarrel in your drink, my friends? ye' abuse
    Glasses, and Wine, made for a better use.
'Tis a Dutch trick; Fie, let your brawling cease,
    And from your Wine and Olives learn both mirth and
        peace.

Your swords drawn in a Tavern, whilest the hand
   That holds them shakes, and he that fights cann't stand,
Sheath 'um for shame, embrace, kiss, so away,
   Sit down, and ply the business of the day.
But I'le not drink, unless T.S. declares
10   Who is his Mistress, and whose wounds he wears,
Whence comes the glance, from what sweet-killing-Eye,
   That sinks his Hope so low, and mounts his Muse so high!
Wilt thou not tell? Drawer, what's to pay?
   If you're reserv'd I'le neither drink nor stay:
Or let me go, or out w'it; she must be
   Worth naming, sure; whose Fate it was to conquer thee:
Speak softly, — She! forbid it Heaven above!
   Unhappy youth! unhappy in thy love;
Oh how I pity thy Eternal pain!
20   Thou never can'st get loose, thou never canst obtain;
Lets talk no more of love, my friends, lets drink again.   (1666)

RICHARD CRASHAW (1612/3–1649)

Attended Pembroke College, Cambridge, and was subsequently a Fellow of Peterhouse. Took part in the religious life of Little Gidding, but turned to Rome and brought into English verse the extremities of continental devotion. Author of *Steps to the Temple* (1646, enlarged 1648). What Hazlitt called 'his usual *hectic* manner' becomes this peculiar ode – lurid denunciation of the villain who planted the tree that nearly did for Horace, leading to a vision of poets in the underworld whose strains caused Cerberus to hang his black lugs. Horace can get away with a great deal, but perhaps not quite this much.

---

9 *T.S.* Thomas Sprat?

Ode II.13

Shame of thy mother soyle! ill-nurtur'd tree!
Sett to the mischeife of posteritie!
That hand, (what e're it were) that was thy nurse,
Was sacrilegious, (sure) or somewhat worse.
Black, as the day was dismall, in whose sight
Thy rising topp first staind the bashfull light.
That man (I thinke) wrested the feeble life
From his old father. That mans barbarous knife
Conspir'd with darknes 'gainst the strangers throate;
(Whereof the blushing walles tooke bloody note)
Huge high-floune poysons, ev'n of Colchos breed,
And whatsoe're wild sinnes black thoughts doe feed,
His hands have padled in; his hands, that found
Thy traiterous root a dwelling in my ground.
Perfidious totterer! longing for the staines
Of thy kind Master's well-deserving braines.
Mans daintiest care, and caution cannot spy
The subtile point of his coy destiny,
Which way it threats. With feare the merchants mind
Is plough'd as deepe, as is the sea with wind,
(Rowz'd in an angry tempest); Oh the sea!
Oh! that's his feare; there flotes his destiny:
While from another (unseene) corner blowes
The storme of fate, to which his life he owes.
By Parthians bow the soldjer lookes to die,
(Whose hands are fighting, while their feet doe flie.)
The Parthian starts at Rome's imperiall name,
Fledg'd with her Eagles wing; the very chaine
Of his captivity rings in his eares.
Thus, o thus fondly doe wee pitch our feares
Farre distant from our fates. Our fates, that mocke
Our giddy feares with an unlook't for shocke.

    A little more, and I had surely seene

Thy greisly Majesty, Hell's blackest Queene;
And Aeacus on his Tribunall too,
Sifting the soules of guilt; and you, (oh you!)
You ever-blushing meads, where doe the Blest
Farre from darke horrors home appeale to rest.
There amorous Sappho plaines upon her Lute
40 Her loves crosse fortune, that the sad dispute
Runnes murmuring on the strings. Alcaeus there
In high-built numbers wakes his golden lyre,
To tell the world, how hard the matter went,
How hard by sea, by warre, by banishment.
There these brave soules deale to each wondring eare
Such words, soe precious, as they may not weare
Without religious silence; above all
Warres ratling tumults, or some tyrants fall.
The thronging clotted multitude doth feast.
50 What wonder? when the hundred-headed beast
Hangs his black lugges, stroakt with those heavenly lines;
The Furies curl'd snakes meet in gentle twines,
And stretch their cold limbes in a pleasing fire.
Prometheus selfe, and Pelops sterved Sire
Are cheated of their paines; Orion thinkes
Of Lions now noe more, or spotted Linx. (undated)

SIR EDWARD SHERBURNE
(1616–1702)

Fought on the King's side in the Civil War. Translated widely from Greek and Latin.

Ode I.9

   Seest thou not, how Soractes Head,
(For all it's Height) stands covered
With a white Perriwigg of Snow?
Whilst the labouring Woods below
Are hardly able to sustain
The Weight of Winters feather'd Rain;
And the arrested Rivers stand
Imprison'd in an Icy Band?
Dispell the Cold; and to the Fire
10 Add fuell, large as it's Desire;
And from the Sabine Casque let fly
(As free as Liberality)
The Grapes rich blood, kept since the sun
His Annuall Course foure times hath run.
Leave to the Gods the rest, who have
Allay'd the Winds, did fiercely rave
In Battail on the Billowy main,
Where they did blustring tug for Raign.
So that no slender Cypress now,
20 It's Spirelike Crown does tott'ring, bow:
Nor aged Ashtrees, with the shock
Of Blasts impetuous, doe rock.
   Seek not to morrow's Fate to know;
But what day Fortune shall bestow,
Put to a discreet Usurie.
Nor (gentle youth!) so rigid be
With froward scorn to disapprove
The sweeter Blandishments of Love.
Nor mirthfull Revels shun, whilst yet
30 Hoary Austerity is set
Far from thy greener years; the Field
Or Cirque should now thy Pastime yield:

Now nightly at the Howre select,
And pointed Place, Loves Dialect,
Soft whispers, should repeated be;
And that kind Laughters Treacherie,
By which some Virgin closely layd
In dark Confinement, is betrayd:
And now from some soft Arm, or Wrist,
40   A silken Braid, or silver Twist,
Or Ring from Finger, should be gain'd,
By that too nicely not retain'd.   (pub. 1651)

Ode IV.10

Cruel, and fair! when this soft down,
    (Thy Youths bloom,) shall to bristles grow;
And these fair Curls thy shoulders crown,
    Shall shed, or cover'd be with snow:

When those bright Roses that adorn
    Thy Cheeks shall wither quite away,
And in thy Glass (now made Time's scorn)
    Thou shalt thy changed Face survey.

Then, ah then (sighing) thou'lt deplore
10   Thy Ill-spent Youth; and wish, in vain,
Why had I not those thoughts before?
    Or come not my first Looks again?   (pub. 1651)

ABRAHAM COWLEY (1618–1667)

Educated at Westminster School, and Scholar and Fellow of Trinity College, Cambridge. Cowley's oeuvre is hard to characterize, ranging from the unbridled *fougue* of his imitations of Pindar to the quietly reflective tone of his *Essays*. The fame he enjoyed as a poet in his own century (Milton is said to have declared that the three greatest English poets were Spenser, Shakespeare and Cowley) declined in the next century and has never really revived.

Ode I.5 An imitation

I
To whom now Pyrrha, art thou kind?
   To what heart-ravisht Lover,
Dost thou thy golden locks unbind,
   Thy hidden sweets discover,
     And with large bounty open set
All the bright stores of thy rich Cabinet?

II
Ah simple Youth, how oft will he
   Of thy chang'd Faith complain?
And his own Fortunes find to be
10   So airy and so vain,
     Of so Cameleon-like an hew;
That still their colour changes with it too?

III
How oft, alas, will he admire
   The blackness of the Skies?
Trembling to hear the Winds sound higher,
   And see the billows rise;
     Poor unexperienc'd He
Who ne're, alas, before had been at Sea!

IV

He'enjoyes thy calmy Sun-shine now,
   And no breath stirring hears,
In the clear heaven of thy brow,
   No smallest Cloud appears.
   He sees thee gentle, fair, and gay,
And trusts the faithless April of thy May.

V

Unhappy! thrice unhappy He,
   T' whom Thou untry'ed dost shine!
But there's no danger now for Me,
   Since o're Loretto's Shrine
   In witness of the Shipwrack past
My consecrated Vessel hangs at last.   (pub. 1656)

Ode III. 1 'Not exactly copyed, but rudely imitated.'

I

   Hence, ye Profane; I hate ye all;
   Both the Great, Vulgar, and the small.
To Virgin Minds, which yet their Native whiteness hold,
Not yet Discolour'd with the Love of Gold,
   (That Jaundice of the Soul,
Which makes it look so Guilded and so Foul)
To you, ye very Few, these truths I tell;
The Muse inspires my Song, Heark, and observe it well.

II

We look on Men, and wonder at such odds
   'Twixt things that were the same by Birth;
We look on Kings as Giants of the Earth,
These Giants are but Pigmeys to the Gods.
   The humblest Bush and proudest Oak,
Are but of equal proof against the Thunder-stroke.

Beauty, and Strength, and Wit, and Wealth, and Power
    Have their short flourishing hour;
    And love to see themselves, and smile,
And joy in their Preeminence a while;
    Even so in the same Land,
20 Poor Weeds, rich Corn, gay Flowers together stand;
Alas, Death Mowes down all with an impartial Hand.

III
And all you Men, whom Greatness does so please,
    Ye feast (I fear) like Damocles:
    If you your eyes could upwards move,
(But you (I fear) think nothing is above)
You would perceive by what a little thread
    The Sword still hangs over your head.
No Title of Wine would drown your cares;
No Mirth or Musick over-noise your feares.
30 The fear of Death would you so watchfull keep,
As not t' admit the Image of it, sleep.

IV
Sleep is a God too proud to wait in Palaces
And yet so humble too as not to scorn
    The meanest Country Cottages;
    His Poppey grows among the Corn.
The Halcyon sleep will never build his nest
    In any stormy breast.
    'Tis not enough that he does find
    Clouds and Darkness in their Mind;
40   Darkness but half his work will do.
'Tis not enough; he must find Quiet too.

V
The man, who in all wishes he does make,
    Does onely Natures Counsel take.
That wise and happy man will never fear
    The evil Aspects of the Year;

Nor tremble, though two Comets should appear;
He does not look in Almanacks to see,
    Whether he Fortunate shall be;
Let Mars and Saturn in th' Heavens conjoyn,
50 And what they please against the World design,
    So Jupiter within him shine.

VI
If of your pleasures and desires no end be found,
God to your Cares and Fears will set no bound.
    What would content you? Who can tell?
Ye fear so much to lose what you have got,
    As if you lik'd it well.
Ye strive for more, as if ye lik'd it not.
    Go, level Hills, and fill up Seas,
Spare nought that may your wanton Fancy please
60   But trust Me, when you 'have done all this,
Much will be Missing still, and much will be Amiss.

(pub. 1668)

Ode III.16 A paraphrase

I
    A Tower of Brass, one would have said,
        And Locks, and Bolts, and Iron bars,
And Guards, as strict as in the heat of wars,
Might have preserv'd one Innocent Maiden-head.
The jealous Father thought he well might spare,
        All further jealous Care,
And as he walkt, t' himself alone he smil'd,
        To think how Venus Arts he had beguil'd;
        And when he slept, his rest was deep,
10 But Venus laugh'd to see and hear him sleep.

She taught the Amorous Jove
A Magical receit in Love,
Which arm'd him stronger, and which help'd him more,
Than all his Thunder did, and his Almighty-ship before.

II
She taught him Loves Elixar, by which Art,
His Godhead into Gold he did convert,
No Guards did then his passage stay,
He pass'd with ease; Gold was the Word;
Subtle as Lightning, bright and quick and fierce,
20   Gold through Doors and Walls did pierce;
And as that works sometimes upon the sword,
Melted the Maiden-head away,
Even in the secret scabbard where it lay.
The prudent Macedonian King,
To blow up Towns, a Golden Mine did spring.
He broke through Gates with this Petar,
'Tis the great Art of Peace, the Engine 'tis of War;
And Fleets and Armies follow it afar,
The Ensign 'tis at Land, and 'tis the Seamans Star.

III
30 Let all the World, slave to this Tyrant be,
Creature to this Disguised Deitie,
Yet it shall never conquer me.
A Guard of Virtues will not let it pass,
And wisdom is a Tower of stronger brass.
The Muses Lawrel round my Temples spread,
'T does from this Lightnings force secure my head.
Nor will I lift it up so high,
As in the violent Meteors way to lye.
Wealth for its power do we honour and adore?
40 The things we hate, ill Fate, and Death, have more.

IV

From Towns and Courts, Camps of the Rich and Great,
The vast Xerxean Army I retreat,
And to the small Laconick forces fly,
    Which hold the straights of Poverty.
Sellars and Granaries in vain we fill,
    With all the bounteous Summers store,
If the Mind thirst and hunger still.
    The poor rich Man's emphatically poor.
    Slaves to the things we too much prize,
50 We Masters grow of all that we despise.

V

A Field of Corn, a Fountain and a Wood,
    Is all the Wealth by Nature understood,
The Monarch on whom fertile Nile bestows
    All which that grateful Earth can bear,
    Deceives himself, if he suppose
  That more than this falls to his share.
Whatever an Estate does beyond this afford,
    Is not a rent paid to the Lord;
But is a Tax illegal and unjust,
60 Exacted from it by the Tyrant Lust.
    Much will always wanting be,
    To him who much desires. Thrice happy He
To whom the wise indulgency of Heaven,
  With sparing hand, but just enough has given.   (pub. 1668)

From Ode IV.2 An imitation

Appropriately rendered in Pindariques since it was from lines 11–12 of this ode (*numerisque fertur lege solutis,* 'is borne along in measures free from rule') that Horace was understood to say that Pindar composed in irregular stanzas. For a closer reading see the translation by Philip Francis (pp. 179–81).

FROM ODE IV.2 · ABRAHAM COWLEY

The Praise of Pindar

I
Pindar is imitable by none;
The Phoenix Pindar is a vast Species alone.
Who e're but Daedalus with waxen wings could fly
And neither sink too low, nor soar too high?
    What could he who follow'd claim,
But of vain boldness the unhappy fame,
    And by his fall a Sea to name?
    Pindars unnavigable Song
Like a swoln Flood from some steep Mountain pours along,
    The Ocean meets with such a Voice
From his enlarged Mouth, as drowns the Oceans noise.

II
So Pindar does new Words and Figures roul
Down his impetuous Dithyrambique Tide,
    Which in no Channel deigns t' abide,
    Which neither Banks nor Dikes controul.
    Whether th' Immortal Gods he sings
    In a no less Immortal strain,
Or the great Acts of God-descended Kings,
Who in his Numbers still survive and Reign.
    Each rich embroidered Line,
    Which their triumphant Brows around,
    By his sacred Hand is bound,
Does all their starry Diadems outshine.

III
Whether at Pisa's race he please
To carve in polisht Verse the Conque'rors Images,
Whether the Swift, the Skilful, or the Strong,
Be crowned in his Nimble, Artful, Vigorous Song:
Whether some brave young man's untimely fate
In words worth Dying for he celebrate,

24   Such mournful, and such pleasing words,
As joy to'his Mothers and his Mistress grief affords:
       He bids him Live and Grow in fame,
       Among the Stars he sticks his Name:
The Grave can but the Dross of him devour,
So small is Deaths, so great the Poets power.

IV
Lo, how th' obsequious Wind, and swelling Ayr
       The Theban Swan does upwards bear
Into the walks of Clouds, where he does play,
And with extended Wings opens his liquid way.
40   Whilst, alas, my tim'erous Muse
       Unambitious tracks pursues;
       Does with weak unballast wings,
       About the mossy Brooks and Springs;
       About the Trees new-blossom'ed Heads,
       About the Gardens painted Beds,
       About the Fields and flowry Meads,
       And all inferior beauteous things
          Like the laborious Bee,
       For little drops of Honey flee,
50 And there with Humble Sweets contents her Industrie.
                                                                                    (pub. 1656)

JOHN DRYDEN (1631–1700)

Poet, dramatist, critic, and one of the greatest verse translators. He worked mainly with the Latin poets (Ovid, Juvenal, Persius, Virgil), but also translated Homer and Theocritus. About Horace he had

---

24 *Pisa's* Olympia's

mixed feelings: 'I must confess that the delight which [he] gives me is but languishing.' That he could respond more strongly is shown by his translations, notably of the Ode to Maecenas of which he wrote, 'I have endeavour'd to make it my masterpiece in English.'

Ode I.3
Inscrib'd to the Earl of Roscommon, on his intended Voyage to Ireland

So may th' auspitious Queen of Love,
And the twin Stars, (the Seed of Jove,)
And he, who rules the rageing wind
To thee, O sacred Ship, be kind,
And gentle Breezes fill thy Sails,
Supplying soft Etesian Gales,
As thou to whom the Muse commends,
The best of Poets and of Friends,
Dost thy committed Pledge restore:
10   And land him safely on the shore:
And save the better part of me,
From perishing with him at Sea.
Sure he, who first the passage try'd,
In harden'd Oak his heart did hide,
And ribs of Iron arm'd his side!
Or his at least, in hollow wood,
Who tempted first the briny Floud:
Nor fear'd the winds contending roar,
Nor billows beating on the shore;
20   Nor all the Tyrants of the Main.
What form of death cou'd him affright,
Who unconcern'd with stedfast sight,

---

6 *Etesian* summer wind from the north-east

Cou'd view the Surges mounting steep,
And monsters rolling in the deep?
Cou'd thro' the ranks of ruin go,
With Storms above, and Rocks below!
In vain did Natures wise command,
Divide the Waters from the Land,
If daring Ships, and Men prophane,
30 Invade th' inviolable Main:
Th' eternal Fences over leap;
And pass at will the boundless deep.
No toyl, no hardship can restrain
Ambitious Man inur'd to pain;
The more confin'd, the more he tries,
And at forbidden quarry flies.
Thus bold Prometheus did aspire,
And stole from heaven the seed of Fire:
A train of Ills, a ghastly crew,
40 The Robbers blazing track persue;
Fierce Famine, with her Meagre face,
And Feavours of the fiery Race,
In swarms th' offending Wretch surround,
All brooding on the blasted ground:
And limping Death, lash'd on by Fate,
Comes up to shorten half our date.
This made not Dedalus beware,
With borrow'd wings to sail in Air:
To Hell Alcides forc'd his way,
50 Plung'd thro' the Lake, and snatch'd the Prey
Nay scarce the Gods, or heav'nly Climes
Are safe from our audacious Crimes;
We reach at Jove's Imperial Crown,
And pull the unwilling thunder down.   (pub. 1685)

Ode I.9

Behold yon' Mountains hoary height
    Made higher with new Mounts of Snow;
Again behold the Winters weight
    Oppress the lab'ring Woods below:
And streams with Icy fetters bound,
Benum'd and crampt to solid ground.

With well heap'd Logs dissolve the cold,
    And feed the genial hearth with fires;
Produce the Wine, that makes us bold,
    And sprightly Wit and Love inspires:
For what hereafter shall betide,
God, if 'tis worth his care, provide.

Let him alone with what he made,
    To toss and turn the World below;
At his command the storms invade;
    The winds by his Commission blow
Till with a Nod he bids 'em cease,
And then the Calm returns, and all is peace.

To morrow and her works defie,
    Lay hold upon the present hour,
And snatch the pleasures passing by,
    To put them out of Fortunes pow'r:
Nor love, nor love's delights disdain,
What e're thou get'st to day is gain.

Secure those golden early joyes,
    That Youth unsowr'd with sorrow bears,
E're with'ring time the taste destroyes,
    With sickness and unwieldy years!

> For active sports, for pleasing rest,
> 30 This is the time to be possest;
> The best is but in season best.
>
> The pointed hour of promis'd bliss,
>   The pleasing whisper in the dark,
> The half unwilling willing kiss,
>   The laugh that guides thee to the mark,
> When the kind Nymph wou'd coyness feign,
> And hides but to be found again,
> These, these are joyes the Gods for Youth ordain. (pub. 1685)

Ode III.29

Paraphras'd in Pindarique Verse; and Inscrib'd to the Right Honourable Lawrence Earl of Rochester

I

> Descended of an ancient Line,
>   That long the Tuscan Scepter sway'd,
> Make haste to meet the generous wine,
>   Whose piercing is for thee delay'd:
> The rosie wreath is ready made;
>   And artful hands prepare
> The fragrant Syrian Oyl, that shall perfume thy hair.

II

> When the Wine sparkles from a far,
>   And the well-natur'd Friend cries, come away;
> 10 Make haste, and leave thy business and thy care,
>   No mortal int'rest can be worth thy stay.

III

    Leave for a while thy costly Country Seat;
        And, to be Great indeed, forget
    The nauseous pleasures of the Great:
        Make haste and come:
    Come and forsake thy cloying store;
        Thy Turret that surveys, from high,
    The smoke, and wealth, and noise of Rome;
        And all the busie pageantry
20   That wise men scorn, and fools adore:
Come, give thy Soul a loose, and taste the pleasures of the poor.

IV

    Sometimes 'tis grateful to the Rich, to try
    A short vicissitude, and fit of Poverty:
        A savoury Dish, a homely Treat,
        Where all is plain, where all is neat,
        Without the stately spacious Room,
    The Persian Carpet, or the Tyrian Loom,
    Clear up the cloudy foreheads of the Great.

V

        The Sun is in the Lion mounted high;
30   The Syrian Star
            Barks from a far;
    And with his sultry breath infects the Sky;
    The ground below is parch'd, the heav'ns above us fry.
        The Shepheard drives his fainting Flock,
        Beneath the covert of a Rock;
        And seeks refreshing Rivulets nigh:
        The Sylvans to their shades retire,
    Those very shades and streams, new shades and streams require;
And want a cooling breeze of wind to fan the rageing fire.

VI

        Thou, what befits the new Lord May'r,
        And what the City Faction dare,
        And what the Gallique Arms will do,
        And what the Quiver bearing Foe,
        Art anxiously inquisitive to know:
    But God has, wisely, hid from humane sight
        The dark decrees of future fate;
        And sown their seeds in depth of night;
    He laughs at all the giddy turns of State;
When Mortals search too soon, and fear too late.

VII

        Enjoy the present smiling hour;
        And put it out of Fortunes pow'r:
    The tide of bus'ness, like the running stream,
        Is sometimes high, and sometimes low,
        A quiet ebb, or a tempestuous flow,
          And alwayes in extream.
        Now with a noiseless gentle course
        It keeps within the middle Bed;
        Anon it lifts aloft the head,
And bears down all before it, with impetuous force:
        And trunks of Trees come rowling down,
        Sheep and their Folds together drown:
    Both House and Homested into Seas are borne,
    And Rocks are from their old foundations torn,
And woods made thin with winds, their scatter'd honours mourn.

VIII

        Happy the Man, and happy he alone,
        He, who can call to day his own:
        He, who secure within, can say
    To morrow do thy worst, for I have liv'd to day.
        Be fair, or foul, or rain, or shine,

ODE III.29 · JOHN DRYDEN

70   The joys I have possest, in spight of fate are mine.
      Not Heav'n it self upon the past has pow'r;
But what has been, has been, and I have had my hour.

IX

      Fortune, that with malicious joy,
        Does Man her slave oppress,
    Proud of her Office to destroy,
        Is seldome pleas'd to bless:
    Still various and unconstant still;
    But with an inclination to be ill;
    Promotes, degrades, delights in strife,
80   And makes a Lottery of life.
    I can enjoy her while she's kind;
    But when she dances in the wind,
    And shakes her wings, and will not stay,
    I puff the Prostitute away:
The little or the much she gave, is quietly resign'd:
    Content with poverty, my Soul I arm;
    And Vertue, tho' in rags, will keep me warm.

X

      What is 't to me,
    Who never sail in her unfaithful Sea,
90   If Storms arise, and Clouds grow black?
    If the Mast split and threaten wreck,
    Then let the greedy Merchant fear
        For his ill gotten gain;
    And pray to Gods that will not hear,
While the debating winds and billows bear
        His Wealth into the Main.
    For me secure from Fortunes blows,
    (Secure of what I cannot lose,)
    In my small Pinnace I can sail,
100   Contemning all the blustring roar;
      And running with a merry gale,

With friendly Stars my safety seek
Within some little winding Creek;
And see the storm a shore.   (pub. 1685)

WENTWORTH DILLON, EARL OF ROSCOMMON (1633?–1685)

Born in Ireland, travelled in France and Italy, and came to England only after the Restoration. Author of *Horace's Art of Poetry Made English* (1684) in blank verse, and in couplets *An Essay on Translated Verse* (1685), from which Dryden professed to learn much. Accepting 'the judgment of the public', Johnson wrote of him: 'He is elegant, but not great; he never labours after exquisite beauties, and he seldom falls into gross faults.'

Ode I.22

Vertue, Dear Friend, needs no defence,
The surest Guard is innocence:
None knew till Guilt created Fear
What Darts or poyson'd Arrows were.

Integrity undaunted goes
Through Libyan sands or Scythian snows,
Or where Hydaspes wealthy side
Pays Tribute to the Persian pride.

For as (by amorous thoughts betray'd)
10 Careless in Sabin Woods I stray'd,
A Grisly foaming Wolf, unfed,
Met me unarm'd, yet trembling fled.

    No Beast of more Portentous size,
In the Hercinian forest lies;
None fiercer, in Numidia bred,
With Carthage were in Triumph led.

    Set me in the remotest place,
That Neptune's frozen Arms Embrace,
Where Angry Jove did never spare
20 One breath of Kind and temperate Air.

    Set me where on some pathless plain,
The swarthy Africans complain,
To see the Chariot of the Sun
So near their scorching Country run.

    The burning Zone the frozen Isles
Shall hear me sing of Caelia's smiles,
All cold but in her Breast I will despise,
And dare all heat but that of Caelia's Eyes.   (1684)

Ode I.22 An imitation, attributed to Roscommon

I
Vertue (dear Friend) needs no Defence,
No Arms but its own Innocence;
Quivers and Bows, and poison'd Darts,
Are only us'd by Guilty Hearts.

II
An Honest Mind safely alone,
May travel thro' the Burning Zone;
Or thro' the deepest Scythian Snows,
Or where the fam'd Hydaspes flows.

III

    While rul'd by a resistless Fire,
10   Our great Orinda I admire.
    The hungry Wolves that see me stray,
    Unarm'd and single, run away.

IV

    Set me in the Remotest Place,
    That ever Neptune did embrace,
    When there her Image fills my Breast,
    Helicon is not half so blest.

V

    Leave me upon some Lybian Plain,
    So she my Fancy entertain,
    And when the thirsty Monsters meet,
20   They'll all pay homage to my Feet.

VI

    The Magick of Orinda's Name
    Not only can their Fierceness tame,
        But if that mighty Word I once rehearse.
        They seem submissively to roar in Verse.   (1684)

Ode III.6

  Those Ills your Ancestors have done,
    Romans are now become your own;
        And they will cost you dear,
        Unless you soon repair
The falling Temples which the Gods Provoke,
And Statues sully'd yet with Sacraligious smoke.

---

10 *great Orinda* the poet Katherine Philips

ODE III.6 · ROSCOMMON

    Propitious Heaven that rais'd your Fathers high,
        For humble, gratefull Piety,
        (As it rewarded their Respect)
10   Hath sharply punish'd your Neglect;
        All Empires on the Gods depend,
  Begun by their command, at their command they end.

    Let Crassus Ghost and Labienus tell,
   How twice by Jove's revenge our Legions fell,
        And with insulting Pride
Shining in Roman Spoils the Parthian Victors ride.

    The Scythian and Aegyptian Scum
        Had almost ruin'd Rome,
    While our Seditions took their part
20 Fill'd each Aegyptian Sail, and wing'd each Scythian dart.

        First, those Flagitious times,
        (Pregnant with unknown Crimes)
    Conspir'd to violate the Nuptial Bed
        From which polluted head,
  Infectious Streams of Crowding Sins began,
And through the Spurious Breed and guilty Nation ran.

    Behold a Ripe and Melting Maid,
    Bound Prentice to the Wanton Trade;
  Ionian Artists at a mighty price,
30   Instruct her in the Mysteries of Vice,
What Nets to spread, where subtile Baits to lay,
And with an Early hand they form the temper'd Clay.

    Marry'd, their Lessons she improves,
    By practice of Adult'rous Loves,
    And scorns the Common mean design
To take advantage of her Husband's Wine;
        Or snatch in some dark place,
    A hasty Illegitimate Embrace.

No! the Brib'd Husband knows of all,
40   And bids her Rise when Lovers call;
      Hither a Merchant from the Straits,
      Grown wealthy by forbidden Freights,
         Or City Cannibal repairs,
       Who feeds upon the flesh of Heirs:
    Convenient Brutes, whose tributary flame,
Pays the full price of Lust, and guilds the slighted shame.

       'Twas not the Spawn of such as these,
     That Dy'd with Punick bloud the Conquer'd Seas,
          And quash't the stern Aeacides;
50   Made the proud Asian Monarch feel
     How weak his Gold was against Europes steel,
          Forc't e'en dire Hannibal to yield;
And won the long disputed World at Zamas fatal Field.

     But Souldiers of a Rustick Mould
    Rough, hardy, season'd, Manly, bold,
       Either they dug the stubborn Ground,
    Or through hewn Woods their weighty strokes did sound.
       And after the declining Sun
    Had chang'd the shadows, and their Task was done
60 Home with their weary Team they took their way,
    And drownd in friendly Bowles the labour of the day.

     Time sensibly all things impairs
     Our Fathers have been worse than theirs,
     And we than Ours, next Age will see
     A Race more Profligate than we
(With all the pains we take) have skill enough to be.

(1684)

---

49 *Aeacides* – not the grandson of Aeacus (called Pyrrhus) who fought in the Trojan War, but Pyrrhus, king of Epirus, an enemy of Rome.
54 *Zamas fatal Field* traditional site of Hannibal's defeat

SIR CHARLES SEDLEY (1639?–1701)

Author of several comedies and some graceful lyrics. A nineteenth-century editor, T. E. Page, claimed that 'this is perhaps the only Ode of Horace of which there is an adequate English rendering.'

Ode II.8

Did any Punishment attend
    Thy former Perjuries,
I should believe a second time,
    Thy charming Flatteries:
Did but one Wrinkle mark this Face,
Or hadst thou lost one single Grace.

No sooner hast thou, with false Vows,
    Provok'd the Powers above;
But thou art fairer than before,
    And we are more in love,
Thus Heaven and Earth seem to declare,
They pardon Falshood in the Fair.

Sure 'tis no Crime vainly to swear,
    By every Power on high,
And call our bury'd Mother's Ghost
    A Witness to the Lye:
Heaven at such Perjury connives,
And Venus with a Smile forgives.

The Nymphs and cruel Cupid too,
    Sharp'ning his pointed Dart
On a old Hone, besmear'd with Blood,
    Forbear thy perjur'd Heart.
Fresh Youth grows up, to wear thy Chains,
And the old Slave no Freedom gains.

Thee, Mothers for their eldest Sons,
  Thee, wretched Misers fear,
Lest thy prevailing Beauty should
  Seduce the hopeful Heir:
New-marry'd Virgins fear thy Charms
30 Should keep their Bridegroom from their Arms.   (pub. 1701)

APHRA BEHN (1640–1689)

Born in Guiana, came to England in 1658, and was employed by Charles II as a spy in Antwerp during the Dutch War. Wrote a number of plays described as 'typical coarse comedies of contemporary London life'. As other female authors were to do, in her freely expansive version of this ode she switches the sexes and has a pretty young man beguiling a young woman.

Ode I.5 An imitation

I
What mean those Amorous Curles of Jet?
  For what heart-Ravisht Maid
Dost thou thy Hair in order set,
  Thy Wanton Tresses Braid?
And thy vast Store of Beauties open lay,
That the deluded Fancy leads astray.

II
For pitty hide thy Starry eyes,
  Whose Languishments destroy
And look not on the Slave that dyes

10　　　With an Excess of Joy.
　　Defend thy Coral Lips, thy Amber Breath;
　　To taste these Sweets lets in a Certain Death.

III
Forbear, fond Charming Youth, forbear,
　　Thy words of Melting Love:
Thy Eyes thy Language well may spare,
　　One Dart enough can move.
And she that hears thy voice and sees thy Eyes
With too much Pleasure, too much Softness dies.

IV
Cease, Cease, with Sighs to warm my Soul,
20　　Or press me with thy Hand:
Who can the kindling fire controul,
　　The tender force withstand?
Thy Sighs and Touches like wing'd Lightning fly,
And are the Gods of Loves Artillery.　　　　　(pub. 1684)

THOMAS OTWAY (1652–1685)

Known primarily as a tragedian. Of his best play, *Venice Preserv'd*, Johnson wrote that it is the work of a man 'who conceived forcibly, and drew originally, by consulting nature in his own breast'.

Ode II.16

In Storms when Clouds the Moon do hide,
And no kind Stars the Pilot guide,
Shew me at Sea the boldest there,
Who does not wish for quiet here.

---

11 *Amber* scented with ambergris

For quiet (Friend) the Souldier fights,
Bears weary Marches, sleepless nights,
For this feeds hard, and lodges cold,
Which can't be bought with hills of Gold.

Since wealth and power too weak we find
10 To quell the tumults of the mind;
Or from the Monarchs roofs of state
Drive thence the cares that round him wait.

Happy the man with little blest
Of what his Father left possest;
No base desires corrupt his head,
No fears disturb him in his bed.

What then in life, which soon must end,
Can all our vain designs intend?
From shore to shore why should we run
20 When none his tiresome self can shun?

For baneful care will still prevail,
And overtake us under sail,
'Twill dodge the Great mans train behind,
Out run the Roe, out flie the wind.

If then thy soul rejoyce to day,
Drive far to morrows cares away.
In laughter let them all be drown'd,
No perfect good is to be found.

One Mortal feels Fates sudden blow,
30 Another's lingring death comes slow;
And what of life they take from thee,
The Gods may give to punish me.

>   Thy portion is a wealthy stock,
>   A fertile glebe, a fruitful flock,
>   Horses and Chariots for thy ease,
>   Rich Robes to deck and make thee please.
>
>   For me a little Cell I chuse,
>   Fit for my mind, fit for my muse,
>   Which soft content does Best adorn,
> 40 Shunning the Knaves and Fools I scorn.   (pub. 1684)

JOHN OLDHAM (1653–1683)

Son of a Nonconformist minister, educated at St Edmund Hall, Oxford. Supported himself by teaching, first as an usher, then as a tutor. Despite his early death from smallpox – 'too little and too lately known', Dryden wrote – he left a considerable body of work, mostly satirical, of a Juvenalian rather than a Horatian cast. We must lament the loss of what was to come.

Part of Ode I.31 Expansively paraphrased

I

>   What does the Poet's modest Wish require?
>   What Boon does he of gracious Heav'n desire?
>   Not the large Crops of Esham's goodly Soil,
>   Which tire the Mower's and the Reaper's toil:
>   Not the soft Flocks, on hilly Cotswold fed,
>   Nor Lemster Fields with living Fleeces clad:
>   He does not ask the Grounds, where gentle Thames,
>   Or Seavern spread their fat'ning Streams.

    Where they with wanton windings play,
10 And eat their widen'd Banks insensibly away:
    He does not ask the Wealth of Lombard-street,
    Which Consciences and Souls are pawn'd to get.
    Nor those exhaustless Mines of Gold,
14 Which Guinny and Peru in their rich bosoms hold . . .

III

29   He wants no Cyprus Birds, nor Ortolans,
30   Nor Dainties fetch'd from far to please his Sence,
   Cheap wholsom Herbs content his frugal Board,
    The Food of unfaln Innocence,
   Which the mean'st Village Garden does afford:
   Grant him, kind Heav'n, the sum of his desires,
   What Nature, not what Luxury requires:
   He only does a Competency claim,
   And, when he has it, wit to use the same:
   Grant him sound Health, impair'd by no Disease,
    Nor by his own Excess:
40   Let him in strength of Mind and Body live,
   But not his Reason, nor his Sense survive:
   His Age (if Age he e're must live to see)
   Let it from want, Contempt, and Care be free,
 But not from Mirth, and the delights of Poetry.
   Grant him but this, he's amply satisfi'd,
 And scorns whatever Fate can give beside.

Ode II.14 Expansively paraphrased

I

 Alas! dear Friend, alas! time hasts away,
 Nor is it in our pow'r to bribe its stay:
 The rolling years with constant motion run,
 Lo! while I speak, the present minute's gone,
 And following hours urge the foregoing on.

ODE II.14 · JOHN OLDHAM

'Tis not thy Wealth, 'tis not thy Power,
'Tis not thy Piety can thee secure:
They're all too feeble to withstand
Grey Hairs, approaching Age, and thy avoidless end.
When once thy fatal Glass is run,
When once thy utmost Thred is spun,
'Twill then be fruitless to expect Reprieve:
Could'st thou ten thousand Kingdoms give
In purchase for each hour of longer life,
They would not buy one gasp of breath,
Not move one jot inexorable Death.

II

All the vast stock of humane Progeny,
Which now like swarms of Insects crawl
Upon the Surface of Earth's spacious Ball,
Must quit this Hillock of Mortality,
And in its Bowels buried lie.
The mightiest King, and proudest Potentate,
In spight of all his Pomp, and all his State,
Must pay this necessary Tribute unto Fate.
The busie, restless Monarch of the times, which now
Keeps such a pother, and so much ado
To fill Gazettes alive,
And after in some lying Annal to survive;
Ev'n He, ev'n that great mortal Man must die,
And stink, and rot as well as thou, and I,
As well as the poor tatter'd wretch, that begs his bread,
And is with Scraps out of the Common Basket fed.

III

In vain from dangers of the bloody Field we keep,
In vain we scape
The sultry Line, and stormy Cape,

---

25 *restless Monarch* Louis XIV

      And all the treacheries of the faithless Deep:
In vain for health to forein Countries we repair,
      And change our English for Mompellier Air,
      In hope to leave our fears of dying there:
40   In vain with costly far-fetch'd Drugs we strive
      To keep the wasting vital Lamp alive:
      In vain on Doctors feeble Art rely;
Against resistless Death there is no remedy:
      Both we, and they for all their skill must die,
And fill alike the Bedrols of Mortality.

IV

      Thou must, thou must resign to Fate, my Friend,
And leave thy House, thy Wife, and Family behind:
      Thou must thy fair and goodly Mannors leave,
      Of these thy Trees thou shalt not with thee take,
50   Save just as much as will thy Coffin make:
Nor wilt thou be allow'd of all thy Land, to have,
      But the small pittance of a six-foot Grave.
      Then shall thy prodigal young Heir
      Lavish the Wealth, which thou for many a year
      Hast hoarded up with so much pains and care:
      Then shall he drain thy Cellars of their Stores,
Kept sacred now as Vaults of buried Ancestors:
      Shall set th' enlarged Butts at liberty,
      Which there close Pris'ners under durance lie,
60   And wash these stately Floors with better Wine
Than that of consecrated Prelates when they dine. (pub. 1681)

---

45 *Bedrols* bead-rolls, a long list of names

Ode III.9, imitated

A Dialogue betwixt the Poet and Lydia

I
Hor. While you for me alone had Charms,
And none more welcome fill'd your Arms,
Proud with content, I slighted Crowns,
And pitied Monarchs on their Thrones.

II
Lyd. While you thought Lydia only fair,
And lov'd no other Nymph but her,
Lydia was happier in your Love,
Than the bless'd Virgins are above.

III
Hor. Now Chloes charming Voice and Art
Have gain'd the conquest of my Heart:
For whom, ye Fates, I'd wish to die,
If mine the Nymphs dear Life might buy.

IV
Lyd. Thyrsis by me has done the same,
The Youth burns me with mutual Flame:
For whom a double Death I'd bear;
Would Fate my dearest Thyrsis spare.

V
Hor. But say, fair Nymph, if I once more
Become your Captive as before?
Say, I throw off my Chloes chain,
And take you to my Breast again?

VI

Lyd. Why then, tho he more bright appear,
More constant than a fixed Star;
Tho you than Wind more fickle be,
And rougher than the stormy Sea;
    By Heav'n, and all its Pow'rs I vow
    I'd gladly live, and die with you.   (pub. 1681)

RICHARD DUKE (1659?–1711)

Educated at Westminster School and Trinity College, Cambridge. A wit who turned parson, as Swift put it; author of satirical and occasional verse and translator, mainly from Latin.

Ode II.4

Blush not, my friend, to own the Love
Which thy fair Captives eyes do move:
Achilles once the Fierce, the Brave,
Stoopt to the Beauties of a Slave;
Tecmessa's charmes could over-power
Ajax her Lord and Conquerour;
Great Agamemnon, when success
Did all his Arms with Conquest bless;
When Hector's fall had gain'd him more
10 Than ten long rolling years before,
By a bright Captive Virgin's Eyes
E'en in the midst of Triumph dyes.
You know not to what mighty line
The lovely Maid may make you joyn;
See but the charmes her sorrow wears,
No common cause could draw such tears;
Those streams sure that adorn her so
For loss of Royal kindred flow:

Oh! think not so divine a thing
20 Could from the bed of Commons spring;
Whose faith could so unmov'd remain,
And so averse to sordid gain,
Was never born of any race
That might the noblest Love disgrace.
Her blooming Face, her snowey Armes,
Her well shap't Leg, and all her charmes
Of her Body and her Face,
I, poor I, may safely praise.
Suspect not Love the youthfull Rage
30 From Horace's declining Age,
But think remov'd by forty years
All his flames and all thy fears.

(1684)

THOMAS CREECH (1659–1700)

A Fellow of Wadham College, Oxford, his translation of Lucretius (1682) was admired, and Dryden thought it good enough to steal from. With the translation of Horace 'he lost all his laurels', a writer in *The Monthly Review* for 1758 claimed, yet it went into six editions between 1684 and 1743. Supposedly on account of an unhappy love affair, he hanged himself and was found dead in an apothecary's garret.

Ode I.17

Swift Faunus oft Lyceum leaves behind,
   And to my pleasing Farm retreats;
     And from the Summer heats
Defends my Goats, and from the rainy wind.

---

1 *Lyceum* Pan's shrine on Mt Lycaeus in Arcadia

O'er Vales, o'er craggy Rocks, and Hills they stray,
   Seek flowry Thyme, and safely brouze
     And wanton in the boughs;
Nor fear an angry Serpent in the way.

No lurking Venom swells the harmless mold,
10   The Kids are safe, the tender Lambs
     Lie bleating by their Dams,
Nor hear the Evening Wolves grin round the fold.

Soft rural Lays thro every Valley sound;
   By low Ustica's purling Spring
     The Shepherds pipe and sing,
Whilst from the even Rocks the tunes rebound.

Kind Heaven defends my soft aboads,
   I live the Gods peculiar Care,
     Secure and free from fear;
20 My Songs and my Devotion please the Gods.

Here naked Truth, Love, Peace, good Nature reign,
   And here to Thee shall plenty flow,
     And all her Riches show
To raise the honor of the quiet Plain.

Here crooked Vales afford a cool retreat;
   Or underneath an Arbor's shade
     For Love and Pleasure made,
Thou shalt avoid the Dog-Star's raging heat;

And sweetly sing the harmless Wars of Love,
30   How, chast Penelope's desires,
     And wanton Circe's fires
With various heats for one Ulysses strove.

At Noon with Wine the fiery beams asswage
   Beneath a shade on beds of Grass,
      And take a Chirping glass;
But never drink till Mirth boils up to rage.

Ne'er fear thy old Gallant, He's far away,
   He shall not see, nor seize, nor tear
      Thy Chaplet from thy Hair;
40 We shall have leisure, and have room to play.   (pub. 1684)

Ode I.28

In this unusual ode, a development of the Greek sepulchral epigram, a drowned man addresses the drowned Archytas, a distinguished philosopher of the Pythagorean school which believed in reincarnation. The speaker announces that death claims all men, even Pythagoras, who is thus shown to have been wrong. He then turns to a passing seaman and asks that his body be buried. There is a helpful discussion of the ode in Gordon Williams, *Tradition and Originality in Roman Poetry*, pp. 181–5.

    A Narrow Grave by the Matinian Shore
    Confines Thee now, and thou canst have no more,
    Ah! learn'd Architas, ah how small for Thee,
    Whose wond'rous Mind could measure Earth and Sea!
    What Sands make up the Shore minutely teach,
    And count as far as Number's self could reach?
    What did it profit that thy nimble Soul
    Had travell'd Heaven, and oft ran round the Pole,
    Pursu'd the motions of the rowling Light
10 When Death came on, and spread a gloomy Night!
    Wise Tantalus the guest of Gods is dead,
    And on strange wings the chang'd Tithonus fled:
    Jove's Friend, just Minos, hath resign'd his Breath,
    And wise Pythagoras felt a second Death;
    Altho his Trojan Shield, and former State
    Did prove his Soul above the force of Fate;

Withdrew the Mind from Death's black conquering hand,
And left but Skin and Bones at Fate's Command;
In thy Opinion He did most excel,
20 Discover'd Truth, and follow'd Nature well:
But once o'er all long Night her shades will spread,
And all must walk the Valleys of the Dead.
Some Rage spurs on, and Death attends in Wars;
The Sea destroys the greedy Mariners:
The Young and Old confus'd by Numbers fall,
And Death with equal hand doth strike at all:
A boisterous Storm my feeble tackling tore,
And left me naked on the Illyrian shore:
But, Seaman, pray be just, put near the Land,
30 Bestow a Grave, and hide my Limbs in Sand:
So may the threatning East-winds spare the Floods,
And idlely spend their Rage on Hills and Woods;
Whilst you ride safely; so from every Shore
May Gain flow in, and feed thy growing Store.
May Jove and Neptune, soft Tarentum's Guard,
Conspire to Bless, and join in one reward:
Perhaps you scorn, and are design'dly base,
Thy Crime shall Damn thy undeserving Race;
Thy Pride, vain Man, shall on the self return,
40 Thou naked lie, and be the Publick scorn:
My Prayers shall mount, and pull just Vengeance down,
No Offerings shall release, no Vows atone:
Tho hasty now, driven by a prosperous gale,
('Tis quickly done) thrice strew the sand, and sail.   (pub. 1684)

Ode III.18

Faunus that flying Nymphs pursues
And Courts as oft as they refuse,
If Yearly Ridglings stain thy Grove,
If the large Bowl the Friend of Love,

Still flows with Wine; if Prayers invoke,
And thy old Shrines with Odors smoak,
Defend my Fields, and sunny Farm,
And keep my tender Flocks from harm:
O'er grassy Plains the wanton Flocks,
10   The Village with their idle Ox,
Sport o'er the Fields, all finely drest
When cold December doth restore thy Feast:
The Lambs midst ravenous Wolves repose,
The Wood to Thee spreads rustick Boughs,
The Ditcher with his Country Jugg,
Then smiles to Dance where once he dugg.   (pub. 1684)

Ode III.23

A Fat and costly Sacrifice
Is not the welcom'st Tribute to the Skies,
They're more delighted with the small expence
  Of Honesty and Innocence.

Let rustick Phydile prepare
  At each new Moon an humble Prayer,
  And at her old Penates Shrine
  Pour one small bowl of Country Wine,
And stain their Altars with a greedy Swine;
10   No scorching Winds shall blast her fruit,
  Her Corn be free from barren smut;
  Nor let her darling Children fear
The shivering Agues of the dying Year.

The Sacrifice Albanian Pastures feed,
Or Snowy Algidum's cold Mountains breed
  'Midst fruitful Oaks a pamper'd Beast,
  Shall stain the Axes of the Priest:

>   But why should You profusely try
>   With slaughter'd Flocks to bribe the Sky,
> 20   Since Myrtle Crowns, and from the neighbouring Flood,
>   Few sprinkled drops shall please the God
>   More than whole Rivers of their offer'd blood?
>   If with an unpolluted hand,
>   Which neither Blood nor wicked Arts have stain'd,
>   A little Meal and Salt you bring
>   'Twill prove a more provailing Offering
>   Then all the Spices of the Eastern King.   (pub. 1684)

FRANCIS ATTERBURY (1662–1732)

Bishop of Rochester. Deeply involved in religious politics, on friendly terms with the leading writers and intellectuals of the day, and admired for his oratory. Sympathetic to the Jacobite cause, he was arrested in 1722, tried for treason, found guilty and banished. His literary works include a Latin translation of Dryden's *Absalom and Achitophel*, some original Latin poems, and three short treatises on classical subjects.

Ode IV.3

> He, on whose natal Hour the Queen
>   Of Verse hath smil'd, shall never grace
> The Isthmian Gauntlet, or be seen
>   First in the fam'd Olympic Race:
> He shall not after Toils of War,
>   And taming haughty Monarchs' Pride
> With laurel'd Brows conspicuous far,
>   To Jove's Tarpeian Temple ride:

>   But Him, the Streams which warbling flow
> 10   Rich Tibur's fertile Vales along,
>   And shady Groves, his Haunts, shall know
>   The Master of th' Aeolian Song.
>   The Sons of Rome, majestic Rome!
>   Have plac'd Me in the Poet's Quire,
>   And Envy, now or dead or dumb,
>   Forbears to blame what They admire.
>   Goddess of the sweet-sounding Lute,
>   Which thy harmonious Touch obeys,
>   Who canst the finny Race, though mute,
> 20   To Cygnet's dying Accents raise,
>   Thy Gift it is, that all, with Ease,
>   Me Prince of Roman Lyrics own;
>   That, while I live, my Numbers please,
>   If pleasing, is thy Gift alone.   (1746)

RICHARD BENTLEY (1662–1724)

One of the giants of classical scholarship, Bentley's edition of Horace (1711), highly influential throughout the eighteenth century, introduced over 700 emendations into a text held to be remarkably pure. Johnson admired Bentley's poem (the only one he is known to have written in English): 'They are the forcible verses of a man of a strong mind, but not accustomed to write verse; for there is some uncouthness in the expression.' His life is agreeably related by Sir Richard Jebb, *Bentley* (1882).

In response to an undergraduate's imitation of Ode III.2

Who strives to mount Parnassus' hill,
    And thence poetic laurels bring,
Must first acquire due force and skill,
    Must fly with swan's or eagle's wing.

Who Nature's treasures would explore,
    Her mysteries and arcana know,
Must high, as lofty Newton, soar,
    Must stoop, as delving Woodward, low.

Who studies ancient laws and rites,
    Tongues, arts, and arms, all history,
Must drudge, like Selden, days and nights,
    And in the endless labour die.

Who travels in religious jarrs,
    Truth mix'd with error, shade with rays,
Like Whiston, wanting pyx and stars,
    In ocean wide or sinks or strays.

But grant our hero's hope, long toil
    And comprehensive genius crown,
All sciences, all arts his spoil,
    Yet what reward, or what renown?

Envy, innate in vulgar souls,
    Envy steps in and stops his rise;
Envy with poison'd tarnish fouls
    His lustre, and his worth decries.

---

8 *Woodward* geologist   **11** *Selden* jurist and orientalist
13 *travels* travails? (Jebb)   **15** *Whiston* heretical theologian; *pyx* compass

>   He lives inglorious or in want,
>   To college and old books confin'd;
>   Instead of learn'd, he's call'd pedànt;
>   Dunces advanc'd, he's left behind:
>   Yet left content, a genuine stoic he,
> 30 Great without patron, rich without South-sea.   (writ. 1722)

GEORGE STEPNEY (1663–1707)

Educated at Westminster School and Trinity College, Cambridge. A diplomatist rather than a poet, he wrote some occasional verse and translated from Latin. Johnson described him as 'a very licentious translator'.

Ode III.7 An imitation

Compare Stepney's treatment of Horace's scenario for a four-part romantic playlet with the sweetly Victorian version by Austin Dobson (pp. 243–5). For a close translation, see Clough (p. 236).

>   I
>   Dear Molly, why so oft in Tears?
>   Why all these Jealousies and Fears,
>   For thy bold Son of Thunder?
>   Have Patience till we've conquer'd France,
>   Thy Closet shall be stor'd with Nants;
>   Ye Ladies like such Plunder.

---

5 *Nants* brandy

II

Before Toulon thy Yoke-mate lies,
Where all the live-long Night he sighs
   For thee in lowsy Cabbin:
And tho' the Captain's Chloe cries,
''Tis I, dear Bully, prithee rise –'
   He will not let the Drab in.

III

But she, the Cunning'st Jade alive,
Says, 'Tis the ready way to thrive,
   By sharing Female Bounties:
And, if he'll be but kind one Night,
She Vows, He shall be dubb'd a Knight,
   When she is made a Countess.

IV

Then tells of smooth young Pages whipp'd,
Cashier'd, and of their Liv'ries stripp'd,
   Who late to Peers belonging;
Are nightly now compell'd to trudge
With Links, because they would not drudge
   To save their Ladies Longing.

V

But Vol the Eunuch cannot be
A Colder Cavalier than he,
   In all such Love-Adventures:
Then pray do you, dear Molly, take
Some Christian Care, and do not break
   Your Conjugal Indentures.

---

11 *Bully* sweetheart, darling
23 *Links* torches

VI

Bellair! Who does not Bellair know?
The Wit, the Beauty, and the Beau,
   Gives out, He loves you dearly:
And many a Nymph attack'd with Sighs,
And soft Impertinence and Noise,
   Full oft has beat a Parley.

VII

But, pretty Turtle, when the Blade
Shall come with am'rous Serenade,
   Soon from the Window rate him:
40 But if Reproof will not prevail,
And he perchance attempt to scale,
   Discharge the Jordan at him.

(1715)

TOM BROWN (1663–1704)

Knockabout satirist and entertainer, author of *Amusements Serious and Comical*, sketches of the London scene. 'His life,' the *DNB* pronounces, 'was as licentious as his writings.' His inability to love Dr Fell has none the less won him a modest immortality.

Ode I.27 Freely adapted

I

To fight in your Cups, and abuse the good Creature,
Believe it, my Friends, is a sin of that nature,
That were you all damn'd for a tedious long year
To nasty Mundungus, and heath'nish Small Beer,

---

37 *Turtle* turtle-dove
4 *Mundungus* evil-smelling tobacco

Such as after debauches your Sparks of the Town
For a penance next morning devoutly pour down
It would not atone for so vile a Transgression,
You're a scandal to all of the drinking profession.

II
What a pox do ye bellow, and make such a pother,
And throw Candlesticks, Bottles, and Pipes at each other.
Come, keep the Kings Peace, leaving your damning and
    sinking,
And gravely return to good Christian drinking:
He that flinches his Glass, and to drink is not able,
Let him quarrel no more, but knock under the Table.

III
Well, Faith, since you've rais'd my ill nature so high,
I'll drink on no other condition, not I,
Unless my old friend in the corner declares
What Mistress he Courts, and whose colours he wears;
You may safely acquaint me, for I'm none of those
That use to divulge what's spoke under the Rose.
Come, part with't – What she! forbid it ye Powers,
What unfortunate Planet rul'd o'er thy Amours.
Why man she has lain (Oh thy Fate how I pity)
With half the blue Breeches and Wigs in the City.
So thank Mr Parson, give him thanks with a curse,
Oh those damnable words For better for worse.
To regain your old freedom you vainly endeavour,
Your Doxy and You no Priest can dissever,
You must dance in the Circle, you must dance in't for ever.
(pub. 1692)

---

13 *flinches* avoids emptying
14 *knock under the Table* succumb in a drinking bout

Ode II.11 Freely adapted

I
What the Bully of France, and our Friends on the Rhine,
With their stout Grenadiers this Summer design,
Cease over your Coffee, and Wine, to debate:
Why the Devil shou'd you, that live this side the water,
Pore over Gazettes, and be vext at the matter?
Come, come, let alone these Arcana's of State.

II
Alas! while such idle discourse you maintain,
And with Politic Nonsense thus trouble your Brain,
Your Youth flys away on the back of swift hours,
10 Which no praying, no painting, no sighing restores.
Then you'll find, when old Age has discolour'd your head,
Tho a Mistress be wanting, no rest in your Bed.

III
Prithee do but observe how the Queen of the night
Still varies her station, and changes her light:
Now with a full Orb she the darkness does chase,
Now like Whores in the Pit, shews but half of her face.
These Chaplets of Flowers that our Temples adorn,
Now tarnish and fade, that were fresh in the morn.

IV
But to leave off these similes, for Curate in Chamlet,
20 To lard a dry Sermon for grave folks in Hamlet,
While our Vigour remains, we'll our Talents improve,
Dash the pleasures of Wine with the Blessings of Love,
Here, carelessly here, we'll lye down in the shade
Which the friendly kind Poplars and Lime-trees have made.

---

1 *Bully* swashbuckler?
19 *Chamlet* 'a kind of stuff ... made with wool and silk' (Johnson)

V

Your Claret's too hot – Sirrah, Drawer, go bring
A cup of cold Adam from the next purling spring.
And now your hands in, prethee step o're the way
And fetch Madam Tricksy, the brisk and the gay.
Bid her come in her Alamode Manto of Sattin,
30 Two coolers I'm sure with our Wine can be no false Latin.

(1699)

JONATHAN SWIFT (1667–1745)

Born in Dublin, educated at Trinity College. He was a great prose writer, but Dryden is said to have told him, 'Cousin Swift, you will never be a poet.' Perhaps not, but the quality of his best verse, notably his handling of the conversational octosyllabic couplet, makes the distinction between poetry and verse a dangerous one to press, as Eliot acknowledged in his essay on Kipling.

From Ode III.2 Swift omits the first three stanzas

To the Earl of Oxford, Late Lord Treasurer. Sent to him when he was in the Tower, before his Tryal

    How blest is he, who for his Country dies;
Since Death pursues the Coward as he flies.
The Youth, in vain, would fly from Fate's Attack,
With trembling Knees, and Terror at his Back;
Though Fear should lend him Pinions like the Wind,
Yet swifter Fate will seize him from behind.

---

30 *false Latin* breach of manners

Virtue repuls't, yet knows not to repine;
But shall with unattainted Honour shine;
Nor stoops to take the Staff, nor lays it down,
Just as the Rabble please to smile or frown.

Virtue, to crown her Fav'rites, loves to try
Some new unbeaten Passage to the Sky;
Where Jove a Seat among the Gods will give
To those who die, for meriting to live.

Next, faithful Silence hath a sure Reward:
Within our Breast be ev'ry Secret barr'd:
He who betrays his Friend, shall never be
Under one Roof, or in one Ship with me.
For, who with Traytors would his Safety trust,
Lest with the Wicked, Heaven involve the Just?
And, though the Villain 'scape a while, he feels
Slow Vengeance, like a Blood-hound at his Heels. (writ. 1716)

WILLIAM CONGREVE (1670–1729)

Born near Leeds but educated in Ireland where he attended Trinity College. Best known for his comedies (*The Way of the World*, 1700), he wrote a readable version of the Homeric *Hymn to Venus* and translated from Ovid and Horace. Of his imitations of Horace Johnson wrote that they were 'feebly paraphrastical, and the additions which he makes are of little value'. Too severe?

---

9 *Staff* the white staff of the Lord Chancellor

Ode I.19 A paraphrase

I

    The Tyrant Queen of soft desires,
        With the resistless aid of sprightly Wine
        And wanton Ease, conspires
    To make my Heart its peace resign,
And re-admit Loves long rejected Fires.
    For beauteous Glycera, I burn,
The Flames so long repell'd with double force return:
    Endless her Charms appear, and shine more bright
    Than polish'd Marble when reflecting light;
    With winning coyness, she my Soul disarms,
    And when her Looks are coldest, most she warms:
        Her face darts forth a thousand Rays,
    Whose Lustre, an unwary sight betrays,
My Eye-balls swim, and I grow giddy while I gaze.

II

    She comes! she comes! she rushes in my Veins!
    At once all Venus enters, and at large she reigns!
    Cyprus, no more with her abode is blest,
    I am her Palace, and her Throne my Breast.
    Of Savage Scythian Arms, no more I write,
    Or Parthian Archers, who in flying fight
        And make rough War their sport;
      Such idle Themes, no more shall move,
    Nor any thing but what's of high import:
        And what's of high import, but Love?
    Vervain and Gums, and the green Turf prepare;
    With Wine of two years old, your Cups be fill'd:
        After our Sacrifice and Pray'r,
    The Goddess may incline her Heart to yield.   (1693)

---

25 *Vervain and Gums* plant used in sacred rites; gums used for perfume or incense

JOSEPH ADDISON (1672–1719)

Educated at Charterhouse and The Queen's College, Oxford, later a Fellow of Magdalen. Held a number of public positions. An essayist of genius, perhaps, who brought the best thought of the time within the range of the general reader, author of *Cato*, a tragedy much admired in its day, and a competent poet, 'one of our earliest examples of correctness' (Johnson).

Ode III.3 A free translation, much expanded

'Augustus had a design to rebuild Troy, and make it the Metropolis of the Roman Empire, having closetted several Senators on the project: Horace is suppos'd to have written the following Ode on this occasion.' (Addison.) Modern scholarship is not inclined to credit Augustus with so strange a design, and takes the ode's subject to be the future of Rome, not the Trojan past.

    The Man resolv'd and steady to his trust,
Inflexible to ill, and obstinately just,
May the rude rabble's insolence despise,
Their senseless clamours and tumultuous cries;
The tyrant's fierceness he beguiles,
And the stern brow, and the harsh voice defies,
And with superior greatness smiles.

    Not the rough whirlwind, that deforms
Adria's black gulf, and vexes it with storms,
10 The stubborn virtue of his soul can move;
Not the red arm of angry Jove,
That flings the thunder from the sky,
And gives it rage to roar, and strength to fly.

Should the whole frame of nature round him break,
In ruine and confusion hurl'd,
He, unconcern'd, would hear the mighty crack,
And stand secure amidst a falling world.

Such were the godlike arts that led
Bright Pollux to the blest abodes;
20   Such did for great Alcides plead,
And gain'd a place among the Gods;
Where now Augustus, mix'd with heroes, lies,
And to his lips the nectar bowl applies:
His ruddy lips the purple tincture show,
And with immortal stains divinely glow.

By arts like these did young Lyaeus rise:
His Tigers drew him to the skies,
Wild from the desart and unbroke:
In vain they foam'd, in vain they star'd,
30   In vain their eyes with fury glar'd;
He tam'd 'em to the lash, and bent 'em to the yoke.

Such were the paths that Rome's great founder trod,
When in a whirlwind snatch'd on high,
He shook off dull mortality,
And lost the Monarch in the God.
Bright Juno then her awful silence broke,
And thus th' assembled deities bespoke.

Troy, says the Goddess, perjur'd Troy has felt
The dire effects of her proud tyrant's guilt;
40   The towering pile, and soft abodes,
Wall'd by the hand of servile Gods,

---

26 *Lyaeus* Bacchus
32 *great founder* Romulus

ODE III.3 · JOSEPH ADDISON

Now spreads its ruines all around,
And lyes inglorious on the ground.
An umpire, partial and unjust,
And a lewd woman's impious lust,
Lay heavy on her head, and sunk her to the dust.

Since false Laomedon's tyrannick sway,
That durst defraud th' immortals of their pay,
Her guardian Gods renounc'd their patronage,
50 Nor wou'd the fierce invading foe repell;
To my resentments, and Minerva's rage,
The guilty King and the whole People fell.

And now the long protracted wars are o'er,
The soft adult'rer shines no more;
No more do's Hector's force the Trojans shield,
That drove whole armies back, and singly clear'd the field.

My vengeance sated, I at length resign
To Mars his off-spring of the Trojan line:
Advanc'd to god-head let him rise,
60 And take his station in the skies;
There entertain his ravish'd sight
With scenes of glory, fields of light;
Quaff with the Gods immortal wine,
And see adoring nations crowd his shrine:

The thin remains of Troy's afflicted host,
In distant realms may seats unenvy'd find,
And flourish on a foreign coast;
But far be Rome from Troy disjoin'd,
Remov'd by seas, from the disastrous shore,
70 May endless billows rise between, and storms unnumber'd
roar.

Still let the curst detested place,
Where Priam lies, and Priam's faithless race,
Be cover'd o'er with weeds, and hid in grass.
There let the wanton flocks unguarded stray;
Or, while the lonely shepherd sings,
Amidst the mighty ruins play,
And frisk upon the tombs of Kings.

May Tigers there, and all the savage kind,
Sad solitary haunts, and silent desarts find;
80 In gloomy vaults, and nooks of palaces,
May th' unmolested Lioness
Her brinded whelps securely lay,
Or, couch't, in dreadful slumbers waste the day.

While Troy in heaps of ruines lyes,
Rome and the Roman Capitol shall rise;
Th' illustrious exiles unconfin'd
Shall triumph far and near, and rule mankind.

In vain the sea's intruding tide
Europe from Afric shall divide,
90 And part the sever'd world in two:
Through Afric's sands their triumphs they shall spread,
And the long train of victories pursue
To Nile's yet undiscover'd head.

Riches the hardy soldier shall despise,
And look on gold with un-desiring eyes,
Nor the disbowell'd earth explore
In search of the forbidden ore;
Those glitt'ring ills conceal'd within the Mine,
Shall lye untouch'd, and innocently shine.
100 To the last bounds that nature sets,
The piercing colds and sultry heats,

ODE III.3 · JOSEPH ADDISON

    The godlike race shall spread their arms;
Now fill the polar circle with alarms,
'Till storms and tempests their pursuits confine;
Now sweat for conquest underneath the line.

    This only law the victor shall restrain,
On these conditions shall he reign;
If none his guilty hand employ
To build again a second Troy,
110 If none the rash design pursue,
Nor tempt the vengeance of the Gods anew.

    A Curse there cleaves to the devoted place,
That shall the new foundations rase:
Greece shall in mutual leagues conspire
To storm the rising town with fire,
And at their armies head my self will show
What Juno, urged to all her rage, can do.

    Thrice should Apollo's self the city raise,
And line it round with walls of brass,
120 Thrice should my fav'rite Greeks his works confound,
And hew the shining fabrick to the ground;
Thrice should her captive dames to Greece return,
And their dead sons and slaughter'd husbands mourn.

    But hold, my Muse, forbear thy towering flight,
Nor bring the secrets of the Gods to light:
In vain would thy presumptuous verse
Th' immortal rhetoric rehearse;
The mighty strains, in Lyric numbers bound,
Forget their majesty, and lose their sound.   (pub. 1709)

WILLIAM SOMERVILLE
(1675–1742)

Educated at Winchester and New College, Oxford. Lived a rural life improved by literary interests. Author of *The Chase* (1735), a poem about the pleasures of hunting. In this imitation Somerville follows the fashion of substituting English poets for the Greek poets named by Horace, and goes one better by praising not only Milton but his admiring critic Addison, whose Saturday Papers on *Paradise Lost* provided an affable account of the beauties of the poem.

From Ode IV.9 A much expanded imitation

For a translation see Philip Francis (p. 183).

10   What tho' Majestick Milton stands alone
         Inimitably great?
     Bow low ye Bards at his exalted Throne,
        And lay your Labours at his Feet;
     Capacious Soul! whose boundless Thoughts survey
         Heav'n, Hell, Earth, Sea:
           Lo! where th' embattel'd Gods appear,
           The Mountains from their Seats they tear,
     And shake th' eternal Throne with impious War.
         Yet nor shall Milton's Ghost repine
20   At all the Honours we bestow
         On Addison's deserving Brow,
     By whom convinç'd, we own his Work divine,
     Whose skillful Pen has done his Merit right,
     And set the Jewel in a fairer Light.
         Enliven'd by his bright Essay
         Each flow'ry Scene appears more gay,
     New Beauties spring in Eden's fertile Groves,
     And by his Culture Paradise improves ...   (pub. 1715)

WILLIAM OLDISWORTH
(1680–1734)

A political journalist in the Tory interest and miscellaneous author, Oldisworth published his translation of the *Odes* in 1712–13. Pope said of him that he could translate an ode 'the quickest of any man in England'. His version of III.6 perhaps took longer than usual.

Ode III.6

A sombre meditation on the degeneracy of the Roman state, the ode begins with a particular offence, neglect of the temples of the gods. Hence defeat in war abroad, at home a young married woman prostituting herself with her husband's connivance. From this Horace passes to a picture, conventional but deeply felt, of the virtues that once made Rome great.

>   Unhappy Romans! doom'd to bear
>   The Load of your Forefathers Guilt;
>   Till by your Piety and Care
>   Our Shrines and Temples are rebuilt:
>   You reign by bowing to the Gods Commands,
> From this your State arose, on this your Glory stands.
>
>   Your impious Land already wears
>   The Marks of Vengeance from on high
>   Feels the yet smarting Parthian Scars,
> 10   And blushes with ignoble Dye;
>   When from Monaeses' Arms your Squadrons fled,
> And Rome's collected Spoils adorn'd the Victor's Head.
>
>   The Dacian and the sunny Moor
>   By Sea and Land their Forces bent,
>   At once to sink the Roman Pow'r

When Civil Rage the Empire rent;
When like a Deluge Vice triumphant reign'd,
And a degen'rate Race the Marriage Rites prophan'd.

Hence the Contagion first began,
    And reach'd our Blood, and stain'd our Race:
The blooming Virgin, ripe for Man,
    A thousand wanton Airs displays:
Train'd to the Dance her well-taught Limbs she moves,
And sates her wishing Soul with loose Incestuous Loves.

The Bride her lustful Rake invites,
    Before her Husband's Face to toy;
She stays not for his drunken Fits,
    Nor in a Corner tastes the Joy;
But in her Cuckolds Presence sells her Charms,
And grasps the Merchant's Gold, or meets the Captain's Arms.

'Twas not from such a motly Brood
    Those better braver Romans came,
Who dy'd the Punick Seas with Blood,
    And rais'd so high their Countrey's Fame;
By whom Antiochus and Pyrrhus dy'd,
And Hannibal was tam'd, and Carthage lost her Pride.

But hardy Youths inur'd to toil,
    Or fell the Wood, or till the Land,
Or turn with heavy Spades the Soil,
    By a dread Mother's just Command,
Nor ceas'd their Work, 'till down the Azure Way,
Sol rowl'd his beamy Car, and shut the chearful Day.

Time alters all things in its Pace,
    Each Century new Vices owns;
Our Fathers bore an Impious Race,

And we shall have more wicked Sons:
   Impiety still gathers in its Course;
The Present Times are bad, the Future will be worse.

                                          (pub. 1712–13)

Ode III.30

To my own Name this Monument I raise,
High as the Pyramids, and strong as Brass;
Which neither Storms nor Tempests shall deface:

This shall remain, whilst Time glides nimbly by;
And the swift Years in measur'd Stages fly,
For I'll not perish, not entirely die.

My Fame, my better Half, shall never end,
Whilst Mitred Priests before the Altar bend,
And Vestal Nymphs the Capitol ascend.

10 Where Aufidus with rapid Fury flows,
And Daunus heretofore his Dwelling chose,
And from a low Estate to Empire rose:

The distant Race of Latins shall admire
Me the first Bard, who urg'd with Sacred Fire,
Tun'd a Greek Measure to a Roman Lyre.

Be bold, my Muse! to claim the just Renown,
Thy Merits and Immortal Lays have won;
And deck thy Poet with a Laurel Crown.   (pub. 1712–13)

ALLAN RAMSAY (1686–1758)

Born in Lanarkshire, set up shop in Edinburgh as a wig-maker – a scull-thacker (thatcher), to use his own term – and played a lively role in the literary scene. Though confessing that he understood Horace 'but faintly in the Original' (he used a French crib), his translations helped to win for Scottish verse a higher respect among the educated public. See Coda for the series of epistles in the 'Habbie' stanza exchanged with William Hamilton of Gilbertfield, Scotland's spirited response to the Horatian exchanges in vogue among gentlemanly Southrons.

Ode I.1 A free translation

To the Right Honourable William Earl of Dalhousie

    Dalhousie of an auld Descent,
My Chief, my Stoup and Ornament,
For Entertainment a wee while,
Accept this Sonnet with a Smile;
Setting great Horace in my View,
He to Mecenas, I to you:
But that my Muse may sing with Ease,
I'll keep or drap him as I please.

    How differently are Fowk inclin'd,
10 There's hardly twa of the same Mind:
Some like to study, some to play,
Some on the Links to win the Day,
And gar the Courser rin like wood,
A' drapin down with Sweat and Blood:

---

2 *Stoup* pillar   **13** *gar* force; *wood* mad

ODE I.I · ALLAN RAMSAY

The Winner syne assumes a Look
Might gain a Monarch or a Duke.
Neist view the Man with pauky Face
Has mounted to a fashous Place,
Inclin'd by an o'er-ruling Fate,
20 He's pleas'd with his uneasy State:
Glowr'd at a while, he gangs fou braw,
Till frae his kittle Post he fa'.

The Lothian Farmer he likes best
To be of good faugh Riggs possest,
And fen upon a frugal Stock,
Where his Forbeers had us'd the Yoke:
Nor is he fond to leave his Wark,
And venture in a rotten Bark,
Syne unto far aff Countries steer
30 On tumbling Waves to gather Gear.

The Merchant wreck'd upon the Main
Swears he'll never venture on't again;
That he had rather live on Cakes,
And shyrest Swats, with Landart Maiks,
As rin the Risk by Storms to have,
When he is dead, a living Grave.
But Seas turn smooth, and he grows fain,
And fairly takes his Word again:
Tho he shou'd to the Bottom sink,
40 Of Poverty he downa think.

---

16 *gain* fit 17 *pauky* cunning 18 *fashous* troublesome
21 *fou braw* very splendid 22 *kittle* precarious
24 *faugh Riggs* fallow fields 25 *fen* support himself on
34 *shyrest Swats* thinnest beer; *Landart* country

Some like to laugh their Time away,
To dance while Pipes or Fidles play,
And have nae Sense of ony Want
As lang as they can drink and rant.

The rat'ling Drum and Trumpet's Tout
Delight young Swankies that are stout:
What his kind frighted Mother ugs,
Is Musick to the Soger's Lugs.

The Hunter with his Hounds and Hawks
50 Bangs up afore his Wife awakes;
Nor speers gin she has ought to say,
But scowrs o'er Highs and Hows a' Day,
Throw Moss and Moor, nor does he care
Whither the Day be foul or fair,
If he his trusty Hounds can chear
To hunt the Tod or drive the Deer.

May I be happy in my Lays,
And won a lasting Wreath of Bays,
Is a' my Wish; well pleas'd to sing
60 Beneath a Tree, or by a Spring,
While Lads and Lasses on the Mead
Attend my Caledonian Reed,
And with the sweetest Notes rehearse
My Thoughts, and roose me for my Verse.

If you, my Lord, class me amang
Those who have sung baith saft and strang,
Of smiling Love or doughty Deed,
To Starns sublime I'll lift my Head. (pub. 1721)

---

47 *ugs* dreads **51** *speers gin* asks if
52 *Hows* vales **56** *Tod* fox

Ode I.4 A free translation

   Now Gowans sprout and Lavrocks sing,
And welcome West Winds warm the Spring,
O'er Hill and Dale they saftly blaw,
And drive the Winter's Cauld awa.
The Ships lang gyzen'd at the Peer
Now spread their Sails and smoothly steer,
The Nags and Nowt hate wissen'd Strae,
And frisking to the Fields they gae,
Nor Hynds wi' Elson and hemp Lingle,
10 Sit solling Shoon out o'er the Ingle.
Now bonny Haughs their Verdure boast,
That late were clade wi' Snaw and Frost,
With her gay Train the Paphian Queen
By Moon-light dances on the Green,
She leads while Nymphs and Graces sing,
And trip around the Fairy Ring.
Mean Time poor Vulcan hard at Thrift,
Gets mony a sair and heavy Lift,
Whilst rinnen down, his haff-blind Lads
20 Blaw up the Fire, and thump the Gads.

   Now leave your Fitsted on the Dew,
And busk ye'r sell in Habit new.
Be gratefu' to the guiding Powers,
And blythly spend your easy Hours.
O kanny F——! tutor Time,
And live as lang's ye'r in your Prime;
That ill bred Death has nae Regard
To King or Cottar, or a Laird,

---

1 *Gowans* daisies; *Lavrocks* skylarks   **5** *gyzend'd* warpcd, leaky
7 *Nowt* black cattle; *wissen'd* withered   **9** *Elson* awl; *Lingle* thread
11 *Haughs* river-meadows   **21** *Fitsted* footprints

>   As soon a Castle he'll attack,
> 30 As Waus of Divots roof'd wi' Thack.
>   Immediately we'll a' take Flight
>   Unto the mirk Realms of Night,
>   As Stories gang, with Gaists to roam,
>   In gloumie Pluto's gousty Dome;
>   Bid fair Good-day to Pleasure syne
>   Of bonny Lasses and red Wine.
>
>   Then deem ilk little Care a Crime,
>   Dares waste an Hour of precious Time;
>   And since our Life's sae unko short,
> 40 Enjoy it a', ye've nae mair for't.   (pub. 1721)

Ode I.5 Freely Scotticized

> What young Raw Muisted Beau Bred at his Glass
> now wilt thou on a Rose's Bed Carress
> wha niest to thy white Breasts wilt thow intice
> with hair unsnooded and without thy Stays.
> O Bonny Lass wi' thy Sweet Landart Air
> how will thy fikle humour gie him care
> when e'er thou takes the fling strings, like the wind
> that Jaws the Ocean – thou'lt disturb his Mind
> when thou looks smirky kind and claps his cheek
> to poor friends then he'l hardly look or speak,
> 10 the Coof belivest-na but Right soon he'll find
> thee Light as Cork and wavring as the Wind
> on that slid place where I 'maist brake my Bains
> to be a warning I Set up twa Stains
> that nane may venture there as I hae done
> unless wi' frosted Nails he Clink his Shoon.   (undated)

---

30 *Waus* walls; *Divots* turf; *Thack* thatch   **34** *gousty* dreary
1 *Muisted* powdered   **7** *takes the fling strings* loses her temper
8 *Jaws* makes surge   **9** *smirky* flirtatiously   **11** *Coof* simpleton;
belivest-na does not believe   **16** *frosted* spiked; *Clink* clinches

ALEXANDER POPE (1688–1744)

Apart from these two versions, Pope's Horatian verse is to be found in the *Imitations of Horace*, written during the 1730s. In the same decade he produced the four hardly less Horatian *Moral Essays* and *Epistle to Dr Arbuthnot*. Above the entrance to his grotto at Twickenham, Pope had inscribed the Horatian motto *Hic secretum iter et fallentis semita vitae* ('Here is a secluded path along the course of a life unnoticed') from Epistle I.18, line 103.

Ode IV.1

    Again? new Tumults in my Breast?
Ah spare me, Venus! let me, let me rest!
    I am not now, alas! the man
As in the gentle Reign of My Queen Anne.
    Ah sound no more thy soft alarms,
Nor circle sober fifty with thy Charms.
    Mother too fierce of dear Desires!
Turn, turn to willing Hearts your wanton fires.
    To Number five direct your Doves,
There spread round Murray all your blooming Loves;
    Noble and young, who strikes the heart
With every sprightly, every decent part;
    Equal, the injur'd to defend,
To charm the Mistress, or to fix the Friend.
    He, with a hundred Arts refin'd,
Shall stretch thy Conquests over half the kind:
    To him each Rival shall submit,
Make but his riches equal to his Wit.
    Then shall thy Form the Marble grace,
(Thy Graecian Form) and Chloe lend the Face:

---

9 *Number five* Murray's lodgings, in King's Bench Walk

His House, embosom'd in the Grove,
Sacred to social Life and social Love,
   Shall glitter o'er the pendent green,
Where Thames reflects the visionary Scene.
   Thither, the silver-sounding Lyres
Shall call the smiling Loves, and young Desires;
   There, every Grace and Muse shall throng,
Exalt the Dance, or animate the Song;
   There, Youths and Nymphs, in consort gay,
30 Shall hail the rising, close the parting day.
   With me, alas! those joys are o'er;
For me, the vernal Garlands bloom no more.
   Adieu! fond hope of mutual fire,
The still-believing, still-renew'd desire;
   Adieu! the heart-expanding bowl,
And all the kind Deceivers of the soul!
   – But why? ah tell me, ah too dear!
Steals down my cheek th' involuntary Tear?
   Why words so flowing, thoughts so free,
40 Stop, or turn nonsense at one glance of Thee?
   Thee, drest in Fancy's airy beam,
Absent I follow thro' th' extended Dream,
   Now, now I seize, I clasp thy charms,
And now you burst, (ah cruel!) from my arms,
   And swiftly shoot along the Mall,
Or softly glide by the Canal,
   Now shown by Cynthia's silver Ray,
And now, on rolling Waters snatch'd away.   (pub. 1737)

Part of Ode IV.9 Imitated

Pope omits the last six stanzas. For a translation see Philip Francis (p. 183).

> Lest you should think that Verse shall die,
>   Which sounds the Silver Thames along,
> Taught on the Wings of Truth, to fly
>   Above the reach of vulgar Song;
>
> Tho' daring Milton sits Sublime,
>   In Spencer native Muses play;
> Nor yet shall Waller yield to time,
>   Nor pensive Cowley's moral Lay.
>
> Sages and Chiefs long since had birth
> 10   E're Caesar was, or Newton nam'd,
> These rais'd new Empires o'er the Earth,
>   And Those new Heav'ns and Systems fram'd;
>
> Vain was the chief's and sage's pride
>   They had no Poet and they dyd!
> In vain they schem'd, in vain they bled
>   They had no Poet and are dead!   (pub. 1751)

THOMAS TICKELL (1688–1740)

Educated at The Queen's College, Oxford, translated the first book of the *Iliad* and wrote a fine elegy on the death of Addison. Johnson granted him 'a high place among the minor poets'. In this very distant imitation Tickell follows an allegorical interpretation probably dating from the Renaissance, which saw in Horace's fable about the disastrous consequences of Paris's rapture of Helen an allusion to Antony and Cleopatra. Tickell applies it to an event of his own time, the first Jacobite rebellion of 1715 led by the Earl of Mar. See David Ferry's translation of this ode (pp. 270–71).

Ode I.15 An imitation

    As Mar his Round one Morning took,
(Whom some call Earl, and some call Duke)
And his new Brethren of the Blade,
Shiv'ring with Fear and Frost, survey'd,
On Perth's bleak Hills he chanc'd to spy
An Aged Wizard six Foot high,
With bristled Hair, and Visage blighted,
Wall-ey'd, bare-haunch'd, and Second-sighted.

    The grizly Sage in Thought profound
10 Beheld the Chief with Back so Round,
Then roll'd his Eye-balls to and fro
O'er his paternal Hills of Snow,
And into these tremendous Speeches
Broke forth the Prophet without Breeches.

    Into what Ills betray'd, by Thee,
This Auncient Kingdom do I see!
Her Realms un-peopled and forlorn!
Wae's me! that ever thou wert born!
Proud English Loons (our Clans o'ercome)
20 On Scottish Pads shall amble home;

---

2 *some call Duke* the Old Pretender created Mar a Duke just before the rebellion
5 *Perth's bleak hills* Perth was the headquarters of the rebellion
10 *Back so Round* Mar was a hunchback
20 *pads* road-horses

ODE I.15 · THOMAS TICKELL

I see them drest in Bonnets blue,
(The Spoils of thy rebellious Crew)
I see the Target, cast away,
And chequer'd Plad become their Prey,
The chequer'd Plad to make a Gown
For many a Lass in London Town.

In vain thy hungry Mountaineers
Come forth in all their warlike Geers,
The Shield, the Pistol, Durk, and Dagger,
In which they daily wont to swagger,
And oft have sally'd out to pillage
The Hen-roosts of some peaceful Village,
Or, while their Neighbours were asleep,
Have carry'd off a Low-land Sheep.

What boots thy high-born Host of Beggars,
Mac-leans, Mac-kenzies, and Mac-gregors,
With Popish Cut-throats, perjur'd Ruffians,
And Forster's Troop of Raggamuffins?

In vain thy Lads around thee bandy,
Inflam'd with Bag-pipe and with Brandy.
Doth not bold Sutherland the trusty,
With Heart so true, and Voice so rusty,
(A loyal Soul) thy Troops affright,
While hoarsely he demands the Fight?
Do'st thou not gen'rous Ilay dread,
The bravest Hand, the wisest Head?
Undaunted do'st thou hear th' Alarms
Of hoary Athole sheath'd in Arms?

---

23 *Target* small targe
38 *Forster's Troop* Thomas Forster, leader of the English Jacobites
41–57 Scotsmen who opposed the rebellion

Douglas, who draws his Lineage down
50 From Thanes and Peers of high Renown,
Fiery, and young, and un-control'd,
With Knights, and Squires, and Barons bold,
(His noble Houshold-Band) advances,
And on his Milk-white Courser prances.
Thee Forfar to the Combat dares,
Grown swarthy in Iberian Wars:
And Monroe kindled into Rage
Sow'rly defies thee to engage;
He'll rout thy Foot, though ne'er so many,
60 And Horse to boot – if thou had'st any.

But see Argyle, with watchful Eyes,
Lodg'd in his deep Intrenchment lies!
Couch'd like a Lion in thy way,
He waits to spring upon his Prey;
While like a Herd of tim'rous Deer
Thy Army shakes and pants with Fear,
Led, by their doughty Gen'ral's Skill,
From Frith to Frith, from Hill to Hill.

Is thus thy haughty Promise pay'd
70 That to the Chevalier was made,
When thou didst Oaths and Duty barter,
For Dukedom, Gen'ralship, and Garter?
Three Moons thy Jemmy shall command,
With Highland Scepter in his Hand,
Too good for his Pretended Birth.
– Then down shall fall the King of Perth.

---

61 *Argyle* John Campbell, second Duke of Argyll, commanded the Hanoverian forces   **70–73** the Old Pretender, James (hence 'Jemmy') Stuart, was the Chevalier de St George

'Tis so decreed: for George shall Reign,
And Traitours be forsworn in vain.
Heav'n shall for ever on him smile,
80 And bless him still with an Argyle.
While Thou, pursu'd by vengeful Foes,
Condemn'd to barren Rocks and Snows,
And hinder'd passing Inverlocky,
Shalt burn thy Clan, and curse poor Jocke.   (pub. 1715)

LADY MARY WORTLEY MONTAGU (1698–1762)

Best known for her letters, notably those from Constantinople. She learned Turkish, studied the position of women in Turkey, and sought to introduce into England the Turkish practice of inoculation against smallpox. Wrote witty occasional verse and collaborated with Pope and Gay on *Town Eclogues* (1717), a series of satirical poems. At one time on friendly terms with Pope, but the friendship went bad and he directed against her one of his cruellest couplets: 'From furious Sappho scarce a milder Fate, / P–x'd by her Love, or libell'd by her Hate.' She and Lord Hervey (Sporus) struck back with *Verses Address'd to the Imitator of . . . Horace* (1733).

Ode I.4 'Adapted from the Latin'

Sharp winter now dissolved, the linnets sing,
The grateful breath of pleasing Zephyrs bring
The welcome joys of long desired spring.

---

83 *Inverlocky* Fort William

ODE I.4 · LADY MARY WORTLEY MONTAGU

The gallies now for open sea prepare,
The herds forsake their stalls for balmy air,
The fields adorn'd with green th' approaching sun declare.

In shining nights the charming Venus leads
Her troop of Graces, and her lovely maids
Who gaily trip the ground in myrtle shades.

10 The blazing forge her husband Vulcan heats,
And thunderlike the labouring hammer beats,
While toiling Cyclops every stroke repeats.

Of myrtle new the chearful wreath compose,
Or various flowers which opening spring bestows,
Till coming June presents the blushing rose.

Pay your vow'd offering to God Faunus' bower!
Then, happy Sestius, seize the present hour,
'Tis all that nature leaves to mortal power.

The equal hand of strong impartial fate,
20 Levels the peasant and th' imperious great,
Nor will that doom on human projects wait.

To the dark mansions of the senseless dead,
With daily steps our destined path we tread,
Realms still unknown, of which so much is said.

Ended your schemes of pleasure and of pride,
In joyous feasts no one will there preside,
Torn from your Lycidas' beloved side;

Whose tender youth does now our eyes engage,
And soon will give in his maturer age,
30 Sighs to our virgins – to our matrons rage.   (undated)

Ode I.5 An imitation

As Aphra Behn (pp. 120–21) had done in the previous century, Lady Mary reverses the sexes.

>   For whom are now your Airs put on?
>   And what new Beauty doom'd to be undone?
>   That careless Elegance of Dress,
>   This Essence that perfumes the Wind,
>   Your every motion does confess
>   Some secret Conquest is design'd.
>
>   Alas the poor unhappy Maid,
>   To what a train of ills betraid!
>   What fears! what pangs shall rend her Breast!
>10   How will her eyes disolve in Tears!
>   That now with glowing Joy is blest,
>   Charm'd with the faithless vows she hears.
>
>   So the young Sailor on the Summer Sea
>   Gaily persues his destin'd way,
>   Fearless and careless on the deck he stands
>   Till sudden storms arise, and Thunders rowl,
>   In vain he casts his Eye to distant Lands,
>   Distracting Terror tears his timerous Soul.
>
>   For me, secure I view the raging Main,
>20 Past are my Dangers, and forgot my Pain,
>   My Votive Tablet in the temple shews
>   The Monument of Folly past,
>   I paid the bounteous God my gratefull vows
>   Who snatch'd from Ruin sav'd me at the last.

(pub. 1750)

CHRISTOPHER PITT (1699–1748)

Educated at Winchester and New College, Oxford, where he became a Fellow, but withdrew to cultivated rural seclusion on being presented with the rectory of Pimperne in Dorset. Johnson thought well of his translation of the *Aeneid*, though he added: 'Pitt pleases the critics, and Dryden the people ... Pitt is quoted, and Dryden read.'

Ode I.22 A free translation

I
The Man unsully'd with a Crime,
    Disdains the Pangs of Fear,
He scorns to dip the poison'd Shaft,
    Or poise the glittering Spear.

II
Nor with the loaded Quiver goes
    To take the dreadful Field;
His solid Virtue is his Helm,
    And Innocence his Shield.

III
In vain the fam'd Hydaspes' Tides,
10   Obstruct and bar the Road,
He smiles on Danger, and enjoys
    The Roarings of the Flood.

IV
All Climes are Native, and forgets
    Th' Extreams of Heats and Frosts,
The Scythian Caucasus grows warm,
    And cools the Lybian Coasts.

V

For while I wander'd thro' the Woods,
    And rang'd the lonely Grove,
Lost and bewilder'd in the Songs
    And pleasing Cares of Love;

VI

A Wolf beheld me from afar,
    Of monstrous Bulk and Might,
But naked as I was, he fled
    And trembled at the Sight.

VII

A Beast so huge, nor Daunia's Groves,
    Nor Africk ever view'd;
Tho' nurst by Her, the Lion reigns
    The Monarch of the Wood.

VIII

Expose Me in those horrid Climes,
    Where not a gentle Breeze
Revives the Vegetable Race,
    Or chears the drooping Trees.

IX

Where on the World's remotest Verge
    Th' unactive Seasons lie,
And not one genial Ray unbinds
    The Rigor of the Sky.

X

On that unhabitable Shore,
    Expose me all alone,
Where I may view without a Shade,
    The culminating Sun.

XI
Beneath th' Aequator, or the Pole,
  In safety could I rove;
And in a thousand different Climes
  Could live for Her I love. (pub. 1727)

JAMES THOMSON (1700–1748)

A Scotsman who spent his life in England, Thomson is read, when he is read, for *Winter* (1726) – Book I of *The Seasons* – and perhaps for *The Castle of Indolence* (1748). Author of 'Rule, Britannia' from *Alfred: A Masque* (1740). These lines are taken from *Liberty* (1735–6), 'Rome', lines 166–80. For complete translations, see Philip Francis (pp. 173–5) and David Ferry (pp. 274–6).

Ode III.5 A partial retelling

166 Hence Regulus the wavering Fathers firm'd,
    By dreadful Counsel never given before;
    For Roman Honour sue'd, and his own Doom.
    Hence he sustain'd to dare a Death prepar'd
170 By Punic Rage. On Earth his manly Look
    Relentless fix'd, he from a last Embrace,
    By Chains polluted, put his Wife aside,
    His little Children climbing for a Kiss;
    Then dumb thro' Rows of weeping wondering Friends,
    A new illustrious Exile! press'd along.
    Nor less impatient did he pierce the Crouds
    Opposing his Return, than if, escap'd
    From long litigious Suits, he glad forsook
    The noisy Town a while and City Cloud
180 To breathe Venafrian, or Tarentine Air. (pub. 1735)

SAMUEL BOYSE (1708–1749)

Educated at Glasgow University, but 'took no degree, entered no profession, and, bungling all his opportunities, died in poverty' (Bonamy Dobrée). Author of *Deity: A Poem* (1739) which versifies the scientific interests of the day.

Ode I.38

I
Away! my Boy, 'tis needless Toil,
I hate your Essences and Oil,
  And all th' enervate Train!
Leave the nice Flow'r, th' autumnal Rose,
Of Myrtle Twigs the Wreath compose,
  Both beautiful and plain.

II
With this, beneath the friendly Shade,
Surround thy careless Master's Head,
  And then adorn thy own:
10 The fragrant Plant shall gaily shine,
Shall aid the generous Joys of Wine,
  And form a grateful Crown!   (pub. 1738)

PHILIP FRANCIS (1708?–1773)

Born in Dublin where he was ordained and became rector of St Peters. Crossed to England in 1739 where he spent the rest of his contentious, extravagant and largely unsuccessful life. For some years private chaplain to Lord Holland ('the atheist chaplain of an atheist lord', Churchill called him). His one great achievement is the translation of the complete works of Horace which appeared between 1743 and 1747 and went through numerous editions during the second part of the eighteenth century and the first part of the nineteenth.

Ode II.3

In arduous Hours an equal Mind maintain,
    Nor let your Spirit rise too high,
Though Fortune kindly change the Scene,
    Alas! my Dellius, Thou wert born to die,

Whether your Life in sadness pass,
    Or wing'd with Pleasure glide away;
Whether reclining on the Grass,
    You bless with choicer Wine the festal Day,

Where the pale Poplar and the Pine
10   Expel th' inhospitable Beam;
Where in kind Shades their Branches twine,
    And toils, obliquely swift, the purling Stream.

There pour your Wines, your Odours shed,
    Bring forth the rosy, short-liv'd Flower,
While Fate yet spins thy mortal Thread,
    While Youth and Fortune give th' indulgent Hour.

Your purchas'd Woods, your House of State,
    Your Villa wash'd by Tiber's Wave,
You must, my Dellius, yield to Fate,
20   And to your Heir these high-pil'd Treasures leave.

Though you could boast a Monarch's Birth,
    Though wealth unbounded round Thee flows,
Though poor, and sprung from vulgar Earth,
    No Pity for his Victim Pluto knows;

Ode III.5

Horace reads contemporary Rome a lesson from the past, telling how Regulus, captured by the Parthians, came home on parole to negotiate the ransom of prisoners, but instead urged that they be left to die while he himself returned to Carthage to face death by torture. A grand and very skilful ode, difficult of reception today for those who regard patriotism as offensive. Compare the modern version by David Ferry (pp. 274–6).

>   Dread Jove in Thunder speaks his just Domain;
>   On Earth a present God shall Caesar reign,
>   Since World-divided Britain owns his Sway,
> And Parthia's haughty Sons his high Behests obey.
>   O Name of Country, once how sacred deem'd!
>   O sad Reverse of Manners, once esteem'd!
>   While Rome her antient Majesty maintain'd,
>   And in his Capitol while Jove imperial reign'd,
>   Could they to foreign Spousals meanly yield,
> 10   Whom Crassus led with Honour to the Field?
>   Have they, to their Barbarian Lords allied,
> Grown old in hostile Arms beneath a Tyrant's Pride,
>   Basely forgetful of the Roman Name,
>   The Heaven-descended Shields, the Vestal Flame,
>   That wakes eternal, and the peaceful Gown,
> Those Emblems, which the Fates with boundless Empire crown?
>   When Regulus refus'd the Terms of Peace
>   Inglorious, He foresaw the deep Disgrace,
>   Whose foul Example should in Ruin end,
> 20 And even to latest Times our baffled Arms attend,

Unless the captive Youth in servile Chains
Should fall unpitied. In the Punic Fanes
Have I not seen, the Patriot Captain cry'd,
The Roman Ensigns fix'd in monumental Pride?
I saw our Arms resign'd without a Wound;
The free-born Sons of Rome in Fetters bound;
The Gates of Carthage open, and the Plain,
Late by our War laid waste, with Culture cloth'd again.
Ransom'd, perhaps, with nobler Sense of Fame
The Soldier may return – Ye purchase Shame.
When the fair Fleece imbibes the Dyer's Stain,
Its native Colour lost it never shall regain;
And Valour, failing in the Soldier's Breast,
Scorns to resume what Cowardice possest.
If from the Toils escap'd the Hind shall turn
Fierce on her Hunters, He the prostrate Foe may spurn
In second Fight, who felt the Fetters bind
His Arms enslav'd; who tamely hath resign'd
His Sword unstain'd with Blood; who might have died,
Yet on a faithless Foe, with abject Soul, relied;
Who for his Safety mix'd poor Terms of Peace
Even with the Act of War; O foul disgrace!
O Carthage now with rival Glories great,
And on the Ruins rais'd of Rome's dejected State!
The Hero spoke; and from his wedded Dame,
And Infant-Children turn'd, opprest with Shame
Of his fallen State; their fond Embrace repell'd,
And sternly on the Earth his manly Visage held,
'Till, by his unexampled Counsel sway'd,
Their firm Decree the wavering Senate made;
Then, while his Friends the Tears of Sorrow shed,
Amidst the weeping Throng the glorious Exile sped.
Nor did he not the cruel Tortures know,
Vengeful, prepar'd by a Barbarian Foe;
Yet, with a Countenance serenely gay,
He turn'd aside the Croud, who fondly press'd his Stay;

As if, when wearied by some Client's Cause,
After the final Sentence of the Laws
Chearful he hasted to some calm Retreat,
60 To taste the pure Delights, which bless the rural Seat.

(pub. 1746)

Ode III.25

O Bacchus, when by Thee possest,
What hallowed Spirit fills my raving Breast?
   How am I rapt to dreary Glades,
To gloomy Caverns, unfrequented Shades?
   In what Recesses shall I raise
My Voice to sacred Caesar's deathless Praise,
   Amid the Stars to bid him shine,
Rank'd in the Councils of the Powers divine?
   Some bolder Song shall wake the Lyre,
10 And Sounds unknown its trembling Voice inspire.
   Thus o'er the steepy Mountain's Height,
Starting from Sleep, thy Priestess takes her Flight;
   Amaz'd beholds the Thracian Snows,
With languid Streams where icy Heber flows,
   Or Rhodope's high-towering Head,
Where frantick Quires barbarian Measures tread.
   O'er pathless Rocks; through lonely Groves
With what Delight my raptur'd Spirit roves!
   O Thou, who rul'st the Naiad's Breast;
20 By whom the Bacchanalian Maids, possest
   With sacred Rage inspir'd by Thee,
Tear from the bursting Glebe th' uprooted Tree,
   Nothing or low, or mean, I sing,
No mortal Sound shall shake the swelling String.

The venturous Theme my Soul alarms,
But warm'd by thee the Thought of Danger charms.
   When Vine-crown'd Bacchus leads the Way,
What can his daring Votaries dismay?   (pub. 1746)

Ode III.29

Compare Dryden's paraphrase (pp. 110–14).

   Descended from an antient Line,
      That once the Tuscan Sceptre sway'd,
   Haste thee to meet the generous Wine,
      Whose piercing is for Thee delay'd;
   For Thee the fragrant Essence flows,
For Thee, Maecenas, breathes the blooming Rose.

   From the Delights, Oh! break away,
      Which Tibur's marshy Prospect yields,
   Nor with unceasing Joy survey
10   Fair Aesula's declining Fields;
   No more the verdant Hills admire
Of Telegon, who kill'd his aged Sire.

   Instant forsake the joyless Feast,
      Where Appetite in Surfeit dies,
   And from the towered Structure haste,
      That proudly threatens to the Skies;
   From Rome and its tumultuous Joys,
Its Crouds, and Smoke, and Opulence, and Noise.

   To frugal Treats, and humble Cells,
20   With grateful Change the Wealthy fly,
   Where health-preserving Plainness dwells,
      Far from the Carpet's gaudy Dye.
   Such Scenes have charm'd the Pangs of Care,
And smooth'd the clouded Forehead of Despair.

Andromeda's conspicuous Sire
    Now darts his hidden Beams from far;
The Lion shews his madding Fire,
    And barks fierce Procyon's raging Star,
While Phoebus, with revolving Ray,
Brings back the Burnings of the thirsty Day.

Fainting beneath the sweltring Heat,
    To cooling Streams, and breezy Shades
The Shepherd and his Flocks retreat,
    While rustic Sylvans seek the Glades,
Silent the Brook its Borders laves,
Nor curls one vagrant Breath of Winds the Waves.

But you for Rome's imperial State
    Attend with ever-watchful Care,
Or, for the World's uncertain Fate
    Alarm'd, with ceaseless Terrors fear;
Anxious what Eastern Wars impend,
Or what the Scythians in their Pride intend.

But Jove, in Goodness ever wise,
    Hath hid, in Clouds of depthless Night,
All that in future Prospect lies,
    Beyond the Ken of mortal Sight,
And laughs to see vain Man opprest
With idle Fears, and more than Man distrest.

Then wisely form the present Hour;
    Enjoy the Bliss which it bestows;
The rest is all beyond our Power,
    And like the changeful Tiber flows,
Who now beneath his Banks subsides,
And peaceful to his native Ocean glides;

But when descends a sudden Shower
    And wild provokes his silent Flood,
The Mountains hear the Torrent roar,
    And Echoes shake the neighbouring Wood,
Then swollen with Rage He sweeps away
60   Uprooted Trees, Herds, Dwellings to the Sea.

Happy the Man, and he alone,
    Who Master of himself can say,
To-day at least hath been my own,
    For I have clearly liv'd To-day:
Then let To-morrow's Clouds arise,
Or purer Suns o'erspread the chearful Skies.

Not Jove himself can now make void
    The Joy, that wing'd the flying Hour;
The certain Blessings once enjoy'd
70   Is safe beyond the Godhead's Power;
Nought can recall the acted Scene,
What hath been, spite of Jove himself, hath been.

But Fortune, ever-changing Dame,
    Indulges her malicious Joy,
And constant plays her haughty Game,
    Proud of her Office to destroy;
To-day to me her Bounty flows,
And now to others she the Bliss bestows.

I can applaud her while she stays,
80   But if she shake her rapid Wings,
I can resign, with careless Ease,
    The richest Gifts her Favour brings,
Then folded lie in Virtue's Arms,
And honest Poverty's undower'd Charms.

>   Though the Mast howl beneath the Wind,
>   I make no mercenary Prayers,
>   Nor with the Gods a Bargain bind
>   With future Vows, and streaming Tears,
>   To save my Wealth from adding more
> 90 To boundless Ocean's avaricious Store;
>
>   Then in my little Barge I'll ride,
>   Secure amid the foamy Wave,
>   Calm will I stem the threatening Tide,
>   And fearless all its Tumults brave;
>   Even then perhaps some kinder Gale,
>   While the Twin Stars appear, shall fill my joyful Sail.

(pub. 1746)

Ode IV.2

It seems to have been suggested that Horace should compose an ode in Pindaric style to celebrate Augustus' return from a foreign campaign. He in effect writes or sketches the required ode, then, 'a master of the graceful sidestep', protests that the task is beyond him; a fitter celebrant would be Iullus Antonius (his name is omitted in the translation), a young Roman nobleman and amateur poet.

>   He, who to Pindar's Height attempts to rise,
>   Like Icarus, with waxen Pinions tries
>   His pathless Way, and from the venturous Theme
>   Shall leave to azure Seas his falling Name.
>   As when a River, swollen by sudden Showers
>   O'er its known Banks, from some steep Mountain pours,
>   So in profound, unmeasurable Song
>   The deep-mouth'd Pindar, foaming, pours along.
>   Well He deserves Apollo's laurel'd Crown,
> 10 Whether new Words He rolls enraptur'd down
>   Impetuous through the Dithyrambic Strains;
>   Free from all Laws, but what Himself ordains;

Whether in lofty Tone sublime He sings
The deathless Gods, or God-descended Kings,
With Death deserv'd who smote the Centaurs dire,
And quench'd the fierce Chimaera's Breath of Fire;

Or whom th' Olympic Palm, celestial Prize!
Immortal crowns, and raises to the Skies,
Wrestler or Steed – with Honours that outlive
20 The mortal Fame, which thousand Statues give:

Or mourns some hapless Youth in plaintive Lay,
From his fond, weeping Bride, ah! torn away,
His Manners pure, his Courage, and his Name,
Snatch'd from the Grave, He vindicates to Fame.

Thus when the Theban Swan attempts the Skies,
A nobler Gale of Rapture bids Him rise;
But like a Bee, which through the breezy Groves,
With feeble Wing and idle Murmurs roves,

Sits on the Bloom, and with unceasing Toil
30 From Thyme sweet-breathing culls his flowery Spoil;
So I, weak Bard! round Tibur's lucid Spring,
Of humble Strain laborious Verses sing.

'Tis thine with deeper Hand to strike the Lyre,
For Caesar's Glory shall his Bard inspire,
When He, with Laurel crown'd, the Meed of War,
Drags the fierce Gaul at his triumphal Car;

Than whom the Gods ne'er gave, or bounteous Fate
To human Kind a Gift more good or great,
Nor from their Treasures shall again unfold,
40 Though Time roll backward to his antient Gold.

Be thine the festal Days, the City's Joys,
The Forum silenc'd from litigious Noise,
The public Games for Caesar safe restor'd,
A Blessing oft with pious Vows implor'd.

Then, if my Voice can reach the glorious Theme,
Thus I will sing, amid the loud Acclaim –
Hail brightest Sun; in Rome's fair Annals shine,
Caesar returns – eternal Praise be thine.

        As the Procession awful moves along,
50   Let Shouts of Triumph fill our joyful Song;
     Repeated Shouts of Triumph Rome shall raise,
     And to the bounteous Gods our Altars blaze.
        Of thy fair Herds twice ten shall grateful bleed,
     While I, with pious Care, one Steerling feed:
     Wean'd from the Dam, o'er Pastures large he roves,
     And for my Vows his rising Youth he proves;
        His Horns like Luna's bending Fires appear,
     When the third Night she rises to her Sphere;
     And, yellow all the rest, one Mark there glows
60   Full in his Front, and bright as Winter Snows.   (pub. 1746)

Ode IV.5

'... perhaps of all Horace's *Odes* the easiest to read as straightforwardly fascist' – Don Fowler, Fellow and Tutor in Classics at Jesus College, Oxford (*Horace Made New*, p. 273). 'We cannot imagine anything more tender, than the sentiments of this Ode, in which the poet not only shews the Love and Veneration of the Romans for Augustus ... but tells him, why they adore him, and by this means draws a beautiful picture of that Happiness, which they enjoyed under his reign.' Critical comment on the ode quoted by Francis.

        Propitious to the Sons of Earth
           (Best Guardian of the Roman State)
        The heavenly Powers beheld thy Birth,
           And form'd thee glorious, good and great;
     Rome and her holy Fathers cry, thy Stay
     Was promis'd short, ah! wherefore this Delay?

Come then, auspicious Prince, and bring,
    To thy long gloomy Country, Light,
For in thy Countenance the Spring
    Shines forth to chear thy People's Sight;
Then hasten thy Return, for, Thou away,
Nor Lustre has the Sun, nor Joy the Day.

As a fond Mother views with Fear
    The Terrours of the rolling Main,
While envious Winds, beyond his Year,
    From his lov'd Home her Son detain;
To the good Gods with fervent Prayer she cries,
And catches every Omen as it flies;

Anxious she listens to the Roar
    Of Winds that loudly sweep the Sky;
Nor fearful from the winding Shore,
    Can ever turn her longing Eye:
Smit with as faithful and as fond Desires,
Impatient Rome her absent Lord requires.

Safe by thy Cares her Oxen graze,
    And yellow Ceres clothes the Fields:
The Sailor plows the peaceful Seas,
    And Earth her rich Abundance yields;
While nobly conscious of unsullied Fame,
Fair Honour dreads th' imputed Sense of Blame.

By thee our wedded Dames are pure
    From foul Adultery's Embrace;
The conscious Father views secure
    His own Resemblance in his Race:
Thy chaste Example quells the spotted Deed,
And to the Guilt thy Punishments succeed.

Who shall the faithless Parthian dread,
    The freezing Armies of the North,
Or the fierce Youth, to Battle bred,
    Whom horrid Germany brings forth?
Who shall regard the War of cruel Spain,
If Caesar live secure, if Caesar reign?

Safe in his Vineyard toils the Hind,
    Weds to the widow'd Elm his Vine,
'Till the Sun sets his Hill behind,
    Then hastens joyful to his Wine,
And in his gayer Hours of Mirth implores
Thy Godhead to protect and bless his Stores.

To Thee he chaunts the sacred Song,
    To Thee the rich Libation pours;
Thee, plac'd his Houshold Gods among,
    With solemn daily Prayer adores;
So Castor and great Hercules of old
Were with her Gods by grateful Greece enroll'd.

Gracious and good, beneath thy Reign
    May Rome her happy Hours employ,
And grateful hail thy just Domain
    With pious Hymns and festal Joy:
Thus, with the rising Sun we sober pray,
Thus, in our Wine beneath his setting Ray.   (pub. 1746)

Ode IV.9

While with the Grecian Bards I vye,
    And raptur'd tune the social String,
Think not the Song shall ever die,
    Which with no vulgar Art I sing,
Though born where Aufid rolls his sounding Stream,
In Lands far distant from poetic Fame.

What though the Muse her Homer thrones
    High above all th' immortal Quire,
Nor Pindar's Rapture She disowns,
10   Nor hides the plaintive Caean lyre;
Alcaeus strikes the Tyrant's Soul with Dread,
Nor yet is grave Stesichorus unread.

Whatever old Anacreon sung,
    However tender was the Lay,
In spite of Time is ever young,
    Nor Sappho's amorous Flames decay;
Her living Songs preserve their charming Art,
Her Love still breathes the Passions of her Heart.

Helen was not the only Fair,
20   By an unhappy Passion fir'd,
Who the lewd Ringlets of the Hair
    Of an adulterous Beau admir'd;
Court Arts, Gold Lace, and Equipage have Charms
To tempt weak Woman to a Stranger's Arms.

Nor first from Teucer's vengeful Bow
    The feather'd Death unerring flew,
Nor was the Greek the single Foe,
    Whose Rage ill-fated Ilion knew;
Greece had with Heroes fill'd th' embattled Plain,
30 Worthy the Muse in her sublimest Strain.

Nor Hector first transported heard
    With fierce Delight the War's Alarms,
Nor brave Deïphobus appear'd
    Amid the tented Field in Arms,
With glorious Ardour prodigal of Life,
To guard a darling Son, and faithful Wife.

Before great Agamemnon reign'd,
    Reign'd Kings as great as He, and brave,
Whose huge Ambition's now contain'd
40   In the small Compass of a Grave;
In endless Night they sleep, unwept, unknown,
No Bard had They to make all Time their own.

In Earth if it forgotten lies,
    What is the Valour of the Brave?
What difference, when the Coward dies,
    And sinks in Silence to his Grave?
Nor, Lollius, will I not thy Praise proclaim,
But from Oblivion vindicate thy Fame.

Nor shall its livid Power conceal
50   Thy Toils – how glorious to the State!
How constant to the public Weal
    Through all the doubtful Turns of Fate!
Thy steady Soul, by long Experience found
Erect alike, when Fortune smil'd, or frown'd.

Villains, in public Rapine bold,
    Lollius, the just Avenger, dread,
Who never by the Charms of Gold,
    Shining Seducer! was misled;
Beyond thy Year such Virtue shall extend,
60 And Death alone thy Consulate shall end.

Perpetual Magistrate is He,
    Who keeps strict Justice full in Sight;
With scorn rejects th' Offender's Fee,
    Nor weighs Convenience against Right;
Who bids the Crowd at awful Distance gaze,
And Virtue's Arms victoriously displays.

    Not He, of Wealth immense possest,
        Tasteless who piles his massy Gold,
    Among the Number of the Blest
70   Should have his glorious Name enroll'd;
    He better claims the glorious Name, who knows,
    With Wisdom to enjoy what Heaven bestows:

    Who knows the Wrongs of Want to bear,
        Even in its lowest, last Extreme;
    Yet can with conscious Virtue fear,
        Far worse than Death, a Deed of Shame;
    Undaunted, for his Country or his Friend,
    To sacrifice his Life – O glorious End!   (pub. 1746)

Ode IV.10

O Cruel still and vain of Beauty's Charms,
When wintry Age thy Insolence disarms;
When fall those Locks that on thy Shoulders play,
And Youth's gay Roses on thy Cheeks decay;
When that smooth Face shall Manhood's Roughness wear,
And in your Glass another Form appear,
Ah why! you'll say, do I now vainly burn,
Or with my Wishes, not my Youth return?   (pub. 1746)

WILLIAM DUNKIN (1709?–1765)

Educated at Trinity College, Dublin, appointed by Lord Chesterfield to the mastership of Portora Royal School in Enniskillen. A friend of Swift who praised his English and Latin verse and described him as 'a man of genuine true wit and a delightful companion'. A number of his translations are included in Francis' Horace.

Ode III.15

    Thou poor Man's Incumbrance, Thou Rake of a Wife,
At length put an End to this infamous Life;
Now near thy long Home, to be rank'd with the Shades,
Give over to frisk it with buxom young Maids,
And, furrow'd with Wrinkles, profanely to shroud
Those bright Constellations with Age's dark Cloud.
    What Pholoë well, with a Decency free,
Might practise, fits aukward, O Chloris, on Thee;
Like her, whom the Timbrel of Bacchus arouses,
10 Thy Daughter may better lay siege to the Houses
Of youthful Gallants, while she wantonly gambols,
Of Nothus enamour'd, like a Goat in its Rambles;
The Spindle, the Distaff, and Wool-spinning thrifty;
Not musical Instruments fit Thee at Fifty,
Nor Roses impurpled, enriching the Breeze,
Nor Hogsheads of Liquor drunk down to the Lees.

                                              (pub. 1746)

Ode III.26

Horace's theme is the *militia amoris*, the warfare of love designed to bring the beauty to her knees. Dunkin gives it a more chivalrous turn.

    I lately was fit to be call'd upon Duty,
And gallantly fought in the Service of Beauty;
But now crown'd with Conquest I hang up my Arms,
My Harp, that campaign'd it in midnight Alarms.
Here fix on this Wall, here my Ensigns of Wars,
By the Statue of Venus, my Torches and Bars,
And Arrows, which threaten'd by Cupid their Liege,
War, War on all Doors, that dare hold out a Siege.

O Goddess of Cyprus, and Memphis, that know
10   Nor the Coldness or Weight of Love-chilling Snow,
With an high-lifted Stroke, yet gently severe,
Avenge me on Chloe, the proud and the fair.   (pub. 1746)

SAMUEL JOHNSON (1709–1784)

Johnson translated several odes while still at school, among them this version of I.22, the only one he liked well enough to publish in a slightly revised form. Ode IV.7 he translated in the month before his death. He told Boswell that Horace's *Odes* 'were the compositions in which he took most delight, and it was long before he liked His Epistles and Satires.'

Ode I.22

The man, my friend, whose conscious heart
    With virtue's sacred ardour glows,
Nor taints with death the envenom'd dart,
    Nor needs the guard of Moorish bows.

O'er icy Caucusus he treads,
    Or torrid Afric's faithless sands,
Or where the fam'd Hydaspes spreads
    His liquid wealth thro' barbarous lands.

For while in Sabine forests, charm'd
10   By Lalagé, too far I stray'd,
Me singing, careless and unarm'd,
    A furious wolf approach'd, and fled.

No beast more dreadful ever stain'd
    Apulia's spacious wilds with gore;
No beast more fierce Numidia's land,
    The lion's thirsty parent, bore.

Place me where no soft summer gale
    Among the quivering branches sighs,
Where clouds, condens'd, for ever veil
20   With horrid gloom the frowning skies:

Place me beneath the burning zone,
    A clime deny'd to human race;
My flame for Lalagé I'll own;
    Her voice and smiles my song shall grace.

                           (pub. 1743; rev. 1757)

Ode IV.7

Written in the month before his death.

The snow dissolv'd no more is seen,
The fields, and woods, behold, are green,
The changing year renews the plain,
The rivers know their banks again,
The spritely nymph and naked grace
The mazy dance together trace.
The changing year's successive plan
Proclaims mortality to man.
Rough winter's blasts to spring give way,
10 Spring yields to summer's sovereign ray,
Then summer sinks in autumn's reign,
And winter chils the world again.
Her losses soon the moon supplies,
But wretched man, when once he lies

Where Priam and his sons are laid,
Is naught but ashes and a shade.
Who knows if Jove who counts our score
Will toss us in a morning more?
What with your friend you nobly share
20 At least you rescue from your heir.
Not you, Torquatus, boast of Rome,
When Minos once has fix'd your doom,
Or eloquence, or splendid birth,
Or virtue shall replace on earth.
Hippolytus unjustly slain
Diana calls to life in vain,
Nor can the might of Theseus rend
The chains of hell that hold his friend.   (pub. 1787)

CHRISTOPHER SMART
(1722–1771)

Educated at Pembroke College, Cambridge, subsequently becoming a Fellow. Resigned to try his luck as a writer in London. Best known for *A Song to David*, his hymns, and (since its publication in 1939) for *Jubilate Agno*. Published a prose translation of Horace in 1756, followed by one in verse eleven years later. Spent several years in a madhouse and died in a debtors' prison.

Ode II.4 An imitation

Written, like the imitation of III.30, in the 1740s, twenty years before Smart set to work on his complete verse translation of Horace.

The Pretty Chambermaid

Colin, oh! cease thy friend to blame,
Who entertains a servile flame.
Chide not – believe me, 'tis no more
Than great Achilles did before,
Who nobler, prouder far than he is,
Ador'd his chambermaid Briseis.

The thund'ring Ajax Venus lays
In love's inextricable maze.
His slave Tecmessa makes him yield.
Now mistress of the sevenfold shield.
Atrides with his captive play'd,
Who always shar'd the bed she made.

'Twas at the ten years siege, when all
The Trojans fell in Hector's fall,
When Helen rul'd the day and night,
And made them love, and made them fight:
Each hero kiss'd his maid, and why,
Tho' I'm no hero, may not I?

Who knows? Perhaps Polly may be
A piece of ruin'd royalty.
She has (I cannot doubt it) been
The daughter of some mighty queen;
But fate's irremeable doom
Has chang'd her sceptre for a broom.

Ah! cease to think it – how can she,
So generous, charming, fond, and free,
So lib'ral of her little store,
So heedless of amassing more,
Have one drop of plebeian blood
In all the circulating flood?

But you, by carping at my fire,
Do but betray your own desire –
Howe'er proceed – made tame by years,
You'll raise in me no jealous fears.
You've not one spark of love alive,
For, thanks to heav'n, you're forty-five.   (pub. 1746)

Ode III.30 An imitation

On Taking a Batchelor's Degree

'Tis done: – I tow'r to that degree,
   And catch such heav'nly fire,
That Horace ne'er could rant like me,
   Nor is King's-chapel higher.
My name in sure recording page
   Shall time itself o'erpow'r,
If no rude mice with envious rage
   The buttery books devour.
A title too, with added grace,
10   My name shall now attend,
Till to the church with silent pace
   A nymph and priest ascend.
Ev'n in the schools I now rejoice,
   Where late I shook with fear,
Nor heed the Moderator's voice
   Loud thund'ring in my ear.
Then with Aeolian flute I blow
   A soft Italian lay,
Or where Cam's scanty waters flow,
20   Releas'd from lectures, stray.
Meanwhile, friend Banks, my merits claim
   Their just reward from you,

---

21 *Banks* 'a celebrated taylor'

For Horace bids us challenge fame,
    When once that fame's our due.
Invest me with a graduate's gown,
    Midst shouts of all beholders,
My head with ample square-cap crown,
    And deck with hood my shoulders. (pub. 1750)

Ode I.3

This and the following translations belong to Smart's complete Horace of 1767.

    So may the queen of Cyprus' isle
And Helen's brethren in sweet star-light smile,
    And Aeolus the winds arrest,
All but the fav'ring gales of fresh north-west,
    O ship, that ow'st so great a debt,
No less than Virgil, to our fond regret!
    By thee on yon Athenian shore
Let him be safely landed, I implore:
    And o'er the billows, as they roll,
10 Preserve the larger portion of my soul!
    A heart of oak, and breast of brass
Were his, who first presum'd on seas to pass,
    And ever ventur'd to engage,
In a slight skiff, with ocean's desperate rage;
    Nor fear'd to hear the cracking masts,
When Africus contends with northern blasts;
    Nor Hyads, still foreboding storms,
Nor wrathful south, that all the depth deforms;
    Than whom no greater tyrant reigns
20 Whether the waves he ruffles or restrains.
    How dauntless of all death was he,
Whose tearless eyes could such strange monsters see;

      Cou'd see the swelling ocean low'r,
Or those huge rocks, which in Epirus tow'r!
      Dread Providence the land in vain
Has cut from that dissociable main,
      If impious mortals not the less
On this forbidden element transgress:
      Determin'd each extreme to bear,
30 All desp'rate deeds the race of mortals dare.
      Prometheus, with presumptuous fraud,
Stole fire from heav'n, and spread the flame abroad,
      Of which dire sacrilege the fruit,
The lank consumption, and a new recruit
      Of fevers came upon mankind,
And for a long delay at first design'd,
      The last extremity advanc'd,
And urg'd the march of death, and all his pangs inhanc'd.
      With wings, not giv'n a man below,
40 Did Dedalus attempt in air to go.
      Th' Herculean toil, exceeding bound,
Broke through the gulf of Acheron profound.
      Nothing too difficult for man,
He'll scale the skies in folly, if he can;
      Nor by his vices every day
Will give Jove leave his wrathful bolts to stay.   (pub. 1767)

Ode I.5

Say what slim youth, with moist perfumes
    Bedaub'd, now courts thy fond embrace,
There, where the frequent rose-tree blooms,
    And makes the grot so sweet a place?
Pyrrha, for whom with such an air
Do you bind back your golden hair?

So seeming in your cleanly vest,
   Whose plainness is the pink of taste –
Alas! how oft shall he protest
10   Against his confidence misplac't,
And love's inconstant pow'rs deplore,
And wondrous winds, which, as they roar,

Throw black upon the alter'd scene –
   Who now so well himself deceives,
And thee all sunshine, all serene
   For want of better skill believes,
And for his pleasure has presag'd
Thee ever dear and disengag'd.

Wretched are all within thy snares,
20   The inexperienc'd and the young!
For me the temple witness bears
   Where I my dropping weeds have hung,
And left my votive chart behind
To him that rules both wave and wind.   (pub. 1767)

Ode I.8

I charge thee, Lydia, tell me straight,
   Why Sybaris destroy,
Why make love do the deeds of hate,
And to this end precipitate
   The dear enamour'd boy?
Why can he not the field abide,
   From sun and dust recede,
Nor with his friends, in gallant pride,
Dress'd in his regimentals, ride,
10   And curb the manag'd steed?

Why does he now to bathe disdain,
   And fear the sandy flood?
Why from th' athletic oil refrain,
As if its use would be his bane,
   As sure as viper's blood?
No more his shoulders black and blue
   By wearing arms appear;
He, who the quoit so dextrous threw,
And from whose hand the jav'lin flew
20   Beyond a rival's spear;
Why does he skulk, as authors say
   Of Thetis' fav'rite heir
Lest a man's habit should betray,
And force him to his troops away,
   The work of death to share?

(pub. 1767)

Ode II.4

O Phoceus, think it no disgrace
   To love your maid, since Thetis heir,
Tho' proud, of old was in your case,
   Briseis was so fair.
– The slave Tecmessa at her feet
   Saw her lord Ajax – Atreus son
Lov'd his fair captive in the heat
   Of conquest, that he won,
When beat by that Thessalian boy,
10   The Phrygian host was disarray'd,
And Hector's death, the fall of Troy,
   An easy purchase made.
Who knows what wealth thou hast to claim,
   Rich parents may thy Phyllis grace,
Surely the Gods have been to blame
   To one of royal race.

You cannot think her meanly born,
   Nor worthless cou'd her mother be,
Whose heart has such ingenuous scorn
20   For wealth, and love for thee.
Her face, her limbs so form'd t' engage,
   I praise with a safe conscience still –
Shun to suspect a man, whose age
     Is going down the hill.   (pub. 1767)

Ode II.14

   Ah! Posthumus, the years, the years
   Glide swiftly on, nor can our tears
Or piety the wrinkl'd age forfend,
Or for one hour retard th' inevitable end.
   'Twould be in vain, tho' you should slay,
   My friend, three hundred beeves a day
To cruel Pluto, whose dire waters roll,
Geryon's threefold bulk, and Tityus to controul.
   This is a voyage we all must make,
10   Whoe'er the fruits of earth partake,
Whether we sit upon a royal throne,
Or live, like cottage hinds, unwealthy and unknown.
   The wounds of war we scape in vain,
   And the hoarse breakers of the main;
In vain with so much caution we provide
Against the southern winds upon th' autumnal tide.
   The black Cocytus, that delays
   His waters in a languid maze,
We must behold, and all those Danaids fell,
20 And Sysiphus condemn'd to fruitless toil in hell.
   Lands, house, and pleasing wife, by thee
   Must be relinquish'd; nor a tree
Of all your nurseries shall in the end,
Except the baleful cypress, their brief lord attend.

Thy worthier heir the wine shall seize
    You hoarded with a hundred keys,
And with libations the proud pavement dye,
And feasts of priests themselves shall equal and outvie.

(pub. 1767)

Ode II.18

Gold or iv'ry's not intended
   For this little house of mine,
Nor Hymettian arches, bended
   On rich Afric pillars, shine.
For a court I've no ambition,
   As not Attalus his heir,
Nor make damsels of condition
   Spin me purple for my wear.
But for truth and wit respected,
   I possess a copious vein,
So that rich men have affected
   To be number'd of my train.
With my Sabine field contented,
   Fortune shall be dunn'd no more;
Nor my gen'rous friend tormented
   To augment my little store.
One day by the next's abolish'd,
   Moons increase but to decay;
You place marbles to be polish'd
   Ev'n upon your dying day.
Death unheeding, though infirmer,
   On the sea your buildings rise,
While the Baian billows murmur,
   That the land will not suffice.
What tho' more and more incroaching,
   On new boundaries you press,
And in avarice approaching,
   Your poor neighbours dispossess;

The griev'd hind his gods displaces,
   In his bosom to convey,
And with dirty ruddy faces
   Boys and wife are driven away.
Yet no palace grand and spacious
   Does more sure its lord receive,
Than the seat of death rapacious,
   Whence the rich have no reprieve.
Earth alike to all is equal,
   Whither would your views extend?
Kings and peasants in the sequel
   To the destin'd grave descend.
There, tho' brib'd, the guard infernal
   Would not shrewd Prometheus free;
There are held in chains eternal
   Tantalus, and such as he.
There the poor have consolation
   For their hard laborious lot;
Death attends each rank and station,
   Whether he is call'd or not.   (pub. 1767)

Ode IV.13

Lyce, the gods my vows have heard,
   At length they've heard my vows;
You wou'd be beauteous with a beard,
   You romp and you carouse:
And drunk, with trembling voice, you court
   Slow Cupid, prone to seek
For better music, bloom, and sport,
   In buxom Chia's cheek.
For he, a sauce-box, scorns dry chips,
   And teeth decay'd and green;
Where wrinkled forehead, and chapt lips,
   And snowy hairs are seen.
Nor Coan elegance, nor gems,

    Your past years will restore;
Which time to his records condemns,
    With fleeting wings of yore.
Ah! where's that form, complexion, grace,
    That air – where is she, say,
That cou'd my sick'ning soul solace,
20   And stole my heart away?
Blest! who cou'd Cynara succeed,
    As artful and as fair –
But fate, to Cynara, decreed
    Few summers for her share,
That crow-like Lyce might survive,
    'Till lads shou'd laugh and shout,
To see the torch, but just alive,
    So slowly stinking out.   (pub. 1767)

THOMAS WARTON (1728–1790)

An important literary figure in his day: Professor of Poetry at Oxford, later Camden Professor of History, Poet Laureate in 1785. His extensive work *The History of English Poetry* appeared between 1774 and 1781. His two translations are written in the stanza Milton devised for the 'Ode to Pyrrha'. ('Blandusian': a variant reading found in some manuscripts.)

Ode III.13

Ye waves, that gushing fall with purest stream,
Blandusian Fount! to whom the products sweet
    Of richest vines belong,
    And fairest flowers of spring;
To thee, a chosen victim will I slay,
A kid, who glowing in lascivious youth

        Just blooms with budding horn,
        And with vain thought elate
Yet destines future war: but ah! too soon
His reeking blood with crimson shall enrich
        Thy pure translucent flood,
        And tinge thy crystal clear.
Thy sweet recess the sun in mid-day hour
Can ne'er invade, thy streams the labour'd ox
        Refresh with cooling draught,
        And glad the wand'ring herds.
Thy name shall shine with endless honors grac'd,
While on my shell I sing the nodding oak,
        That o'er thy cavern deep
        Waves his embowering head.   (pub. 1746

Ode III.18

Faunus, who lov'st to chase the light-foot Nymphs,
Propitious guard my fields and sunny farm,
        And nurse with kindly care
        The promise of my flock.

So to thy pow'r a Kid shall yearly bleed,
And the full bowl to genial Venus flow;
        And on thy rustic shrine
        Rich odours incense breathe:

So thro' the vale the wanton herds shall bound,
When thy December comes, and on the green
        The steer in traces loose
        With the free village sport:

No more the lamb shall fly th' insidious wolf,
The woods shall shed their leaves, and the glad hind
        The ground, where once he dug,
        Shall beat in sprightly dance.   (1802)

OLIVER GOLDSMITH (1730?–1774)

Educated at Trinity College, Dublin, and the University of Edinburgh. Came to London and lived for a few years as a Jack of all trades, but soon established himself in the literary world. This passage is taken from *The Deserted Village* (1770), lines 275–86. See headnote to C. H. Sisson's translation (p. 258).

Based on Ode II.15

275   The man of wealth and pride,
Takes up a space that many poor supplied;
Space for his lake, his park's extended bounds,
Space for his horses, equipage, and hounds;
The robe that wraps his limbs in silken sloth,
280 Has robbed the neighbouring fields of half their growth;
His seat, where solitary sports are seen,
Indignant spurns the cottage from the green;
Around the world each needful product flies,
For all the luxuries the world supplies.
While thus the land adorned for pleasure all
In barren splendour feebly waits the fall.   (pub. 1770)

WILLIAM COWPER (1731–1800)

Educated privately and at Westminster School. Poet of a strangely varied oeuvre: satires – hardly his *métier* – some fine hymns, the six books of *The Task* containing his most attractive writing, the ballad 'John Gilpin', two poems of religious despair – and the translations of Horace: two from the *Satires* done in his twenties, four from the *Odes* belonging to his maturity. Cowper's was an umbratile, often distressed life with several periods of madness.

Ode I.9 A free translation

See'st thou yon mountain laden with deep snow,
The groves beneath their fleecy burthen bow,
    The streams congeal'd forget to flow;
Come, thaw the cold, and lay a cheerful pile
       Of fuel on the hearth;
Broach the best cask, and make old Winter smile
       With seasonable mirth.
This be our part – let heaven dispose the rest;
  If Jove command, the winds shall sleep,
10   That now wage war upon the foamy deep,
And gentle gales spring from the balmy west.
    E'en let us shift to-morrow as we may,
      When to-morrow's past away,
      We at least shall have to say,
      We have liv'd another day;
Your auburn locks will soon be silver'd o'er,
Old age is at our heels, and youth returns no more.

                              (pub. 1815)

Ode I.38

Boy, I hate their empty shows,
  Persian garlands I detest,
Bring not me the late-blown rose
  Ling'ring after all the rest:

Plainer myrtle pleases me
  Thus out-stretch'd beneath my vine,
Myrtle more becoming thee,
  Waiting with thy master's wine.   (pub. 1815)

Ode II.10

Receive, dear friend, the truths I teach,
So shalt thou live beyond the reach
   Of adverse fortunes pow'r;
Not always tempt the distant deep,
Nor always timorously creep
   Along the treach'rous shore.

He that holds fast the golden mean,
And lives contentedly between
   The little and the great,
10 Feels not the wants that pinch the poor,
Nor plagues that haunt the rich man's door,
   Imbitt'ring all his state.

The tallest pines feel most the pow'r
Of wintry blasts, the loftiest tow'r
   Comes heaviest to the ground,
The bolts that spare the mountains side,
His cloud-capt eminence divide
   And spread the ruin round.

The well inform'd philosopher
20 Rejoices with an wholesome fear,
   And hopes in spite of pain;
If winter bellow from the north,
Soon the sweet spring comes dancing forth,
   And nature laughs again.

What if thine heav'n be overcast,
The dark appearance will not last,
   Expect a brighter sky;
The God that strings the silver bow,
Awakes sometimes the muses too,
30   And lays his arrows by.

If hindrances obstruct thy way,
Thy magnanimity display,
   And let thy strength be seen,
But oh! if Fortune fill thy sail
With more than a propitious gale,
   Take half thy canvass in.   (pub. 1782)

A Reflection on the Foregoing Ode

And is this all? Can reason do no more
Than bid me shun the deep and dread the shore?
Sweet moralist! afloat on life's rough sea
The christian has an art unknown to thee;
He holds no parley with unmanly fears,
Where duty bids he confidently steers,
Faces a thousand dangers at her call,
And trusting in his God, surmounts them all.   (pub. 1782)

Ode II.16

Ease, is the weary Merchant's Pray'r,
   Who Ploughs by Night th' Aegean Flood,
When neither Moon nor Stars appear,
   Or Glimmer faintly thro' the Cloud.

For Ease, the Mede with Quiver graced,
    For Ease, the Thracian Hero Sighs,
Delightfull Ease All Pant to Taste,
    A Blessing which no Treasure buys.

For neither Gold can Lull to Rest,
10   Nor All a Consul's Guard beat off,
The Tumults of a troubled Breast,
    The Cares that Haunt a Gilded Roof.

Happy the Man whose Table shews
    A few clean Ounces of Old Plate,
No Fear intrudes on his Repose,
    No sordid Wishes to be Great.

Poor short-lived things! what Plans we lay,
    Ah why forsake our Native Home,
To distant Climates Speed away,
20   For Self cleaves fast where'er we Roam.

Care follows hard, and soon o'ertakes
    The well-rigg'd Ship, the Warlike Steed,
Her destin'd Quarry ne'er Forsakes,
    Not the Wind flies with half the Speed.

From anxious Fears of future Ill
    Guard well the cheerfull Happy NOW,
Gild ev'n your Sorrows with a Smile,
    No Blessing is unmixt Below.

Some Die in Youth, some Halt Behind
30   And With'ring Wait the slow Decree,
And I perhaps may be Design'd
    For Years, that Heav'n denies to Thee.

Thy Neighing Steeds and Lowing Herds,
   Thy num'rous Flocks around thee Graze,
And the best Purple Tyre affords
   Thy Robe Magnificent displays.

On Me Indulgent Fate bestow'd
   A Rural Mansion, Neat and Small,
This Lyre – and as for yonder Crowd,
40   The Glory to Despise them All.   (pub. 1815)

ROBERT FERGUSSON (1750–1774)

Edinburgh born, attended St Andrews till forced to leave by the poverty that dogged him throughout his brief career. Revivified the Scots literary language, honoured by Burns as his 'elder brother', and now acknowledged as a model by Scots-writing poets. Fell sick and developed manic-depressive symptoms, dying a pauper lunatic in the Edinburgh Bedlam.

Ode I.11

  Ne'er fash your thumb what gods decree
To be the weird o' you or me,
Nor deal in cantrup's kittle cunning
To speir how fast your days are running,
But patient lippen for the best,
Nor be in dowy thought opprest,
Whether we see mare winters come
Than this that spits wi' canker'd foam.

---

1 *fash your thumb* trouble yourself   **3** *cantrup* charm; *kittle* mysterious
4 *speir* enquire   **5** *lippen* trust   **6** *dowy* gloomy

Now moisten weel your geyzen'd wa'as
10 Wi' couthy friends and hearty blaws;
Ne'er lat your hope o'ergang your days,
For eild and thraldom never stays;
The day looks gash, toot aff your horn,
Nor care yae strae about the morn.

(pub. 1773)

RICHARD PORSON (1759–1808)

Housman, in a passage from a speech which the folk memory has perhaps brought to its final perfection, claimed to be a better scholar than Wordsworth and a better poet than the eminent classicist and famous three-bottle man, Richard Porson. Porson's qualifications in the convivial field might have made him the ideal translator of this convivial ode but for his lack of qualifications as a poet.

Ode I.27 An imitation

Fye, friends! were glasses made for fighting,
And not your hearts and heads to lighten?
Quit, quit, for shame, the savage fashion,
Nor fall in such a bloody passion.

'Pistols and ball for six:' what sport!
How distant from – 'Fresh lights and port!'
Get rid of this ungodly rancour,
And bring your – elbows to an anchor.

---

9 *geyzen'd* dry; *wa'as* walls   **10** *couthy* sociable; *blaws* drinks
13 *gash* bright; *toot aff your horn* drain your cup   **14** *strae* straw

Why, though your stuff is plaguy heady,
I'll try to hold one bumper steady:
Let Ned but say, what wench's eyes
Gave him the wound, of which he dies.

You won't? – then, dammee if I drink: –
A proper question this to blink!
Come, come; for whomsoe'er you feel
These pains, you always sin genteel –

And were your girl the dirtiest drab –
(You know I never was a blab).
Out with it; whisper soft and low; –
What! is it she? – the filthy frow!
You've got a roaring sea to tame,
Boy, worthy of a better flame!

What Lapland witch, what cunning man
Can free you from this haridan?
St George himself, who slew the dragon,
Would idly waste his strength this hag on. (pub. 1794)

SUSANNA ROWSON (1762–1824)

Daughter of a British naval officer who settled in New England, but returned when his property was confiscated during the War of Independence, she led a various, energetic, mostly successful life, first in England then in America, as novelist, actress and schoolmistress. Her translations of some odes of Horace, apparently written in her late teens, are included in *Miscellaneous Poems* (Boston, 1804).

Ode II.17

No! my Maecenas, no! the gods and I
Are equally averse, that thou shouldst die;
My best support, my patron, or to blend
Every dear name in one, my honoured friend,
Cease these complaints, it cannot, must not be,
That thou shouldst seek Elysium without me.

Alas! should fate the hasty mandate give,
And my soul's better part should cease to live;
Then for what reason should I tarry here,
10 Not half so good, nor to mankind so dear;
Nor could I long survive, when torn from thee;
The day, which takes thee hence, will ruin me.
In life, in death, resolv'd to follow thee,
Justice demands it, and the fates decree.

Have I not sworn, nor will I break my oath,
The call of death for one will summon both;
When, or howe'er thou may'st the journey make,
I am resolv'd its perils to partake;
We will together, tread the gloomy way,
20 Together, seek the realms of brighter day.

Though to appal me, fell Chimera stands,
Though Gyas rise, and with his hundred hands
Oppose my passage, nought shall have the pow'r,
To tear me from thee in that dreadful hour;
For whether Libra, balance of the earth,
Or the fierce scorpion overruled our birth,
Or the rude tyrant of the western sea;
Certain, our stars most strangely do agree;
Jupiter's guardian glories round thee shine,
30 While light-wing'd Mercury's protection's mine.

For when cold Saturn would repress thy praise,
Thy planet rules, and lo! the people raise
Three shouts of glad applause; and when on me
The fatal sisters hurl'd a falling tree,
Mercury, watchful patron of the learn'd,
Aside by Faunus' hand the danger turn'd.
Remember therefore to the Gods and fate,
Victims to burn, and temples dedicate;
For thee, the smoke of hecatombs shall rise,
40   But for thy Horace one poor lamb suffice.   (pub. 1804)

THE YOUNG GENTLEMEN OF MR RULE'S ACADEMY AT ISLINGTON

Ode I.25 A free translation

These verses may be found in *Poetical Blossoms by the Young Gentlemen of Mr Rule's Academy*.

The bloods and bucks of this lewd town
   No longer shake your windows down
      With knocking;
Your door stands still, no more you hear
'I die for you, O Lydia dear',
      Love's God your slumbers rocking.

Forsaken, in some narrow lane
   You in your turn will loud complain,
      Gallants no more engaging:

10   Whilst north-winds roar, and lust, whose pow'r
     Makes madding mares the meadows scour,
          Is in your bosom raging.

     You're griev'd, and quite eat up with spleen,
          That ivy and sweet myrtle green
               Young men alone long after;
     And that away they dri'd leaves throw,
     And let them down the river go
          With laughter.   (pub. 1766)

JOHN QUINCY ADAMS
(1767–1848)

Author of the most accomplished translation of Horace by an American until the later twentieth century, America's sixth President and one of his country's most distinguished public servants, Adams received a solid classical education in Europe.

Ode I.22 An imitation

To Sally

The man in righteousness array'd,
   A pure and blameless liver,
Needs not the keen Toledo blade,
   Nor venom-freighted quiver.
What though he wind his toilsome way
   O'er regions wild and weary –
Through Zara's burning desert stray;
   Or Asia's jungles dreary:

What though he plough the billowy deep
   By lunar light, or solar,
Meet the resistless Simoon's sweep,
   Or iceberg circumpolar.
In bog or quagmire deep and dank,
   His foot shall never settle;
He mounts the summit of Mont Blanc,
   Or Popocatapetl.

On Chimborazo's breathless height,
   He treads o'er burning lava;
Or snuffs the Bohan Upas blight,
   The deathful plant of Java.
Through every peril he shall pass,
   By Virtue's shield protected;
And still by Truth's unerring glass
   His path shall be directed.

Else wherefore was it, Thursday last,
   While strolling down the valley
Defenceless, musing as I pass'd
   A canzonet to Sally;
A wolf, with mouth protruding snout,
   Forth from the thicket bounded –
I clapped my hands and raised a shout –
   He heard – and fled – confounded.

Tangier nor Tunis never bred
   An animal more crabbed;
Nor Fez, dry nurse of lions, fed
   A monster half so rabid.

---

11 *Simoon* hot dry sandwind
19 *Bohan Upas* a fabulous tree so poisonous it kills all life within fifteen miles

Nor Ararat so fierce a beast
  Has seen, since days of Noah;
Nor strong, more eager for a feast,
40 The fell constrictor boa.

Oh! place me where the solar beam
  Has scorch'd all verdure vernal;
Or on the polar verge extreme,
  Block'd up with ice eternal –
Still shall my voice's tender lays
  Of love remain unbroken;
And still my charming Sally praise,
  Sweet smiling and sweet spoken.   (1848)

WILLIAM WORDSWORTH
(1770–1850)

Ode III.13

For the imprint left by this ode on Wordsworth's mature work, see Introduction, pp. 37–8. ('Blandusian': a variant reading found in some manuscripts.)

Blandusian Spring, than glass more brightly clear,
Worthy of flowers and dulcet wine,
To-morrow shall a kid be thine,
Whose brow, where the first budding horns appear,
Battles and loves portends – portends in vain,
For he shall pour his crimson blood
To stain, bright Spring, thy gelid flood,
Nor e'er shall seek the wanton herd again.
Thee Sirius smites not from his raging star;

10 Thy tempting gloom a cool repose
    To many a vagrant herd bestows,
    And to faint oxen weary of the share;
    Thou too 'mid famous fountains shalt display
    Thy glory while I sing the oak
    That hangs above the hollow rock
    Whence thy loquacious waters leap away.   (writ. 1794?)

GEORGE HOWARD, VISCOUNT MORPETH

later sixth Earl of Carlisle (1773–1848)

Educated at Eton and Christ Church, Oxford, sat in the House of Commons in the Whig interest from 1795, subsequently holding several distinguished official positions. In this imitation of Horace's Ode to Fortune the speaker is an enthusiastic supporter of the French Revolution. Published in *Anti-Jacobin*, no. 9, 8 January 1798.

Distantly suggested by Ode I.35

Ode to Anarchy

    Goddess, whose dire terrific power
    Spreads, from thy much-loved Gallia's plains,
    Where'er her blood-stain'd ensigns lower,
Where'er fell Rapine stalks, or barb'rous Discord reigns!

    Thou, who canst lift to fortune's height
    The wretch by truth and virtue scorn'd,
    And crush, with insolent delight,
All whom true merit raised, or noble birth adorn'd!

   Thee oft the murd'rous band implores,
10   Swift-darting on its hapless prey:
   Thee, wafted from fierce Afric's shores,
  The Corsair chief invokes to speed him on his way.

   Thee the wild Indian tribes revere;
   Thy charms the roving Arab owns;
   Thee kings, thee tranquil nations fear,
  The bane of social bliss, the foe to peaceful thrones.

   For soon as thy loud trumpet calls,
   To deadly rage, to fierce alarms,
   Just order's goodly fabric falls,
20   Whilst the mad people cries, 'to arms, to arms!'

   With thee Proscription, child of strife,
   With death's choice implements, is seen,
   Her murd'rer's gun, assassin's knife,
  And, 'last not least in love,' her darling *Guillotine*.

   Fond hope is thine, – the hope of spoil,
   And faith, – such faith as ruffians keep:
   They prosper thy destructive toil,
  That makes the widow mourn, the helpless orphan weep.

   Then false and hollow friends retire,
30   Nor yield one sigh to soothe despair;
   Whilst crowds triumphant Vice admire,
  Whilst harlots shine in robes that deck'd the great and fair.

   Guard our famed chief to Britain's strand!
   Britain, our last, our deadliest foe:
   Oh, guard his brave associate band!
  A band to slaughter train'd, and 'nursed in scenes of woe.'

What shame, alas! one little Isle
   Should dare its native laws maintain?
At Gallia's threats serenely smile,
40   And, scorning her dread power, triumphant rule the main.

For this have guiltless victims died
   In crowds at thy ensanguined shrine!
For this has recreant Gallia's pride
O'erturn'd religion's fanes, and braved the wrath divine!

What throne, what altar, have we spared
   To spread thy power, thy joys impart?
Ah then, our faithful toils reward?
And let each falchion pierce some loyal Briton's heart.

(pub. 1798)

JAMES AND HORATIO SMITH
(1775–1839 and 1779–1849)

James Smith was solicitor to the Board of Ordnance, and with his brother Horatio wrote *Horace in London* (1813). Their drolleries continued to please through much of the nineteenth century and have their small place in the long story of Horace's reception in England.

Ode I.9 A Regency imitation

See Richmond is clad in a mantle of snow;
   The woods that o'ershadow'd the hill,
Now bend with their load, while the river below,
In musical murmurs forgetting to flow,
   Stands mournfully frozen and still.

Who cares for the winter! *my* sun-beams shall shine
    Serene from a register stove;
With two or three jolly companions to dine,
And two or three bottles of generous wine,
10   The rest I relinquish to Jove.

The oak bows its head in the hurricane's swell,
    Condemn'd in its glory to fall:
The marigold dies unperceiv'd in the dell,
Unable alike to retard or impel,
    The crisis assign'd to us all.

Then banish to-morrow, its hopes and its fears;
    To-day is the prize we have won:
Ere surly old age in its wrinkles appears,
With laughter and love, in your juvenile years
20   Make sure of the days as they run.

The park and the playhouse *my* presence shall greet,
    The opera yield its delight;
Catalani may charm me, but ten times more sweet,
The musical voice of Laurette when we meet
    In tête-à-tête concert at night.

False looks of denial in vain would she fling,
    In vain to some corner be gone;
And if in our kisses I snatch off her ring,
It is, to my fancy, a much better thing
30   Than a kiss after putting one on!   (pub. 1813)

THOMAS MOORE (1779–1852)

Attended Trinity College, Dublin. Moved to London and won much social and literary renown. *Irish Melodies* (1807–35) established him as the national poet of Ireland, *Lalla Rookh* (1817), a series of oriental tales in verse, brought him a European reputation.

Ode I.22 An imitation

Lord Eldon, an inflexible conservative, was Lord Chancellor for most of 1801 to 1827.

'Freely Translated by Lord Eld–n'

The man who keeps a conscience pure,
    (If not his own, at least his Prince's,)
Through toil and danger walks secure,
    Looks big and black, and never winces.

No want has he of sword or dagger,
    Cock'd hat or ringlets of Geramb;
Though Peers may laugh, and Papists swagger,
    He doesn't care one single d-mn.

Whether midst Irish chairmen going,
10   Or through St Giles's alleys dim,
'Mid drunken Sheelahs, blasting, blowing,
    No matter, 'tis all one to him.

For instance, I, one evening late,
    Upon a gay vacation sally,
Singing the praise of Church and State,
    Got (Gods know how) to Cranbourne Alley.

When lo! an Irish Papist darted
    Across my path, gaunt, grim, and big –
I did but frown, and off he started,
20   Scar'd at me, even without my wig.

Yet a more fierce and raw-bon'd dog
    Goes not to mass in Dublin City,
Nor shakes his brogue o'er Allen's Bog,
    Nor spouts in Catholic Committee.

Oh! place me midst O'Rourkes, O'Tooles,
    The ragged royal-blood of Tara;
Or place me where Dick M-rt-n rules
    The houseless wilds of Connemara;

Of Church and State I'll warble still
30   Though ev'n Dick M-rt-n's self should grumble;
Sweet Church and State, like Jack and Jill,
    So lovingly upon a hill –
Ah! ne'er like Jack and Jill to tumble!   (pub. 1812)

LEIGH HUNT (1784–1859)

Educated at Christ's Hospital. In 1808 he launched the *Examiner* (where this translation was first published, in 1812), the liberal journal whose adverse judgements on the Prince Regent cost Hunt two and a half years' imprisonment. On friendly terms with leading literary figures of the day, he brought about a meeting between Keats and Shelley.

---

27 *Dick M-rt-n* Richard Martin, MP, a firm supporter of Roman Catholic emancipation

Ode II.12

To Maecenas

No; ask no more so soft a lyre
As mine to strain its simple wire,
And tell of wild Numantian wars,
Nor Hannibal and all our scars,
Nor yet of that Sicilian tide
With Carthaginian blood bedyed,
Nor of the fierce Pirithoan stir
That crushed the jovial ravisher,
Nor giant sieges of the sky,
10   Herculean strife, that shook on high
Old Saturn's glorious dynasty.

You, dear Maecenas, shall rehearse,
In prose much better than my verse,
The battles that our Caesar gains,
And threatening kings led up in chains: —
Me the fond Muse engrosses still
With my Licymnia's warbling skill,
And those two eyes of cordial fire,
That speak the faith which they inspire.
20   How lightsome in the dance is she,
How sparkling sweet her raillery,
And what a shape her arm of snow,
When upon days of sacred show
Entwined the glancing maidens go!

Would you, if you adored like me,
For all that Monarchs hold in fee,
Exchange, or even think to share,
One lock of such a charmer's hair,
When back she throws that sweep of bliss,
30   Her neck, to meet a headlong kiss,

Or cruel for relenting's sake,
Denies what you should rather take, –
Turning at last, with smile and start,
And kissing you with all her heart? (pub. 1812)

JOHN CAM HOBHOUSE, LORD BROUGHTON (1786–1869)

Educated at Westminster and Trinity College, Cambridge. Politically an aristocratic radical, poetically the author of a free, scurrilous translation of Juvenal. These verses were written shortly before he set out with Byron on a journey to Albania.

Ode II.6 An imitation

To Byron, on their departure for Greece

Though we, my friend! prepare to roam
   From happy Britain's native shore,
And leave the dear delights of home,
   To hear the loud Atlantic roar:

Though to the distant lands we fly,
   Where desolation widely reigns,
Where Tadmor's lonely ruins lie
   On Syria's wild unpeopled plains:

This is my secret wish, to close
   My days in some secure retreat,
And from the toils of life repose,
   Content with my maternal seat.

>   Or if my follies or my fate
>   Should that my own resort deny,
>   Then let me rent a small estate,
>   Fast by the banks of lovely Wye.
>
>   Retir'd near Clongher's secret bowers,
>   Oh! may that nook for life be mine,
>   Where honey drops from all the flowers,
> 20   And orchard trees excel the vine!
>
>   Where lasting frosts and tempests wild
>   Nor bind the earth, nor cloud the sky,
>   But summers long and winters mild
>   The genial tepid airs supply.
>
>   Thou too, my B——n, shalt be near
>   To sooth my life, my death attend;
>   And weep, for thou canst weep, one tear,
>   To mourn the poet and the friend.   (pub. 1809)

GEORGE GORDON, LORD BYRON (1788–1824)

From Ode III.3

Apart from *Hints from Horace*, his racy imitation of *Ars Poetica*, this translation is Byron's only tribute to the poet he 'hated so' as a schoolboy.

>   I
>   The man of firm, and noble soul,
>   No factious clamours can controul;
>   No threat'ning tyrant's darkling brow,

    Can swerve him from his just intent;
Gales the warring waves which plow,
    By Auster on the billows spent,
To curb the Adriatic main,
Would awe his fix'd determined mind in vain.

II
Aye, and the red right arm of Jove,
10 Hurtling his lightnings from above,
With all his terrors there unfurl'd,
    He would, unmov'd, unaw'd, behold;
The flames of an expiring world,
    Again in crashing chaos roll'd
In vast promiscuous ruin hurl'd,
Might light his glorious funeral pile,
Still dauntless midst the wreck of earth he'd smile.

                          (writ. *c.* 1806)

ALEXANDER PUSHKIN
(1799–1837)
and VLADIMIR NABOKOV
(1899–1977)

Ode III.30, extra-territorialized

Horace moves east in the hands of Russia's greatest poet ('that god before whom all Russian authors bow' – Isaiah Berlin), gaining readers in regions hitherto unfamiliar to him. Nabokov's translation was published in *Three Russian Poets* (1944).

EXEGI MONUMENTUM

'No hands have wrought my monument; no weeds
will hide the nation's footpath to its site.
Tsar Alexander's column it exceeds
   in splendid insubmissive height.

'Not all of me is dust. Within my song,
safe from the worm, my spirit will survive,
and my sublunar fame will dwell as long
   as there is one last bard alive.

'Throughout great Rus' my echoes will extend,
and all will name me, all tongues in her use:
the Slavs' proud heir, the Finn, the Kalmuk, friend
   of steppes, the yet untamed Tunguz.

'And to the people long shall I be dear
because kind feelings did my lyre extoll,
invoking freedom in an age of fear,
   and mercy for the broken soul.'

Obey thy God, and never mind, O Muse,
the laurels or the stings: make it thy rule
to be unstirred by praise as by abuse,
   and do not contradict the fool.   (pub. 1836 and trans. 1944)

EDWARD BULWER-LYTTON, LORD LYTTON (1803–1873)

Educated successively at both Trinity College and Trinity Hall, Cambridge. Entered Parliament in 1831; Secretary for the Colonies, 1858–9. He was a prolific novelist, but only his *Last Days of Pompeii*

(1834) has to some extent survived. Metrically unusual, this translation is written in an unrhymed equivalent (not imitation) of Horace's alcaic metre.

Ode II.14

Postumus, Postumus, the years glide by us,
Alas! no piety delays the wrinkles,
   Nor old age imminent,
      Nor the indomitable hand of Death.

Though thrice each day a hecatomb were offered,
Friend, thou couldst soften not the tearless Pluto,
   Encoiling Tityos vast,
      And Geryon, triple giant, with sad waves –

Waves over which we all of us must voyage,
All whosoe'er the fruits of earth have tasted;
   Whether that earth we ruled
      As kings, or served as drudges of its soil.

Vainly we shun Mars and the gory battle,
Vainly the Hadrian hoarse with stormy breakers,
   Vainly, each autumn's fall,
      The sicklied airs through which the south wind sails.

Still the dull-winding ooze of slow Cocytus,
The ill-famed Danaids, and, to task that ends not
   Sentenced, Aeolides;
      These are the sights on which we all must gaze.

Lands, home, and wife, in whom thy soul delighteth,
Left; and one tree alone of all thy woodlands,
   Loathed cypress, faithful found,
      Shall follow to the last the brief-lived lord.

The worthier heir thy Caecuban shall squander,
Bursting the hundred locks that guard its treasure,
   And wines more rare than those
     Sipped at high feast by pontiffs, dye thy floors.

(pub. 1869)

ALFRED TENNYSON later Alfred Lord Tennyson (1809–1892)

In no great English poet is the whole range of classical poetry, Greek and Latin equally, more richly present, echoed without a touch of pedantry and transformed into his own substance. If Virgil and Theocritus influenced him most profoundly, Horace always came at call. This translation, together with those of Ode III.3 and the opening of Epode 5, was written during his schooldays.

Ode I.9

See! how Soracte's hoary brow
   And melancholy crags uprear
Their weight of venerable snow:
   And scarce the groaning forests bear
The burthen of the gloomy year
   And motionless the stream remains
   Beneath the weight of icy chains.
Thou of the social banquet King,
Now store of welcome faggots bring,
   Now bid a brighter flame arise,
Now let the rich and rosy wine
Within the joyful goblets shine,
That wine whose age hath seen the ray
Of four long summers roll away
   Along yon wintry skies.

Leave to the Gods the rest – whose force
  Can stay the whirlwind's wasting course;
  When they have soothed the maddening jar
  Of mingled elemental war,
20 Nor those tall ash-trees dread the storm
  Nor cypress bows his shadowy form.
  Why should we fear tomorrow's woe?
     Whatever day the Powers above
  Have given, rejoice: nor, while the flow
     Of joy and golden youth delight
     Thy soul – while age avoids thee – slight
  The mazy dance – the power of love.   (writ. *c*.1822)

W. E. GLADSTONE (1809–1898)

The great Liberal statesman found the time to keep more than abreast with classical, notably Homeric, scholarship. It is fitting that Horace's poem on the ship of state should be robustly translated by the man who, as Prime Minister four times, guided England's ship of state.

Ode I.14

Oh Ship! new billows sweep thee out
Seaward. What wilt thou? Hold the port, be stout:
     See'st not thy mast
How rent by stiff Southwestern blast?

Thy side, of rowers how forlorn?
Thine hull, with groaning yards, with rigging torn,
     Can ill sustain
The fierce, and ever fiercer main;

Thy gods, no more than sails entire,
10 From whom yet once thy need might aid require,
    Oh Pontic Pine,
The first of woodland stocks is thine,

Yet race and name are but as dust.
Not painted sterns give storm-tost seamen trust;
    Unless thou dare
To be the sport of storms, beware.

O fold at best a weary weight,
A yearning care and constant strain of late,
    O shun the seas
20 That gird those glittering Cyclades.   (1863)

Ode III.30

Now have I reared a monument
    more durable than brass,
And one that doth the royal scale
    of pyramids surpass,
Nor shall defeated Aquilo
    destroy, nor soaking rain,
Nor yet the countless tide of years,
    nor seasons in their train.
Not all of me shall die: my praise
10   shall grow, and never end,
While pontiff and mute vestal shall
    the Capitol ascend,
And so a mighty share of me
    shall Libitina foil.
Where bellows headstrong Aufidus,
    where, on his arid soil,
King Daunus ruled a rural folk,
    of me it shall be told

>   That, grown from small to great, I first
> 20   of all men subtly wrought
>   Aeolian strains to unison
>   with our Italian thought.
>   So take thine honours earned by deeds;
>   and graciously do thou,
>   Melpomenè, with Delphic bays
>   adorn thy poet's brow.   (1863)

SIR STEPHEN DE VERE (1812–1904)

Educated at Trinity College, Dublin, and called to the Irish bar in 1836. Encouraged emigration to Canada during the Irish famine, but learning of the sufferings of steerage passengers on these voyages went steerage himself, and on his return was able to see that better accommodation was provided for emigrants. His *Translations from Horace* was published in 1885.

Ode II.16

>   When the pale moon is wrapt in cloud,
>   And mists the guiding stars enshroud;
>   When on the dark Aegaean shore
>   The bursting surges flash and roar;
>   The mariner with toil opprest
>   Sighs for his home, and prays for rest:
>   So pray the warrior sons of Thrace;
>   So pray the quivered Mede's barbaric race:
>   Grosphus, not gold nor gems can buy
> 10   That peace which in brave souls finds sanctuary;

Nor Consul's pomp, nor treasured store,
Can one brief moment's rest impart,
Or chase the cares that hover o'er
The fretted roof, the wearied heart.

Happy is he whose modest means afford
Enough – no more: upon his board
Th' ancestral salt-vase shines with lustre clear,
Emblem of olden faith and hospitable cheer;
Nor greed, nor doubt, nor envy's curses deep
20   Disturb his innocent sleep.
Why waste on doubtful issues life's short years?
Why hope that foreign suns can dry our tears?
    The Exile from his country flies,
Not from himself, nor from his memories.

Care climbs the trireme's brazen sides;
Care with the serried squadron rides;
Outstrips the cloud-compelling wind
And leaves the panting stag behind:
But the brave spirit, self-possest,
30   Tempers misfortune with a jest,
With joy th' allotted gift receives,
The gift denied to others frankly leaves.

A chequered life the Gods bestow:
Snatched by swift fate Achilles died:
Time-worn Tithonus, wasting slow,
Long wept a death denied:
    A random hour may toss to me
Some gifts, my friend, refused to thee.

A hundred flocks thy pastures roam:
40 Large herds, deep-uddered, low around thy home
    At the red close of day:
    The steed with joyous neigh

>   Welcomes thy footstep: robes that shine
>   Twice dipt in Afric dyes are thine.
>   To me kind Fate with bounteous hand
>   Grants other boon; a spot of land,
>   A faint flame of poetic fire,
>   A breath from the Aeolian lyre,
>   An honest aim, a spirit proud
> 50 That loves the truth, and scorns the crowd.   (pub. 1885)

PATRICK BRANWELL BRONTË (1817–1848)

Brother of and overshadowed by his famous sisters, as a child he was held to be the family genius, but he made a mess of his life with opium and drink, and died of consumption. He translated the first book of the *Odes* (omitting the final poem) probably in his early twenties.

Ode I.16

> O Lovely Girl, whose bloom outshines
>   Thy lovely Mothers fame,
> To ocean give my angry lines,
>   Or cast them in the flame;
>
> But know, that neither wrapt Apollo,
>   Nor He who rules the bowl,
> Nor Ceres priests with tymbals hollow,
>   Like Wrath can shake the soul;

Whose direful might, nor sword can fright,
    Nor floods, nor fires, nor Jove
Descending on our blasted sight
    In Thunder from above.

When man Prometheus made from clay,
    In fashioning each part,
The Lions rage he stole away
    And fixed it in his heart.

'Twas wrath that hurled Thyestes down
    With heavy overthrow;
'Tis wrath, oer many a mighty town,
    That drives the foeman's plough;

And me, while young, that wrath beguiled
    In furious rhymes to range,
But Satires wild to songs more mild
    My melting muse shall change;

While Thou – thy passion laid aside
    With vows of amity –
Shall hush the urgings of thy pride,
    And back return to me! (writ. 1840)

Ode I.21

Virgins, sing the Virgin Huntress;
    Youths, the youthful Phoebus, sing;
Sing Latona, she who bore them
    Dearest to the eternal King:
Sing the heavenly maid who roves
Joyous, through the mountain groves;
She who winding waters loves;
    Let her haunts her praises ring!

Sing the vale of Peneus' river;
10   Sing the Delian deity;
The shoulder glorious with its quiver;
    And the Lyre of Mercury.
From our country, at our prayer –
Famine, plague, and tearful war
These, benign, shall drive afar
    To Persias plains or Britains sea.   (writ. 1840)

ARTHUR HUGH CLOUGH
(1819–1861)

Educated at Rugby under Dr Arnold and at Balliol, he was elected to a fellowship at Oriel College, Oxford, but soon resigned and became an examiner in the Education Office. The translation of this and of the following ode seeks to follow the word order of the Latin.

Ode I.3

        So may the Cyprian Queen,
    So Helena's brethren, constellations bright,
        And the winds' father guide
    Thy course, the rest refraining save Iapyx!
        O ship, that for our trust,
    Our Virgil, debtor art! to Attic shores
        Him render safe, I pray;
    And save alive my own life's better part!
        Strong oak and triple brass
10 His heart did case about, who, frail to fierce,

---

4 *Iapyx* north-west wind

ODE I.3 · ARTHUR HUGH CLOUGH

        Committed bark to billow,
First mariner; nor feared the heady south
        In deadly fight with the north,
Nor the sad Hyades, nor the wild south-west,
        Of Hadria's stormy main,
Chief autocrat, to rouse it or to lull.
        What shape of death feared he,
Who unabashed the floating monster forms,
        The swelling seas beheld,
20 And of sad fame the Acroceraunian rocks?
        Vainly did heaven dispart,
Wise, by the uncompanionable deep,
        The lands, if rashly still
Bound o'er forbidden gulfs the godless bark.

        Defying, daring all,
Our human race through sin runs blindly on:
        Iapet's daring blood
Fire with ill guile among the nations brought;
        Fire from the heavenly home
30 Once come, came leanness, and of fevers came
        An army on the earth,
And, distant until then, death's tardy doom
        Did quicken straight his pace;
The vacant air did Daedalus essay
        With wings for man unmeant;
Through Acheron Herculean labour broke.
        To mortals nought is hard,
The very heaven our folly fain would scale,
        Nor let we through our crimes,
40 His wrathful thunders Jupiter lay by.   (pub. 1847)

---

27 *Iapet* father of Prometheus

Ode III.7

Compare the imitations by George Stepney (pp. 137–9) and Austin Dobson (pp. 243–5).

    Him wherefore weep, Asteria, whom bright airs
    With early spring, Favonian, shall restore,
        Rich with Bithynian ware,
           A lover true to troth,
    Thy Gyges? He to Oricum with the south
    Borne on, the stormy goatstar overhead,
        The cold night wakeful spends,
           Wakeful and weeping tears.
    Though he whom stranger maid importunate
10 Deputes to say how Chloe pants, on fire
        For thine own passion, ply
           Ten thousand subtlest arts;
    How Proetus, lending to a lying wife
    Easy belief, misguided was against
        Bellerophon, o'er-chaste,
           Death to devise, relate;
    And tell of Peleus, scarce from Tartarus saved
    The Magnessian queen, Hippolyta, denying;
        And cite with wily tongue,
20   The tales that teach to sin.
    In vain; for deafer than Icarian rocks
    Him court they still thine own. But thou the while,
        Lest thee Enipeus please
           Too well, thy neighbour, look!
    Though ne'er another skilled to rein the steed
    Like him, be marked upon the turf of Mars,
        Nor any swift as he
           Do swim the Tiber tide;
    Close thou thine house with early dusk, nor let
30 The plaintive pipe unto thy window bring thee;
        Let him that oft shall call
           Thee cruel, find thee chaste!   (pub. 1847)

Ode III.4, lines 58-64

Visiting the Pantheon in Rome, Claude, the protagonist of *Amours de Voyage* (1858), imagines himself (Canto I, lines 161-7) repeopling the Christian images in the niches with 'the mightier forms of an older, austerer worship', and recites these lines from Horace's ode:

161
    Eager for battle here
Stood Vulcan, here matronal Juno,
  And with the bow to his shoulder faithful
He who with pure dew laveth of Castaly
His flowing locks, who holdeth of Lycia
The oak forest and the wood that bore him,
  Delos' and Patara's own Apollo.   (pub. 1858)

JOHN CONINGTON (1825-1869)

A distinguished classical scholar, Conington was the first to hold the Corpus chair of Latin at Oxford. Engaged energetically in university business and the movement for reform. Edited Virgil and translated the *Aeneid* in Scott's ballad metre. His translation of the *Odes* was published in 1863, that of Horace's hexameter poems in 1870.

Ode II.9

The rain, it rains not every day
 On the soak'd meads; the Caspian main
Not always feels the unequal sway
 Of storms, nor on Armenia's plain,
Dear Valgius, lies the cold dull snow
 Through all the year; nor northwinds keen

Upon Garganian oakwoods blow,
    And strip the ashes of their green.
You still with tearful tones pursue
10   Your lost, lost Mystes; Hesper sees
Your passion when he brings the dew,
    And when before the sun he flees.
Yet not for loved Antilochus
    Grey Nestor wasted all his years
In grief; nor o'er young Troilus
    His parents' and his sisters' tears
For ever flow'd. At length have done
    With these soft sorrows; rather tell
Of Caesar's trophies newly won,
20   And hoar Niphates' icy fell,
And Medus' flood, 'mid conquer'd tribes
    Rolling a less presumptuous tide,
And Scythians taught, as Rome prescribes,
    Henceforth o'er narrower steppes to ride.   (pub. 1863)

Ode II.11

In the last line Conington's 'wild' translates *incomptum . . . nodum* ('disorderly', 'untidy') not *in comptum*, 'in a neat', found in most texts).

O ask not what those sons of war,
    Cantabrian, Scythian, each intend,
Disjoin'd from *us* by Hadria's bar,
    Nor puzzle, Quintius, how to spend
A life so simple. Youth removes,
    And Beauty too; and hoar Decay
Drives out the wanton tribe of Loves
    And Sleep, that came or night or day.
The sweet spring-flowers not always keep
10   Their bloom, nor moonlight shines the same

Each evening. Why with thoughts too deep
    O'ertask a mind of mortal frame?
Why not, just thrown at careless ease
    'Neath plane or pine, our locks of grey
Perfumed with Syrian essences
    And wreathed with roses, while we may,
Lie drinking? Bacchus puts to shame
    The cares that waste us. Where's the slave
To quench the fierce Falernian's flame
20   With water from the passing wave?
Who'll coax coy Lyde from her home?
    Go, bid her take her ivory lyre,
The runaway, and haste to come,
    Her wild hair bound with Spartan tire.   (pub. 1863)

Ode III.12

The metre, unusually jaunty for Conington, imitates the light, dancing movement of the original, written in a metre Horace uses nowhere else, ionics *a minore* (∪∪− − ∪∪− −, cf. *Hiawatha*).

How unhappy are the maidens who with Cupid may not
        play,
Who may never touch the wine-cup, but must tremble all
        the day
    At an uncle, and the scourging of his tongue!
Neobule, there's a robber takes your needle and your thread,
Lets the lessons of Minerva run no longer in your head;
    It is Hebrus, the athletic and the young!
O, to see him when anointed he is plunging in the flood!
What a seat he has on horseback! was Bellerophon's as good?
    As a boxer, as a runner, past compare!
10 When the deer are flying blindly all the open country o'er,
He can aim and he can hit them; he can steal upon the boar,
    As it couches in the thicket unaware.   (pub. 1863)

C. S. CALVERLEY (1831–1884)

Educated at Harrow and Balliol from where, proving too witty and obstreperous to please constituted authority, he migrated to Christ's College, Cambridge. Admitted to the bar in 1865, he fell heavily on his head while skating and was forced to retire and devote the rest of his life to polite letters. A type of the highly cultivated Victorian amateur, Calverley wrote occasional verse in English and Latin, parodies (notably of Browning), and translations of Homer, Virgil, Theocritus, and fifteen odes of Horace.

Ode I.9

One dazzling mass of solid snow
   Soracte stands; the bent woods fret
   Beneath their load; and, sharpest-set
With frost, the streams have ceased to flow.

Pile on great faggots and break up
   The ice: let influence more benign
   Enter with four-years-treasured wine,
Fetched in the ponderous Sabine cup:

Leave to the gods all else. When they
   Have once bid rest the winds that war
   Over the passionate seas, no more
Gray ash and cypress rock and sway.

Ask not what future suns shall bring.
   Count to-day gain, whate'er it chance
   To be: nor, young man, scorn the dance,
Nor deem sweet Love an idle thing,

Ere Time thy April youth hath changed
   To sourness. Park and public walk
   Attract thee now, and whispered talk
20 At twilight meetings pre-arranged;

Hear now the pretty laugh that tells
   In what dim corner lurks thy love;
   And snatch a bracelet or a glove
From wrist or hand that scarce rebels. (1861)

Ode I.11

Seek not, for thou shalt not find it, what my end, what thine
   shall be;
Ask not of Chaldaea's science what God wills, Leuconöe:
Better far, what comes, to bear it. Haply many a wintry blast
Waits thee still; and this, it may be, Jove ordains to be thy
   last,
Which flings now the flagging sea-wave on the obstinate
   sandstone-reef.
Be thou wise: fill up the wine-cup; shortening, since the time
   is brief,
Hopes that reach into the future. While I speak, hath stol'n
   away
Jealous Time. Mistrust To-morrow, catch the blossom of
   To-day. (1861)

Ode I.24

Unshamed, unchecked, for one so dear
   We sorrow. Lead the mournful choir,
   Melpomene, to whom thy sire
Gave harp, and song-notes liquid-clear!

Sleeps He the sleep that knows no morn?
　　Oh Honour, oh twin-born with Right
　　Pure Faith, and Truth that loves the light,
When shall again his like be born?

Many a kind heart for Him makes moan;
10　　Thine, Virgil, first. But ah! in vain
　　Thy love bids heaven restore again
That which it took not as a loan:

Were sweeter lute than Orpheus given
　　To thee, did trees thy voice obey;
　　The blood revisits not the clay
Which He, with lifted wand, hath driven

Into his dark assemblage, who
　　Unlocks not fate to mortal's prayer.
　　Hard lot! Yet light their griefs who BEAR
20　The ills which they may not undo.　　　　　　(1861)

AUSTIN DOBSON (1840–1921)

Modestly educated, he worked from 1856 to 1901 in the Board of Trade, principally in the marine department. A shy, bookish man, his tastes led him to the eighteenth century about which he was quietly learned. The titles he chose for his books of verse, *Vignettes in Rhymes*, *Proverbs in Porcelain*, *Old World Idylls*, reveal the nature of his fragile, delicate gift. 'The Ballad of "Beau Brocade"' still makes agreeable reading.

Ode I.23

You shun me, Chloe, wild and shy
    As some stray fawn that seeks its mother
Through trackless woods. If spring-winds sigh,
    It vainly strives its fears to smother; –

Its trembling knees assail each other
    When lizards stir the bramble dry; –
    You shun me, Chloe, wild and shy
As some stray fawn that seeks its mother.

And yet no Libyan lion I, –
10   No ravening thing to rend another;
Lay by your tears, your tremors by –
    A Husband's better than a brother;
Nor shun me, Chloe, wild and shy
    As some stray fawn that seeks its mother.   (pub. 1877)

Ode III.7 An imitation

Compare the Restoration version by George Stepney (pp. 137–9).

Outward Bound

Come, Laura, patience. Time and Spring
Your absent Arthur back shall bring,
Enriched with many an Indian thing
        Once more to woo you;
Him neither wind nor wave can check,
Who, cramped beneath the 'Simla's' deck,
Still constant, though with stiffened neck,
        Makes verses to you.

Would it were wave and wind alone!
The terrors of the torrid zone,
The indiscriminate cyclone,
    A man might parry;
But only faith, or 'triple brass',
Can help the 'outward-bound' to pass
Safe through that eastward-faring class
    Who sail to marry.

For him fond mothers, stout and fair
Ascend the tortuous cabin stair
Only to hold around his chair
    Insidious sessions;
For him the eyes of daughters droop
Across the plate of handed soup,
Suggesting seats upon the poop,
    And soft confessions.

Nor are these all his pains, nor most.
Romancing captains cease to boast –
Loud majors leave their whist – to roast
    The youthful griffin;
All, all with pleased persistence show
His fate, – 'remote, unfriended, slow', –
His 'melancholy' bungalow, –
    His lonely tiffin.

In vain. Let doubts assail the weak;
Unmoved and calm as 'Adam's Peak',
Your 'blameless Arthur' hears them speak
    Of woes that wait him;

---

28 *griffin* a newcomer to India   **32** *tiffin* luncheon
34 *Adam's Peak* sacred mountain in Ceylon

Naught can subdue his soul secure;
'Arthur will come again,' be sure,
Though matron shrewd and maid mature
    Conspire to mate him.

But, Laura, on your side, forbear
To greet with too impressed an air
A certain youth with chestnut hair, –
    A youth unstable;
Albeit none more skilled can guide
The frail canoe on Thamis tide,
Or, trimmer-footed, lighter glide
    Through 'Guards' or 'Mabel'.

Be warned in time. Without a trace
Of acquiescence on your face,
Hear, in the waltz's breathing-space,
    His airy patter;
Avoid the confidential nook;
If, when you sing, you find his look
Grow tender, close your music book,
    And end the matter.   (pub. 1870)

GERARD M. HOPKINS (1844–1889)

Read Classics at Balliol, received by Newman into the Catholic church in 1866, entered the novitiate of the Society of Jesus two years later, and ordained as a priest in 1877. His poems, unpublished during his lifetime, were collected by Robert Bridges who edited the first edition in 1918. The translations from Horace were probably written between 1866 and 1868.

Ode I.38

Ah child, no Persian – perfect art!
Crowns composite and braided bast
They tease me. Never know the part
    Where roses linger last.

Bring natural myrtle, and have done:
Myrtle will suit your place and mine:
And set the glasses from the sun
    Beneath the tackled vine.   (writ. *c.* 1868)

Ode III.1 Left incomplete

Tread back – and back, the lewd and lay! –
Grace guard your tongues! – what never ear
Heard yet, the Muses' man, today
I bid the boys and maidens hear.

Kings herd it on their subject droves
But Jove's the herd that keeps the kings –
Jove of the Giants: simple Jove's
Mere eyebrow rocks this round of things.

Say man than man may more enclose
In rankèd vineyards; one with claim
Of blood to our green hustings goes;
One with more conscience, cleaner fame;

One better backed comes crowding by: –
That level power whose word is Must
Dances the balls for low or high:
Her urn takes all, her deal is just.

Sinner who saw the blade that hung
Vertical home, could Sicily fare
Be managed tasty to that tongue?
20 Or bird with pipe, viol with air

Bring sleep round then? – sleep not afraid
Of country bidder's calls or low
Entries or banks all over shade
And Tempe with the west to blow.

Who stops his asking mood at par
The burly sea may quite forget
Nor fear the violent calendar
At Haedus-rise, Arcturus-set,

For hail upon the vine nor break
30 His heart at farming, what between
The dog-star with the fields abake
And spitting snows to choke the green.

Fish feel their waters drawing to
With our abutments: there we see
The lades discharged and laded new,
And Italy flies from Italy.

But fears, fore-motions of the mind,
Climb quits: one boards the master there
On brazèd barge and hard behind
40 Sits to the beast that seats him – Care.

O if there's that which Phrygian stone
And crimson wear of starry shot
Not sleek away; Falernian-grown
And oils of Shushan comfort not,

Why.........................
....
Why should I change a Sabine dale
For wealth as wide as weariness?   (writ. *c.* 1868)

A. E. HOUSMAN (1859–1937)

'The leading classic of his generation', as Auden called him, Housman failed in Greats and left Oxford without taking a degree, but a series of outstanding papers written while he was a civil servant in the Patent Office led in 1911 to his appointment as Professor of Latin at Cambridge. Of this translation (which he placed with his poems, not among his translations), published in 1897, it is recorded that during a lecture 'he read the ode aloud with deep emotion, first in Latin and then in an English translation of his own. "That," he said hurriedly, almost like a man betraying a secret, "I regard as the most beautiful poem in ancient literature," and walked quickly out of the room.'

Ode IV.7

The snows are fled away, leaves on the shaws
   And grasses in the mead renew their birth,
The river to the river-bed withdraws,
   And altered is the fashion of the earth.

The Nymphs and Graces three put off their fear
   And unapparelled in the woodland play.
The swift hour and the brief prime of the year
   Say to the soul, *Thou wast not born for aye.*

Thaw follows frost; hard on the heel of spring
10   Treads summer sure to die, for hard on hers
Comes autumn, with his apples scattering;
    Then back to wintertide, when nothing stirs.

But oh, whate'er the sky-led seasons mar,
    Moon upon moon rebuilds it with her beams;
Come *we* where Tullus and where Ancus are,
    And good Aeneas, we are dust and dreams.

Torquatus, if the gods in heaven shall add
    The morrow to the day, what tongue has told?
Feast then thy heart, for what thy heart has had
20   The fingers of no heir will ever hold.

When thou descendest once the shades among,
    The stern assize and equal judgment o'er,
Not thy long lineage nor thy golden tongue,
    No, nor thy righteousness, shall friend thee more.

Night holds Hippolytus the pure of stain,
    Diana steads him nothing, he must stay;
And Theseus leaves Pirithöus in the chain
    The love of comrades cannot take away.   (pub. 1897)

G. M. and G. F. WHICHER
(1860–1937 and 1889–1954)

G. M. Whicher was Professor of Greek and Latin at Hunter College, New York. His son G. F. wrote several books on New England writers. This translation was published in *On the Tibur Road* (1911). By their success with the last line and a half of the fourth stanza, the neatest turn to date of *ingenuoque semper amore peccas*, the translators do something to atone for rhyming 'sirrah' with 'Chimera'.

Ode I.27

Come, comrades, cease your Thracian fights
    O'er cups designed for better uses,
For moderate Bacchus ne'er delights
    In bloody quarrels o'er his juices.

How far removed from lamps and wine
    Should be the Median dagger keen!
Hush drunken clamor, friends of mine;
    In quiet on your elbows lean.

. . . You wish to have me taste my share
10   Of strong Falernian with the rest? . . .
Megilla's brother must declare
    First, by what mortal wound he's blest.

Falters his will? . . . Then I'll not drink . . .
    Come, tell us by what love you're swayed,
What fire consumed; . . . tut, man, don't shrink
    To own an honest escapade!

Trust it to safe ears; 't is no sin
    But to impart your sweetheart's name. –
Ah! What Charybdis are you in,
20   Youth worthy of a nobler flame!

What witch, what wizard's potent brew,
    What god can save you this time, sirrah?
Scarce Pegasus could rescue you,
    Entrapped by such three-fold Chimera.   (pub. 1911)

RUDYARD KIPLING (1865–1936)

Insufficiently recognized as one of our great Horatian poets, Kipling first read Horace at school and did not like him. Chided for not having prepared this ode, he made good by imitating it in broad Devonshire dialect.

Ode III.9 An imitation

HE
So long as 'twuz me alone
    An' there wasn't no other chaps,
I was praoud as a King on 'is throne –
    Happier tu, per'aps.

SHE
So long as 'twuz only I
    An' there wasn't no other she
Yeou cared for so much – sure*ly*
    I was glad as could be.

HE
But now I'm in lovv with Jane Pritt –
    She can play the piano, she can;
An' if dyin' 'ud 'elp 'er a bit
    I'd die laike a man.

SHE
Yeou'm like me. I'm in lovv with young Frye –
    Him as lives out tu Appledore Quay;
An' if dyin' 'ud 'elp 'im I'd die –
    Twice ovver for he.

HE

But s'posin' I threwed up Jane
    An' niver went walkin' with she –
And come back to yeou again –
20   How 'ud that be?

SHE

Frye's sober. Yeou've allus done badly –
    An' yeou shifts like cut net-floats, yeou du:
But – I'd throw that young Frye ovver gladly
    An' lovv 'ee right thru!   (pub. 1882)

EZRA POUND (1885–1973)

Having been grudging to Horace throughout his career, Pound turned to him, perhaps in the 1950s, and translated these three odes, his final contribution to the art he transformed and dominated, surpassing even Dryden in his ability to devise radically different styles for different kinds of poetry. There is a useful discussion of these translations in Daniel M. Hooley, *The Classics in Paraphrase* (1988), pp. 109–21.

Ode I.11

Ask not ungainly askings of the end
Gods send us, me and thee, Leucothoë;
Nor juggle with the risks of Babylon,
    Better to take whatever,
Several, or last, Jove sends us. Winter is winter,
Gnawing the Tyrrhene cliffs with the sea's tooth.

Take note of flavors, and clarity's in the wine's manifest.
Cut loose long hope for a time.
We talk. Time runs in envy of us,
10 Holding our day more firm in unbelief. (pub. 1963)

Ode I.31

By the flat cup and the splash of new vintage
What, specifically, does the diviner ask of Apollo? Not
Thick Sardinian corn-yield nor pleasant
Ox-herds under the summer sun in Calabria, nor
Ivory nor gold out of India, nor
Land where Liris crumbles her bank in silence
Though the water seems not to move.

Let him to whom Fortune's book
Gives vines in Oporto, ply pruning hook, to the
10 Profit of some seller that he, the seller,
May drain Syra from gold out-size basins, a
Drink even the Gods must pay for, since he found
It is merchandise, looking back three times,
Four times a year, unwrecked from Atlantic trade-routes.

Olives feed me, and endives and mallow roots.
Delight had I healthily in what lay handy provided.
Grant me now, Latoe:
                Full wit in my cleanly age,
Nor lyre lack me, to tune the page. (pub. 1964)

Ode III.30

This monument will outlast metal and I made it
More durable than the king's seat, higher than pyramids.
Gnaw of the wind and rain?
                      Impotent
The flow of the years to break it, however many.

Bits of me, many bits, will dodge all funeral,
O Libitina-Persephone and, after that,
Sprout new praise. As long as
Pontifex and the quiet girl pace the Capitol
I shall be spoken where the wild flood Aufidus
Lashes, and Daunus ruled the parched farmland:

Power from lowliness: 'First brought Aeolic song to Italian
    fashion' –
Wear pride, work's gain! O Muse Melpomene,
By your will bind the laurel.
                      My hair, Delphic laurel.

(pub. 1964)

BASIL BUNTING (1900–1985)

A Northumbrian who spent much of his life abroad while keeping his native accent, Bunting began as a protégé of Pound. A strict experimental formalist, he wrote poetry all his life, publishing it often in obscure places, but won wide recognition only with *Briggflatts* (1966). Translated Persian and Latin poetry, Catullus and Lucretius in addition to Horace.

Ode II.14

You cant grip years, Postume,
that ripple away nor hold back
wrinkles and, soon now, age,
nor can you tame death,

not if you paid three hundred
bulls every day that goes by
to Pluto, who has no tears,
who has dyked up

giants where we'll go aboard,
10 we who feed on the soil,
to cross, kings some, some
penniless plowmen.

For nothing we keep out of war
or from screaming spindrift
or wrap ourselves against autumn,
for nothing, seeing

we must stare at that dark, slow
drift and watch the damned
toil while all they build
20 tumbles back on them.

We must let earth go and home,
wives too, and your trim trees,
yours for a moment, save one
sprig of black cypress.

Better men will empty
bottles we locked away,
wine puddle our table,
fit wine for a pope.

(pub. 1971)

J. V. CUNNINGHAM (1911–1985)

Poet, translator, critic, taught at Brandeis and several other universities. A poet who stood at some deliberate remove from the main streams of modern writing, his *Collected Poems and Epigrams* was published in 1971.

Ode I.9

See how resplendent in deep snow
Soracte stands, how straining trees
   Scarce can sustain their burden
     Now that the rivers congeal and freeze.

Thaw out the chill, still heaping more
Wood on the hearth; ungrudgingly
   Pour forth from Sabine flagons,
     O Thaliarchus, the ripened wine.

Leave all else to the gods. They soon
10 Will level on the yeasty deep
   Th' embattled tempests, stirring
     Cypress no more, nor agèd ash.

Tomorrow may no man divine.
This day that Fortune gives set down
   As profit, nor while young still
     Scorn the rewards of sweet dancing love,

So long as from your flowering days
Crabbed age delays. Now through the parks
   Soft whisperings toward nightfall
20   Visit again at the trysting hour;

Now from her bower comes the charmed laugh,
Betrayer of the hiding girl;
   Now from her arm the forfeit
     Plundered, her fingers resisting not.   (pub. 1950)

C. H. SISSON (1914–)

Author of *The Spirit of British Administration* – Sisson describes himself as 'primarily a civil servant – like Chaucer' – and of numerous volumes of verse. His *Collected Poems* were published in 1984. Has translated Heine, Catullus, Dante, Lucretius, Racine and Virgil in addition to Horace. His essays on translation are included in *Two Minds: Guesses at Other Writers* (1990).

Ode II.14

The years go by, the years go by you, nameless,
I cannot help it nor does virtue help.
   Wrinkles are there, old age is at your elbow,
   Death on the way, it is indomitable.

Not if you choose, as you will choose, to doctor
Yourself with hope, will you weep out your pain.
   The underworld is waiting. There are monsters
   Such as distended you before you died.

The subterranean flood is there for every-
one who has taken food and drink on earth.
   A light skiff will put out, you will be on it –
   And, win the pools, you still will go aboard.

The blood dried on you and you came home safely
– Useless. You blew out an Atlantic storm.
  – No need to fear the wind, it can do no harm.
  It brings you where you will be brought at last.

The dark, the black and, in the blackness, water,
A winding stream, it will not matter to you.
  The fifty murderesses are there, the toiler,
20   Exhaustion beyond hope, condemned to dreams.

Your house, your wife, and the familiar earth,
All will recede, and of the trees you prune
  Only the cypress follow you, ill-omened.
  You were here briefly, you are here no more.

The heir you leave is better than yourself,
What you kept closest he will throw away.
  Your books are on the pavement, and his laughter
  Sounding like broken glass through all the rooms.

(pub. 1974)

Freely rendered from Ode II.15

Just as Goldsmith did in 'The Deserted Village' (p. 202), Sisson gives the theme of Horace's ode a contemporary application, but on a narrower front. Note how 'nothing soon for the plough' is quickly reduced to nothing for 'the nostrils' – of urban man hoping to enjoy a ramble in the country. Still narrower is Larkin's treatment of the theme in 'Going, Going': 'I thought it would last my time – / The sense that, beyond the town, / There would always be fields and farms . . .' But before long 'the whole / Boiling will be bricked in / Except for the tourist parts . . . / And that will be England gone, / The shadows, the meadows, the lanes, / The guildhalls, the carved choirs. / There'll be books; it will linger on / In galleries; but all that remains / For us will be concrete and tyres.'

There will be nothing soon for the plough
But huge bulks everywhere. On all sides
    Wider than lakes, the city
    Lamp-standards drive out the elms,

Planes, beeches. Once it was fertile here.
Edges of violets circumscribed
    The grove; there was everywhere something for the
    Nostrils, but now there is nothing.

Where there were once forests a region of
Concrete. Until quite recently
    There were meadows at Westminster.
    The salmon leaped where Raleigh was beheaded.

Once there was only nature for ornament.
Then there was ornament and art flourished;
    Now there is only the South Bank
    And, of course, the Arts Council.

It was not laws but a less abstract
Technology made the turf spring.
    The churches in those days, you may
    Remember, were built of stone.   (pub. 1974)

Carmen Saeculare An imitation

For a translation of this ode, see James Michie (pp. 290–93) and for a discussion of Sisson's imitation, Introduction, pp. 51–3.

O sun, and moonlight shining in the woods,
The best things in heaven, always to be worshipped
As long as they give us exactly what we want

Now, at this season when selected girls
And the boys who are about to venture upon them,
Though still in bud, sing what will please London,

As you bring out one day and conceal another
Shine on the arms and legs and make them brown.
May all you see be greater than we are.

10 The time will come to open thighs in child-birth.
Gently, supervising god, look after the mothers.
Bringing to light is the true meaning of genitals.

Could you bring up these children without laws?
The statute-book is crowded, what wonder therefore
If all that interests them is an obscure kindness?

A hundred and ten years it may easily be
Before songs and games which come as speedily
As these three days, ah, and delicious nights.

You have sung truthfully enough, O fates.
20 Once it was ordained that everything should be stable
And will be again, but not now, or for ever.

Rich in apples, yes, and seething with cattle,
The succulent earth is dressed in barley whiskers.
And grow plump, embryo, from the natural gifts.

The sun will shine, as long as the boys are suppliant,
That will keep sickness away; and you girls,
Listen, for the moon will hear you if you do.

If you made London, as before it Engelland,
The Jutes coming over in ships, but only to be Romans,
30 Part of that remnant to join this one

The ways that have led here are multifarious,
Even Brutus from Troy, our ancestors believed,
But whatever they left they found better here.

You cannot credit the wish, that the young should be
    teachable
And old age quiet. Yet it is these wishes
Spring from the earth at last, when the country flowers.

Might you not even remember the old worship?
I could name ancestors, it is not done any more.
It remains true that, before you are king, you must win.

40 We have been through it all, victory on land and sea,
These things were necessary for your assurance.
The King of France. Once there was even India.

Can you remember the expression 'Honour'?
There was, at one time, even Modesty.
Nothing is so dead it does not come back.

There is God. There are no Muses without him.
He it is who raises the drug-laden limbs
Which were too heavy until he stood at Saint Martin's.

It is he who holds London from Wapping to Richmond,
50 May he hold it a little longer, Saint George's flag
Flap strenuously in the wind from the west country.

Have you heard the phrase: 'the only ruler of princes'?
Along the Thames, in the Tower, there is the crown.
I only wish God may hear my children's prayers.

He bends now over Trafalgar Square.
If there should be a whisper he would hear it.
Are not these drifting figures the chorus?   (pub. 1974)

ROBERT LOWELL (1917–1977)

A poet who stood so high in his day (*Time* magazine put him on the cover wearing a laurel wreath resembling a crown of barbed-wire thorns) that some inevitable diminution, surely to be adjusted, has set in. A translator or imitator (*Imitations*, 1961) of licentious genius when his original could be turned into Lowell.

Ode II.7

Serving under Brutus

O how often with me in the forlorn hope
under the proconsulship of Marcus Brutus,
Citizen! Who brought you back to Rome,
to our sultry gods and hot Italian sky?

My first friend, and my best, O Pompey,
how often have we drawn out the delaying day
with wine, and brightened our rough hair,
with Syrian nard!

With you too at Philippi, at that hysterical
10 mangling of our legions, when we broke
like women. Like an Egyptian,
I threw away my little shield.

I was afraid, but Mercury, the quick,
the subtle, found a way for me to escape.
And you? The wave of battle drew you under,
knocked you down into its troubled, bleeding surf.

Offer the Sky-god then this meal,
spread out your flesh worn out by war.
Enjoy this laurel tree, and don't forget me,
20 or spare the wine jars set aside for you.

Fill the frail goblets with red wine,
pour perfume from the fragile shells!
Who'll be the first to twist parsley
and myrtle with the coronets?

Throw down the dice. Throw down the dice –
Venus has chosen her master of the feast.
I'll drink like Alexander. It is sweet
to drink to fury when a friend's reprieved.   (pub. 1967)

ANTHONY HECHT (1923–)

Studied at Bard College and Columbia University. Has held various academic positions. Author of several volumes of verse: *A Summoning of Stones* (1954), *The Seven Deadly Sins* (1958), *The Hard Hours* (1967), and most recently *The Transparent Man* (1990). Applied successfully for a Guggenheim Fellowship in 1954 and 1959.

Ode I.1 An imitation

Application for a Grant

Noble executors of the munificent testament
Of the late John Simon Guggenheim, distinguished bunch
Of benefactors, there are certain kinds of men
Who set their hearts on being bartenders,
For whom a life upon duck-boards, among fifths,
Tapped kegs and lemon twists, crowded with lushes

Who can master neither their bladders nor consonants,
Is the only life, greatly to be desired.
There's the man who yearns for the White House, there to compose
10 Rhythmical lists of enemies, while someone else
Wants to be known to the *Tour d'Argent*'s head waiter.
As the Sibyl of Cumae said: It takes all kinds.
Nothing could bribe your Timon, your charter member
Of the Fraternal Order of Grizzly Bears to love
His fellow, whereas it's just the opposite
With interior decorators; that's what makes horse races.
One man may have a sharp nose for tax shelters,
Screwing the IRS with mirth and profit;
Another devote himself to his shell collection,
20 Deaf to his offspring, indifferent to the feast
With which his wife hopes to attract his notice.
Some at the Health Club sweating under bar bells
Labor away like grunting troglodytes,
Smelly and thick and inarticulate,
Their brains squeezed out through their pores by sheer exertion.
As for me, the prize for poets, the simple gift
For amphibrachs strewn by a kind Euterpe,
With perhaps a laurel crown of the evergreen
Imperishable of your fine endowment
30 Would supply my modest wants, who dream of nothing
But a pad on Eighth Street and your approbation. (pub. 1979)

JOHN HERINGTON (1924–)

Talcott Professor of Greek Emeritus of Yale University, author of *Poetry into Drama* (1985).

Ode I.11

You must not ask the end (to know is wickedness)
that God has set for you and me,
Lynne, my white heart: Leuconoe: you must not

search in our horoscopes. Let's take what comes; maybe
this stormwind is the last that God
will let us feel, us together, this same wind

which even now is breaking the rampant Tuscan seas
in foam against embattled rock.
Now have some sense, pour the wine! And cut away

long ages of our hope in the brief slash of love.
While you and I are talking, were
talking, Time envies, envied, comes and went; oh

pick today's flower! As little as you can
trust in tomorrow, Leuconoe. White heart. Lynne.

(pub. 1970)

DAVID FERRY (1924–)

Sophie Chantal Hart Professor of English Emeritus at Wellesley College, author of three books of verse, *On the Way to the Island* (1960), *Strangers: A Book of Poems* (1983), and *Dwelling Places* (1993). His *Gilgamesh: A New Rendering in English Verse* was published in 1992. Has also written a study of Wordsworth, *The Limits of Mortality* (1959). Absence of a publication date in the following poems indicates that this is the first time in print.

Ode I.1

Maecenas, you, descended from many kings,
O you who are my stay and my delight,
There is the man whose glory it is to be
So famous even the gods have heard the story

Of how his chariot raised Olympic dust,
The dazzling wheel making the smoking turn;
And there is he whose bliss it is to be carried
Up to the honors of office on the shifting

Shoulders of the crowd; and he whose pride
Is that his barns hold everything that can
Be gathered from the Libyan fields of grain.
And there's the man who with his little hoe

Breaks the hard soil of his poor father's farm,
But all the money there is could never persuade
That man to cross the sea, a quaking sailor.
And the fearful merchant in his wallowing vessel,

As the storm comes on longs for his native village
And longs for the quiet fields surrounding it –
And then of course next year refits his ship,
Unable to forgo the profit of it.

And there's the man who likes his cup of wine,
Taking his ease in the busiest time of the day,
Under the shady boughs of the green arbutus
Or near the secret source of some murmuring brook.

There are those who love encampments, and love the
    confused
Music of trumpet and clarion sounding together
And are in love with the wars their mothers hate.
And all the night long, out in the bitter cold,

If his faithful dogs have startled up a deer
30 Or if a wild boar has broken through the snare,
The hunter waits, forgetful of his bride;
All night the bride at home waits for the hunter.

What links *me* to the gods is that I study
To wear the ivy wreath that poets wear;
The cool sequestered grove, in which I play
For nymphs and satyrs dancing to my music,

Is where I am set apart from other men –
Unless the muse Euterpe takes back the flute
Or Polyhymnia untunes the lyre.
40 But if *you* say I am truly among the poets,

Then my exalted head will knock against the stars.

Ode I.4

Now the hard winter is breaking up with the welcome
    coming
  Of spring and the spring winds; some fishermen,
Under a sky that looks changed, are hauling their caulked
    boats
  Down to the water; in the winter stables the cattle
Are restless; so is the farmer sitting in front of his fire;
  They want to be out of doors in field or pasture;
The frost is gone from the meadowgrass in the early
    mornings.

    Maybe, somewhere, the nymphs and graces are dancing,
Under the moon the goddess Venus and her dancers;
    Somewhere far in the depth of a cloudless sky
Vulcan is getting ready the storms of the coming summer.
    Now is the time to garland your shining hair
With myrtle and with the flowers the free-giving earth has
      given;
    Now is the right time to offer the kid or lamb
In sacrifice to Faunus in the firelit shadowy grove.
    Revenant whitefaced Death is walking not knowing
      whether
He's going to knock at a rich man's door or a poor man's.
    O goodlooking fortunate Sestius, don't put your hope in
      the future;
The night is falling; the shades are gathering around;
    The walls of Pluto's shadowy house are closing you in.
There who will be lord of the feast? What will it matter,
    What will it matter there, whether you fell in love
With Lycidas, this or that girl with him, or he with her?

                                        (pub. 1983)

Ode I.10

O fluent Mercury, grandchild of Atlas, you
Who gave the means of order to the ways
Of early men by giving speech to them
And laying down the rules of the wrestling-floor,

Where grace is learned in the intricacy of play.
It is your praise I sing, O messenger
Of Jupiter and of the other gods,
Clever deviser of the curvèd lyre,

Hider away of anything you please
10 It pleases you to hide. The day you were born
You stole away from him Apollo's cattle;
Apollo had to laugh when he found out

That while he stormed and threatened you'd stolen away
His quiver and arrows too; you stole away
Priam of Troy from Troy bearing possessions,
Guiding him past the light of Thessalian watchfires,

Past the enemy camp of the arrogant Greeks.
You guide the pious dead to their place of bliss;
With your wand you shepherd the ghostly unruly flock.
20 You please both the gods above and those below.

Ode I.11

Don't be too eager to ask
    What the gods have in mind for us,
What will become of you,
    What will become of me,
What you can read in the cards,
    Or spell out on the ouija board,
It's better not to know.
    Either Jupiter says
This coming winter is not
10   After all going to be
The last winter you have,
    Or else Jupiter says
This winter that's coming soon,
    Eating away the cliffs
Along the Tyrrhenian Sea,
    Is going to be the final
Winter of all. Be mindful.
    Take good care of your vineyard.

The time we have is short.
        Cut short your hopes for longer.
Now as I say these words,
        Time has already fled
Backwards away —
        Leuconoë —
                Hold on to the day.

Ode I.15

As Paris, beautiful treacherous shepherd youth,
Betrayer of Menelaus, fled with his Helen

Over the waves to safety, or so they thought,
Nereus, prophetic god, stilled the sea-winds,

And, becoming a sea-bird, sang of things to come.
The little boat, becalmed, rocked in the water.

'Bad luck for Troy that this adventure brings.
The woman you are bringing home will bring

Against your home how many Grecian heroes
Determined to undo what you have done

And to bring down the city of your father.
Alas, what dolorous work for men and horses

You are the cause of. Already I see the goddess,
Pallas Athena, as she is putting on

Her glittering helmet and getting ready her shining
Chariot and shield, preparing her rage.

ODE I.15 · DAVID FERRY

What good will it do to sit in your lady's chamber,
Venus's hero, combing your beautiful hair

And playing a tune on the cithara, of the sort
That women like? What good will it do to try,

In a palace room to avoid the noise of battle,
The spears and the arrows and Ajax in pursuit?

It won't be long, although, alas, too late,
Before your beautiful hair gets dirty enough

When you lie down in the dirt. Haven't you heard
Of Laertes' son, the scourge of the Trojan people?

Haven't you heard of Nestor? And don't you know
That Salaminian Teucer, brother of Ajax,

Deterred by nothing, is on the hunt for you?
And, undeterred, Sthelenus too, and he,

Tydides' terrible son, more terrible than
His terrible father, is hot to hunt you down?

And you, like a grazing deer that when it sees
A wolf on the other side of the valley coming

Forgets to graze and runs as fast as it can,
Head back and panting hard, heart throbbing, you

Will run away as fast as you can, head back
And panting hard, how much unlike the way

You promised her that you were going to be,
Heart throb with Helen in the palace chamber.'

Ode II.3

When things are bad, be steady in your mind;
    Dellius, do not be
Too unrestrainedly joyful in good fortune.
    You are going to die.

It does not matter at all whether you spend
    Your days and nights in sorrow,
Or, on the other hand, in holiday pleasure,
    Drinking Falernian wine

Of an excellent vintage year, on the river bank.
10   Why is it, do you suppose,
That the dark branches of those tall pines and those
    Poplars' silvery leafy

Branches love to join, coming together,
    Creating a welcoming shade?
Have you not noticed how in the quiet river
    The current shows signs of hurry,

Urging itself to go forward, going somewhere,
    Making its purposeful way?
By all means tell your servants to bring you wine,
20   Perfumes, and the utterly lovely

Too briefly blossoming flowers of the villa garden;
    Yes, of course, while youth,
And circumstance, and the black threads of the Sisters
    Suffer this to be so.

You are going to have to yield those upland pastures,
    The ones you bought just lately;
You are going to yield the town house, and the villa,
    The country place whose margin

The Tiber washes as it moves along.
    Heirs will possess all that
Which you have gathered. It does not matter at all
    If you are rich, with kings

Forefathers of your pride; no matter; or poor,
    Fatherless under the sky.
You will be sacrificed to Orcus without pity.
    All of us together

Are being gathered; the lot of each of us
    Is in the shaken urn
With all the other lots, and like the others
    Sooner or later our lot

Will fall out from the urn; and so we are chosen to take
    Our place in that dark boat,
In that dark boat, that bears us all away
    From here to where no one comes back from ever.

Ode II.7

Dear friend who fought so often together with me
In the ranks of Brutus in hardship and in danger,
Under whose sponsorship have you come back,
A citizen again, beneath our sky?

O Pompey, we drank together so many times,
And we were together in the Philippi fight,
The day I ran away, leaving my shield,
And Mercury got me out of it, carrying me

In a cloud, in a panic, right through the enemy rage;
But the undertow of a wave carried you back
Into the boiling waters of the war.
So, come then, let us dedicate a feast

To Jupiter, just as we told each other we'd do;
Come, stretch your weary legs out under this tree;
I've got good food to eat, good wine to drink.
Come, celebrate old friendship under the laurel.

Ode III.5

The Example of Regulus

The way we know that Jove is king in heaven
Is by his manifestation in what he does:
Listen! Jove is thundering in the sky.
Augustus too will show his godlike power

In what he does: and so the Britons will be
Put down by him, and the frightening Medes also.
Is it not true that soldiers of Crassus's army
Lowered themselves to marry barbarian wives

(O Rome disgraced in such disgraceful ways)
10 And served their time out in the army of
Their fathers-in-law, the enemies of Rome?
Imagine! Roman soldiers willing to serve

Under the orders of Medes, forgetting that
They bore the name of Roman, forgetting about
The temple of Vesta and the sacred shields,
Although their city still needed their defense.

This is what Regulus saw and why he refused
To accept the bargain of easy shameful terms.
He saw that a peace thus bargained for would be
20 A precedent for how the glory of Rome

Would come in future days to final ruin,
Unless our Roman soldiers, if they are captured,
Are left – to die if they must – in the enemy camp.
'With my own eyes,' he said, 'I have seen our banners

Hung up on the walls in shame in Punic shrines,
And I have seen our weapons given over,
Without a struggle, into Punic hands;
With my own eyes I have seen our young men standing,

Their arms pinioned in shame behind their backs,
The gates of Carthage confidently open,
Unthreatened now, the fields we put in danger
Growing their peaceful grain, fearless of Rome.

What makes you think that he, the ransomed soldier,
Brought safely back to Rome by payment of gold
Will bravely fight in battle a second time?
What makes you think he will get his manhood back

Once he has stood tied up there, trembling with fear?
A man like that, confused about who he is,
Confuses peace and war. O shame of Rome!
O greatness of Carthage built on Roman shame!'

It is said that Regulus shunned his wife's embraces
And the kisses of his weeping little children,
As if he had no right to them, and stood,
Gaze fixed upon the ground, waiting for

The wavering Roman fathers in their Senate
To come to understand his argument.
And then – oh yes, he knew that torture and death
Were ready for him when he went back to Carthage,

As he had promised – Regulus shouldered his way
50 Through the protesting crowd of friends and relations,
Looking as if he had just completed a case
In court or some other tedious legal chore,

And was off for a weekend at his place in the country.

Ode III.6

To the Romans

It is not a question of whether or not you are guilty,
    Roman, yourself.
The transgressions of your fathers must be paid for.
    You must rebuild
The broken-down temples and the toppled altars;
    You must restore,
Also, the fallen statues, cleaned of their grime.

The only way to rule is to serve the gods.
    All things begin
10 From them; and it is only the gods who know
    How all things will end.
Neglected, the gods brought down upon the Romans
    All the misfortunes
Sorrowing Italy suffers from in these days.

Twice now the Parthians have crushed our army,
    Turning us back
Under a bad star's sign; how they must grin,
    The Parthian warriors,
So pleased to have added Roman trophies to all
20   The others that dangle
And glitter on their savage necklaces.

ODE III.6 · DAVID FERRY

Confused, bewildered by internal conflict,
    The city of Rome
Just barely escaped destruction by the Dacians,
    Formidable and fearsome
Because of the skills of their famous ranks of archers,
    Or by the Egyptians,
Formidable as they, but because of their ships.

Prolific with vileness this generation has soiled
30   The marriage bed,
And then corrupted the children in the home;
    And from this source,
Reeking, polluted, and degenerate,
    Calamity
Flows out infecting everything there is

In the Roman state. The young woman eager for love
    And eager for pleasure
First takes her pleasure in learning how to dance
    In the lascivious
40 Grecian way, and practices her skills,
    Her mind alive
With images of the unchaste loves to come.

It isn't long before, in her husband's house,
    At the drinking parties,
She's on the lookout, and not without his knowledge,
    For younger lovers,
Nor is she choosy about whoever it is
    When the lights are low,
Some visiting salesman, maybe, or maybe some Spanish

50 Shipcaptain or other. Dealers in shame. In the old days,
    The days of the fathers
Of those because of whom the sea ran red
    With Punic blood

And of those because of whom great Herod fell
    And Hannibal
The Terrible, it wasn't like this. Those virtuous

Romans were taught how to use the Sabine hoe
    To till the soil
Of their father's farm and at their mother's call
60   To carry in
The cut wood when the shadows shifted on the hill
    As the sun went down.
It was the hour of rest for man and beast.

What is there that has been left unruined?
    Our parents' time
Was worse than was their parents' time, and then
    They brought forth us,
Worse than they were, and after us will be
    Our sons and daughters,
70 Worse than we are, then theirs, still worse than they.

Ode III.22

Virgin, goddess, goddess of the groves
And of the hills, goddess to whom the young
Mother in her labor cries out three times

And then again, three times, cries out O goddess,
Goddess, to hear and rescue her from death,
O goddess triple-formed, I dedicate

This pine-tree by my dwelling-house to you,
And promise to offer every year the blood
Of a young boar just learning to use its tusks.

Ode IV.3

He whom you looked upon,
>Melpomene, at his birth,
With gentle approving eyes,
>Sitting beside his cradle,
Will not be drawn in triumph
>In the festive Achaean car,
Victor in games, nor shall
>Long practice in the skill
Make him a famous boxer;
>Nor at the Capitol,
Returning from a war
>With Delian garlands crowned,
And drawn by nodding horses,
>Shall crowds applaud how he
Defeated haughty kings;
>No, it is he whom the nurturing
Waters that flow past Tibur
>And the leafy and shadowy groves
Shall bring to fame for those
>Aeolian songs he sang.

Apparently the children
>Of Rome, the queen of cities,
Grant me their approbation
>To sing among the poets;
Now do I feel less often
>How envy's tooth can bite.
Melpomene, O muse,
>Knowing how to adjust
And regulate to sweetness
>The notes of the golden shell,
You could, if you so chose,
>Instruct the silent fish

How to sing as well as the swan.
    It is entirely by
Your favoring gift that others,
    Seeing me on the street,
Point me out as he
    Who plays the Roman lute;
It is your gift if I
40   Should please, if I do please.

Ode IV.11

I have saved for the day a full bottle of old
Wine from the Alban hills. Phyllis, out in the garden
  There's parsley, and ivy, for fillets and coronets
To bind up your hair and make you look still more
  Beautiful than you looked even before.

The household is getting ready; the silver is polished,
The cups and flagons gleam; the household altar,
  Adorned with leaves, is ready, awaiting the offerings.
Everyone hurries. The servants, the boys and girls,
10 Going this way and that, getting everything ready.
The air is alive with the smoke of fiery wreaths.

Today is the Ides of April, the month of Venus,
A festival day for me because of Maecenas,
  Who celebrates today his natal day,
The onward flowing of another year.

I have to tell you something. Telephus,
The highborn boy you love, loves somebody else.
  She is wanton, young, and rich; he is fettered to her
By chains of delight. Scorched Phaethon flew too high,
20 And wingèd Pegasus flying toward heaven shook
The burden of Bellerophon from his back.
  There is a lesson in this. Learn from example.

Love only as it is fitting; do not desire
That which you ought not to have. Phyllis, listen to me:
    You are the last of my loves; there will be no others.
Come, learn a new song and sing it to me; for song
    Is the means, in your beautiful voice, to lighten black cares.

Ode IV.13

The gods have certainly given me what I asked for,
Lycia. Lycia, yes, they have certainly done so:
Lycia is getting old, and Lycia wants to be
Still beautiful, and still she goes to parties,

And drinks too much, and a little teary, sings
A tremulous song meant for the ears of Cupid;
But Cupid's eyes are on Chia playing the lyre,
For Cupid scorns the old. So tell me, Lycia,

What is it you expect? Cupid scorns you.
10 He scorns your graying hair and yellowing teeth.
Old crow that watches from a dead oak tree
As wingèd Love flies by to another tree,

Neither your purple gowns of silk from Cos
Nor the costly jewels with which they are adorned
Can ever bring you back the things that time
Has locked away for good in its well-known box.

Where has your beauty gone, where has it gone,
Where is your fair complexion, where, alas,
The grace with which you walked? Lycia, you,
20 Whose breath was the very breath of love itself,

Who stole me from myself, oh, Lycia, you
Who exulted so when beautiful Cinara died,
Leaving your beauty unrivalled, where has it gone,
What is there left? When Cinara died young

The gods gave early death to her as a gift,
And Lycia, they gave all your years to you
To give the young men something for them to laugh at,
Old crow, old torch burned out, fallen away to ashes.

K. W. GRANSDEN (1925–)

Emeritus Reader in English and Comparative Literature, University of Warwick. His publications include *The Aeneid: Landmarks in World Literature* (1990), *Virgil's Iliad* (1984), and *The Last Picnic: Poems* (1981). The following poem appears here in print for the first time.

After Ode I.34

A Funny Thing Happened . . .

I, master of philosophy,
Ex-adept of an idiot's creed,
Lax and infrequent churchgoer,
Am now compelled to turn again
By something that I cannot read:
Thunder in blue skies, and no rain!
Whatever can so freak the weather
Must be the god of earth and sea
And hell and heaven, I now concede.
10 Jehovah, Paradox or Luck
Pulls down the proud, promotes the meek:
What changes all, now changes me.

CHRISTOPHER MIDDLETON
(1926–)

English poet long resident in Austin, Texas. Of his many books of verse, the earliest is *Poems* (1944), the most recent *The Balcony Tree* (1992). Has translated widely from German, both verse and prose. The following poem appears here in print for the first time.

Ode III.13

O Bandusian spring, than glass more bright,
Of sweet wine worthy, of flowers no less,'
   Come the morn a kid will be given thee,
      One whose brow, with budding horns,

His first, predestines him for loves and fights –
But no: Thy chill cascades his crimson
   Blood will fleck, a youngling torn
      From his frisky flock.

By the black time untouched, when Dog Star rays
10 Blaze and scorch, for toilworn oxen
   Cool thou dost provide, cool again
      For vagabond cows, their herd.

Thee, too, one of the world's famed fountains
I will make, telling of the oak, how it broods
   Over the rock hollow whence
      Thy waters, talking always, leap.

JAMES MICHIE (1927–)

Educated at Marlborough and Trinity College, Oxford, where he read Classics. Publications include *Possible Laughter* and a translation of Martial. His Horace was first published in 1963.

Ode I.20

My dear Maecenas, noble knight,
You'll drink cheap Sabine here tonight
From common cups. Yet I myself
Sealed it and stored it on the shelf
In a Greek jar that day the applause
Broke out in your recovery's cause,
So that the compliment resounded
Through the full theatre and rebounded
From your own Tiber's banks until
The echo laughed on Vatican hill.
At your house you enjoy the best –
Caecuban or the grape that's pressed
At Cales. But whoever hopes
My cups will taste of Formian slopes
Or of the true Falernian
Must leave a disappointed man.

(pub. 1963)

Ode II.11

'Is warlike Spain hatching a plot?'
You ask me anxiously. 'And what
Of Scythia?' My dear Quinctius,
There's a whole ocean guarding us.
Stop fretting: life has simple needs.
Behind us smooth-cheeked youth recedes,

Good looks go too, and in our beds
Dry wizened skins and grizzled heads
Wait to put easy sleep to rout
10 And drive love's sensuous pleasures out.
Buds lose their springtime gloss, and soon
The full becomes the thin-faced moon.
Futurity is infinite:
Why tax the brain with plans for it?
Better by this tall plane or pine
To sprawl and, while we may, drink wine
And grace with Syrian balsam drops
And roses these fast-greying tops.
Bacchus shoos off the wolves of worry.
20 Ho, slaves! Which one of you will hurry
Down to the nearby brook to tame
The heat of this Falernian's flame?
Who'll coax from home to join our feast
Lyde, of easy girls the least
Easy to get? Bid her bestir
Herself and bring along with her
The ivory lyre, wearing her curls
Neat-braided like a Spartan girl's.   (pub. 1963)

Ode II.15

Horace criticizes the fashionable mania for ostentatious buildings
and the use of once productive land as a playground for the rich.

Soon I foresee few acres for harrowing
Left once the rich men's villas have seized the land;
   Fishponds that outdo Lake Lucrinus
     Everywhere; bachelor plane-trees ousting

Vine-loving elms; thick myrtle-woods, violet-beds,
All kinds of rare blooms tickling the sense of smell,
    Perfumes to drown those olive orchards
        Nursed in the past for a farmer's profit;

Quaint garden-screens, too, woven of laurel-boughs
10 To parry sunstroke. Romulus never urged
    This style of life; rough-bearded Cato
        Would have detested the modern fashions.

Small private wealth, large communal property –
So ran the rule then. No one had porticoes
    Laid out with ten-foot builder's measures,
        Trapping the cool of the northern shadow.

No one in those days sneered at the turf by the
Roadside; yet laws bade citizens beautify
    Townships at all men's cost and quarry
20   Glorious marble to roof the temples.   (pub. 1963)

Ode III.4

For a reading of this ode, see Fraenkel's *Horace*, pp. 273–85.

Descend, divine Calliope, from heaven
And play a long, a solemn song, with flute as
    Accompaniment or else
Apollo's lyre, or sing, clear-voiced, alone.

Listen! Or is it kind hallucination
Deceiving me? I seem to glimpse her music,
    I roam through hallowed groves
Where pleasant winds and waters wander too.

ODE III.4 · JAMES MICHIE

    Signs marked my boyhood. Once, on pathless Vultur,
10 Beyond the borders of my nurse Apulia,
       Play-worn and sleep-inclined
    I lay down and the legendary doves

    Wove me a blanket of the leaves just fallen.
    In Bantia's glades, high in the village-eyrie
       Of Acherontia
    And through Forentum's fertile valleys, folk

    Marvelled at how the bears and black snakes left me
    Tucked in my coverlet of bay and myrtle
       To sleep on, safe, a babe
20 And unafraid, watched over by the gods.

    Whether I climb my own steep slopes or pass time
    In hill-perched Tibur or cool-aired Praeneste
       Or Baiae's cloudless bay,
    Dear Muses, I am yours, fatefully yours.

    Because I love your fountains and your dances,
    You saved me when the ranks broke at Philippi,
       And when that cursed tree tried
    To murder me, and when the sea ran high

    Off Palinurus' cape. With you beside me
30 I'll undertake great explorations, gladly
       Sail the wild Bosphorus, cross
    The torrid deserts of the Persian Gulf,

    Travel among the stranger-hating Britons,
    See quivered Scythians camping on the Don's banks,
       Or Concani who gulp
    The blood of horses, and return unharmed.

When he has hidden his war-weary cohorts
Among the towns, who gives great Caesar solace
   In the Pierian cave
40 And longed-for rest from government but you,

Kind ones, who prompt us gently and rejoice in
The wisdom we accept? We know the story
   Of how He who controls
The brute earth and the wind-stirred sea and rules,

Just and supreme, the cities of the living,
The sad realm of the dead and all immortal
   And mortal gatherings,
Felled the massed impious Titans with his flung

Thunderbolt when that young crew raised defiant
50 Fists and the brothers piled pine-dark Olympus
   On Pelion and built
Mutiny to the height of Jove's dismay.

Yet how could mighty Mimas or Typhoeus
Or Rhoetus or Porphyrion for all his
   Colossal rage or fierce
Enceladus who tore up trees for darts

Succeed? Their charge wilted against the ringing
Shield of Athene. Battle-hungry Vulcan
   Stood by, Queen Juno too,
60 And he who never leaves his arm bow-bare,

Who bathes his loose hair in the pure Castalian
Fountain – Apollo, lord of Lycia's thickets,
   Guardian of Patara
And Delos, where his native woodlands are.

Primitive force topples to its own ruin,
But when the mind guides power it prospers; heaven
    Helps it: the gods abhor
Brute strength devoted to malignant ends.

Gyas the hundred-handed and Orion,
70 Who laid hands on inviolable Diana
    And died by her chaste shaft,
Bear witness to the truth I have set down.

Earth, heaped over her monsters, groans and curses
The bolt that hurled them into pallid Hades;
    The Giant that Etna pins
Still spouts up fire to eat away his tomb;

Even now the vulture, lust's appointed jailer,
Tears at the liver of incontinent Tityos;
    Hundreds of chains still bind
80 Pirithous whose passion broke the law.   (pub. 1963)

Ode III.10

If you were a Scythian squaw and the river
Don was your drink, you'd relent before
Letting me lie stretched out to shiver
In the blizzard beside your hard hut-door.

Can you hear the gate creak in the wind and the trees in
Your elegant villa's courtyard bower
Groan, Lyce? Feel Jupiter freezing
The fallen snow with his pure, clear power?

Venus hates pride; so enough of this hauteur,
10 Or the wheel may spin back and the rope go too.
No Tuscan could ever have fathered a daughter
As stiff and Penelope-cold as you.

Though you're proof against presents and prayers and the ashen
Cheeks of adorers ill with distress,
Unmoved by even your husband's passion
For a slut from Thessaly, nonetheless

Spare us poor suitors, O hard heart tougher
Than oak, as mild as a Moorish snake.
Not for ever will these bones suffer
20 The rain and the doorstep for your sake. (pub. 1963)

Carmen Saeculare

For an account of this ode, commissioned by Augustus for a great public ceremony, see Introduction, pp. 51–2.

The Centennial Hymn

Diana, queen of forests, and Apollo,
O honoured and for ever to be honoured
Twin glories of the firmament, accord us
    All we beseech today –

Day of devotion, when the Sibyl's verses
Enjoin the chaste, the chosen youths and maidens
To chant their hymns of worship to the patron
    Gods of our seven hills.

Kind sun, bright charioteer, bringer and hider
10 Of light, newborn each morning yet each morning
Unaltered, may thou never view a city
    Greater on earth than Rome.

Moon, gentle midwife, punctual in thy office,
Lucina, Ilithyia, Genitalis –
Be called whichever title is most pleasing –
    Care for our mothers' health.

Goddess, make strong our youth and bless the Senate's
Decrees rewarding parenthood and marriage,
That from the new laws Rome may reap a lavish
    Harvest of boys and girls

So that the destined cycle of eleven
Decades may bring again great throngs to witness
The games and singing: three bright days and three long
    Nights of the people's joy.

And you, O Fates, who have proved truthful prophets,
Your promise stands – and may time's sacred landmarks
Guard it immovably: to our accomplished
    Destiny add fresh strength.

May Mother Earth, fruitful in crops and cattle,
Crown Ceres' forehead with a wreath of wheat-ears,
And dews and rains and breezes, God's good agents,
    Nourish whatever grows.

Sun-god, put by thy bow and deign to listen
Mildly and gently to the boys' entreaties.
Moon, crescent sovereign of the constellations,
    Answer the virgins' prayers.

Rome is your handiwork; in your safe-keeping
The Trojan band reached an Etruscan haven,
That remnant which, at your command, abandoned
    City and hearth to make

The auspicious voyage, those for whom pure-hearted
Aeneas, the last pillar of royal manhood
Left standing in burnt Troy, paved paths to greater
    Fame than they left behind.

Gods, by these tokens make our young quick pupils
Of virtue, give the aged peace and quiet,
Rain on the race of Romulus wealth, offspring,
    Honours of every kind;

And when, tonight, with blood of milk-white oxen
50 The glorious son of Venus and Anchises
Invokes you, grant his prayers. Long may Augustus
    Conquer but spare the foe.

Now Parthia fears the fist of Rome, the fasces
Potent on land and sea; now the once haughty
Ambassadors from the Caspian and the Indus
    Sue for a soft reply.

Now Faith and Peace and Honour and old-fashioned
Conscience and unremembered Virtue venture
To walk again, and with them blessed Plenty,
60   Pouring her brimming horn.

Apollo, augur, bright-bowed archer, well-loved
Music-master of the nine Muses, healer
Whose skill in medicine can ease the body's
    Ills and infirmities,

By thy affection for the Palatine altars
Prolong, we pray, the Roman State and Latium's
Prosperity into future cycles, nobler
    Eras, for evermore.

Diana, keeper of the sacred hilltops
70 Of Aventine and Algidus, be gracious
To the prayers of the Fifteen Guardians, to the children
    Bend an attentive ear.

That Jove and all the gods approve these wishes
We, the trained chorus, singers of the praises
Of Phoebus and Diana, carry homewards
    Happy, unshaken hope. (1963)

CHARLES TOMLINSON (1927–)

His *Collected Poems* first appeared in 1985. His most recent publications are *The Door in The Wall* (1992) and *Selected Poems of Attilio Bertolucci* (1990). Editor of *The Oxford Book of Verse in English Translation* (1980). Emeritus Professor of Bristol University. The following two poems appear here in print for the first time.

Ode I.37

Cleopatra

Let's drink, my friends, and let us beat
The pulsing ground with nimble feet,
And let the dancing priests of Mars
Set delicacies before his altars.
To bring up vintage from our store
Would have been sacrilege before:
Drunk on their dream of mastery,
Her crew of decadents and she,
Their aim was to destroy the state,
10 Subvert the empire, burn the senate.
His galleys following behind,
Caesar has brought down her mind
Out of its fumes to solid things.
Her fleet's in flames, and still he clings –

Close as the hawk pursuing doves
Or as the huntsman where he moves
On hare tracks through Thessalian snows –
To load with chains this monster who
Has a nobler death in view
20 And neither holds the sword in dread
Nor to some hidden harbour's fled.
She sees the ruins of her palace
With steady eye and unmoved face,
Applies the asp and finds that vein
Where poison swiftest can get in.
Her much premeditated end
Measures the greatness of her mind,
That in its privacy now hears
No taunts of crude Liburnian tars:
30 Refusing to be shipped to Rome,
She scorns their triumph from her tomb.

Ode II.20

No ordinary wing shall bear
Me, poet-bird, through liquid air;
I'll linger upon earth no more,
Unenvying, quit the cities there.
The blood of humble parents, I
My dear Maecenas, shall not die,
Nor sink into the Stygian wave.
Look at *me* – I already have
A roughish skin about my feet,
10 Above, a white bird grows complete
And downy feathers and a wing
From fingers and from shoulders spring.
A song-bird and more expeditious
Than Daedalus's Icarus,

ODE II.20 · CHARLES TOMLINSON

  Gentle reader, I'll be found
  Where the Bosphorus murmurs round,
  Gaetulian regions I shall pass
  And the far fields of Boreas.
  Barbarian tribes will watch me go
20 And even painted Scythians know
  The bird I am, and Spain shall own
  And he that drinks beside the Rhone.
  No dirges and no lamentation
  At my imaginary cremation,
  Suppress your mourning and forbear
  A superfluous sepulchre.

EPODES

BEN JONSON

Epode 2

The praises of a Countrie life

Happie is he, that from all Businesse cleere,
    As the old race of Mankind were,
With his owne Oxen tills his Sires left lands,
    And is not in the Usurers bands:
Nor Souldier-like started with rough alarmes,
    Nor dreads the Seas inraged harmes:
But flees the Barre and Courts, with the proud bords,
    And waiting Chambers of great Lords.
The Poplar tall, he then doth marrying twine
    With the growne issue of the Vine;
And with his hooke lops off the fruitlesse race,
    And sets more happy in the place:
Or in the bending Vale beholds a-farre
    The lowing herds there grazing are:
Or the prest honey in pure pots doth keepe
    Of Earth, and sheares the tender Sheepe:
Or when that Autumne, through the fields, lifts round
    His head, with mellow Apples crown'd,
How plucking Peares, his owne hand grafted had,
    And purple-matching Grapes, hee's glad!
With which, Priapus, he may thanke thy hands,
    And, Sylvane, thine, that keptst his Lands!

Then now beneath some ancient Oke he may,
  Now in the rooted Grasse him lay,
Whilst from the higher Bankes doe slide the floods;
  The soft birds quarrell in the Woods,
The Fountaines murmure as the streames doe creepe,
  And all invite to easie sleepe.
Then when the thundring Jove his Snow and showres
30 Are gathering by the Wintry houres;
Or hence, or thence, he drives with many a Hound
  Wild Bores into his toyles pitch'd round:
Or straines on his small forke his subtill nets
  For th' eating Thrush, or Pit-falls sets:
And snares the fearfull Hare, and new-come Crane,
  And 'counts them sweet rewards so ta'en.
Who (amongst these delights) would not forget
  Loves cares so evil, and so great?
But if, to boot with these, a chaste Wife meet
40 For houshold aid, and Children sweet;
Such as the Sabines, or a Sun-burnt-blowse,
  Some lustie quick Apulians spouse,
To deck the hallow'd Harth with old wood fir'd
  Against the Husband comes home tir'd;
That penning the glad flock in hurdles by,
  Their swelling udders doth draw dry:
And from the sweet Tub Wine of this yeare takes,
  And unbought viands ready makes:
Not Lucrine Oysters I could then more prize,
50 Nor Turbot, nor bright Golden-eyes:
If with bright floods, the Winter troubled much,
  Into our Seas send any such:
Th' Ionian God-wit, nor the Ginny hen
  Could not goe downe my belly then

---

41 *blowse* 'a ruddy, fat-faced wench'

More sweet then Olives, that new gather'd be
    From fattest branches of the Tree:
Or the herb Sorrell, that loves Meadows still,
    Or Mallowes loosing bodyes ill:
Or at the Feast of Bounds, the Lambe then slaine,
60   Or Kid forc't from the Wolfe againe.
Among these Cates how glad the sight doth come
    Of the fed flocks approaching home!
To view the weary Oxen draw, with bare
    And fainting necks, the turned Share!
The wealthy houshold swarme of bondmen met,
    And 'bout the steeming Chimney set!
These thoughts when Usurer Alphius, now about
    To turne mere farmer, had spoke out,
'Gainst th' Ides, his moneys he gets in with paine,
70   At th' Calends, puts all out againe.   (pub. 1640)

SIR JOHN BEAUMONT

Epode 2

He happy is, who farre from busie sounds,
    (As ancient mortals dwelt)
With his owne Oxen tills his Fathers grounds,
    And debts hath never felt.
No warre disturbes his rest with fierce alarmes,
    Nor angry Seas offend:
He shunnes the Law, and those ambitious charmes,
    Which great mens doores attend.
The lofty Poplers with delight he weds
10   To Vines that grow apace,
And with his hooke unfruitfull branches shreds,
    More happy sprouts to place,

Or else beholds, how lowing heards astray,
    In narrow valleys creepe,
Or in cleane pots, doth pleasant hony lay,
    Or sheares his feeble Sheepe.
When Autumne from the ground his head upreares,
    With timely Apples chain'd,
How glad is he to plucke ingrafted Peares,
20   And Grapes with purple stain'd?
Thus he Priapus, or Sylvanus payes,
    Who keepes his limits free,
His weary limbes, in holding grasse he layes,
    Or under some old tree,
Along the lofty bankes the waters slide,
    The Birds in woods lament,
The Springs with trickling streames the Ayre divide,
    Whence gentle sleepes are lent.
But when great Jove, in winters dayes restores
30   Unpleasing showres and snowes,
With many Dogs he drives the angry Bores
    To snares which them oppose.
His slender nets dispos'd on little stakes,
    The greedy Thrush prevent:
The fearefull Hare, and forraine Crane he takes,
    With this reward content.
Who will not in these joyes forget the cares,
    Which oft in love we meete:
But when a modest wife the trouble shares
40   Of house and children sweete,
Like Sabines, or the swift Apulians wives,
    Whose cheekes the Sun beames harme,
When from old wood she sacred fire contrives,
    Her weary mate to warme,
When she with hurdles, her glad flockes confines,
    And their full undders dries,
And from sweet vessels drawes the yearely wines,
    And meates unbought supplies;

No Lucrine Oysters can my palate please,
   Those fishes I neglect,
Which tempests thundring on the Easterne Seas
   Into our waves direct.
No Bird from Affrike sent, my taste allowes,
   Nor Fowle which Asia breeds:
The Olive (gather'd from the fatty boughes)
   With more delight me feeds.
Sowre Herbs, which love the Meades, or Mallowes good,
   To ease the body pain'd:
A Lambe which sheds to Terminus her blood,
   Or Kid from Wolves regain'd.
What joy is at these Feasts, when well-fed flocks
   Themselves for home prepare!
Or when the weake necke of the weary Oxe
   Drawes back th' inverted share!
When Slaves (the swarmes that wealthy houses charge)
   Neere smiling Lar, sit downe.
This life when Alphius hath describ'd at large,
   Inclining to the Clowne,
He at the Ides calles all that money in,
   Which he hath let for gaine:
But when the next month shall his course begin,
   He puts it out againe.   (pub. 1629)

SIR RICHARD FANSHAWE

Epode 2

Happy is he, that far from mental toil,
   Like the old Mortals, ploughs his Native soil
With his own Oxen; out of debt: Nor leads
   A souldiers life, still in alarms; nor dreads

Th' enraged sea: and flies at any rate
 From Law-suits, and the proud porch of the Great.
What does he then? He, lofty poplars joyns
 Unto adult and marriageable Vines;
And the wild branches with his Sickle lopt,
10 Doth better children in their rooms adopt;
Or in a hollow valley, from above,
 Beholds his lowing herds securely rove;
Or, his best Honey, which he means to keep,
 Puts in clean pots: or shears his tender sheep.
Or when plump Autumn shews his bending head
 With mellow Apples beautifully red,
With what a gust his grafted Pears he pulls;
 And Grapes, the poor mans purple! whence he culls
The fairest, for thee Priap; and for thee
20 Sylvanus, Guardian of his husbandry.
Under an aged Oak he loves to pass
 The heates; or lolling on the matted grass.
Between deep bankes a river rowls the while;
 The birds they prattle to the trees that smile;
A purling brook runs chiding all the way,
 Which gentle slumbers to his eyes convey.
But when rough Winter thundring comes, to throw
 The treasures open of the rain and snow;
Either with dogs, behind him and before
30 He drives into his toils the tusked Boar;
Or spreads his thinner Nets beside some bush,
 An ambuscado for the greedie Thrush,
And (dear delights) inveigles in his snare
 The Travailer-Wood cock, and the Coward-Hare,
Who at these sports, evades not all those darts,
 With which loose love assaults our vacant hearts.
But if a vertuous Wife, that bears sweet fruit
 Yearly to one, and guides the house to boot:

(Such as the Sabine, or the Sun-burnt froe
40   Of him, that was chose Consul from the plough)
Build of old logs, 'gainst her good man comes home
    Weary, a fire as high as half the room;
And shutting in knit hurdles the glad beasts,
    With her own hand unlade their swagging breasts,
And drawing this years Wine from the sweet Butt,
    Dainties unbought upon the Table put;
Your Lucrine Oysters cannot please me more,
    Nor a fresh Sturgion frighted to our shore,
Nor any rarer fish. No Pheasant Hen,
50   Or Quayl, go down my throat more savoury; then
An Olive, gather'd from the fattest bough;
    Cool Endive, wholsome Mallows; or allow
A Lamb upon some mighty Festival;
    Or Kid from the Wolfs jaws; that's worth them all!
Amid these feasts, how sweet 'tis to behold
    The well-fed sheep run wadling to their fold?
To see the wearied Oxe come trayling back
    Th' inverted Plough upon his drooping neck;
And the Plough-boyes (the swarm that makes us thrive)
60   Surround the shining Hearth, content and blith!
All this the Us'rer Alpheus having sed,
    Resolv'd (what else?) a Country life to lead;
At Michaelmas calls all his Moneys in,
    But at Our Lady puts them out agin.   (pub. 1652)

---

39 *froe* wife   **64** *Our Lady* one of the feasts of the Virgin

THOMAS CREECH

Epode 13

Dark Clouds have thickned all the Sky,
    And Jove descends in Rain;
With frightful noise rough Storms do fly
Thro Seas and Woods, and humble Plain.

My noble Friends the Day perswades,
    Come, come, let's use the Day;
Whilst we are strong, ere Age invades,
Let Mirth our coming years delay.

Put briskly round the noble Wine,
10   And leave the rest to Fate,
Jove, chance, will make the Evening shine,
And bring it to a clearer State.

Now, now your fragrant Odours spread,
    Your merry Harps prepare;
'Tis time to cleanse my aking Head,
And purge my drooping thoughts from Care.

Thus Chiron sang in lofty strain
    And taught Achilles Youth;
Great Thetis Son, the pride of Man,
20   Observe, I tell Thee fatal truth.

Thee, Thee for Troy the Gods design
    Where Simois streams do play,
Scamander's thro the Vallies twine
And softly eat their easy way:

And there thy thread of Life must end
   Drawn o'er the Trojan Plain;
In vain her Waves shall Thetis send
To bear Thee back to Greece again:

Therefore, Great Son, my Precepts hear;
30   Let Mirth, and Wine, and Sport,
And merry Talk divert thy Care,
And make Life pleasant, since 'tis short.   (pub. 1684)

JOHN DRYDEN

Epode 2

How happy in his low degree
How rich in humble Poverty, is he,
Who leads a quiet country life!
Discharg'd of business, void of strife,
And from the gripeing Scrivener free.
(Thus e're the Seeds of Vice were sown,
Liv'd Men in better Ages born,
Who Plow'd with Oxen of their own
Their small paternal field of Corn.)
10 Nor Trumpets summon him to War
   Nor drums disturb his morning Sleep,
Nor knows he Merchants gainful care,
   Nor fears the dangers of the deep.
The clamours of contentious Law,
   And Court and state he wisely shuns,
Nor brib'd with hopes nor dar'd with awe
   To servile Salutations runs:

---

5 *Scrivener* money-lender

But either to the clasping Vine
   Does the supporting Poplar Wed,
Or with his pruneing hook disjoyn
   Unbearing Branches from their Head,
   And grafts more happy in their stead:
Or climbing to a hilly Steep
   He views his Herds in Vales afar
Or Sheers his overburden'd Sheep,
   Or mead for cooling drink prepares,
   Of Virgin honey in the Jars.
Or in the now declining year
   When bounteous Autumn rears his head,
He joyes to pull the ripen'd Pear,
   And clustring Grapes with purple spread.
The fairest of his fruit he serves,
   Priapus thy rewards:
Sylvanus too his part deserves,
   Whose care the fences guards.
Sometimes beneath an ancient Oak,
   Or on the matted grass he lies;
No God of Sleep he need invoke,
   The stream that o're the pebbles flies
   With gentle slumber crowns his Eyes.
The Wind that Whistles through the sprays
   Maintains the consort of the Song;
And hidden Birds with native layes
   The golden sleep prolong.
But when the blast of Winter blows,
   And hoary frost inverts the year,
Into the naked Woods he goes
   And seeks the tusky Boar to rear,
   With well mouth'd hounds and pointed Spear:
Or spreads his subtile Nets from sight
   With twinckling glasses to betray
The Larkes that in the Meshes light,
   Or makes the fearful Hare his prey.

EPODE 2 · JOHN DRYDEN

    Amidst his harmless easie joys
        No anxious care invades his health,
    Nor Love his peace of mind destroys,
        Nor wicked avarice of Wealth.
    But if a chast and pleasing Wife,
    To ease the business of his Life,
60   Divides with him his houshold care,
    Such as the Sabine Matrons were,
    Such as the swift Apulians Bride,
        Sunburnt and Swarthy tho' she be,
    Will fire for Winter Nights provide,
        And without noise will oversee,
        His Children and his Family,
    And order all things till he come,
    Sweaty and overlabour'd, home;
    If she in pens his Flocks will fold,
70   And then produce her Dairy store,
    With Wine to drive away the cold,
        And unbought dainties of the poor;
    Not Oysters of the Lucrine Lake
        My sober appetite wou'd wish,
        Nor Turbet, or the Foreign Fish
    That rowling Tempests overtake,
        And hither waft the costly dish.
    Not Heathpout, or the rarer Bird,
        Which Phasis, or Ionia yields,
80   More pleasing morsels wou'd afford
        Than the fat Olives of my fields;
    Than Shards or Mallows for the pot,
        That keep the loosen'd Body sound,
    Or than the Lamb that falls by Lot,
        To the just Guardian of my ground.
    Amidst these feasts of happy Swains,
        The jolly Shepheard smiles to see
    His flock returning from the Plains;
        The Farmer is as pleas'd as he

90   To view his Oxen, sweating smoak,
       Bear on their Necks the loosen'd Yoke;
       To look upon his menial Crew,
          That sit around his cheerful hearth,
       And bodies spent in toil renew
          With wholesome Food and Country Mirth.
       This Morecraft said within himself;
          Resolv'd to leave the wicked Town,
          And live retir'd upon his own;
       He call'd his Mony in:
100   But the prevailing love of pelf,
          Soon split him on the former shelf,
       And put it out again.   (pub. 1685)

THOMAS YALDEN (1670–1736)

High-Churchman, held a number of ecclesiastical positions and lived for the most part an uneventful life. His poetry shows the influence of Cowley, notably the 'Hymn to Darkness' which Johnson thought his best performance, 'imagined with great vigour and expressed with great propriety'.

Epode 15 An expansive translation

To His Perjur'd Mistress

   It was one evening, when the rising Moon
Amidst her Train of Stars distinctly shone:
Serene and calm was the inviting Night,
And Heav'n appear'd in all its lustre bright;
When you, Neaera, you my perjur'd Fair,
Did, to abuse the Gods and me, prepare.
Twas then you swore, remember faithless Maid,
With what indearing Arts you then betray'd:

EPODE 15 · THOMAS YALDEN

  Remember all the tender things that past,
10 When round my neck your willing arms were cast
  The circkling Ivys when with Oaks they joyn,
  Seem loose, and coy, to those fond Arms of thine.

   Believe, you cry'd, this solemn Vow believe,
  The noblest Pledge that Love and I can give:
  Or if there's ought more sacred here below,
  Let that confirm my Oath to Heav'n and you.
  If e're my Breast a guilty Flame receives,
  Or covets Joys, but what thy presence gives:
  May ev'ry injur'd Pow'r assert thy Cause,
20 And Love avenge his violated Laws:
  While cruel Beasts of Prey infest the Plain,
  And Tempests rage upon the faithless Main:
  While Sighs and Tears shall listning Virgins move,
  So long, ye Powers, will fond Neaera love.

   Ah faithless Charmer, lovely perjur'd Maid!
  Are thus my Vows, and generous Flame repay'd?
  Repeated slights I have too tamely bore,
  Still doated on, and still been wrong'd the more.
  Why do I listen to that Syrens Voice,
30 Love ev'n thy Crimes, and fly to guilty Joys!
  Thy fatal Eyes my best Resolves betray,
  My Fury melts in soft desires away:
  Each look, each glance, for all thy Crimes attone,
  Elude my Rage, and I'm again undone.

   But if my injur'd Soul dares yet be brave,
  Unless I'm fond of Shame, confirm'd a Slave:
  I will be deaf to that enchanting Tongue,
  Nor on thy Beauties gaze away my Wrong.
  At length I'll loath each prostituted Grace,
40 Nor court the leavings of a cloy'd Embrace;
  But show, with manly Rage, my Soul's above
  The cold returns of thy exhausted Love.

Then, thou shalt justly Mourn at my disdain,
Find all thy Arts, and all thy Charms in vain:
Shalt Mourn, whilst I, with nobler Flames, pursue
Some Nymph as fair, tho' not unjust, as you;
Whose Wit, and Beauty, shall like thine excel,
But far surpass in Truth, and loving well.

But wretched thou who e're my Rival art,
50 That fondly boast an Empire o're her Heart:
Thou that enjoy'st the fair inconstant Prize,
And vainly triumph'st with my Victories;
Unenvy'd now, o're all her Beauties rove,
Enjoy thy Ruin, and Neaera's Love:
Tho' Wealth, and Honours grace thy nobler Birth,
To bribe her Love, and fix a wand'ring Faith:
Tho' ev'ry Grace, and ev'ry Virtue joyn,
T' inrich thy Mind, and make thy Form divine:
Yet blest with endless Charms, too soon you'l prove
60 The Treacheries of false Neaera's Love.
Lost, and abandon'd by th' ungrateful Fair,
Like me you'l Love, be Injur'd, and Despair.
When left th' unhappy Object of her Scorn,
Then shall I smile to see the Victor mourn,
Laugh at thy Fate, and triumph in my turn. (1694)

C. H. SISSON

Epode 2

Happy the man who, free from business
    As Adam was when innocent,
Pretends to farm paternal acres
    And never thinks of the investment.

EPODE 2 · C. H. SISSON

    Nobody sends him tiresome papers
        Which leave him utterly at sea;
    He is not harried by his brokers
        Or people better off than he.
    Oh no! He cultivates his vineyard
10   And lets his vines get out of hand;
    His cattle graze without regard
        To the condition of the land.
    In pruning, he will always sever
        The fruiting branch, and leave the new;
    At shearing, finds the sheep so clever
        He likes their wool best where it grew;
    Finds honey sticky in the autumn
        And fruit a bit above his head;
    He does not pick the pears, they all come
20   Bouncing on top of him instead.
    His wine is fit for a libation
        Upon the ground, but not to drink;
    He much enjoys the preparation
        And he is proud if it is pink.
    His private stream meanwhile runs purling,
        The birds sing as they're paid to do;
    His fountains never tired of plashing
        And they are soporific too.
    But when the proper sporting weather
30   Arrives, he has to take a gun
    And stir up something in the heather
        As gentlemen have always done,
    Or even venture out on horse-back
        And hope a fox will come his way;
    How awkward he should lose the pack
        So very early in the day!
    With such delights he can forget
        That tiresome girl at the week-end:
    He plans to have, but not just yet,
40   A wife on whom he can depend.

>   – Children perhaps – some sunburnt lady,
>   He'd feel a proper farmer then;
> She'd bring in firewood, have tea ready,
>   He'd come in tired, not curious when
> She penned the geese or milked the cows,
>   So long as she'd drawn cider and,
> From home-grown chicken and potatoes,
>   Prepared a meal with her own hands.
> No Yarmouth oysters could be sweeter,
>   Smoked salmon, turbot, what you please,
> Not any delicacy caught here
>   Or found, long dead, in the deep freeze.
> It's not too bad to dine off pheasant
>   But home-grown olives do as well,
> And what he finds extremely pleasant
>   Is chewing meadow-sweet and sorrel:
> Which one of course can supplement
>   By hedgerow herbs that taste of tar,
> Or better, when such boons are sent
>   A lamb run over by a car.
> 'Amidst such treats as these, how fine
>   To see beasts by your own front door,
> The latest plough, the latest combine,
>   And plan what you will use them for.'
>
> So spoke the city man, and sold
>   The lot, preferring stocks and shares.
> Too bad that he had not been told
>   The full extent of rural cares.

(pub. 1993)

SATIRES

BEN JONSON

Satire II.1

From *The Poetaster*, Act III, Scene 5.

HORACE, TREBATIUS

    There are, to whom I seeme excessive sower;
And past a satyres law, t' extend my power:
Others, that thinke what ever I have writ
Wants pith, and matter to eternise it;
And that they could, in one daies light, disclose
A thousand verses, such as I compose.
What shall I doe, Trebatius? say. *Treb.* Surcease.
    Hora. And shall my Muse admit no more encrease?
    Treb. So I advise. *Hora.* An ill death let mee die,
10 If 'twere not best; but sleepe avoids mine eye:
And I use these, lest nights should tedious seeme.
    Treb. Rather, contend to sleepe, and live like them,
That holding golden sleepe in speciall price,
Rub'd with sweet oiles, swim silver Tyber thrice,
And every ev'en, with neat wine steeped be:
Or, if such love of writing ravish thee,
Then dare to sing unconquer'd Caesar's deeds;
Who cheeres such actions, with aboundant meeds.

Hora. That, father, I desire; but when I trie,
I feele defects in every facultie:
Nor is't a labour fit for every pen,
To paint the horid troups of armed men;
The launces burst, in Gallia's slaughtred forces;
Or wounded Parthians, tumbled from their horses:
Great Caesars warres cannot be fought with words.
   Treb. Yet, what his vertue in his peace affords,
His fortitude, and justice thou canst show;
As wise Lucilius, honor'd Scipio.
   Hora. Of that, my powers shall suffer no neglect,
When such sleight labours may aspire respect:
But, if I watch not a most chosen time,
The humble wordes of Flaccus cannot clime
The' attentive eare of Caesar; nor must I
With lesse observance shunne grosse flatterie:
For he, reposed safe in his owne merit,
Spurnes backe the gloses of a fawning spirit.
   Treb. But, how much better would such accents sound,
Then, with a sad, and serious verse to wound
Pantolabus, railing in his sawcie jests?
Or Nomentanus spent in riotous feasts?
In satyres, each man (though untoucht) complaines
As he were hurt; and hates such biting straines.
   Hora. What shall I doe? Milonius shakes his heeles
In ceaselesse dances, when his braine once feeles
The stirring fervour of the wine ascend;
And that his eyes false number apprehend.
Castor his horse; Pollux loves handie fights:
A thousand heads, a thousand choise delights.
My pleasure is in feet, my words to close,
As, both our better, old Lucilius does:
He, as his trustie friends, his bookes did trust
With all his secrets; nor, in things unjust,
Or actions lawfull, ran to other men:
So, that the old mans life, describ'd was seene

SATIRE II.I · BEN JONSON

As in a votive table in his lines;
And to his steps my Genius inclines,
Lucanian, or Apulian, I not whether;
For the Venusian colonie plowes either:
Sent thither, when the Sabines were forc'd thence
60 (As old fame sings) to give the place defence
'Gainst such, as seeing it emptie, might make rode
Upon the empire; or there fixe abode:
Whether th' Apulian borderer it were,
Or the Lucanian violence they feare.
But this my stile no living man shall touch,
If first I be not forc'd by base reproch;
But, like a sheathed sword, it shall defend
My innocent life; for, why should I contend
To draw it out, when no malicious thiefe
70 Robs my good name, the treasure of my life?
O Jupiter, let it with rust be eaten,
Before it touch, or insolently threaten
The life of any with the least disease;
So much I love, and woe a generall peace.
But, he that wrongs me (better, I proclame,
He never had assai'd to touch my fame.)
For he shall weepe, and walke with every tongue
Throughout the citie, infamously song.
Servius, the Praetor, threats the lawes, and urne,
80 If any at his deeds repine or spurne;
The witch, Canidia, that Albucius got,
Denounceth witch-craft, where shee loveth not:
Thurius, the judge, doth thunder worlds of ill,
To such, as strive with his judicial will;
All men affright their foes in what they may,
Nature commands it, and men must obey.

---

57 *not whether* know not whether
73 *disease* annoyance

Observe with me; The wolfe his tooth doth use:
The bull his horne. And, who doth this infuse,
But nature? There's luxurious Scaeva; Trust
His long-liv'd mother with him; His so just
And scrupulous right hand no mischiefe will;
No more, then with his heele a wolfe will kill,
Or Oxe with jaw: Mary, let him alone
With temper'd poison to remove the croane.
   But, briefly, if to age I destin'd bee,
Or that quick deaths black wings inviron me;
If rich, or poore; at Rome; or fate command
I shall be banish't to some other land;
What hiew soever, my whole state shall beare,
I will write satyres still, in spight of feare.
   Treb. Horace; I feare, thou draws't no lasting breath:
And that some great mans friend will be thy death.
   Hora. What? when the man that first did satyrise,
Durst pull the skin over the eares of vice;
And make, who stood in outward fashion cleare,
Give place, as foule within; shall I forbeare?
Did Laelius, or the man, so great with fame,
That from sackt Carthage fetcht his worthy name,
Storme, that Lucilius did Metellus pierce?
Or bury Lupus quick, in famous verse?
Rulers, and subjects, by whole tribes he checkt;
But vertue, and her friends did still protect:
And when from sight, or from the judgement seat,
The vertuous Scipio, and wise Laelius met,
Unbrac't, with him in all light sports, they shar'd;
Till, their most frugall suppers were prepar'd.
What e're I am, though both for wealth, and wit,
Beneath Lucilius, I am pleas'd to sit;
Yet, envy (spight of her empoisoned brest)
Shall say, I liv'd in grace here, with the best;
And, seeking in weake trash to make her wound,
Shall find me solid, and her teeth unsound:

'Lesse, learn'd Trebatius censure disagree.

   Treb. No, Horace, I of force must yeeld to thee;
Only, take heed, as being advis'd by mee,
Lest thou incurre some danger: Better pause,
Then rue thy ignorance of the sacred lawes;
There's justice, and great action may be su'd
'Gainst such, as wrong mens fames with verses lewd.

   Hora. I, with lewd verses; such as libels bee,
And aym'd at persons of good qualitie.
I reverence and adore that just decree:
But if they shall be sharp, yet modest rimes
That spare mens persons, and but taxe their crimes,
Such, shall in open court, find currant passe;
Were Caesar judge, and with the makers grace.

   Treb. Nay, I'le adde more; if thou thy selfe being cleare,
Shalt taxe in person a man, fit to beare
Shame, and reproch; his sute shall quickly bee
Dissolv'd in laughter, and thou thence sit free.   (pub. 1616)

SIR JOHN BEAUMONT

Satire II.6

This was my wish: no ample space of ground,
T' include my Garden with a mod'rate bound,
And neere my house a Fountaine never dry,
A little Wood, which might my wants supply,
The gods have made me blest with larger store:
It is sufficient, I desire no more,
O sonne of Maia, but this grant alone,
That quiet use may make these gifts mine owne.
If I increase them by no lawlesse way,
Nor through my fault will cause them to decay.

If not to these fond hopes my thoughts decline,
O that this joyning corner could be mine,
Which with disgrace deformes, and maimes my field,
Or Fortune would a pot of silver yeeld,
(As unto him who being hir'd to worke,
Discover'd treasure, which in mold did lurke,
And bought the Land, which he before had till'd,
Since friendly Hercules his bosome fill'd).
If I with thankfull minde these blessings take,
20   Disdaine not this petition which I make.
Let fat in all things, but my wit, be seene,
And be my safest guard as thou hast been.
When from the Citty I my selfe remove
Up to the hills, as to a towre above,
I find no fitter labours, nor delights
Then Satyres, which my lowly Muse indites.
No foule ambition can me there expose
To danger, nor the leaden wind that blowes
From Southerne parts, nor Autumnes grievous raine,
30   Whence bitter Libitina reapes her gaine.
O father of the mornings purple light!
Or if thou rather would'st be Janus hight,
From whose divine beginning, mortalls draw
The paines of life, according to the law,
Which is appointed by the Gods decree,
Thou shalt the entrance of my verses be.
At Rome thou driv'st me, as a pledge to goe,
That none himselfe may more officious show.
Although the fury of the Northerne blast
40   Shall sweepe the earth; or Winters force hath cast
The snowy day, into a narrow Sphere,
I must proceede, and having spoken cleare
And certaine truth, must wrestle in the throng,
Where by my haste, the slower suffer wrong,
And crie, 'What ayles the mad man? whither tend
His speedy steps?' while mine imperious frend

SATIRE II.6 · SIR JOHN BEAUMONT

    Intreates, and chafes, admitting no delay,
    And I must beate all those, that stop my way.
    The glad remembrance of Mecaenas lends
50 A sweete content: but when my journey bends
    To blacke Esquiliae, there a hundred tides
    Of strangers causes presse my head and sides.
    'You must, before the second houre, appeare
    In Court to morrow, and for Roscius sweare.'
    'The Scribes desire you would to them repaire,
    About a publike, great, and new affaire.'
    'Procure such favour, from Mecaenas hand,
    As that his seale may on this paper stand.'
    I answer, 'I will trie': he urgeth still,
60 'I know you can performe it if you will.'
    Sev'n yeeres are fled, the eighth is almost gone,
    Since first Mecaenas tooke me for his owne,
    That I with him might in his chariot sit,
    And onely then would to my trust commit
    Such toyes as these: 'What is the time of day?'
    'The Thracian is the Syrians match in play.'
    'Now carelesse men are nipt with morning cold':
    And words which open eares may safely hold.
    In all this space for ev'ry day and houre
70 I grew more subject to pale envies pow'r.
    'This sonne of Fortune to the Stage resorts,
    And with the fav'rite in the field disports.'
    Fame from the pulpits runnes through ev'ry streete,
    And I am strictly askt by all I meete:
    'Good Sir (you needes must know, for you are neare
    Unto the Gods) doe you no tidings heare
    Concerning Dacian troubles?' 'Nothing I.'
    'You alwayes love your friends with scoffes to try.'
    'If I can tell, the Gods my life confound.'
80 'But where will Caesar give his souldiers ground,
    In Italie, or the Trinacrian Ile?'
    I sweare I know not, they admire the while,

And thinke me full of silence, grave and deepe,
The onely man that should high secrets keepe,
For these respects (poore wretch) I lose the light,
And longing thus repine: when shall my sight
Againe bee happy in beholding thee
My countrey farme? or when shall I be free
To reade in bookes what ancient writers speake,
90 To rest in sleepe, which others may not breake,
To taste (in houres secure from courtly strife)
The soft oblivion of a carefull life?
O when shall beanes upon my boord appeare,
Which wise Pythagoras esteem'd so deare?
Or when shall fatnesse of the Lard anoint
The herbes, which for my table I appoint?
O suppers of the Gods! O nights divine!
When I before our Lar might feast with mine,
And feede my prating slaves with tasted meate,
100 As ev'ry one should have desire to eate.
The frolike guest not bound with heavy lawes,
The liquor from unequall measures drawes:
Some being strong delight in larger draughts,
Some call for lesser cups to cleere their thoughts.
Of others house and lands no speaches grow,
Nor whether Lepos danceth well or no.
We talke of things which to our selves pertaine,
Which not to know would be a sinfull staine.
Are men by riches or by vertue blest?
110 Of friendships ends is use or right the best?
Of good what is the nature, what excells?
My neighbour Cervius old wives fables tells,
When any one Arellius wealth admires,
And little knowes what troubles it requires.
He thus beginnes: 'Long since a countrey Mouse
Receav'd into his low and homely house
A Citty Mouse, his friend and guest before;
The host was sharpe and sparing of his store,

SATIRE II.6 · SIR JOHN BEAUMONT

  Yet much to hospitality inclin'd:
120 For such occasions could dilate his mind.
  He Chiches gives for winter layd aside,
  Nor are the long and slender Otes deny'd:
  Dry Grapes he in his lib'rall mouth doth beare,
  And bits of Bacon which halfe eaten were:
  With various meates to please the strangers pride,
  Whose dainty teeth through all the dishes slide.
  The Father of the family in straw
  Lies stretcht along, disdaigning not to gnaw
  Base corne or darnell, and reserves the best,
130 To make a perfect banquet for his guest.
  To him at last the Citizen thus spake,
  "My friend, I muse what pleasure thou canst take,
  Or how thou canst endure to spend thy time
  In shady Groves, and up steepe hills to clime.
  In savage Forrests build no more thy den:
  Goe to the City, there to dwell with men.
  Begin this happy journey, trust to me,
  I will thee guide, thou shalt my fellow be.
  Since earthly things are ty'd to mortall lives,
140 And ev'ry great, and little creature strives,
  In vaine the certaine stroke of death to flie,
  Stay not till moments past thy joyes denie.
  Live in rich plenty, and perpetuall sport:
  Live ever mindfull, that thine age is short."
  The ravisht field-mouse holds these words so sweet,
  That from his home he leapes with nimble feet.
  They to the Citie travaile with delight,
  And underneath the walles they creepe at night.
  Now darkenesse had possest heav'ns middle space,
150 When these two friends their weary steps did place
  Within a wealthy Palace, where was spred
  A scarlet cov'ring on an Iv'ry bed:
  The baskets (set farre off aside) contain'd
  The meates, which after plenteous meales remain'd:

The Citie Mouse with courtly phrase intreates
His Country friend to rest in purple seates;
With ready care the Master of the feast
Runnes up and downe to see the store increast:
He all the duties of a servant showes,
160 And tastes of ev'ry dish, that he bestowes.
The poore plaine Mouse, exalted thus in state,
Glad of the change, his former life doth hate,
And strives in lookes and gesture to declare
With what contentment he receives this fare.
But straight the sudden creaking of a doore
Shakes both these Mice from beds into the floore.
They runne about the roome halfe dead with feare,
Through all the house the noise of dogs they heare.
The stranger now counts not the place so good,
170 He bids farewell, and saith, "The silent Wood
Shall me hereafter from these dangers save,
Well pleas'd with simple Vetches in my Cave.'"   (pub. 1629)

ABRAHAM COWLEY

Satire I.1, lines 1–79

I 'dmire, Mecaenas, how it comes to pass,
That no man ever yet contented was,
Nor is, nor perhaps will be with that state
In which his own choice plants him or his Fate.
Happy their Merchant, the old Soldier cries;
The Merchant beaten with tempestuous skies,
Happy the Soldier one half hour to thee
Gives speedy Death or Glorious victory.

The Lawyer, knockt up early from his rest
10   By restless Clyents, calls the Peasant blest,
The Peasant when his Labours ill succeed,
Envys the Mouth which only Talk does feed,
'Tis not (I think you'l say) that I want store
Of Instances, if here I add no more,
They are enough to reach at least a mile
Beyond long Orator Fabias his Stile,
But, hold, you whom no Fortune e're endears
Gentlemen, Malecontents, and Mutineers,
Who bounteous Jove so often cruel call,
20   Behold, Jove's now resolv'd to please you all.
Thou Souldier be a Merchant, Merchant, Thou
A Souldier be; and, Lawyer, to the Plow.
Change all their stations strait, why do they stay?
The Devil a man will change, now when he may,
Were I in General Jove's abused case,
By Jove I'de cudgel this rebellious race:
But he's too good; Be all then as you were,
However make the best of what you are,
And in that state be chearful and rejoyce,
30   Which either was your Fate, or was your Choice.
No, they must labour yet, and sweat and toil,
And very miserable be a while.
But 'tis with a Design only to gain
What may their Age with plenteous ease maintain.
The prudent Pismire does this Lesson teach
And industry to Lazy Mankind preach.
The little Drudge does trot about and sweat,
Nor does he strait devour all he can get,
But in his temperate Mouth carries it home
40   A stock for Winter which he knows must come.

---

35 *Pismire* ant

And when the rowling World to Creatures here
Turns up the deform'd wrong side of the Year,
And shuts him in, with storms, and cold, and wet,
He chearfully does his past labours eat:
O, does he so? your wise example, th' Ant,
Does not at all times Rest, and Plenty want.
But weighing justly 'a mortal Ants condition
Divides his Life 'twixt Labour and Fruition.
Thee neither heat, nor storms, nor wet, nor cold
50 From thy unnatural diligence can withhold,
To th' Indies thou wouldst run rather then see
Another, though a Friend, Richer then Thee.
Fond man! what Good or Beauty can be found
In heaps of Treasure buried under ground?
Which rather then diminisht e're to see
Thou wouldst thy self too buried with them be:
And what's the difference, is't not quite as bad
Never to Use, as never to have Had?
In thy vast Barns millions of Quarters store,
60 Thy Belly for all that will hold no more
Then Mine does; every Baker makes much Bread,
What then? He's with no more then others fed.
Do you within the bounds of Nature Live,
And to augment your own you need not strive,
One hundred Acres will no less for you
Your Life's whole business then ten thousand do.
But pleasant 'tis to take from a great store;
What, Man? though you'r resolv'd to take no more
Then I do from a small one? if your Will
70 Be but Pitcher or a Pot to fill
To some great River for it must you go,
When a clear spring just at your feet does flow?
Give me the Spring which does to humane use
Safe, easie, and untroubled stores produce,
He who scorns these, and needs will drink at Nile
Must run the danger of the Crocodile,

And of the rapid stream it self which may
At unawares bear him perhaps away.
In a full Flood Tantalus stands, his skin
80 Washt o're in vain, for ever, dry within;
He catches at the Stream with greedy lips,
From his toucht Mouth the wanton Torment slips:
You laugh now, and expand your careful brow;
Tis finely said, but what's all this to you?
Change but the Name, this Fable is thy story,
Thou in a Flood of useless Wealth dost Glory,
Which thou canst only touch but never taste;
Th' abundance still, and still the want does last.
The Treasures of the Gods thou wouldst not spare,
90 But when they'r made thine own, they Sacred are,
And must be kept with reverence, as if thou
No other use of precious Gold didst know,
But that of curious Pictures to delight
With the fair stamp thy Virtuoso sight.
The only true, and genuine use is this,
To buy the things which Nature cannot miss
Without discomfort, Oyl, and vital Bread,
And Wine by which the Life of Life is fed.
And all those few things else by which we live;
100 All that remains is Giv'n for thee to Give;
If Cares and Troubles, Envy, Grief and Fear,
The bitter Fruits be, which fair Riches bear,
If a new Poverty grow out of store;
The old plain way, ye Gods, let me be Poor. (pub. 1668)

Satire II.6, lines 79–117 A paraphrase

At the large foot of a fair hollow tree,
Close to plow'd ground, seated commodiously,
His antient and Hereditary House,
There dwelt a good substantial Country-Mouse:

Frugal, and grave, and careful of the main,
Yet, one, who once did nobly entertain
A City Mouse well coated, sleek, and gay,
A Mouse of high degree, which lost his way,
Wantonly walking forth to take the Air,
10 And arriv'd early, and belighted there,
For a days lodging: the good hearty Hoast,
(The antient plenty of his hall to boast)
Did all the stores produce, that might excite,
With various tasts, the Courtiers appetite.
Fitches and Beans, Peason, and Oats, and Wheat,
And a large Chesnut, the delicious meat
Which Jove himself, were he a Mouse, would eat.
And for a Haut goust there was mixt with these
The swerd of Bacon, and the coat of Cheese.
20 The precious Reliques, which at Harvest, he
Had gather'd from the Reapers luxurie.
Freely (said he) fall on and never spare,
The bounteous Gods will for to morrow care.
And thus at ease on beds of straw they lay,
And to their Genius sacrific'd the day.
Yet the nice guest's Epicurean mind,
(Though breeding made him civil seem and kind)
Despis'd this Country feast, and still his thought
Upon the Cakes and Pies of London wrought.
30 Your bounty and civility (said he)
Which I'm surpriz'd in these rude parts to see,
Shews that the Gods have given you a mind,
Too noble for the fate which here you find.
Why should a Soul, so virtuous and so great,
Lose it self thus in an Obscure retreat?
Let savage Beasts lodg in a Country Den,
You should see Towns, and Manners know, and men:
And taste the generous Lux'ury of the Court,
Where all the Mice of quality resort;

40   Where thousand beauteous shees about you move,
     And by high fare, are plyant made to love.
     We all e're long must render up our breath,
     No cave or hole can shelter us from death.
         Since Life is so uncertain, and so short,
     Let's spend it all in feasting and in sport.
     Come, worthy Sir, come with me, and partake,
     All the great things that mortals happy make.
         Alas, what virtue hath sufficient Arms,
     T' oppose bright Honour, and soft Pleasures charms?
50   What wisdom can their magick force repel?
     It draws this reverend Hermit from his Cel.
     It was the time, when witty Poets tell,
     That Phoebus into Thetis bosom fell:
     She blusht at first, and then put out the light,
     And drew the modest Curtains of the night.
     Plainly, the troth to tell, the Sun was set,
     When to the Town our wearied Travellers get,
     To a Lords house, as Lordly as can be
     Made for the use of Pride and Luxury,
60   They come; the gentle Courtier at the door
     Stops and will hardly enter in before.
     But 'tis, Sir, your command, and being so,
     I'm sworn t' obedience, and so in they go.
     Behind a hanging in a spacious room,
     (The richest work of Mortclakes noble Loom)
     They wait awhile their wearied limbs to rest,
     Till silence should invite them to their feast.
     About the hour that Cynthia's Silver light,
     Had touch'd the pale Meridies of the night;
70   At last the various Supper being done,
     It happened that the Company was gone,
     Into a room remote, Servants and all,
     To please their nobles fancies with a Ball.
     Our host leads forth his stranger, and do's find,
     All fitted to the bounties of his mind.

Still on the Table half fill'd dishes stood,
And with delicious bits the floor was strow'd.
The courteous mouse presents him with the best,
And both with fat varieties are blest,
80 Th' industrious Peasant every where does range,
And thanks the gods for his Life's happy change.
Loe, in the midst of a well fraited Pye,
They both at last glutted and wanton lye.
When see the sad Reverse of prosperous fate,
And what fierce storms on mortal glories wait.
With hideous noise, down the rude servants come,
Six dogs before run barking into th' room;
The wretched gluttons fly with wild affright,
And hate the fulness which retards their flight.
90 Our trembling Peasant wishes now in vain,
That Rocks and Mountains cover'd him again.
Oh how the change of his poor life he curst!
This, of all lives (said he) is sure the worst.
Give me again, ye gods, my Cave and wood;
With peace, let tares and acorns be my food.   (pub. 1668)

JOHN WILMOT, EARL OF ROCHESTER (1647–1680)

Educated at Wadham College, Oxford. Courtier, prominent among the wits surrounding Charles II, fought bravely at sea in the second Dutch War. Libertine, devoted husband of a wife he had to abduct to marry, brawler given to acts of scandalous violence that would probably have cost him his life had he been a commoner, poet of lyrical grace, satiric wit, notable obscenity, and philosophic depth ('A Satyr against Reason and Mankind', 'Upon Nothing'). Physically worn out, Rochester died devout at the age of thirty-three.

Satire I.10 A free imitation

Discussing Roman satire, Horace points to the failings of the older satirist Lucilius and turns a critical eye on some writers of the day. Rochester follows suit, substituting Dryden for Lucilius. Compare the translation by Francis Howes (pp. 384–8).

    Well Sir, 'tis granted, I said Dryden's Rhimes,
Were stoln, unequal, nay dull many times:
What foolish Patron, is there found of his,
So blindly partial, to deny me this?
But that his Plays, Embroider'd up and downe,
With Witt, and Learning, justly pleas'd the Towne,
In the same paper, I as freely owne:
Yet haveing this allow'd, the heavy Masse,
That stuffs up his loose Volumes must not passe:
10 For by that Rule, I might as well admit,
Crownes tedious Scenes, for Poetry, and Witt.
'Tis therefore not enough, when your false Sense
Hits the false Judgment of an Audience
Of Clapping-Fooles, assembling a vast Crowd
'Till the throng'd Play-House, crack with the dull Load;
Tho' ev'n that Tallent, merrits in some sort,
That can divert the Rabble and the Court:
Which blundring Settle, never cou'd attaine,
And puzling Otway, labours at in vaine.
20 But within due proportions, circumscribe
What e're you write; that with a flowing Tyde,
The Stile, may rise, yet in its rise forbeare,
With uselesse Words, t' oppresse the wearyed Eare:
Here be your Language lofty, there more light,
Your Rethorick, with your Poetry, unite:
For Elegance sake, sometimes alay the force
Of Epethets; 'twill soften the discourse;
A Jeast in Scorne, poynts out, and hits the thing,
More home, than the Morosest Satyrs Sting.

30 Shakespeare, and Johnson, did herein excell,
And might in this be Immitated well;
Whom refin'd Etheridge, Coppys not at all,
But is himself a Sheere Originall:
Nor that Slow Drudge, in swift Pindarique straines,
Flatman, who Cowley imitates with paines,
And rides a Jaded Muse, whipt with loose Raines.
When Lee, makes temp'rate Scipio, fret and Rave,
And Haniball, a whineing Am'rous Slave;
I laugh, and wish the hot-brain'd Fustian Foole,
40 In Busbys hands, to be well lasht at Schoole.
Of all our Moderne Witts, none seemes to me,
Once to have toucht upon true Comedy,
But hasty Shadwell, and slow Witcherley.
Shadwells unfinisht workes doe yet impart,
Great proofes of force of Nature, none of Art.
With just bold Stroakes, he dashes here and there,
Shewing great Mastery with little care;
And scornes to varnish his good touches o're,
To make the Fooles, and Women, praise 'em more.
50 But Witcherley, earnes hard, what e're he gaines,
He wants noe Judgment, nor he spares noe paines;
He frequently excells, and at the least,
Makes fewer faults, than any of the best.

    Waller, by Nature for the Bayes design'd,
With force, and fire, and fancy unconfin'd,
In Panigericks does Excell Mankind:
He best can turne, enforce, and soften things,
To praise great Conqu'rours, or to flatter Kings.

    For poynted Satyrs, I wou'd Buckhurst choose,
60 The best good Man, with the worst Natur'd Muse:
    For Songs, and Verses, Mannerly Obscene,
That can stirr Nature up, by Springs unseene,
And without forceing blushes, warme the Queene:
Sidley, has that prevailing gentle Art,
That can with a resistlesse Charme impart,

The loosest wishes to the Chastest Heart,
Raise such a Conflict, kindle such a fire
Betwixt declineing Virtue, and desire,
Till the poor Vanquisht Maid, dissolves away,
70 In Dreames all Night, in Sighs, and Teares, all Day.
    Dryden, in vaine, try'd this nice way of Witt,
For he, to be a tearing Blade thought fit,
But when he wou'd be sharp, he still was blunt,
To friske his frollique fancy, hed cry Cunt;
Wou'd give the Ladyes, a dry Bawdy bob,
And thus he got the name of Poet Squab:
But to be just, twill to his praise be found,
His Excellencies, more than faults abound.
Nor dare I from his Sacred Temples teare,
80 That Lawrell, which he best deserves to weare.
But does not Dryden find ev'n Johnson dull?
Fletcher, and Beaumont, uncorrect, and full
Of Lewd lines as he calls em? Shakespeares Stile
Stiffe, and Affected? To his owne the while
Allowing all the justnesse that his Pride,
Soe Arrogantly, had to these denyd?
And may not I, have leave Impartially
To search, and Censure, Drydens workes, and try,
If those grosse faults, his Choyce Pen does Commit
90 Proceed from want of Judgment, or of Witt.
Or if his lumpish fancy does refuse,
Spirit, and grace to his loose slatterne Muse?
Five Hundred Verses, ev'ry Morning writ,
Proves you noe more a Poet, than a Witt.
Such scribling Authors, have beene seene before,
Mustapha, the English Princesse, Forty more,
Were things perhaps compos'd in Half an Houre.
To write what may securely stand the test
Of being well read over Thrice at least
100 Compare each Phrase, examin ev'ry Line,
Weigh ev'ry word, and ev'ry thought refine;

    Scorne all Applause the Vile Rout can bestow,
    And be content to please those few, who know.
    Canst thou be such a vaine mistaken thing
    To wish thy Workes might make a Play-house ring,
    With the unthinking Laughter, and poor praise
    Of Fopps, and Ladys, factious for thy Plays?
    Then send a cunning Friend to learne thy doome,
    From the shrew'd Judges in the Drawing-Roome.
110 I've noe Ambition on that idle score,
    But say with Betty Morice, heretofore
    When a Court-Lady, call'd her Buckleys Whore,
    I please one Man of Witt, am proud on't too,
    Let all the Coxcombs, dance to bed to you.
    Shou'd I be troubled when the Purblind Knight
    Who squints more in his Judgment, than his sight,
    Picks silly faults, and Censures what I write?
    Or when the poor-fed Poets of the Towne
    For Scrapps, and Coach roome cry my Verses downe?
120 I loath the Rabble, 'tis enough for me,
    If Sidley, Shadwell, Shepherd, Witcherley,
    Godolphin, Buttler, Buckhurst, Buckingham,
    And some few more, whom I omit to name
    Approve my Sense, I count their Censure Fame.   (pub. 1680)

JOHN OLDHAM

Satire I.9 An imitation. Here abridged

Too freely inventive to be properly called an imitation, this is rather a Restoration poem suggested by a Latin poem written 1600 years before. Horace's satire enjoyed great popularity in the seventeenth century. Jonson included a prose version in *The Poetaster*, Donne drew on it in his fourth and perhaps in his first satire. There is

SATIRE I.9 · JOHN OLDHAM

also a version by Thomas Sprat from which Oldham borrowed or adapted a number of phrases. See the translation by Francis Howes (pp. 380–84).

> As I was walking in the Mall of late,
> Alone, and musing on I know not what;
> Comes a familiar Fop, whom hardly I
> Knew by his name, and rudely seizes me:
> 'Dear Sir, I'm mighty glad to meet with you:
> And pray, how have you done this Age, or two?'
> 'Well I thank God,' said I, 'as times are now:
> I wish the same to you.' And so past on,
> Hoping with this the Coxcomb would be gone.
> 10 But when I saw I could not thus get free;
> I ask'd, what business else he had with me?
> 'Sir,' answer'd he, 'if Learning, Parts, or Sence
> Merit your friendship; I have just pretence.'
> 'I honor you,' said I, 'upon that score,
> And shall be glad to serve you to my power.'
> Mean time, wild to get loose, I try all ways
> To shake him off: Sometimes I walk apace,
> Sometimes stand still: I frown, I chafe, I fret,
> Shrug, turn my back, as in the Bagnio, sweat:
> 20 And shew all kind of signs to make him guess
> At my impatience and uneasiness.
> 'Happy the folk in Newgate!' whisper'd I,
> 'Who, tho in Chains are from this torment free:
> Wou'd I were like rough Manly in the Play,
> To send Impertinents with kicks away.'
>   He all the while baits me with tedious chat,
> Speaks much about the drought, and how the rate
> Of Hay is rais'd, and what it now goes at:
> Tells me of a new Comet at the Hague,
> 30 Portending God knows what, a Dearth, or Plague:
> Names every Wench, that passes through the Park,
> How much she is allow'd, and who the Spark

That keeps her: points, who lately got a Clap,
And who at the Groom-Porters had ill hap
Three nights ago in play with such a Lord:
When he observ'd, I minded not a word,
And did no answer to his trash afford;
'Sir, I perceive you stand on Thorns,' said he,
'And fain would part: but, faith, it must not be:
40 Come, let us take a Bottle.' I cried 'No;
Sir, I am in a Course, and dare not now.'
'Then tell me whither you design to go:
I'll wait upon you.' 'Oh! Sir, 'tis too far:
I visit cross the Water: therefore spare
Your needless trouble.' 'Trouble! Sir, 'tis none:
'Tis more by half to leave you here alone.
I have no present business to attend,
At least which I'll not quit for such a Friend:
Tell me not of the distance: for I vow,
50 I'll cut the Line, double the Cape for you,
Good faith, I will not leave you: make no words:
Go you to Lambeth? Is it to my Lords?
His Steward I most intimately know,
Have often drunk with his Comptroller too.'
By this I found my wheadle would not pass,
But rather serv'd my suff'rings to increase:
And seeing 'twas in vain to vex, or fret,
58 I patiently submitted to my fate . . .

87   By this time we were got to Westminster,
Where he by chance a Trial had to hear,
And, if he were not there, his Cause must fall:
90 'Sir, if you love me, step into the Hall
For one half hour.' 'The Devil take me now,'
Said I, 'if I know anything of Law:

---

41 *in a Course* under a doctor

SATIRE I.9 · JOHN OLDHAM

  Besides I told you whither I'm to go.'
Hereat he made a stand, pull'd down his Hat
Over his eyes, and mus'd in deep debate:
'I'm in a strait,' said he, 'what I shall do:
Whether forsake my business, Sir, or you.'
'Me by all means,' say I. 'No,' says my Sot,
'I fear you'l take it ill, if I should do't:
100 I'm sure, you will.' 'Not I, by all that's good.'
'But I've more breeding, than to be so rude.'
'Pray, don't neglect your own concerns for me:
Your Cause, good Sir!' 'My Cause be damn'd,' says he,
'I value't less than your dear Company.'
With this he came up to me, and would lead
106 The way: I sneaking after hung my head . . .

159   While at this Savage rate he worried me;
160 By chance a Doctor, my dear Friend came by,
That knew the Fellow's humor passing well:
Glad of the sight, I joyn him; we stand still:
'Whence came you, Sir? and whither go you now?'
And such like questions past betwixt us two:
Straight I begin to pull him by the sleeve,
Nod, wink upon him, touch my Nose, and give
A thousand hints, to let him know, that I
Needed his help for my delivery:
He, naughty Wag, with an arch fleering smile
170 Seems ignorant of what I mean the while:
I grow stark wild with rage. 'Sir, said not you,
You'd somewhat to discourse, not long ago,
With me in private?' 'I remember't well:
Some other time, be sure, I will not fail:
Now I am in great hast upon my word:
A messenger came for me from a Lord,
That's in a bad condition, like to die.'
'Oh! Sir, he can't be in a worse, than I:
Therefore, for Gods sake do not stir from hence.'

180   'Sweet Sir! your pardon: 'tis of consequence:
       I hope you're kinder than to press my stay,
       Which may be Heav'n knows what out of my way.'
       This said, he left me to my murderer:
       Seeing no hopes of my relief appear;
       'Confounded by the Stars,' said I, 'that sway'd
       This fatal day! would I had kept my Bed
       With sickness, rather than been visited
       With this worse Plague! what ill have I e're done
       To pull this curse, this heavy Judgment down?'
190   While I was thus lamenting my ill hap,
       Comes aid at length: a brace of Bailiffs clap
       The Rascal on the back: 'Here, take your Fees,
       Kind Gentlemen,' said I, 'for my release.'
       He would have had me Bail. 'Excuse me, Sir,
       I've made a Vow ne're to be surety more:
       My Father was undone by't heretofore.'
           Thus I got off, and blest the Fates that he
           Was Pris'ner made, I set at liberty.   (pub. 1681)

THOMAS CREECH

Satire II.2, lines 112–36

The speaker recalls a rustic sage named Ofellus who, once well-to-do, had his estate confiscated and handed over to a veteran, leaving him to work as a tenant-farmer on the land he once owned. 'This Roman portrait of a great and simple individual, who had seen his world crash about his ears and had calmly pieced it together into another, tolerable, pattern ... is a moving portrait of a great and simple ideal.' (Gordon Williams, *Tradition and Originality in Roman Poetry*, 315 f.)

SATIRE II.2, LINES 112-36 · THOMAS CREECH

166 I knew Ofellus when I was a youth;
Then He was Rich, yet 'midst his greatest Store,
He liv'd as now, since Rapine made him Poor:
Now you may see him with his Wife and Son,
170 Till that Estate for hire which was his own:
He Plows, he Sweats, and stoutly digs for Bread,
Contented still, and as he wrought, He said,
On working Days I never us'd to eat
But Cale and Bacon, that was all my Meat:
But when an old and honest Friend of mine,
Or else my welcome Neighbours came to dine;
When it was rainy, or my work was done,
We feasted not on costly Fish from Town;
But took what I could easily provide
180 From my own Field, a Pullet or a Kid:
And then for second course some Grapes were press'd,
Or Nuts, and Figs, and that was all my Feast:
And after this we drank a Health or two,
As far as harmless sober mirth would go;
And then thank'd Ceres for our present cheer,
And beg'd a plenteous Crop the following year:
And now let Fortune frown, I scorn her force,
How can she make our way of living worse?
Have we not had enough since we grew poor,
190 Have we liv'd worse, My Sons, than heretofore,
Before a Stranger came, and seiz'd my store?
For Nature doth not Me or Him create
The proper Lord of such and such Estate:
He forc'd us out, and doth possess my Plain;
Another cheat shall force him out again,
Or quircks in Law, or when those fears are past,
His long-liv'd Heir shall force him out at last:
That which was once Ofellus Farm is gone,
Now call'd Umbrena's, but 'tis no Mans own:
200 None hath the Property: it comes and goes,
As merry Chance, or stubborn Fates dispose,

As God thinks fit, and his firm Nods Decree,
Now to be us'd by Others, now by Me:
Then live resolv'd, my Sons, refuse to yield,
And when Fates press make Constancy your Shield.

(pub. 1684)

JONATHAN SWIFT and ALEXANDER POPE

Satire II.6 An imitation

The first part of the poem is by Swift. Pope takes over at line 133, 'O charming Noons! and Nights divine!' For a closer rendering see the translation by Sir John Beaumont (pp. 321–6).

> I've often wish'd that I had clear
> For life, six hundred pounds a year,
> A handsome House to lodge a Friend,
> A River at my garden's end,
> A Terras-walk, and half a Rood
> Of Land, set out to plant a Wood.
>   Well, now I have all this and more,
> I ask not to increase my store;
> But here a Grievance seems to lie,
> All this is mine but till I die;
> I can't but think 'twould sound more clever,
> To me and to my Heirs for ever.
>   If I ne'er got, or lost a groat,
> By any Trick, or any Fault;
> And if I pray by Reason's rules,
> And not like forty other Fools:

As thus, 'Vouchsafe, oh gracious Maker!
To grant me this and t' other Acre:
Or if it be thy Will and Pleasure
20 Direct my Plow to find a Treasure:'
But only what my Station fits,
And to be kept in my right wits.
Preserve, Almighty Providence!
Just what you gave me, Competence:
And let me in these Shades compose
Something in Verse as true as Prose;
Remov'd from all th' ambitious Scene,
Nor puff'd by Pride, nor sunk by Spleen.
   In short, I'm perfectly content,
30 Let me but live on this side Trent;
Nor cross the Channel twice a year,
To spend six months with Statesmen here.
   I must by all means come to town,
'Tis for the Service of the Crown,
'Lewis, the Dean will be of use,
Send for him up, take no excuse.'
The toil, the danger of the Seas;
Great Ministers ne'er think of these;
Or let it cost five hundred pound,
40 No matter where the money's found;
It is but so much more in debt,
And that they ne'er consider'd yet.
'Good Mr Dean go change your gown,
Let my Lord know you've come to town.'
I hurry me in haste away,
Not thinking it is Levee-day;
And find his Honour in a Pound,
Hemm'd by a triple Circle round,
Chequer'd with Ribbons blue and green;
50 How should I thrust my self between?
Some Wag observes me thus perplext,
And smiling, whispers to the next,

'I thought the Dean had been too proud,
To justle here among a croud.'
Another in a surly fit,
Tells me I have more Zeal than Wit,
'So eager to express your love,
You ne'er consider whom you shove,
But rudely press before a Duke.'
60 I own, I'm pleas'd with this rebuke,
And take it kindly meant to show
What I desire the World should know.

    I get a whisper, and withdraw;
When twenty Fools I never saw
Come with Petitions fairly penn'd,
Desiring I would stand their friend.

    This, humbly offers me his Case –
That, begs my int'rest for a Place –
A hundred other Men's affairs
70 Like Bees are humming in my ears.
'Tomorrow my Appeal comes on,
Without your help the Cause is gone' –
'The Duke expects my Lord and you,
About some great Affair, at Two –'
'Put my Lord Bolingbroke in mind,
To get my Warrant quickly sign'd:
Consider, 'tis my first request.' –
Be satisfy'd, I'll do my best: –
Then presently he falls to teize,
80 'You may for certain, if you please;
I doubt not, if his Lordship knew –
And, Mr Dean, one word from you' –

    'Tis (let me see) three years and more,
(October next it will be four)
Since Harley bid me first attend,
And chose me for an humble friend;
Wou'd take me in his Coach to chat,
And question me of this and that;

As, 'What's o'clock?' And, 'How's the Wind?'
90 'Who's Chariot's that we left behind?'
Or gravely try to read the lines
Writ underneath the Country Signs;
Or, 'Have you nothing new to-day
From Pope, from Parnel, or from Gay?'
Such tattle often entertains
My Lord and me as far as Stains,
As once a week we travel down
To Windsor, and again to Town,
Where all that passes, *inter nos*,
100 Might be proclaim'd at Charing-Cross.
    Yet some I know with envy swell,
Because they see me us'd so well:
'How think you of our Friend the Dean?
I wonder what some people mean;
My Lord and he are grown so great,
Always together, *tête à tête*,
What, they admire him for his jokes –
See but the fortune of some Folks!'
There flies about a strange report
110 Of some Express arriv'd at Court,
I'm stopp'd by all the fools I meet,
And catechis'd in ev'ry street.
'You, Mr Dean, frequent the great;
Inform us, will the Emp'ror treat?
Or do the Prints and Papers lye?'
Faith, Sir, you know as much as I.
'Ah Doctor, how you love to jest?
'Tis now no secret' – I protest
'Tis one to me – 'Then tell us, pray,
120 When are the Troops to have their pay?'
And, tho' I solemnly declare
I know no more than my Lord Mayor,
They stand amaz'd, and think me grown
The closest mortal ever known.

            Thus in a sea of folly toss'd,
        My choicest Hours of life are lost;
        Yet always wishing to retreat,
        Oh, could I see my Country Seat!
        There, leaning near a gentle Brook,
130   Sleep, or peruse some ancient Book,
        And there in sweet oblivion drown
        Those Cares that haunt the Court and Town.
            O charming Noons! and Nights divine!
        Or when I sup, or when I dine,
        My Friends above, my Folks below,
        Chatting and laughing all-a-row,
        The Beans and Bacon set before 'em,
        The Grace-cup serv'd with all decorum:
        Each willing to be pleas'd, and please,
140   And even the very Dogs at ease!
        Here no man prates of idle things,
        How this or that Italian sings,
        A Neighbour's Madness, or his Spouse's,
        Or what's in either of the Houses:
        But something much more our concern,
        And quite a scandal not to learn:
        Which is the happier, or the wiser,
        A man of Merit, or a Miser?
        Whether we ought to chuse our Friends,
150   For their own Worth, or our own Ends?
        What good, or better, we may call,
        And what, the very best of all?
            Our Friend Dan Prior told, (you know)
        A Tale extreamly *a propos*:
        Name a Town Life, and in a trice,
        He had a Story of two Mice.
            Once on a time (so runs the Fable)
        A Country Mouse, right hospitable,
        Receiv'd a Town Mouse at his Board,
160   Just as a Farmer might a Lord.

A frugal Mouse upon the whole,
Yet lov'd his Friend, and had a Soul;
Knew what was handsome, and wou'd do't,
On just occasion, *coute qui coute*.
He brought him Bacon (nothing lean)
Pudding, that might have pleas'd a Dean;
Cheese, such as men in Suffolk make,
But wish'd it Stilton for his sake;
Yet to his Guest tho' no way sparing,
170 He eat himself the Rind and paring.
Our Courtier scarce could touch a bit,
But show'd his Breeding, and his Wit,
He did his best to seem to eat,
And cry'd, 'I vow you're mighty neat.
As sweet a Cave as one shall see!
A most Romantic hollow Tree!
A pretty kind of savage Scene!
But come, for God's sake, live with Men:
Consider, Mice, like Men, must die,
180 Both small and great, both you and I:
Then spend your life in Joy and Sport,
(This doctrine, Friend, I learnt at Court.)'

 The veriest Hermit in the Nation
May yield, God knows, to strong Temptation.
Away they come, thro thick and thin,
To a tall house near Lincoln's-Inn:
('Twas on the night of a Debate,
When all their Lordships had sate late.)

 Behold the place, where if a Poet
190 Shin'd in Description, he might show it,
Tell how the Moon-beam trembling falls
And tips with silver all the walls:
Palladian walls, Venetian doors,
Grotesco roofs, and Stucco floors:

But let it (in a word) be said,
The Moon was up, and Men a-bed,
The Napkins white, the Carpet red:
The Guests withdrawn had left the Treat,
And down the Mice sate, *tête à tête*.
Our Courtier walks from dish to dish,
Tastes for his Friend of Fowl and Fish;
Tells all their names, lays down the law,
'*Que ça est bon! Ah goutez ça!*
That Jelly's rich, this Malmsey healing,
Pray dip your Whiskers and your Tail in'.
Was ever such a happy Swain?
He stuffs and swills, and stuffs again.
'I'm quite asham'd – 'tis mighty rude
To eat so much – but all's so good.
I have a thousand thanks to give –
My Lord alone knows how to live'.
    No sooner said, but from the Hall
Rush Chaplain, Butler, Dogs and all:
'A Rat, a Rat! clap to the door' –
The Cat comes bouncing on the floor.
O for the Heart of Homer's Mice,
Or Gods to save them in a trice!
(It was by Providence, they think,
For your damn'd Stucco has no chink)
'An't please your Honour, quoth the Peasant,
This same Dessert is not so pleasant:
Give me again my hollow Tree!
A Crust of Bread, and Liberty.'   (pub. 1727/pub. 1738)

ALEXANDER POPE

Satire II.1 An imitation

Compare the close translation by Jonson (pp. 317–21).

To Mr. Fortescue

P. There are (I scarce can think it, but am told)
There are to whom my Satire seems too bold,
Scarce to wise Peter complaisant enough,
And something said of Chartres much too rough.
The Lines are weak, another's pleas'd to say,
Lord Fanny spins a thousand such a Day.
Tim'rous by Nature, of the Rich in awe,
I come to Council learned in the Law.
You'll give me, like a Friend both sage and free,
10   Advice; and (as you use) without a Fee.
   F. I'd write no more.
                    P. Not write? but then I *think*,
And for my Soul I cannot sleep a wink.
I nod in Company, I wake at Night,
Fools rush into my Head, and so I write.
   F. You could not do a worse thing for your Life.
Why, if the Nights seem tedious – take a Wife;
Or rather truly, if your Point be Rest,
Lettuce and Cowslip Wine; *Probatum est*.
But talk with Celsus, Celsus will advise
20   Hartshorn, or something that shall close your Eyes.
Or if you needs must write, write Caesar's Praise:
You'll gain at least a Knighthood, or the Bays.
   P. What? like Sir Richard, rumbling, rough and fierce,
With Arms, and George, and Brunswick crowd the Verse?
Rend with tremendous Sound your ears asunder,
With Gun, Drum, Trumpet, Blunderbuss and Thunder?

Or nobly wild, with Budgell's Fire and Force,
Paint Angels trembling round his falling Horse?
   F. Then all your Muse's softer Art display,
Let Carolina smooth the tuneful Lay,
Lull with Amelia's liquid Name the Nine,
And sweetly flow through all the Royal Line.
   P. Alas! few Verses touch their nicer Ear;
They scarce can bear their Laureate twice a Year:
And justly Caesar scorns the Poet's Lays,
It is to History he trusts for Praise.
   F. Better be Cibber, I'll maintain it still,
Than ridicule all Taste, blaspheme Quadrille,
Abuse the City's best good Men in Metre,
And laugh at Peers that put their Trust in Peter.
Ev'n those you touch not, hate you.
                             P. What should ail 'em?
   F. A hundred smart in Timon and in Balaam:
The fewer still you name, you wound the more;
Bond is but one, but Harpax is a Score.
   P. Each Mortal has his Pleasure: None deny
Scarsdale his Bottle, Darty his Ham-Pye;
Ridotta sips and dances, till she see
The doubling Lustres dance as fast as she;
F— loves the Senate, Hockley-Hole his Brother
Like in all else, as one Egg to another.
I love to pour out all myself, as plain
As downright Shippen, or as old Montagne.
In them, as certain to be lov'd as seen,
The Soul stood forth, nor kept a Thought within;
In me what Spots (for Spots I have) appear,
Will prove at least the Medium must be clear.
In this impartial Glass, my Muse intends
Fair to expose myself, my Foes, my Friends;
Publish the present Age, but where my Text
Is Vice too high, reserve it for the next:

My Foes shall wish my Life a longer date,
And ev'ry Friend the less lament my Fate.

    My Head and Heart thus flowing thro' my Quill,
Verse-man or Prose-man, term me which you will,
Papist or Protestant, or both between,
Like good Erasmus in an honest Mean,
In Moderation placing all my Glory,
While Tories call me Whig, and Whigs a Tory.

    Satire's my Weapon, but I'm too discreet
70 To run a Muck, and tilt at all I meet;
I only wear it in a Land of Hectors,
Thieves, Supercargoes, Sharpers, and Directors.
Save but our Army! and let Jove incrust
Swords, Pikes, and Guns, with everlasting Rust!
Peace is my dear Delight – not Fleury's more:
But touch me, and no Minister so sore.
Who-e'er offends, at some unlucky Time
Slides into Verse, and hitches in a Rhyme,
Sacred to Ridicule! his whole Life long,
80 And the sad Burthen of some merry Song.

    Slander or Poyson, dread from Delia's Rage,
Hard Words or Hanging, if your Judge be Page.
From furious Sappho scarce a milder Fate,
P—x'd by her Love, or libell'd by her Hate:
Its proper Pow'r to hurt, each Creature feels,
Bulls aim their horns, and Asses lift their heels,
'Tis a Bear's Talent not to kick, but hug,
And no man wonders he's not stung by Pug:
So drink with Waters, or with Chartres eat,
90 They'll never poison you, they'll only cheat.

    Then learned Sir! (to cut the Matter short)
What-e'er my Fate, or well or ill at Court,
Whether old Age, with faint, but chearful Ray,
Attends to gild the Evening of my Day,
Or Death's black Wing already be display'd
To wrap me in the Universal Shade;

Whether the darken'd Room to muse invite,
Or whiten'd Wall provoke the Skew'r to write,
In Durance, Exile, Bedlam, or the Mint,
100 Like Lee or Budgell, I will Rhyme and Print.
　　F. Alas young Man! your Days can ne'r be long,
In Flow'r of Age you perish for a Song!
Plums, and Directors, Shylock and his Wife,
Will club their Testers, now, to take your Life!
　　P. What? arm'd for Virtue when I point the Pen,
Brand the bold Front of shameless, guilty Men,
Dash the proud Gamester in his gilded Car,
Bare the mean Heart that lurks beneath a Star;
Can there be wanting to defend Her Cause,
110 Lights of the Church, or Guardians of the Laws?
Could pension'd Boileau lash in honest Strain
Flatt'rers and Bigots ev'n in Louis' Reign?
Could Laureate Dryden Pimp and Fry'r engage,
Yet neither Charles nor James be in a Rage?
And I not strip the Gilding off a Knave,
Un-plac'd, un-pension'd, no Man's Heir, or Slave?
I will, or perish in the gen'rous Cause.
Hear this, and tremble! you, who 'scape the Laws.
Yes, while I live, no rich or noble knave
120 Shall walk the World, in credit, to his grave.
To VIRTUE ONLY and HER FRIENDS, A FRIEND,
The World beside may murmur, or commend.
Know, all the distant Din that World can keep
Rolls o'er my Grotto, and but sooths my Sleep.
There, my Retreat the best Companions grace,
Chiefs, out of War, and Statesmen, out of Place.
There St John mingles with my friendly Bowl,
The Feast of Reason and the Flow of Soul:
And He, whose Lightning pierc'd th' Iberian Lines,
130 Now, forms my Quincunx, and now ranks my Vines,
Or tames the Genius of the stubborn Plain,
Almost as quickly, as he conquer'd Spain.

>   Envy must own, I live among the Great,
> No Pimp of Pleasure, and no Spy of State,
> With Eyes that pry not, Tongue that ne'er repeats,
> Fond to spread Friendships, but to cover Heats,
> To help who want, to forward who excel;
> This, all who know me, know; who love me, tell;
> And who unknown defame me, let them be
> Scriblers or Peers, alike are Mob to me.
> This is my Plea, on this I rest my Cause –
> What saith my Council learned in the Laws?
>   *F.* Your Plea is good. But still I say, beware!
> Laws are explain'd by Men – so have a care.
> It stands on record that in Richard's Times
> A Man was hang'd for very honest Rhymes.
> Consult the Statute: *quart.* I think it is,
> *Edwardi Sext.* or *prim. & quint. Eliz*:
> See Libels, Satires – here you have it – read.
>   *P.* Libels and Satires! lawless Things indeed!
> But grave Epistles, bringing Vice to light,
> Such as a King might read, a Bishop write,
> Such as Sir Robert would approve –
>
>   *F.* Indeed?
> The Case is alter'd – you may then proceed.
> In such a Cause the Plaintiff will be hiss'd,
> My Lords the Judges laugh, and you're dismiss'd.   (pub. 1733)

(lines 140, 150)

GEORGE OGLE (1704–1746)

Ogle was a gentleman classicist and translator from Greek and Latin. Horace's satire is a travesty of the dialogue in Book XI of the *Odyssey* between Odysseus and Tiresias in Hades. Returning home poor, Odysseus wants to know how to become rich again. Ogle's version, like Oldham's of Satire I.9, is full of free invention, sometimes answering to nothing in the Latin.

Satire II.5 Here abridged

Of Legacy-Hunting
A Dialogue between Sir Walter Raleigh, and Merlin the Prophet

Sir Walter Raleigh. Indulge this Favor, Merlin, and impart,
As once before, the Secrets of thy Art.
Teach me the Means my Losses to repair —
But why that Smile? — 'Tis no such trivial Care.
    Merlin. Is't not enough, that rescued from the Main,
You tread your native Soil? The Land of Gain!
Here, can you fail, your Coffers to refill?
A Man of your Accomplishment and Skill!
    Sir W. R. Unerring Seer! My wretched State behold,
10 Distress'd, abandon'd, just as you foretold.
My Country claim'd my Studies and my Toils;
And late Posterity shall reap the Spoils.
Yet see me plunder'd by rapacious Hands,
Of Furniture, of Stock, of Houses, Lands.
And, What is Virtue, Valor, Genius, Race,
What better, without Wealth, than tarnish'd Lace?
    Mer. Well! Poverty you dread without Disguise,
Then listen, where the Road to Fortune lies.
Possess you ought, or wonderful, or rare,
20 Send it your old rich Neighbour; pass it there.
If Grape or Melon your small Garden yields,
If Hare or Partridge traverses your Fields,
Quick let them follow; thus begin to hoard,
A surer Way, than Lending to the Lord!
Payments of Heav'n come late. Nor think it odd —
Still offer to the Rich, before thy God.
If but his Bags are equal to his Years,
No Matter, tho' the Pillory claim his Ears;
His guilty Hand, tho' distant India plead,
30 Skill'd in all Poisons of the learned Mead;

SATIRE II.5 · GEORGE OGLE

Tho' basely got, and yet more basely bred;
Tho' Tyburn stands defrauded of his Head;
No Matter! at his Beck, sit, walk, or stand,
And be the outward 'Squire of his Left Hand.

Sir W. R. I, meanly stoop to ev'ry Fool or Knave;
Wont to oppose the Great, and check the Brave!
I, that bold Truths at Risque of Life maintain'd,
With Cecil, Essex, when Eliza reign'd.

Mer. Oh! if this Task, too haughty to endure,
40 'Tis in your Choice, live honorably poor!

Sir W. R. Well! I will curb the Soul within my Breast,
And bear this Hardship as I bore the rest.
But say, O Merlin, say, my best Divine,
Where, quickly, may I raise this golden Mine?

Mer. Know (to begin again where I began)
The Man of Policy should prey on Man.
The Shoal of Batchelors with glitt'ring Gills
Observe, and slily angle at their Wills.
Tho' one, or two, of penetrating Look,
50 May nibble at the Bait, and fly the Hook;
Quit not thy Hope, nor of thy Art despair,
Others shall swallow down a Length of Hair.

Frequent the Courts, Prerogative and Hall;
Inquire, 'What Cause has Clerk? What Plea has Paul?
Who are the Parties? When the Merit's try'd?'
And lift you on the beneficial Side.
If one be rich, and rich without an Heir,
Advance thy genuin Proof, and boldly swear.
Mind not or whence, or what be the Dispute,
60 Tho' some litigious Villain rais'd the Suit;
No Favor let the injur'd Party claim,
Tho' Man of Probity, tho' Man of Fame;
Thy Care he forfeits by his Choice of Life;
If he has healthy Child, or breeding Wife.

This done; proceed your Service to inforce,
And oil his tender Ear with soft Discourse.

Never direct to Master, but to 'Squire,
For what we want the most, we most admire.
Now call him, my Sweet Sir, now, good my Lord,
70 But let your Honour be the plainest Word.
For Compliments, tho' blunder'd or misplac'd,
Like high-forc'd Sauces, please the vitious Taste.
He'll never see your indirecter View,
And, tho' he has no Title, 'tis his Due.

    Then warmly swear, or solemnly protest,
'Cou'd your Eyes penetrate my naked Breast,
There you might read these Characters engrav'd,
That, by your Virtues I am bound! inslav'd!
I know the double Windings of the Laws,
80 No Man alive can better serve your Cause;
Leave it, Dear Sir, but leave it to my Care,
I'd lose both Eyes, e're you should lose a Hair;
E're you shou'd prove at last the publick Sport,
Or stand the Loss of being cast in Court.
No Sir! Enjoy your Pleasure, and your Wealth,
86 Go Home, and take your Ease; and mind your Health!' . . .

101   Yet the same beaten Path not always run;
Try some old Father of one sickly Son.
Lest your Pursuit of Batchelors get vent,
And you grow noted as the Priest on Trent.
Slow, as obsequious, yet as sure as slow,
Thro' all Degrees of his Devises go;
Till, after his weak Boy, and Issue Male,
At last he names you, second in Intail;
Then when the Youth (no doubt) shall run his Race,
110 With easy Slide you fill his vacant Place:
Millions have profited by this Device;
There is no surer Cast in all the Dice!

    If any Dotard, where these Arts succeed,
Gives his last Will and Testament to read;

SATIRE II.5 · GEORGE OGLE

      To read the Notice of his Death, deny!
      Yet course it with the Corner of an Eye!
      Mark the Round Letters, the Proviso Lines;
      Three Looks will certify what he enjoins;
      If common, or particular his Care;
120   Whether he leaves you joint, or single Heir.
      Let this be acted with a passive Hand;
122   And ev'ry Muscle of your Face command . . .

159   Have you digested what was giv'n before?
160   Then to the former add one Precept more.
      Observe the Servants of thy Friend decay'd,
      The leading Footman, or the fav'rite Maid;
      Court all or any of the menial Crew,
      If they but know the Measure of his Shoe;
      Her Honesty, his Diligence commend,
      And florish on these Topics, while they tend.
      Their Int'rest serv'd, your Int'rest they will raise,
      And, in your Absence, pay you Praise for Praise.
        'Tis something, Inch by Inch to gain your Ground,
170   And win the Outworks which the Fort surround;
      With Safety hence your Forces may be led,
      But let your strong Attack be at the Head.
      Discover where his ruling Foible lies,
      And how, and when to enter by Surprise.
      Loves he his own dull Verses to repeat,
      That creep or hobble on unequal Feet;
      Admire their Flow! Be lavish of thy Tropes!
      Swear they transcend all Dryden's, and all Pope's!
      If to Intrigue his Inclination turns;
180   Then watch the Crisis when the Fever burns.
      Wait not his Asking. No, his Wish prevent,
      And be thy own lov'd Raleigh freely lent.
        Sir W.R. Raleigh! Of virtuous Wives the standing Rule!
      Turn Prostitute to ev'ry Knave or Fool!

Who to her Lord, in other Worlds detain'd,
For Years inviolable Faith maintain'd;
And, when return'd he felt the Hands of Power,
Greatly forsook the Palace for the Tower!
   Mer. Those were rude Manners of Eliza's Age,
190 E're Youths yet learn'd with Presents to engage.
When Lovers, who to widow'd Wives drew near,
Sought little Venery, but much good Chear;
Unknown, the Party square, or private Treat:
Their Bent, not half so strong to court, as eat.
Hence mere Oeconomy, averse to Waste,
First made her frugal, and then kept her chaste.
But had she tasted once the rich and old,
Who what they fail in Love supply in Gold;
Raleigh herself had never left the Scent,
200 And you, to share the Prey, had liv'd content.
Staunch as a Hound new-blooded to the Sport,
Ev'n she had drove the Chace thro' Town and Court;
Where many a Wife of Industry adorns
204 Her patient Knight or Peer, with gilded Horns . . .

247 But when the End of all thy Cares appears,
Thy long Servility of Hopes and Fears;
When the brib'd Lawyer lodges in thy Hands,
250 'To Raleigh, Half of all my Goods and Lands' –
Then, broad awake, his hapless Death deplore,
And cry, with Budgel, 'Is he then no more?'
Or, in a later Strain, 'where shall I find
A Friend so good, so singularly kind!'
Then, all the Pow'r of Artifice imploy,
To mask the Countenance discov'ring Joy;
And, if 'tis possible to drive so near,
Stop the broad Grin, and squeeze a little Tear.
   Is the last Charge committed to thy Care?
260 Tho', in thy Soul a Miser, nothing spare.

On the best feather'd Undertaker fix;
Let his Hearse lead the Twentieth Coach-and-Six.
Let Fifty, on a Side, the sable Bands
Attend, with golden Truncheons in their Hands.
Let not his House the signal Hatchment lack,
Put ev'ry Servant, to the Boy, in black.
Black, as his Will, let mourning Rings be sent
To all his Friends, to his next Heirs present.
This Generosity shall blaze thee forth,
270 And the World own, you are a Man of Worth.
    One Caution more e're yet you leave the Stage,
Is your Co-partner more advanc'd in Age?
Plagued with a Cough, or dry comsumptive Wheeze?
Marks him for Death some slow but sure Disease?
Offer the Lodge not far from Lincoln Down;
"Tis yours for one conditionary Crown;
My Lawyer shall release it without Fees;
Or take the Welch Estate, or what you please.'
    But hold! Adieu! I hear th' infernal Bell;
280 Imperious Satan calls me back to Hell.
We sit in Council there on Markham's Will –
Observe these Maxims, and be wealthy still.   (pub. 1737)

PHILIP FRANCIS

Satire I.6, lines 45–131 Addressed to Maecenas

61   As for myself, a Freed-man's Son confest,
A Freed-man's Son, the public Scorn and Jest,
That now with you I joy the social Hour,
That once a Roman Legion own'd my Power;
But though they envy'd my Command in War
Justly perhaps, yet sure 'tis different far

To gain your Friendship, where no servile Art,
Where only Men of Merit, claim a Part.
Nor yet to Chance this Happiness I owe;
70 Friendship like your's she had not to bestow.
My best-lov'd Virgil first, then Varius told
Among my Friends what Character I hold:
When introduc'd, in few and faultring Words
(Such as an infant Modesty affords)
I did not tell you my Descent was great,
Or that I wander'd round my Country Seat
On a proud Steed in richer Pastures bred:
But what I really was I frankly said.

Short was your Answer, in your usual Strain;
80 I take my Leave, nor wait on you again,
Till, nine Months past, engag'd and bid to hold
A Place among your nearer Friends enroll'd.
An Honour this, methinks of nobler Kind,
That innocent of Heart and pure of Mind,
Though with no titled Birth, I gain'd his Love,
Whose Judgment can discern, whose Choice approve.

If some few, trivial Faults deform my Soul
(Like a fair Face when spotted with a Mole)
If none with Avarice justly brand my Fame
90 With Sordidness, or Deeds too vile to name:
If pure and innocent: if dear (forgive
These little Praises) to my Friends I live,
My Father was the Cause, who, though maintain'd
By a lean Farm but poorly, yet disdain'd
The Country-Schoolmaster, to whose low Care
The mighty Captain sent his high-born Heir
With Satchel, Copy-book, and Pelf to pay
The wretched Teacher on th' appointed Day.

To Rome by this bold Father was I brought
100 To learn those Arts, which well-born Youth are taught,
So drest and so attended, you would swear
I was some wealthy Lord's expensive Heir;

SATIRE I.6, LINES 45–131 · PHILIP FRANCIS

    Himself my Guardian, of unblemish'd Truth,
Among my Tutors would attend my Youth,
And thus preserv'd my Chastity of Mind
(That prime of Virtue in its highest Kind)
Not only pure from Guilt, but even the Shame,
That might with vile Suspicion hurt my Fame;
Nor fear'd to be reproach'd, although my Fate
Should fix my Fortune in some meaner State,
From which some trivial Perquisites arise,
Or make me, like himself, Collector of Excise.
   For this my Heart far from complaining pays
A larger Debt of Gratitude and Praise;
Nor, while my Senses hold, shall I repent
Of such a Father, nor with Pride resent,
As many do, th' involuntary Disgrace,
Not to be born of an illustrious Race,
But not with theirs my Sentiments agree,
Or Language; for if nature should decree,
That we from any stated Point might live
Our former Years, and to our Choice should give
The Sires, to whom we wish'd to be allied,
Let others chuse to gratify their Pride:
While I, contented with my own, resign
The titled Honours of an antient Line.
This may be Madness in the People's Eyes,
But in your Judgment not, perhaps, unwise;
That I refuse to bear a Pomp of State,
Unus'd and much unequal to the Weight.
   Instant a larger Fortune must be made,
To purchase Votes my low Addresses paid;
Whether a Jaunt or Journey I propose
With me a Croud of new Companions goes,
While, anxious to compleat a Length of Train,
Domestics, Horses, Coaches I maintain.
But now as Chance or Pleasure is my Guide,
Upon my bob-tail'd Mule alone I ride.

Gall'd in his Crupper with my Wallet's Weight;
140 His Shoulder shews his Rider's aukward Seat.
    Yet no penurious Vileness e'er shall stain
My Name, as when, great Praetor, with your Train
Of five poor Slaves, you carry where you dine
Your travelling Kitchen, and your Flask of Wine.
    Thus have I greater Blessings in my Power,
Than you, proud Senator, and thousands more.
Alone I wander, as by Fancy led,
I cheapen Herbs, or ask the Price of Bread;
I listen, while Diviners tell their Tale,
150 Then homeward hasten to my frugal Meal,
Herbs, Pulse, and Pancakes; each a separate Plate:
While three Domestics at my Supper wait.
A Bowl on a white Marble Table stands,
Two Goblets, and a Ewer to wash my Hands;
An hallow'd Cup of true Campanian Clay
My pure Libations to the Gods to pay.
I then retire to Rest, nor anxious fear
Before dread Marsyas early to appear,
Whose very Statue swears it cannot brook
160 The Meanness of that slave-born Judge's Look.
I sleep till ten; then take a Walk, or chuse
A Book, perhaps, or trifle with the Muse:
For chearful Exercise and manly Toil
Anoint my Body with the pliant Oil,
But not with such as Natta's, when he vamps
His filthy Limbs, and robs the public Lamps.
    But when the Sun pours down his fiercer Fire,
And bids me from the toilsome Sport retire,
I haste to bathe and decently regale
170 My craving Stomach with a frugal Meal;
Enough to nourish Nature for a Day,
Then trifle my Domestic Hours away.

    Such is the Life from bad Ambition free;
Such Comfort has the Man low-born like me;
With which I feel myself more truly blest,
Than if my Sires the Quaestor's Power possest.   (pub. 1747)

WILLIAM COWPER

Satire I.5, omitting lines 51–70

The Journey to Brundusium

'Twas a long Journey lay before us,
When I and honest Heliodorus,
(Who far in Point of Rhetoric
Surpasses every living Greek),
Each leaving our respective Home,
Together sally'd forth from Rome.
    First at Aricia we alight,
And there refresh, and pass the Night.
Our Entertainment? rather coarse
10 Than sumptuous, but I've met with worse.
    Thence o'er the Causeway, soft and fair,
To Appii-forum we repair.
But as this Road is well supply'd
(Temptation strong!) on either Side
With Inns commodious, snug and warm,
We split the Journey, and perform
In two Days time, what's often done
By brisker Travellers in one.
    Here rather chusing not to sup
20 Than with bad Water mix my Cup,
After a warm Debate, in spite
Of a provoking Appetite,

SATIRE I.5, OMITTING LINES 51—70 · WILLIAM COWPER

    I sturdily resolve at last
To balk it, and pronounce a Fast;
And, in a moody Humour, wait
While my less dainty Comrades bait.
    Now o'er the spangled Hemisphere
Diffus'd, the starry Train appear,
When there arose a desperate Brawl;
30 The Slaves and Bargemen, one and all,
Rending their Throats (have Mercy on us!)
As if they were resolv'd to stun us.
'Steer the Barge this Way to the Shore!'
'I tell you, we'll admit no more —
Plague! will you never be content!'
Thus a whole Hour at least is spent,
While they receive the several Fares,
And kick the Mule into his Gears.
Happy! these Difficulties past,
40 Could we have fall'n asleep at last;
But, what with humming, croaking, biting,
Gnats, Frogs, and all their Plagues uniting,
These tuneful Natives of the Lake
Conspir'd to keep us broad awake.
Besides, to make the Concert full,
Two maudlin Wights, exceeding dull,
The Bargeman and a Passenger,
Each in his Turn essay'd an Air
In Honour of his absent Fair.
50 At length, the Passenger, opprest
With Wine, left off, and snor'd the rest.
The weary Bargeman too gave o'er,
And, hearing his Companion snore,
Seiz'd the Occasion, fix'd the Barge,
Turn'd out his Mule to graze at large,
And slept, forgetful of his Charge.
    And now the Sun, o'er Eastern Hill,
Discover'd that our Barge stood still;

When one, whose Anger vex'd him sore,
60 With Malice fraught, leaps quick on Shore;
Plucks up a Stake; with many a Thwack
Assails the Mule and Driver's Back.

   Then, slowly moving on, with Pain,
At ten, Feronia's Stream we gain,
And in her pure and glassy Wave
Our Hands and Faces gladly lave.
Climbing three Miles, fair Anxur's Height
We reach, with stony Quarries white.

   While here, as was agreed, we wait,
70 'Till, charg'd with Business of the State,
Maecenas and Cocceius come,
(The Messengers of Peace) from Rome;
My Eyes, by watry Humours blear
And sore, I with black Balsam smear.
At length they join us, and with them
Our worthy Friend Fonteius came;
A Man of such complete Desert,
Antony lov'd him at his Heart.

   At Fundi we refus'd to bait,
80 And laugh'd at vain Aufidius' State;
A Praetor now (a Scribe before)
The purple-border'd Robe he wore;
His Slave the smoking Censer bore.

   Tir'd, at Muraena's we repose
At Formia; sup at Capito's.

   With Smiles the rising Morn we greet;
At Sinuessa pleas'd to meet
With Plotius, Varius, and the Bard,
Whom Mantua first with Wonder heard.
90 The World no purer Spirits knows,
For none my Heart more warmly glows.
O what Embraces we bestow'd,
And with what Joy our Breasts o'erflow'd!
Sure, while my Sense is sound and clear,
Long as I live, I shall prefer

A gay, good-natur'd, easy Friend
To every Blessing Heaven can send!
   At a small Village, the next Night,
Near the Vulturnus we alight;
100 Where, as employ'd on State Affairs,
We were supply'd by the Purvey'rs
Frankly at once, and without Hire,
With Food for Man and Horse, and Fire.
   Capua, next Day, betimes we reach,
Where Virgil and myself, who each
Labour'd with different Maladies,
His such a Stomach, mine such Eyes,
As would not bear strong Exercise,
In drowsy Mood to Sleep resort;
110 Maecenas to the Tennis-court . . .

158   To Beneventum next we steer,
Where our good Host, by over-care
160 In roasting Thrushes, lean as Mice,
Had almost fall'n a Sacrifice.
The Kitchen soon was all on Fire,
And to the Roof the Flames aspire.
There might you see each Man and Master
Striving, amidst this sad Disaster,
To save the Supper – then they came
With Speed enough to quench the Flame.
   From hence we first at Distance see
Th' Apulian Hills, well known to Me,
170 Parch'd by the sultry Western Blast,
And which we never should have past,
Had not Trivicus, by the Way,
Receiv'd us at the Close of Day:
But each was forc'd, at entering here,
To pay the Tribute of a Tear;
For more of Smoke than Fire was seen,
The Hearth was pil'd with Logs so green.

From hence in Chaises we were carry'd
Miles twenty-four, and gladly tarry'd
At a small Town, whose Name my Verse
(So barbarous is it!) can't rehearse.
Know it you may by many a Sign;
Water is dearer far than Wine;
Their Bread is deem'd such dainty Fare,
That every prudent Traveller
His Wallet loads with many a Crust;
For, at Canusium, you might just
As well attempt to gnaw a Stone,
As think to get one Morsel down.
That too with scanty Streams is fed:
Its Founder was brave Diomed.
Good Varius (ah! that Friends must part!)
Here left us all with aching Heart.

At Rubi we arriv'd that Day,
Well jaded by the Length of Way;
And sure poor Mortals ne'er were wetter.
Next Day, no Weather could be better,
No Roads so bad; we scarce could crawl
Along to fishy Barium's Wall.

Th' Egnatians next, who, by the Rules
Of Common-sense, are Knaves or Fools,
Made all our Sides with Laughter heave;
Since we with them must needs believe
That Incense in their Temples burns,
And, without Fire, to Ashes turns.
To Circumcision's Bigots tell
Such Tales. For Me, I know full well
That in high Heaven, unmov'd by Care,
The Gods eternal Quiet share;
Nor can I deem their Spleen the Cause
Why fickle Nature breaks her Laws.

Brundusium last we reach, and there
Stop short the Muse and Traveller.

(pub. 1759)

FRANCIS HOWES (1776–1844)

Educated at Trinity College, Cambridge, held various curacies and in 1815 became a minor canon of Norwich Cathedral. He translated the *Satires* of Persius in 1809, and his *Epodes, Satires and Epistles* of Horace appeared in 1845. Conington in the 1860s described Howes' Horace as 'forgotten but highly meritorious', praising the 'unforced, idiomatic, and felicitous' quality of the writing. Buried today in still deeper oblivion.

Satire I.1

Whence comes it, dear Maecenas, that we find
Each to applaud his neighbour's lot inclined –
Each to repine at that which chance has thrown
Into his lap, or choice ordain'd his own?
Blest is the merchant's fate, the soldier cries,
As bow'd with years the toilsome march he plies:
Again, the merchant tost by storms at sea
Exclaims, – *The soldier's is the life for me;*
For why – the trumpet summons to the fray,
10 *And death or glory quickly crowns the day.*
The lawyer, when ere cock-crow at his gate
Loud clients knock, applauds the peasant's fate:
Dragg'd from the country by a writ, the clown
Swears none are blest but those that dwell in town.
So many like examples wait our call,
Scarce prating Fabius could recount them all.
   But (not to tire myself and you) 'twere best
At once to bring the matter to the test.
Suppose some god should cry, 'Lo, it shall be
20 Ev'n as ye list: you, soldier, off to sea!
You, lawyer, go and plough! advance, retire,
Change sides, and be at last what ye desire!'

Why all draw back! – Was ever whim like this? –
Retract their wishes, and renounce their bliss!
What hinders but that Jove, with burly scowl
(As limners paint him) and inflated jowl,
In vengeance swear, that never will he deign
A patient hearing to such suits again?
    But, not to treat my subject as in jest –
30 (Albeit why may not truth in smiles be drest,
As gentle teachers lure the child to come
And learn his horn-book, with a sugar plum?) –
Joking apart – he that with restless toil
Urges his ploughshare through the stubborn soil,
This tapster-like retailer of the laws,
This veteran champion of his country's cause,
And this stout seaman who in quest of gain
Unfurls his sail and braves the boisterous main,
All with one view profess to labour on –
40 That, when at last the spring of life is gone
And strength declines, of ample stores possest
They may retire to competence and rest.
'So the small ant' (the precedent they plead),
'Patient of toil and provident of need,
Drags in her mouth whatever spoil she meets,
And adds it to her stock of hoarded sweets.'
    Yet that same ant, when wintry clouds appear,
And grim December's blasts deform the year,
Creeps not from home; but temperately wise
50 Unlocks her hoard and feeds on her supplies:
While *you* nor summer's heat nor winter's cold
Can tear asunder from the search of gold;
Fire, water, steel must yield to sordid pelf,
'Till not a wretch is wealthier than yourself.
Say, what avails it thus to drudge and sweat
For all the gold and silver you can get, –
And, when the silver and the gold are found,
To delve a pit and hide them underground?

The heap, once touch'd, soon dwindles to an end.
But wherefore was it heap'd, unless to spend?
Ten thousand coombs are thresh'd upon your floor; —
What follows? not that you can *eat* the more.
Thus, were it yours to bear upon your head
Amid a train of slaves the sack of bread,
Not one loaf more would to your portion fall
Than to the rest who carried none at all.
Whoe'er to nature's wants conforms his will,
Say, what imports it whether that man till
Ten — or ten thousand — rood? *A pleasure lies*
In drawing what one wants from large supplies.
This we can draw, too, from our humbler store;
And what can all your granaries do more?
As if you should of water clear and sweet
Need but a pitcher-full (while at your feet
Bubbled a spring) and say, 'My cup I'll fill
From yon deep river, not from this poor rill.'
So shall the slippery bank your foot betray,
And you by Aufidus be swept away;
While he, who wisely studies to confine
His wishes there, where nature draws the line,
Quaffs pure his beverage from the fountain's side,
Nor tempts the perils of the boisterous tide.

Yet thousands, duped by avarice in disguise,
Intrench themselves in maxims sage and wise.
Go on, they say, *and hoard up all you can;*
For wealth is worth, and money makes the man!
What shall we say to such? Since 'tis their will
Still to be wretched, let them be so still! —
Self-curst as that same miser must have been,
Who lived at Athens, rich as he was mean, —
Who, when the people hiss'd, would turn about
And drily thus accost the rabble-rout:
'Hiss on; I heed you not, ye saucy wags,
While self-applauses greet me o'er my bags.'

Poor Tantalus attempts in vain to sip
The flattering stream that mocks his thirsty lip.
You smile, as if the story were not true!
Change but the name, and it applies to *you*.
O'er countless heaps in nicest order stored
100 You pore agape, and gaze upon the hoard,
As relicks to be laid with reverence by,
Or pictures only meant to please the eye.

With all your cash, you seem not yet to know
Its proper use, or what it can bestow!
"Twill buy me herbs, a loaf, a pint of wine, –
All, which denied her, Nature would repine.'
But what are *your* indulgencies? All day,
All night, to watch and shudder with dismay,
Lest ruffians fire your house, or slaves by stealth
110 Rifle your coffers, and abstract your wealth?
If this be affluence – this her boasted fruit,
Of all such joys may I live destitute!

'Yet if a cold' (you urge) 'or aching head
Or other ill confine you to your bed,
With wealth you'll never want some faithful friend
Or civil neighbour, zealous to attend,
Sit by you, mix your cordials, and request
The doctor to beware and do his best, –
Your precious health, if possible, restore,
120 And give you to your weeping friends once more.'

Vain thought! for you nor daughter, son, nor wife
Puts up the prayer, or cares about your life.
Relations and acquaintance, great and small,
Female and male, despise – detest you all.
Nor wonder if, while gold is all your care,
That love, you feel not, neither must you share.
But if you think to win, by wealth alone,
The love of them whom nature made your own,
'Tis labor lost, – as if one strove to train
130 The ass to prance and curvet to the rein.

Push not your wishes then to this excess;
But, as you have the more, fear want the less.
You are what once you wish'd: – then wisely cease
All further trouble, and repose in peace:
Lest the same doom be yours, which, as we're told,
Befel a rich curmudgeon once of old,
Possest (my tale is short) of so much treasure
That he could count it only by the measure;
And yet withal so eager still to save,
140   He drest, he fared, scarce better than a slave, –
Nay, to his death was haunted with the dread
Of want and beggary hanging o'er his head.
At last a wench of true *Tyndarid* vein
Took up an axe and clave the churl in twain.
    But must I waste, like Naevius, my estate?
Like Nomentanus, live a profligate? –
Why deal in such extremes? what need to place
These opposite excesses face to face?
I blame the niggard; but it follows not
150   That I commend the rake-hell and the sot.
Much as they differ, Tanais I admire
As little as I do Visellius' fire.
Some bound there ever is, some rule of right,
Which parts each error from its opposite:
Folly and vice on either side are seen,
While justice, truth, and virtue lie between.
    Thus – (to revert to what was said at first) –
All view their own condition as the worst;
And, meanly envious of another's lot,
160   Scorn what they have and praise what they have not.
If but some luckier neighbour's ewes or kine
Yield more than theirs, they murmur and repine:
And, while insatiate avarice bids them pant
First one and then another to supplant,
However rich, some richer still they find,
Toil after *them*, nor heed the poor behind.

          So in the race, when starting from the bar
          The furious coursers urge the rapid car,
          To pass the next on speeds the charioteer,
170   Disdaining him that lingers in the rear.
          Hence few are found, who dying can declare
          That theirs was comfort unalloy'd with care;
          Or, rising from life's banquet, quit their seat,
          Like cheerful guests, contented with the treat.
              But hold! – You'll think I've pillaged the scrutoir
          Of blear Crispinus: – Not one word then more!   (pub. 1845)

Satire I.4

Horace discursively defends his satires, discusses the proper stylistic level of the genre (nearer prose than poetry), and traces its descent from the Greek comic poets and the older Roman writer Lucilius, whose slapdash composition he criticizes. The satirist should not be accused of malice; his purpose is not to brand individuals but to point in good-humoured fashion to the social failings of the time – and to his own.

          Cratinus, Eupolis, with some few more
          Who trod the comic stage in days of yore,
          Was there a knave or scoundrel of their time,
          Rake, ruffian, thief – whatever were his crime,
          On him their honest indignation hurl'd,
          And lash'd with freedom a licentious world.
              Close to their steps and studious of their fame,
          His numbers different – but his scope the same,
          Lucilius follow'd, skill'd in taunts severe
10   To point at trembling vice the caustic jeer.
          Yet, with address and pleasantry enough,
          His style was awkward and his verses rough.
          For all his pride unhappily was plac'd
          In this – that what he wrote, he wrote with haste;

And had, while standing on one foot, the power
To spin his lines two hundred in the hour.
No wonder sure, if such a rapid flood
Bore in its current no small share of mud:
No wonder if the hand, which only cared
20 For writing fast, wrote much that might be spared.
The toil of writing well is death to such:
Yet, if not *well*, what matters it *how much*?

    See, bold Crispinus boasts such fluent ease,
He'll write a race with me for what I please!
'Come on! Take you your tablets,' he will say,
'And I'll take mine; appoint your place and day:
Let umpires watch us both; and let us try
Which can compose the faster – you or I.'

    Thanks to my stars that made me of a mind
30 To brawls and babbling never much inclined, –
Patient and poor in spirit, slow to boast,
And oft, when most contemn'd, contented most!
Go on then, ye that list, to give free vent
To every thought within your bosoms pent!
Go, ape the blacksmith's leathern lungs that blow
Till the fused mass in ruddy current flow.
Blest Fannius, whose kind friends, unask'd, combine
To bear his bust and books to Phoebus' shrine,
The world applauding! – while, whate'er I write,
40 Before that world I tremble to recite, –
Aware that satire suits not gentle ears,
And each man hates it – because each man fears.

    Pick me a man at random from the throng; –
My life upon't, there's something in him wrong:
Base envy sours him, or ambition fires;
He burns with lawless love or worse desires;
Or pines the sculptured silver to amass,
Or dotes with Albius on Corinthian brass;
Or traffics from the climes of orient day
50 To realms that glow beneath the setting ray:

See how from port to port, from shore to shore,
Urged headlong by the restless thirst of more, –
And, tho' still saving, eager still to save, –
Like dust before the wind, he skims the wave!
No wonder sure if these and such as these
The poet and his verse alike displease.

    Like a mad bull, they shun him thro' the streets;
'Beware,' they cry: 'he butts at all he meets!
And, if he can but let his spleen o'erflow,
60 The spiteful creature spares nor friend nor foe:
Besides, whate'er he once has written down,
He's wretched 'till 'tis known to half the town,
And at the baker's shop or public well
Men – women – boys the witty slander tell.'

    A few plain words in my defence I claim:
First from the list of *Poets* strike my name.
For not the merely smooth and flowing line –
Much less such loose pedestrian verse as mine –
Confers that title. No – the *Bard* is he
70 Who boasts a genius bold, creative, free;
Whose fancy, when diviner thoughts inspire,
Springs up aloft to soar on wings of fire;
Whose words in more than mortal accents roll,
And echo back the greatness of his soul.

    Hence some have doubted if 'twere right to call
The Comic Drama poetry at all;
Since nor its style nor matter is imprest
With that fine rage which fills the poet's breast, –
And, save that all in measured cadence flows,
80 Its diction differs not from simple prose.
'Yet,' you object, 'the father stamps the stage
And rates his son with more than prose-like rage,
When the gay stripling, deaf to wisdom's lore,
Slights the rich heiress for the thriftless whore;
Or staggering forth, 'ere night obscures the sky,
Waves in the open street his torch on high.'

But, were Pomponius' sire his son to see,
Would he not rave and scold as loud as he?
'Tis not enough then merely to inclose
Plain sense in numbers, – which if you transpose,
The words were such as any man might say,
Just like the ranting father in the play.
Take but from mine or old Lucilius' rhime
This regular return of measured time, –
Let every line's arrangement be reversed,
And place the first word last – the last word first;
What's the result? – 'Tis poetry no more,
And therefore was not poetry before.
Not so – *When Discord brake the ponderous bar*
And oped the adamantine gates of War:
Here dislocate – distort him, as you will; –
Tho' piecemeal torn, you see the *Poet* still.

    How far this kind of writing forms or no
A proper poem, we may elsewhere show:
Proceed we now to that more serious head –
How far it forms an object of just dread.
Caprius and Sulcius with their bags and books,
Writs in their hands and gibbets in their looks,
Walk forth and strike, wherever they appear,
The felon and the thief with conscious fear.
Yet he whose hands are pure, who keeps his oath,
Nor wrongs his neighbour, may despise them both.
Now tho' a rogue, like Caelius, you may be,
It follows not that Caprius is like me.
My books on no vile stall or column stand,
Soil'd by Tigellius' and each vulgar hand.
When I recite them (which I seldom do),
'Tis but in private to a friend or two, –

99–100 '*When Discord . . .*' From the early epic poet Ennius

At their request, not of my own free grace, –
120 Not before all, not yet in every place.
I grant that some less delicate there are,
Who spout their poems in the public square, –
Or in the bath, where sweetly floats the sound
Re-echo'd by the vaulted roof around.
Coxcombs, thus eager to obtrude their rhime,
Feel little scruple about place and time.

I write (you tell me) with a base design,
And spiteful rancour dictates every line.
Whence and from whom do these foul charges flow?
130 Can any, that have known me, tell you so?
The wretch who can revile an absent friend,
Or, when reviled, is backward to defend; –
Who thinks ill-nature wit; and, poorly proud
To catch the laughter of a grinning croud,
Bids from his lips the hallow'd secret fly,
Or, when truth fails him, coins the blackening lie:
If such there be, *him*, Romans! it were well
To mark: *his* touch is death, *his* heart is hell!

Go, scan a party but of twelve, reclined
140 Around the genial board, and you shall find
That some more pert and overbearing guest
With saucy jokes bespatters all the rest; –
All but his host, – and him too, when the bowl
Gives licence to the tongue and bares the soul.
Yet he's a boon companion, frank and free;
While every jest is blasphemy in me:
And if perchance I smiling say – *The fop
Rufillus breathes of perfume from the shop,
Gorgonius glories in a goat-like smell,* –
150 Oh! tis such scandal as no tongue can tell!

Mention perhaps is in your presence made
Of him who filch'd the crown from Jove's own head.
Now hear the censor of the' envenom'd page!
Now see him glow with friendship's generous rage!

Not so; he damns, while seeming to defend: —
'Petillius was my very worthy friend;
From early youth I've been his frequent guest,
And many has he served at my request:
So after all he lives, and lives at large; —
Well, 'troth I'm glad; but 'twas an ugly charge.'
Here is the honey'd lip and heart of coal,
The canker-juice and night-shade of the soul.
Now, spite like this, I'll venture to engage,
Ne'er stained my heart, nor e'er shall stain my page.

   But if I jest more freely now and then,
And give a larger licence to my pen,
Some early habits wrought into my frame
Plead my excuse — if not support my claim.
A tender father taught my youthful breast
To mark the vice he wish'd me to detest,
And warn'd me what to shun and what pursue
By holding apt examples to my view.
If he would have me frugally inclined,
Content with what himself could leave behind,
'Look,' he would say, 'at Albius' ruin'd son;
See Barrus by his own excess undone!
An useful lesson this to all young heirs
To guard against extravagance like theirs.'
If he would arm me 'gainst the wanton's eye,
'Take warning from Sectanus,' he would cry;
And that I might not woo the wedded dame,
While safety recommends a sanctioned flame,
'Trebonius,' he would hint, 'kick'd out of doors,
Gain'd little credit by his loose amours.
The lectures of the wise, my son, 'erelong
Will point you out the grounds of right and wrong.
Enough for me if my poor art inspires
Plain rules of life transmitted from our sires,
Which, while you need a guardian, may secure
Your morals chaste, your reputation pure:

When manhood gives your mind a firmer tone,
You'll drop these corks and stem the tide alone.'
  With such monitions providently kind
He moulded to his will my youthful mind:
And if he urged me to a virtue, 'See,
For this you've good authority,' said he;
'Copy that man's example,' – holding forth
Some judge or statesman of acknowledged worth.
If he would frighten me from something base,
200 'Twas then – 'That such things lead but to disgrace
Henceforth you cannot doubt; for mark, my son,
The bad repute of such or such an one.'
Just as a neighbour's funeral passing near
Strikes the sick glutton with a wholesome fear,
So, when it meets the tender stripling's eyes,
Another's shame oft warns him to be wise.
  Well, thanks then to a parent's timely care,
Such crimes as tend to ruin and despair
Taint not my soul. To some small faults indeed,
210 Some venial frailties, guilty still I plead.
And haply these too may in time be brought
To yield to friendly counsel and sage thought:
For, whether on my couch supinely laid
Or sauntering in the public colonnade,
Still to myself some lesson I impart,
And thus in secret commune with my heart:
Here duty points; – this path to comfort tends; –
Thus I may win the' affections of my friends; –
This or that folly be it mine to shun
220 *Taught by the fate of such or such an one.*
  Such are my dumb soliloquies: when time
Permits, I pen them down in sportive rhime;
A practice to be number'd, I allow,
Among those lighter faults I named just now.
But if, extreme to mark what is amiss,
You stoop to censure such a fault as this,

A host of verse-men to my aid I'll call,
(And trust my word, our forces are not small)
Who, like the Jews, if still our sect you slight,
Shall drag you off a trembling proselyte.   (pub. 1845)

Satire I.9

Along the Sacred Street I chanced to stray
Musing I know not what, as is my way,
And wholly wrapt in thought – when up there came
A fellow scarcely known to me by name:
Grasping my hand, 'My dear friend, how d'ye do?
And pray,' he cried, 'how wags the world with you?'
I thank you, passing well, as times go now;
Your servant: – And with that I made my bow.
But finding him still dangle at my sleeve
Without the slightest sign of taking leave,
I turn with cold civility and say –
Any thing further, Sir, with me to-day?
'Nay, truce with this reserve! it is but fit
We two were friends, since I'm a brother-wit.'
Here some dull compliment I stammer'd out,
As, *That, Sir, recommends you much no doubt.*

    Vex'd to the soul and dying to be gone,
I slacken now my pace, now hurry on;
And sometimes halt at once in full career,
Whispering some trifle in my lackey's ear.
But when he still stuck by me as before, –
Sweating with inward spleen at every pore,
Oh! how I long'd to let my passion pass,
And sigh'd, Bolanus, for thy front of brass!

    Meanwhile he keeps up one incessant chat
About the streets, the houses, and all that:
Marking at last my silence – 'Well,' said he,
''Tis pretty plain you're anxious to get free:

But patience, darling Sir! so lately met –
Odslife! I cannot think of parting yet.
Inform me, whither are your footsteps bound?'
To see (but pray don't let me drag you round)
A friend of mine, who lies extremely ill
A mile beyond the bridge, or further still.
'Nay then, come on! I've nothing else to do;
And as to distance, what is that – with *you*!'

On hearing this, quite driven to despair,
Guess what my looks and what my feelings were!
Never did ass upon the public road,
When on his back he felt a double load,
Hang both his ears so dismal and so blank.
'In me, Sir,' he continues, 'to be frank,
You know not what a friend you have in store:
Viscus and Varius will not charm you more.
For as to dancing, who with me can vie?
Or who can scribble verse so fast as I?
Again, in powers of voice so much I shine
Hermogenes himself must envy mine.'

Here for a moment, puff'd with self-applause,
He stopp'd; I took advantage of the pause:
These toils will shorten, sure, your precious life;
Have you no loving mother, friend, or wife
Who takes an interest in your fate? – 'Oh, no;
Thank heaven! they're all disposed of long ago.'

Good luck (thought I), by thee no longer vex'd!
So I, it seems, must be *disposed of* next:
Well, let me but at once resign my breath;
To die by inches thus were worse than death.
Now, now I see the doom approaching near,
Which once was told me by a gossip seer:
While yet a boy, the wrinkled beldame shook
Her urn, and, eyeing me with piteous look,
'Poor lad!' she cried, 'no mischief shalt thou feel
Or from the poison'd bowl or hostile steel;

Nor pricking pleurisy, nor hectic cough,
Nor slow-consuming gout shall take thee off:
'Tis thy sad lot, when grown to man's estate,
To fall the victim of a puppy's prate:
Go, treasure in thy mind the truths I've sung,
And shun, if thou art wise, a chattering tongue.'
  At Vesta's temple we arrived at last;
And now one quarter of the day was past –
When by the greatest luck he had, I found,
To stand a suit, and by the law was bound
Either to answer to the charges brought,
Or else to suffer judgment by default.
'I'm sorry to detain you here,' he cried;
'But might I ask you just to step aside?'
You must excuse me; legs so cramp'd with gout
As mine, I fear, could never stand it out:
Then, may I perish if I've skill or taste
For law; besides, you know I am in haste.
'Faith, now you make me doubtful what to do;
Whether to sacrifice my cause or you.'
Me, by all means, Sir! – me, I beg and pray.
'Not for the world,' cried he, and led the way.
Convinced all further struggle was but vain,
I follow like a captive in his train.
  'Well' – he begins afresh – 'how stand you, Sir,
In the good graces of our Minister?'
His favorites are but few, and those select:
Never was one more nice and circumspect.
'Enough – In all such cases I'm the man
To work my way! In short, to crown your plan,
You need some *second*, master of his art,
To act, d'ye see, a sort of under-part.
Now what is easier? – Do but recommend
Your humble servant to this noble friend; –
And, take my word, the coast we soon should clear,
And you 'erelong monopolize his ear.'

Tush! matters go not there as you suppose;
No roof is purer from intrigues like those:
Think not, if such and such surpass myself
In wealth or wit, I'm laid upon the shelf:
Each has his place assign'd. – 'Why, this is new
And passing strange!' – *Yet not more strange than true.*
'Gods! how you whet my wishes! well, I vow,
I long to know him more than ever now.'
Assail him then; the will is all you need;
With prowess such as yours, you must succeed:
He's not impregnable; but (what is worst)
He knows it, and is therefore shy at first.
'If that's his humour, trust me, I shall spare
No kind of pains to win admittance there:
I'll bribe his porter; if denied to-day,
I'll not desist, but try some other way:
I'll watch occasions – linger in his suite,
Waylay, salute, huzzah him through the street.
Nothing of consequence beneath the sun
Without great labour ever yet was done.'
  Thus he proceeded prattling without end,
When – who should meet us but my worthy friend,
Aristius Fuscus, one who knew the fop
And all his humours: up he comes – we stop.
'Whence now, good Sir, and wither bound?' he cries,
And to like questions, put in turn, replies.
In hopes he'd take the hint and draw me off,
I twitch his listless sleeve – nod – wink – and cough.
He, feigning ign'rance what my signals mean,
With cruel waggery smiles: – I burn with spleen.
  Fuscus (said I), *you mention'd t' other day*
Something particular you wish'd to say
Betwixt ourselves. – 'Perhaps I might: 'tis true:
But never mind; some other time will do:
This is the Jews' grand feast; and I suspect
You'd hardly like to spurn that holy sect.'

Nay, for such scruples, 'troth I feel not any.
'Well, but I do, and, like the vulgar many,
Am rather tender in such points as these:
140 So by and bye of that, Sir, if you please.'
Ah me! that e'er so dark a sun should rise!
Away the pitiless barbarian flies,
And leaves me baffled, half bereft of life,
All at the mercy of the ruthless knife.

With hue and cry the plaintiff comes at last;
'Soho there, sirrah! whither now so fast?
Sir,' – he address'd me – 'You'll bear witness here?'
Aye, that I will, quoth I, and turn'd my ear.
Anon he's dragg'd to court; on either side
150 Loud shouts ensue, and uproar lords it wide:
While I, amid the hurly-burly riot,
Thanks to Apollo's care! walk off in quiet. (pub. 1845)

Satire I.10

Yes, I did say that old Lucilius' song
In rough unmeasur'd numbers halts along:
And who so blindly partial to his verse,
That dares to call Lucilius smooth and terse?
Yet that with ridicule's keen gibe he knew
To lash the town, I gave him honour due.
Let then his humorous talent stand confest;
Still granting this, I must withhold the rest:
For, if mere wit all excellence combine,
10 The farces of Laberius were divine.
'Tis not sufficient with broad mirth to win
The laugh convulsive and distended grin;
And though to set an audience in a roar
Be something, still we look for something more.
'Mid other needfuls brevity we place,
That all your thoughts may flow with ease and grace;

Not wildly rambling, but compact and clear,
Nor clogg'd with words that load the labouring ear.
The style must vary too from grave to gay,
20 Just as the varying subject points the way;
Now rouse the poet's fire, the speaker's art —
Now stoop to act the humourist's lighter part,
Like one who, to give play, retreating cowers,
And purposely puts forth but half his powers:
For oft a smile beyond a frown prevails,
And raillery triumphs where invective fails.
In this the earlier comic bards excel,
In this deserve our imitation well; —
Those wits whom nor Hermogenes the fair
30 Nor that pert jackanapes e'er made his care,
Who only knows Catullus' strains to sing
And troll soft Calvus to the warbling string.

But 'tis alleged, 'that old Lucilius shines
In mingling Greek with Latin in his lines.'
Ye puny pedants! seems it strange to you
What ev'n Pitholeon of Rhodes could do? —
'Yet there's a sweetness in this blended speech
Which neither tongue (say they) apart can reach,
Like that rich zest which nicer tastes discern,
40 In mellow Chian mix'd with rough Falern.'
Talk you of verse alone? Or (let me ask)
Were you engaged in the more arduous task
Of pleading for Petillius, would you speak
A motley brogue, half Latin and half Greek?
And, while our Pedius and Messala toil
In the pure idiom of their native soil,
Spurning your birthright, would you at the Bar
Mix terms outlandish with vernacular, —
And, like Canusium's amphibious sons,
50 Jabber a brace of languages at once?

In early youth, when strong was my desire
With Latian hand to smite the Attic lyre,

Rome's founder, at the hour when dreams are true,
Rose in a vision to my wondering view:
'Horace!' – said he in accents deep and slow,
'Horace! the fruitless enterprise forego:
To swell the host of Grecians were as vain
As adding water to the boundless main.'
Hence, while Alpinus in bombastic line
60 Lays Memnon low and mars the head of Rhine,
These sportive lays I sing, ne'er meant to vie
For ivy crowns 'neath Tarpa's critic eye,
Nor fraught with ribald mirth or tragic rage
Night after night to figure on the stage.

    To paint the lavish stripling's crafty girl
Plotting with Davus to outwit the churl –
This is a branch of art, Fundanius, known
Of modern wits to you and you alone,
Whose pencil to the prattling scene can give
70 The air of truth which bids the picture live:
In stately trimeters proud Pollio sings
The tragic fates of heroes and of kings:
Varius in matchless numbers full and grand
Pours his bold epic with a master's hand;
While every muse that haunts the sylvan plain
Breathes grace and elegance in Virgil's strain.
In Satire only, which with some few more
Varro had tried (but vainly tried) before,
Could I succeed; though sure that no success
80 Of mine could make its first inventor less:
For never from his brows would Horace tear
The wreath he wears and well deserves to wear.

    'Tis true I said that like a rapid flood
He carries in his course a train of mud,
And that his happier lines are few compared
With those loose stragglers that might well be spared.
And do not you, ye critics! now and then
Peck at the foibles ev'n of Homer's pen?

Dares not your loved Lucilius to correct
In older Accius many a gross defect?
Of Ennius does he not with laughter speak,
Where'er his verse is lame – his language weak?
Talks he not of himself, when self he names,
As one superior far to those he blames?
What then forbids us, when we con him o'er,
To use that freedom which he used before?
Ask if his ruggedness of numbers seem
Due to the slov'nly pen or stubborn theme? –
And doubt if patience may not give the strain
A smoother flow than that man can attain,
Who (deeming that his lines, however rough,
While each contains six feet, run smooth enough)
Scribbles before his supper twice five score,
And after supper scribbles twice five more; –
Like Tuscan Cassius whose exuberant song
Swift as a mountain torrent sweeps along;
Of whom fame tells, so rapid was his style,
That his own volumes form'd his funeral pile?
    But grant Lucilius is polite and chaste; –
Grant that he took more pains and shews more taste
Than that rude bard who by a lucky hit
First dared a path unknown to Grecian wit,
Or than our older minstrels: – Yet, could fate
To times more modern have prolong'd his date,
How would he toil each roughness to refine,
To nerve the weak and point the lagging line!
Each crude excrescence, each redundant spray,
As false luxuriance, he would prune away,
Nor amid fancy's wildest raptures fail
To scratch the brow and gnaw the bleeding nail.
    Spare not erasion, ye that wish your strain,
When once perused, to be perused again;
Nor court the mob, – contented if those few
Can praise, whose judgment speaks their praises true.

Let others more ambitious joy to see
Their works the school-boy's talk! Enough for me
If Knights applaud, as once with saucy pride
To hissing crouds Arbuscula replied.
    What – shall the bug Pantilius move my spleen?
130 Or shall I fret because unheard, unseen,
Demetrius aims his pitiful attack
And spurts his venom'd slime behind my back?
Shall sneers from Fannius, or his dangling guest,
The pert Hermogenes, disturb my rest?
No – let Maecenas smile upon my lays, –
Let Plotius, Varius, Valgius, Virgil praise, –
Let Fuscus and the good Octavius deign
With either Viscus to approve the strain; –
And, far from idle dreams of vulgar fame,
140 You, Pollio! you, Messala! let me name,
Nor less your brother; candid Furnius too,
And you, my Bibulus! and Servius! you:
Such, with some others whom I here omit,
Such are the friends whose taste I fain would hit;
Mine be the boast to win the smiles of these,
Nor e'er to please them less than now I please!
But you, Demetrius, and your stupid gang –
I bid you, with Tigellius all go hang
And scribble tasks for school-girls! – Boy, pen down
150 These lines, and let them know I scorn their frown.

(pub. 1845)

Satire II.3, lines 1–18

So seldom now you court the Muse, I hear,
You call for parchment scarcely thrice a year;
On dull revisal while you waste your pow'rs,
And, sleep or wine engrossing all your hours,

SATIRE II.3, LINES 1–18 · FRANCIS HOWES

Vex'd with yourself you peevishly complain
That you can hammer out no living strain.
How now! from Saturn's revels you withdrew,
As one resolved to carol something new.
Here then, all sober, keep your promise; come,
Begin, compose – Alas! you still are dumb.
In vain you curse the pen, and in a rage
Pour your resentment on the luckless page.
Poor innocents! regardless of their worth
Sure Gods and Poets frown'd upon their birth.
Methought your looks bespoke some wondrous feat
If e'er you reach'd your villa's snug retreat.
Why else, as if to' indulge a studious fit,
Heap Plato's wisdom on Menander's wit!
Why take Archilochus, a goodly load,
With Eupolis, companions on the road?
Think you the wrath of envy to appease,
By quitting virtue for inglorious ease?
Poor wretch! contempt awaits you. Scorn the smiles
Of Siren Sloth and her insidious wiles, –
Or tamely forfeit all your claim to praise,
The meed of toil and fruits of better days.

    Your counsel, Damasippus, I must own,
Is just: And for the wisdom you have shown
Heaven send you a good barber –! But pray tell
How wist you me and my concerns so well?   (pub. 1845)

EPISTLES

JOHN MILTON

Epistle I.16, lines 40–45

from *Tetrachordon*, 1645

Whom doe we count a good man, whom but he
Who keepes the lawes and statutes of the Senate,
Who judges in great suits and controversies,
Whose witnesse and opinion winnes the cause;
But his owne house, and the whole neighbourhood
Sees his foule inside through his whited skin. (pub. 1645)

ABRAHAM COWLEY

Epistle I.10 A paraphrase

Health, from the lover of the Country me,
Health, to the lover of the City thee,
A difference in our souls, this only proves,
In all things else, w' agree like marryed doves.
But the warm nest, and crowded dove-house thou
Dost like; I loosly fly from bough to bough,

And Rivers drink, and all the shining day,
Upon fair Trees, or mossy Rocks I play;
In fine, I live and reign when I retire
From all that you equal with Heaven admire.
Like one at last from the Priests service fled,
Loathing the honie'd Cakes, I long for Bread.
Would I a house for happines erect,
Nature alone should be the Architect.
She'd build it more convenient, then great,
And doubtless in the Country choose her seat.
Is there a place, doth better helps supply,
Against the wounds of Winters cruelty?
Is there an Ayr that gentl'er does asswage
The mad Celestial Dogs, or Lyons rage?
Is it not there that sleep (and only there)
Nor noise without, nor cares within does fear?
Does art through pipes, a purer water bring,
Then that which nature straines into a spring?
Can all your Tap'stries, or your Pictures show
More beauties then in herbs and flowers do grow?
Fountains and trees our wearied Pride do please,
Even in the midst of gilded Palaces.
And in your towns that prospect gives delight,
Which opens round the country to our sight.
Men to the good, from which they rashly fly,
Return at last, and their wild Luxury
Does but in vain with those true joyes contend,
Which Nature did to mankind recommend.
The man who changes gold for burnisht Brass,
Or small right Gems, for larger ones of glass:
Is not, at length, more certain to be made
Ridiculous, and wretched by the trade,
Than he, who sells a solid good, to buy
The painted goods of Pride and Vanity.
If thou be wise, no glorious fortune choose,
Which 'tis but pain to keep, yet grief to loose.

EPISTLE I.10 · ABRAHAM COWLEY

> For, when we place even trifles, in the heart,
> With trifles too, unwillingly we part.
> An humble Roof, plain bed, and homely board,
> More clear, untainted pleasures do afford,
> Then all the Tumult of vain greatness brings
> To Kings, or to the favorites of Kings.
> The horned Deer by Nature arm'd so well,
> Did with the Horse in common pasture dwell;
> And when they fought, the field it alwayes wan,
> Till the ambitious Horse begg'd help of Man,
> And took the bridle, and thenceforth did reign
> Bravely alone, as Lord of all the plain:
> But never after could the Rider get
> From off his back, or from his mouth the bit.
> So they, who poverty too much do fear,
> T' avoid that weight, a greater burden bear;
> That they might Pow'r above their equals have,
> To cruel Masters they themselves enslave.
> For Gold, their Liberty exchang'd we see,
> That fairest flow'r, which crowns Humanity.
> And all this mischief does upon them light,
> Only, because they know not how, aright,
> That great, but secret, happiness to prize,
> That's laid up in a Little, for the Wise:
> That is the best, and easiest Estate,
> Which to a man sits close, but not too strait;
> 'Tis like a shooe; it pinches, and it burns,
> Too narrow; and too large it overturns.
> My dearest friend, stop thy desires at last,
> And chearfully enjoy the wealth thou hast.
> And, if me still seeking for more you see,
> Chide, and reproach, despise and laugh at me.
> Money was made, not to command our will,
> But all our lawful pleasures to fulfil.
> Shame and wo to us, if we' our wealth obey;
> The Horse doth with the Horse-man run away. (pub. 1668)

50

60

70

THOMAS CREECH

Epistle I.6

Not to admire, as most are wont to do,
It is the only method that I know,
To make Men happy, and to keep 'em so.
Some view this glittering Sun, and glorious Stars,
And all the various Seasons free from fears;
Well then, those Gifts of Earth the Gums and Gold,
Which sweet Arabia, and the Indies hold,
Applause and Office, that mistaken good,
That great Preferment of the Roman Crowd;
When these are view'd with all their gawdy show,
How calm should be our Thoughts, how smooth our Brow!
Now those that fear their Opposites, admire
These Toys, as much as He that doth desire;
For both sides fear lest Things their Hopes deceive,
And both at sudden disappointments grieve.
Whether one joy or grieve, or hate or love,
Or strive to shun, or eagerly approve,
'Tis all alike if the Event appears,
Or worse or better than He hopes or fears,
He stands amaz'd with fix'd and staring Eyes,
His Limbs and Soul grow stiff at the surprise:
The just will be unjust, wise void of Wit,
That seek e'en Vertue more than what is fit:
Now go, let Gold and Statues charm thine Eyes,
Go, and admire thy Gems and Tyrian Dyes:
Rejoice that when you speak Men gape and wait;
Go to the Court betimes, and come home late;
Lest Mutius reap a greater Crop of Corn,
For 'tis unfit, since not so nobly born.

EPISTLE I.6 · THOMAS CREECH

30 Rather let him be wonder'd at by you,
    Than you by him, 'tis better of the Two:
    Whatever's under Ground Age brings to light,
    And that will bury too, and hide the bright?
    When Appius way, and Grippa's Porch shall know,
    And see thee famous, thou must walk below,
    As Numa, and as Ancus long ago.
    If vexing pains thy Sides, or Kidneys seize,
    Then seek some present Cure for thy Disease.
    Would'st thou live well? Who not? Then quickly strive,
40 And now since Vertue only this can give,
    Then leave thy false delights, and that pursue:
    But if you think their wild Opinion true,
    (As heedless Minds the vainest things approve)
    That Words make Vertue just as Trees a Grove,
    Then follow Wealth, make that thy chiefest Care,
    See none forestal, and none ingross the Fair,
    Or bate the prizes of thy precious Ware.
    Then get one Thousand Talents, then one more,
    And then Another, and then square the Store;
50 For by this Empress Wealth is all bestow'd,
    A rich and honest Wife, and every Good,
    As Beauty, Friends, and nobleness of Blood:
    The Rich and Moneyed Man hath every grace,
    Perswasion in his Tongue, and Venus in his Face.
    The Cappodocian King is poor in Coin,
    Tho rich in Slaves, let not his way be Thine:
    Lucullus once desir'd to lend the Stage
    A Thousand Suits, says, 'How can I engage,
    So many Suits? And yet I'll quickly send,
60 I'll search my store, and see what I can lend':
    And streight writes Word, 'I have five thousand good,
    And they might take as many as They wou'd.'
    That's an unfurnish'd House, that Master poor,
    Which hath Things necessary, and no more,

And whole Superfluous plenty not deceives,
And scapes the Master's Eye, and profits Thieves.
If Wealth can make Thee blest, and keep Thee so,
Mind it the first, and the last Thing you do.
If Offices, and all their gawdy Pride,
70 Then buy a witty Slave to guard thy side;
To tell Thee great Mens Names, and Nobles show,
And warn Thee to bow Popularly low;
'Sir, that's a Lord, and this, Sir's such a One,
He bears the greatest sway in all the Town:
Unless you cringe and get his Voice, despair,
His Vote disposes of the Consul's Chair:
Sir, as their Years require some Fathers call,
Some Sons, and pleasantly adopt them all':
If He lives well that eats well, come 'tis light,
80 Let's go, led by our ruling Appetite.
Let's Fish and Hunt as Gargil us'd to do,
Who every morning bad his Servants go,
With Poles, and Nets, and Spears, and march along
The well fill'd Market place, and busie throng,
That One of many Mules might carry home,
A Boar, that he had bought, thro gazing Rome.
Let's Bath e'en whilst the undigested load,
Lies crude, forgetting what is just and good:
Fit to be wax'd, Ulysses Mates outright,
90 Who lov'd their Country less than base delight.
If nothing, as Mimnermus strives to prove,
Can e'er be pleasant without wanton Love;
Then live in wanton Love, thy Sport pursue,
Let that employ thy precious Time; Adieu.
If you know better Rules than these, be free,
Impart them, but if not, use these with Me. (pub. 1684)

ALEXANDER POPE

Epistle I.1 An imitation

For a close rendering, compare Conington (pp. 443–7).

> St John, whose love indulg'd my labours past
> Matures my present, and shall bound my last!
> Why will you break the Sabbath of my days?
> Now sick alike of Envy and of Praise.
> Publick too long, ah let me hide my Age!
> See modest Cibber now has left the Stage:
> Our Gen'rals now, retir'd to their Estates,
> Hang their old Trophies o'er the Garden gates,
> In Life's cool evening satiate of applause,
> Nor fond of bleeding, ev'n in Brunswick's cause.
>   A Voice there is, that whispers in my ear,
> ('Tis Reason's voice, which sometimes one can hear)
> 'Friend Pope! be prudent, let your Muse take breath,
> And never gallop Pegasus to death;
> Lest stiff, and stately, void of fire, or force,
> You limp, like Blackmore, on a Lord Mayor's horse.'
>   Farewell then Verse, and Love, and ev'ry Toy,
> The rhymes and rattles of the Man or Boy:
> What right, what true, what fit, we justly call,
> Let this be all my care – for this is All:
> To lay this harvest up, and hoard with haste
> What ev'ry day will want, and most, the last.
>   But ask not, to what Doctors I apply?
> Sworn to no Master, of no Sect am I:
> As drives the storm, at any door I knock,
> And house with Montagne now, or now with Lock.
> Sometimes a Patriot, active in debate,
> Mix with the World, and battle for the State,

Free as young Lyttleton, her cause pursue,
Still true to Virtue, and as warm as true:
Sometimes, with Aristippus, or St Paul,
Indulge my Candor, and grow all to all;
Back to my native Moderation slide,
And win my way by yielding to the tyde.

　　Long, as to him who works for debt, the Day;
Long as the Night to her whose love's away;
Long as the Year's dull circle seems to run,
When the brisk Minor pants for twenty-one;
So slow th' unprofitable Moments roll,
That lock up all the Functions of my soul;
That keep me from Myself; and still delay
Life's instant business to a future day:
That task, which as we follow, or despise,
The eldest is a fool, the youngest wise;
Which done, the poorest can no wants endure,
And which not done, the richest must be poor.

　　Late as it is, I put my self to school,
And feel some comfort, not to be a fool.
Weak tho' I am of limb, and short of sight,
Far from a Lynx, and not a Giant quite,
I'll do what Mead and Cheselden advise,
To keep these limbs, and to preserve these eyes.
Not to go back, is somewhat to advance,
And men must walk at least before they dance.

　　Say, does thy blood rebel, thy bosom move
With wretched Av'rice, or as wretched Love?
Know, there are Words, and Spells, which can controll
(Between the Fits) this Fever of the soul:
Know, there are Rhymes, which (fresh and fresh apply'd)
Will cure the arrant'st Puppy of his Pride.
Be furious, envious, slothful, mad or drunk,
Slave to a Wife or Vassal to a Punk,
A Switz, a High-dutch, or a Low-dutch Bear –
All that we ask is but a patient Ear.

'Tis the first Virtue, Vices to abhor;
And the first Wisdom, to be Fool no more.
But to the world, no bugbear is so great,
As want of figure, and a small Estate.
To either India see the Merchant fly,
Scar'd at the spectre of pale Poverty!
See him, with pains of body, pangs of soul,
Burn through the Tropic, freeze beneath the Pole!
Wilt thou do nothing for a nobler end,
Nothing, to make Philosophy thy friend?
To stop thy foolish views, thy long desires,
And ease thy heart of all that it admires?

 Here, Wisdom calls: 'Seek Virtue first! be bold!
As Gold to Silver, Virtue is to Gold.'
There, London's voice: 'Get Mony, Mony still!
And then let Virtue follow, if she will.'
This, this the saving doctrine, preach'd to all,
From low St James's up to high St Paul;
From him whose quills stand quiver'd at his ear,
To him who notches Sticks at Westminster.

 Barnard in spirit, sense, and truth abounds.
'Pray then what wants he?' fourscore thousand pounds,
A Pension, or such Harness for a slave
As Bug now has, and Dorimant would have.
Barnard, thou art a Cit, with all thy worth;
But wretched Bug, his Honour, and so forth.

 Yet every child another song will sing,
'Virtue, brave boys! 'tis Virtue makes a King.'
True, conscious Honour is to feel no sin,
He's arm'd without that's innocent within;
Be this thy Screen, and this thy Wall of Brass;
Compar'd to this, a Minister's an Ass.

 And say, to which shall our applause belong,
This new Court jargon, or the good old song?
The modern language of corrupted Peers,
Or what was spoke at Cressy and Poitiers?

Who counsels best? who whispers, 'Be but Great,
With Praise or Infamy, leave that to fate;
Get Place and Wealth, if possible, with Grace;
If not, by any means get Wealth and Place.'
For what? to have a Box where Eunuchs sing,
And foremost in the Circle eye a King.
Or he, who bids thee face with steddy view
Proud Fortune, and look shallow Greatness thro':
And, while he bids thee, sets th' Example too?
110 If such a Doctrine, in St James's air,
Shou'd chance to make the well-drest Rabble stare;
If honest S*z take scandal at a spark,
That less admires the Palace than the Park;
Faith I shall give the answer Reynard gave,
'I cannot like, Dread Sir! your Royal Cave;
Because I see by all the Tracks about,
Full many a Beast goes in, but none comes out.'
Adieu to Virtue if you're once a Slave:
Send her to Court, you send her to her Grave.
120 Well, if a King's a Lion, at the least
The People are a many-headed Beast:
Can they direct what measures to pursue,
Who know themselves so little what to do?
Alike in nothing but one Lust of Gold,
Just half the land would buy, and half be sold:
Their Country's wealth our mightier Misers drain,
Or cross, to plunder Provinces, the Main:
The rest, some farm the Poor-box, some the Pews;
Some keep Assemblies, and wou'd keep the Stews;
130 Some with fat Bucks on childless Dotards fawn;
Some win rich Widows by their Chine and Brawn;
While with the silent growth of ten per Cent,
In Dirt and darkness hundreds stink content.
    Of all these ways, if each pursues his own,
Satire be kind, and let the wretch alone.
But show me one, who has it in his pow'r

        To act consistent with himself an hour.
        Sir Job sail'd forth, the evening bright and still,
        'No place on earth (he cry'd) like Greenwich hill!'
140   Up starts a Palace, lo! th' obedient base
        Slopes at its foot, the woods its sides embrace,
        The silver Thames reflects its marble face.
        Now let some whimzy, or that Dev'l within
        Which guides all those who know not what they mean
        But give the Knight (or give his Lady) spleen;
        'Away, away! take all your scaffolds down,
        For Snug's the word: My dear! we'll live in Town.'
          At am'rous Flavio is the Stocking thrown?
        That very night he longs to lye alone.
150   The Fool whose Wife elopes some thrice a quarter,
        For matrimonial Solace dies a martyr.
        Did ever Proteus, Merlin, any Witch,
        Transform themselves so strangely as the Rich?
        'Well, but the Poor' – the Poor have the same itch:
        They change their weekly Barber, weekly News,
        Prefer a new Japanner to their shoes,
        Discharge their Garrets, move their Beds, and run
        (They know not whither) in a Chaise and one;
        They hire their Sculler, and when once aboard,
160   Grow sick, and damn the Climate – like a Lord.
          You laugh, half Beau half Sloven if I stand,
        My Wig all powder, and all snuff my Band;
        You laugh, if Coat and Breeches strangely vary,
        White Gloves, and Linnen worthy Lady Mary!
        But when no Prelate's Lawn with Hair-shirt lin'd,
        Is half so incoherent as my Mind,
        When (each Opinion with the next at strife,
        One ebb and flow of follies all my Life)
        I plant, root up, I build, and then confound,
170   Turn round to square, and square again to round;
        You never change one muscle of your face,
        You think this Madness but a common case,

Nor once to Chanc'ry, nor to Hales apply;
  Yet hang your lip, to see a Seam awry!
  Careless how ill I with myself agree;
  Kind to my dress, my figure, not to Me.
  Is this my Guide, Philosopher, and Friend?
  This, He who loves me, and who ought to mend?
  Who ought to make me (what he can, or none,)
180 That Man divine whom Wisdom calls her own,
  Great without Title, without Fortune bless'd,
  Rich ev'n when plunder'd, honour'd while oppress'd,
  Lov'd without youth, and follow'd without power,
  At home tho' exil'd, free, tho' in the Tower.
  In short, that reas'ning, high, immortal Thing,
  Just less than Jove, and much above a King,
  Nay half in Heav'n – except (what's mighty odd)
  A Fit of Vapours clouds this Demi-god.   (pub. 1738)

Epistle I.6 An imitation

Compare the translation by Creech (pp. 396–8). For Pope's misquotation of Creech, see Introduction, p. 22.

  'Not to Admire, is all the Art I know,
  To make men happy, and to keep them so.'
  [Plain Truth, dear Murray, needs no flow'rs of speech,
  So take it in the very words of Creech.]
    This Vault of Air, this congregated Ball,
  Self-centred Sun, and Stars that rise and fall,
  There are, my Friend! whose philosophic eyes
  Look thro', and trust the Ruler with his Skies,
  To him commit the hour, the day, the year,
10 And view this dreadful All without a fear.
    Admire we then what Earth's low entrails hold,
  Arabian shores, or Indian seas infold?
  All the mad trade of Fools and Slaves for Gold?

EPISTLE I.6 · ALEXANDER POPE

>   Or Popularity, or Stars and Strings?
>   The Mob's applauses, or the gifts of Kings?
>   Say with what eyes we ought at Courts to gaze,
>   And pay the Great our homage of Amaze?
>   If weak the pleasure that from these can spring,
>   The fear to want them is as weak a thing:
> 20 Whether we dread, or whether we desire,
>   In either case, believe me, we admire;
>   Whether we joy or grieve, the same the curse,
>   Surpriz'd at better, or surpriz'd at worse.
>   Thus good, or bad, to one extreme betray
>   Th' unbalanc'd Mind, and snatch the Man away;
>   For Vertue's self may too much Zeal be had;
>   The worst of Madmen is a Saint run mad.
>   Go then, and if you can, admire the state
>   Of beaming diamonds, and reflected plate;
> 30 Procure a Taste to double the surprize,
>   And gaze on Parian Charms with learned eyes:
>   Be struck with bright Brocade, or Tyrian Dye,
>   Our Birth-day Nobles splendid Livery:
>   If not so pleas'd, at Council-board rejoyce,
>   To see their Judgments hang upon thy Voice;
>   From morn to night, at Senate, Rolls, and Hall,
>   Plead much, read more, dine late, or not at all.
>   But wherefore all this labour, all this strife?
>   For Fame, for Riches, for a noble Wife?
> 40 Shall One whom Nature, Learning, Birth, conspir'd
>   To form, not to admire, but be admir'd,
>   Sigh, while his Chloë, blind to Wit and Worth,
>   Weds the rich Dulness of some Son of earth?
>   Yet Time ennobles, or degrades each Line;
>   It brighten'd Crags's, and may darken thine:
>   And what is Fame? the Meanest have their day,
>   The Greatest can but blaze, and pass away.
>   Grac'd as thou art, with all the Pow'r of Words,
>   So known, so honour'd, at the House of Lords;

50 Conspicuous Scene! another yet is nigh,
    (More silent far) where Kings and Poets lye;
    Where Murray (long enough his Country's pride)
    Shall be no more than Tully, or than Hyde!
        Rack'd with Sciatics, martyr'd with the Stone,
    Will any mortal let himself alone?
    See Ward by batter'd Beaus invited over,
    And desp'rate Misery lays hold on Dover.
    The case is easier in the Mind's disease;
    There, all Men may be cur'd, whene'er they please.
60 Would ye be blest? despise low Joys, low Gains;
    Disdain whatever Cornbury disdains;
    Be Virtuous, and be happy for your pains.
        But art thou one, whom new opinions sway,
    One, who believes as Tindal leads the way,
    Who Virtue and a Church alike disowns,
    Thinks that but words, and this but brick and stones?
    Fly then, on all the wings of wild desire!
    Admire whate'er the maddest can admire.
    Is Wealth thy passion? Hence! from Pole to Pole,
70 Where winds can carry, or where waves can roll,
    For Indian spices, for Peruvian gold,
    Prevent the greedy, and out-bid the bold:
    Advance thy golden Mountain to the skies;
    On the broad base of fifty thousand rise,
    Add one round hundred, and (if that's not fair)
    Add fifty more, and bring it to a square.
    For, mark th' advantage; just so many score
    Will gain a Wife with half as many more,
    Procure her beauty, make that beauty chaste,
80 And then such Friends – as cannot fail to last.
    A Man of wealth is dubb'd a Man of worth,
    Venus shall give him Form, and Anstis Birth.
    (Believe me, many a German Prince is worse,
    Who proud of Pedigree, is poor of Purse)

EPISTLE I.6 · ALEXANDER POPE

    His Wealth brave Timon gloriously confounds;
Ask'd for a groat, he gives a hundred pounds;
Or if three Ladies like a luckless Play,
Takes the whole House upon the Poet's day.
Now, in such exigencies not to need,
Upon my word, you must be rich indeed;
A noble superfluity it craves,
Not for your self, but for your Fools and Knaves;
Something, which for your Honour they may cheat,
And which it much becomes you to forget.
If Wealth alone then make and keep us blest,
Still, still be getting, never, never rest.

    But if to Pow'r and Place your Passion lye,
If in the Pomp of Life consist the Joy;
Then hire a Slave, (or if you will, a Lord)
To do the Honours, and to give the Word;
Tell at your Levee, as the Crouds approach,
To whom to nod, whom take into your Coach,
Whom honour with your hand: to make remarks,
Who rules in Cornwall, or who rules in Berks;
'This may be troublesome, is near the Chair;
That makes three Members, this can chuse a May'r.'
Instructed thus, you bow, embrace, protest,
Adopt him Son, or Cozen at the least,
Then turn about, and laugh at your own Jest.

    Or if your life be one continu'd Treat,
If to live well means nothing but to eat;
Up, up! cries Gluttony, 'tis break of day,
Go drive the Deer, and drag the finny-prey;
With hounds and horns go hunt an Appetite –
So Russel did, but could not eat at night,
Call'd happy Dog! the Beggar at his door,
And envy'd Thirst and Hunger to the Poor.

    Or shall we ev'ry Decency confound,
Thro' Taverns, Stews, and Bagnio's take our round,

120　　Go dine with Chartres, in each Vice out-do
　　　　K—l's lewd Cargo, or Ty—y's Crew,
　　　　From Latian Syrens, French Circaean Feasts,
　　　　Return well travell'd, and transform'd to Beasts,
　　　　Or for a Titled Punk, or Foreign Flame,
　　　　Renounce our Country, and degrade our Name?
　　　　　　If, after all, we must with Wilmot own,
　　　　The Cordial Drop of Life is Love alone,
　　　　And Swift cry wisely, 'Vive la Bagatelle!'
　　　　The Man that loves and laughs, must sure do well.
130　　Adieu – if this advice appear the worst,
　　　　E'en take the Counsel which I gave you first:
　　　　Or better Precepts if you can impart,
　　　　Why do, I'll follow them with all my heart.　　　(pub. 1738)

Epistle II.1

Imitation by Alexander Pope
en face translation by Colin Macleod

Epistle II.1 An imitation

A close translation is printed *en face* to show what Pope is doing with his original.

    While You, great Patron of Mankind, sustain
    The balanc'd World, and open all the Main;
    Your Country, chief, in Arms abroad defend,
    At home, with Morals, Arts, and Laws amend;
    How shall the Muse, from such a Monarch, steal
    An hour, and not defraud the Publick Weal?
      Edward and Henry, now the Boast of Fame,
    And virtuous Alfred, a more sacred Name,
    After a Life of gen'rous Toils endur'd,
10   The Gaul subdu'd, or Property secur'd,
    Ambition humbled, mighty Cities storm'd,
    Or Laws establish'd, and the World reform'd;
    Clos'd their long Glories with a sigh, to find
    Th' unwilling Gratitude of base mankind!
    All human Virtue to its latest breath
    Finds Envy never conquer'd, but by Death.
    The great Alcides, ev'ry Labour past,
    Had still this Monster to subdue at last.
    Sure fate of all, beneath whose rising ray
20   Each Star of meaner merit fades away;
    Oppress'd we feel the Beam directly beat,
    Those Suns of Glory please not till they set.
      To Thee, the World its present homage pays,
    The Harvest early, but mature the Praise:
    Great Friend of Liberty! in Kings a Name
    Above all Greek, above all Roman Fame:

COLIN MACLEOD (1943–1981)

University Lecturer in Greek and Latin Literature and Student of Christ Church, Oxford, until his early death. Macleod's publications include a commentary on *Iliad* XXIV and *Collected Essays* (1983).

Epistle II.1

When you bear alone so great a load of duties,
protect the land with arms, improve its morals
with laws, I should defy the national interest
if my *causeries* detained you long, Augustus.
Romulus and Bacchus, the twins Castor and Pollux,
who after their mighty deeds were enshrined with the gods,
at the time they walked on earth caring for men,
settling wars, allotting lands, founding cities,
moaned that the gratitude they hoped for did not meet
10   their services. The man who crushed the hydra
and quelled great monsters in his destined labours
found out that envy is only tamed by death.
Such brilliance, weighing on talents placed beneath it,
inflames them: once extinguished, it's admired.
You receive honours when they are due, in your lifetime:
we set up altars where we invoke your godhead,
we admit you have no equal, past or future.

Whose Word is Truth, as sacred and rever'd,
As Heav'n's own Oracles from Altars heard.
Wonder of Kings! like whom, to mortal eyes
30 None e'er has risen, and none e'er shall rise.

Just in one instance, be it yet confest
Your People, Sir, are partial in the rest.
Foes to all living worth except your own,
And Advocates for Folly dead and gone.
Authors, like Coins, grow dear as they grow old;
It is the rust we value, not the gold.
Chaucer's worst ribaldry is learn'd by rote,
And beastly Skelton Heads of Houses quote:
One likes no language but the Faery Queen;
40 A Scot will fight for Christ's Kirk o' the Green;
And each true Briton is to Ben so civil,
He swears the Muses met him at the Devil.

Tho' justly Greece her eldest sons admires,
Why should not we be wiser than our Sires?
In ev'ry publick Virtue we excell,
We build, we paint, we sing, we dance as well,
And learned Athens to our Art must stoop,
Could she behold us tumbling thro' a hoop.

If Time improve our Wit as well as Wine,
50 Say at what age a Poet grows divine?
Shall we, or shall we not, account him so,
Who dy'd, perhaps, an hundred years ago?
End all dispute; and fix the year precise
When British bards begin t' Immortalize?

'Who lasts a Century can have no flaw,
I hold that Wit a Classick, good in law.'

Suppose he wants a year, will you compound?
And shall we deem him Ancient, right and sound,
Or damn to all Eternity at once,
60 At ninety nine, a Modern, and a Dunce?

'We shall not quarrel for a year or two;
By Courtesy of England, he may do.'

But this people of yours, so wise and just in putting
you only above our own and the Grecian heroes,
20 by no means use that judgement on other things,
and view with contempt and disgust whatever has not
completed its time and left the land of the living.
So fond are they of antiquity, they insist
that the Twelve Tables, the pacts which set the kings
at one with Gabii or the stiff-necked Sabines,
the priestly books, the aged tomes of prophecy,
came from the Muses' lips on the Alban hill.
If, because the oldest writings of the Greeks
are also the best, we weigh our Roman writers
30 on the same scales, then there's little to be said:
a nut must be soft outside and an olive inside;
we have reached the top in wealth, therefore as artists
and as athletes we outdo the well-oiled Greeks.
If time makes poems better as it does wine,
tell me what age claims value for a book.
Does a writer who went down a century back
belong with the faultless ancients or debased
moderns? Draw a line to stop disputes.
'Age and quality start at a hundred years.'
40 What if one's end was a month or a year too late?
Where does *he* belong, with the ancient poets,
or those whom the present and posterity would spurn?
'Well, we can decently reckon among the ancients
one who is just a month or a whole year younger.'

Then, by the rule that made the Horse-tail bare,
I pluck out year by year, as hair by hair,
And melt down Ancients like a heap of snow:
While you, to measure merits, look in Stowe,
And estimating Authors by the year,
Bestow a Garland only on a Bier.

Shakespear, (whom you and ev'ry Play-house bill
70 Style the divine, the matchless, what you will)
For gain, not glory, wing'd his roving flight,
And grew Immortal in his own despight.
Ben, old and poor, as little seem'd to heed
The Life to come, in ev'ry Poet's Creed.
Who now reads Cowley? if he pleases yet,
His moral pleases, not his pointed wit;
Forgot his Epic, nay Pindaric Art,
But still I love the language of his Heart.

'Yet surely, surely, these were famous men!
80 What Boy but hears the sayings of old Ben?
In all debates where Criticks bear a part,
Not one but nods, and talks of Johnson's Art,
Of Shakespear's Nature, and of Cowley's Wit;
How Beaumont's Judgment check'd what Fletcher writ;
How Shadwell hasty, Wycherly was slow;
But, for the Passions, Southern sure and Rowe.
These, only these, support the crouded stage,
From eldest Heywood down to Cibber's age'.

All this may be; the People's Voice is odd,
90 It is, and it is not, the voice of God.
To Gammer Gurton if it give the bays,
And yet deny the Careless Husband praise,
Or say our fathers never broke a rule;
Why then I say, the Publick is a fool.
But let them own, that greater faults than we
They had, and greater Virtues, I'll agree.
Spenser himself affects the obsolete,
And Sydney's verse halts ill on Roman feet:

EPISTLE II.I · COLIN MACLEOD

Thank you for your permission: bit by bit
I pluck the horse's tail, hair after hair,
till the dilemma of the 'sinking heap' floors
those who burrow in records to judge merit
and admire only what graveyards consecrate.
50 Ennius, noble and profound, 'a second Homer',
to the critics, seems not to worry what the dream
which claims he reincarnates his model comes to.
Is Naevius not in everyone's hands and hearts,
as good as new? So sacred are old poems.
When their standings are discussed, Pacuvius
is dubbed most polished, Accius most sublime,
Afranius' Roman costumes fit Menander,
Plautus bustles along like Epicharmus,
Caecilius is grandest, Terence subtlest.
60 These writers mighty Rome learns up and watches
squashed into the theatre; these it counts
its poets from Livius' time down to our own.
Sometimes the public sees straight, but not always.
If this passion for old poets means it believes
there are none better or equal, it is wrong.
If it thinks its heroes now and then archaic,
and sometimes rough, it grants they're often slack,
it sides with sense and me, and God is with it.

Milton's strong pinion now not Heav'n can bound,
Now serpent-like, in prose he sweeps the ground,
In Quibbles, Angel and Archangel join,
And God the Father turns a School-Divine.
Not that I'd lop the Beauties from his book,
Like slashing Bentley with his desp'rate Hook;
Or damn all Shakespear, like th' affected fool
At Court, who hates whate'er he read at School.

But for the Wits of either Charles's days,
The Mob of Gentlemen who wrote with Ease;
Sprat, Carew, Sedley, and a hundred more,
(Like twinkling Stars the Miscellanies o'er)
One Simile, that solitary shines
In the dry Desert of a thousand lines,
Or lengthen'd Thought that gleams thro' many a page,
Has sanctify'd whole Poems for an age.

I lose my patience, and I own it too,
When works are censur'd, not as bad, but new;
While if our Elders break all Reason's laws,
These fools demand not Pardon, but Applause.

On Avon's bank, where flow'rs eternal blow,
If I but ask, if any weed can grow?
One Tragic sentence if I dare deride
Which Betterton's grave Action dignify'd,
Or well-mouth'd Booth with emphasis proclaims,
(Tho' but, perhaps, a muster-roll of Names)
How will our Fathers rise up in a rage,
And swear, all shame is lost in George's Age!
You'd think no Fools disgrac'd the former Reign,
Did not some grave Examples yet remain,
Who scorn a Lad should teach his Father skill,
And, having once been wrong, will be so still.
He, who to seem more deep than you or I,
Extols old Bards, or Merlin's Prophecy,
Mistake him not; he envies, not admires,
And to debase the Sons, exalts the Sires.

I do not hound down Livius, or want his work
70 burned (I recall Orbilius, that great caner,
dictating him at school); but how can they think him
correct, artistic, all but perfectly finished?
If here and there a choice word flashes out,
if a line or two is slightly neater than most,
it drags the whole work with it into the book-shops.
I fume when something's criticized not because
it's crudely or harshly written, but recently,
when praise, and not indulgence, is sought for the ancients.
If I doubted Atta's plays should stroll flat-footed
80 on our flowered stage, most of the old would cry
'There's no respect these days!', when I tried to blame
what grand Aesopus or subtle Roscius acted:
either they only approve of what they like
or they will not obey their juniors, grant in old age
that what they learnt as striplings should be scrapped.
The admirer of the chant of Numa's priesthood
who tries to pass, where he shares my ignorance,
for the sole expert, does not applaud the dead
and buried, but shoots enviously at us.

      Had ancient Times conspir'd to dis-allow
      What then was new, what had been ancient now?
      Or what remain'd, so worthy to be read
      By learned Criticks, of the mighty Dead?
         In Days of Ease, when now the weary Sword
140   Was sheath'd, and Luxury with Charles restor'd;
      In every Taste of foreign Courts improv'd,
      'All, by the King's Example, liv'd and lov'd.'
      Then Peers grew proud in Horsemanship t' excell,
      New-market's Glory rose, as Britain's fell;
      The Soldier breath'd the Gallantries of France,
      And ev'ry flow'ry Courtier writ Romance.
      Then Marble soften'd into life grew warm,
      And yielding Metal flow'd to human form:
      Lely on animated Canvas stole
150   The sleepy Eye, that spoke the melting soul.
      No wonder then, when all was Love and Sport,
      The willing Muses were debauch'd at Court;
      On each enervate string they taught the Note
      To pant, or tremble thro' an Eunuch's throat.
      But Britain, changeful as a Child at play,
      Now calls in Princes, and now turns away.
      Now Whig, now Tory, what we lov'd we hate;
      Now all for Pleasure, now for Church and State;
      Now for Prerogative, and now for Laws;
160   Effects unhappy! from a Noble Cause.
         Time was, a sober Englishman wou'd knock
      His servants up, and rise by five a clock,
      Instruct his Family in ev'ry rule,
      And send his Wife to Church, his Son to school.
      To worship like his Fathers was his care;
      To teach their frugal Virtues to his Heir;
      To prove, that Luxury could never hold;
      And place, on good Security, his Gold.
      Now Times are chang'd, and one Poetick Itch
170   Has seiz'd the Court and City, Poor and Rich:

90 But had the Greeks loathed novelty as we do,
    what whould now be old for the general public
    to read in private and to thumb to tatters?
    When Greece had put away war for childish things
    and welfare levelled the path of her decline,
    she fell in love with athletics and with racing,
    doted on work in marble, ivory, bronze,
    pinned her gaze and her whole heart on painting,
    revelled in instrumentalists or actors —
    like a baby girl in the nursery, grabbed a toy
100 with glee, but was soon satisfied and dropped it.
    Such were the blessings of peace and of fair winds.
    At Rome, it was long men's practice and their pleasure
    to receive at home from dawn, advise dependants,
    to dole out loans secured by a good name,
    to hear the elders, tell the young how capital
    could be increased and costly whims cut down.
    The fickle people changed their habits, now

Sons, Sires, and Grandsires, all will wear the Bays,
Our Wives read Milton, and our Daughters Plays,
To Theatres, and to Rehearsals throng,
And all our Grace at Table is a Song.
I, who so oft renounce the Muses, lye,
Not —'s self e'er tells more Fibs than I;
When, sick of Muse, our follies we deplore,
And promise our best Friends to ryme no more;
We wake next morning in a raging Fit,
180 And call for Pen and Ink to show our Wit.

    He serv'd a 'Prenticeship, who sets up shop;
Ward try'd on Puppies, and the Poor, his Drop;
Ev'n Radcliff's Doctors travel first to France,
Nor dare to practise till they've learn'd to dance.
Who builds a Bridge that never drove a pyle?
(Should Ripley venture, all the World would smile)
But those who cannot write, and those who can,
All ryme, and scrawl, and scribble, to a man.

    Yet Sir, reflect, the mischief is not great;
190 These Madmen never hurt the Church or State:
Sometimes the Folly benefits mankind;
And rarely Av'rice taints the tuneful mind.
Allow him but his Play-thing of a Pen,
He ne'er rebels, or plots, like other men:
Flight of Cashiers, or Mobs, he'll never mind;
And knows no losses while the Muse is kind.
To cheat a Friend, or Ward, he leaves to Peter;
The good man heaps up nothing but mere metre,
Enjoys his Garden and his Book in quiet;
200 And then – a perfect Hermit in his Diet.
Of little use the Man you may suppose,
Who says in verse what others say in prose;
Yet let me show, a Poet's of some weight,
And (tho' no Soldier) useful to the State.
What will a Child learn sooner than a song?
What better teach a Foreigner the tongue?

their only passion's writing; boys and stern fathers
dine and dictate with laurels on their brows.
110 I too, who swear I am not writing, faithless
as a Parthian am up before the sun
calling for my equipment, pen and paper.
Land-lubbers shun the helm, only an expert
dares prescribe to the sick, surgeons profess
surgery, metal-workers work in metal:
skilled and unskilled alike, we all write poems.
But look at the virtues of the aberration,
this mild form of madness. A bard is not
a money-grubber; his only love is verse.
120 He laughs off losses, runaway slaves and fires,
he would never do down a partner or a ward,
he lives on bean-pods and black bread, an idle
and worthless soldier, but useful to his country
if you grant that great affairs can be helped by small ones.

What's long or short, each accent where to place,
And speak in publick with some sort of grace.
I scarce can think him such a worthless thing,
210　Unless he praise some monster of a King,
Or Virtue, or Religion turn to sport,
To please a lewd, or un-believing Court.
Unhappy Dryden! – In all Charles's days,
Roscommon only boasts unspotted Bays;
And in our own (excuse some Courtly stains)
No whiter page than Addison remains.
He, from the taste obscene reclaims our Youth,
And sets the Passions on the side of Truth;
Forms the soft bosom with the gentlest art,
220　And pours each human Virtue in the heart.
Let Ireland tell, how Wit upheld her cause,
Her Trade supported, and supply'd her Laws;
And leave on Swift this grateful verse ingrav'd,
The Rights a Court attack'd, a Poet sav'd.
Behold the hand that wrought a Nation's cure,
Stretch'd to relieve the Idiot and the Poor,
Proud Vice to brand, or injur'd Worth adorn,
And stretch the Ray to Ages yet unborn.
Not but there are, who merit other palms;
230　Hopkins and Sternhold glad the heart with Psalms;
The Boys and Girls whom Charity maintains,
Implore your help in these pathetic strains:
How could Devotion touch the country pews,
Unless the Gods bestow'd a proper Muse?
Verse chears their leisure, Verse assists their work,
Verse prays for Peace, or sings down Pope and Turk.
The silenc'd Preacher yields to potent strain,
And feels that grace his pray'r besought in vain,
The blessing thrills thro' all the lab'ring throng,
240　And Heav'n is won by violence of Song.
　　Our rural Ancestors, with little blest,
Patient of labour when the end was rest,

The poet moulds our tender, fumbling lips
in childhood, tweaks our ears away from smut;
later he shapes our hearts with kind advice,
corrects our roughness, envy and bad temper,
records good deeds, supplies the age with models
130 from the past, consoles the poor and the despondent.
How would the choirs of virgin girls and boys
learn to sing prayers, if the Muse had made no bards?
They call for help, they feel the godhead's presence,
they beg for rain with prayers that art has sweetened,
keep off plagues, drive away grave danger,
secure both peace and autumns rich in fruit.
Heaven and underworld are appeased by song.
The sturdy farmers of old, happy and poor,
when after harvest-home they refreshed their bodies

Indulg'd the day that hous'd their annual grain,
With feasts, and off'rings, and a thankful strain:
The joy their wives, their sons, and servants share,
Ease of their toil, and part'ners of their care:
The laugh, the jest, attendants on the bowl,
Smooth'd ev'ry brow, and open'd ev'ry soul:
With growing years the pleasing Licence grew,
And Taunts alternate innocently flew.
But Times corrupt, and Nature, ill-inclin'd,
Produc'd the point that left a sting behind;
Till friend with friend, and families at strife,
Triumphant Malice rag'd thro' private life.
Who felt the wrong, or fear'd it, took th' alarm,
Appeal'd to Law, and Justice lent her arm.
At length, by wholesom dread of statutes bound,
The Poets learn'd to please, and not to wound:
Most warp'd to Flatt'ry's side; but some, more nice,
Preserv'd the freedom, and forbore the vice.
Hence Satire rose, that just the medium hit,
And heals with Morals what it hurts with Wit.

    We conquer'd France, but felt our captive's charms;
Her Arts victorious triumph'd o'er our Arms:
Britain to soft refinements less a foe,
Wit grew polite, and Numbers learn'd to flow.
Waller was smooth; but Dryden taught to join
The varying verse, the full resounding line,
The long majestic march, and energy divine.
Tho' still some traces of our rustic vein
And splay-foot verse, remain'd, and will remain.
Late, very late, correctness grew our care,
When the tir'd nation breath'd from civil war.
Exact Racine, and Corneille's noble fire
Show'd us that France had something to admire.
Not but the Tragic spirit was our own,
And full in Shakespear, fair in Otway shone:

140 and hearts, sustained by thoughts of the holiday,
with their children who had helped and faithful wives,
offered a pig to the Earth, milk to Silvanus,
flowers and wine to the Sharer of life's brief joys.
From this practice flowed a form of licensed insult
in which uncouth remarks were exchanged in verse.
Such freedom of speech, welcome once a year,
was a likeable game, until the fun turned savage,
bared its teeth and prowled through noble houses
unchecked. Those whose blood it had drawn felt sore,
150 and even those whom it had left unscathed
were concerned for the common good; indeed, a law
and sanctions were set up precluding poets
from personal abuse. They changed their tune,
for fear of the stick, turned pleasant and well-spoken.
The capture of Greece took her brutish victor captive
and civilized rustic Latium. Thus the crude
Saturnian verse ran out, good taste expelled
the smell of muck; and yet for years the traces
of rusticity remained, and still remain.
160 For it was late when they trained their minds on Greek:
at peace after the Punic wars, they started
to see what the tragedians could teach them.
They tried their hand at composing too, and well,
in their own eyes; to soar came naturally,
they had inspiration and a happy boldness –
but also a foolish horror of crossing out.

But Otway fail'd to polish or refine,
And fluent Shakespear scarce effac'd a line.
Ev'n copious Dryden, wanted, or forgot,
The last and greatest Art, the Art to blot.

    Some doubt, if equal pains or equal fire
The humbler Muse of Comedy require?
But in known Images of life I guess
The labour greater, as th' Indulgence less.
Observe how seldom ev'n the best succeed:
Tell me if Congreve's Fools are Fools indeed?
What pert low Dialogue has Farqu'ar writ!
How Van wants grace, who never wanted wit!
The stage how loosely does Astraea tread,
Who fairly puts all Characters to bed:
And idle Cibber, how he breaks the laws,
To make poor Pinky eat with vast applause!
But fill their purse, our Poet's work is done,
Alike to them, by Pathos or by Pun.

    O you! whom Vanity's light bark conveys
On Fame's mad voyage by the wind of Praise;
With what a shifting gale your course you ply;
For ever sunk too low, or born too high!
Who pants for glory finds but short repose,
A breath revives him, or a breath o'erthrows!
Farewel the stage! if just as thrives the Play,
The silly bard grows fat, or falls away.

    There still remains to mortify a Wit,
The many-headed Monster of the Pit:
A sense-less, worth-less, and unhonour'd crowd;
Who to disturb their betters mighty proud,
Clatt'ring their sticks, before ten lines are spoke,
Call for the Farce, the Bear, or the Black-joke.
What dear delight to Britons Farce affords!
Farce once the taste of Mobs, but now of Lords;
(For Taste, eternal wanderer, now flies
From heads to ears, and now from ears to eyes.)

Comedy, since it draws on common life,
is thought to need less sweat; but it's the harder
for deserving less allowances. Take Plautus –
170 he plays the part of the amorous young man,
the tight-fisted father or wily pimp,
he clowns in the great line of comic spongers,
he bustles across the boards with his shoes flapping.
For his aim's to fill his purse, and after that,
he's not concerned if his play stands up or falls.
When a man sails to the stage in Ambition's car,
dull audiences make him sag and keen ones
swell him; if hearts are greedy for applause,
they're crushed or revived by so little. Not drama, thanks,
180 if I'm to be wasted by failure or puffed with laurels!
Often the boldest poet can be routed
when he sees superior numbers – worthless people,
uncultured boors, ready to fight it out
if their betters disagree – demand in mid-play
a bear or boxers (that's what thrills the mob).
But enjoyment has fled from even their betters' ears
to that dubious judge, the eye, and empty pleasures.

The Play stands still; damn action and discourse,
Back fly the scenes, and enter foot and horse;
Pageants on pageants, in long order drawn,
Peers, Heralds, Bishops, Ermin, Gold, and Lawn;
The Champion too! and, to complete the jest,
Old Edward's Armour beams on Cibber's breast!
320   With laughter sure Democritus had dy'd,
Had he beheld an Audience gape so wide.
Let Bear or Elephant be e'er so white,
The people, sure, the people are the sight!
Ah luckless Poet! stretch thy lungs and roar,
That Bear or Elephant shall heed thee more
While all its throats the Gallery extends,
And all the Thunder of the Pit ascends!
Loud as the Wolves on Orcas' stormy steep,
Howl to the roarings of the Northern deep.
330   Such is the shout, the long-applauding note,
At Quin's high plume, or Oldfield's petticoat,
Or when from Court a birth-day suit bestow'd
Sinks the lost Actor in the tawdry load.
Booth enters – hark! the Universal Peal!
'But has he spoken?' Not a syllable.
'What shook the stage, and made the people stare?'
Cato's long Wig, flowr'd gown, and lacquer'd chair.

   Yet lest you think I railly more than teach,
Or praise malignly Arts I cannot reach,
340   Let me for once presume t' instruct the times,
To know the Poet from the Man of Rymes:
'Tis He, who gives my breast a thousand pains,
Can make me feel each Passion that he feigns,
Inrage, compose, with more than magic Art,
With Pity, and with Terror, tear my heart;
And snatch me, o'er the earth, or thro' the air,
To Thebes, to Athens, when he will, and where.

   But not this part of the poetic state
Alone, deserves the favour of the Great:

The back-drop stays in place for a good four hours
while troops of footmen or cavalry stampede;
190 then glorious kings are dragged along in manacles,
chariots, carriages, waggons, ships strain past
with captured ivory, all the loot from Corinth.
If Democritus returned to earth, he'd laugh
when a crossbred mixture of a panther with a camel
or a white elephant turned the public's heads;
he would watch the audience closer than the show
as a far richer source of entertainment;
but the playwrights he would think were wasting words
on a stone-deaf ass. What voice can overcome
200 our reverberating theatres? You would think
Garganus' woods or the Tuscan sea were rearing;
such is the noise that greets the show with its
exotic trappings; when an actor enters
bedizened with them, right and left hand clash.
'Has he spoken yet?' No, no. 'What's pleased them, then?'
The dye that stains his cloak with bogus violets.
And do not think that I am mean with praise
when others succeed where I refuse to try:
to me, he's nothing short of a tight-rope walker,
210 the poet who wrings my heart with empty sorrows,
stirs, soothes, fills it with false terrors
like a wizard, and transports me to Thebes or Athens.
But there are also those who confide in readers
rather than be scorned by the proud spectator:

430] EPISTLE II.I · ALEXANDER POPE

350 Think of those Authors, Sir, who would rely
More on a Reader's sense, than Gazer's eye.
Or who shall wander where the Muses sing?
Who climb their Mountain, or who taste their spring?
How shall we fill a Library with Wit,
When Merlin's Cave is half unfurnish'd yet?
    My Liege! why Writers little claim your thought,
I guess; and, with their leave, will tell the fault:
We Poets are (upon a Poet's word)
Of all mankind, the creatures most absurd:
360 The season, when to come, and when to go,
To sing, or cease to sing, we never know;
And if we will recite nine hours in ten,
You lose your patience, just like other men.
Then too we hurt our selves, when to defend
A single verse, we quarrel with a friend;
Repeat unask'd; lament, the Wit's too fine
For vulgar eyes, and point out ev'ry line.
But most, when straining with too weak a wing,
We needs will write Epistles to the King;
370 And from the moment we oblige the town,
Expect a Place, or Pension from the Crown;
Or dubb'd Historians by express command,
T' enroll your triumphs o'er the seas and land;
Be call'd to Court, to plan some work divine,
As once for Louis, Boileau and Racine.
    Yet think great Sir! (so many Virtues shown)
Ah think, what Poet best may make them known?
Or chuse at least some Minister of Grace,
Fit to bestow the Laureat's weighty place.
380   Charles, to late times to be transmitted fair,
Assign'd his figure to Bernini's care;
And great Nassau to Kneller's hand decreed
To fix him graceful on the bounding Steed:
So well in paint and stone they judg'd of merit:
But Kings in Wit may want discerning spirit.

spare them a moment, if you wish Apollo's library
to be filled as it deserves and to spur our bards
to fresh efforts in the race for leafy Helicon.
We poets are often our worst enemies
(to hack at my own vines): when we show you books,
220 though you are preoccupied or tired; when we take offence
at a friend who dares object to one single verse;
when we unroll our unsolicited encores;
when we lament that our labours, fine-spun webs
of poetry, have simply gone unnoticed;
when we hope it will come to the point that as soon as you know
we are practising poets, you kindly send for us,
cast out our poverty and drive us into writing.
But it's as well to ask what sort of attendant
merit in peace and war should have for its temple;
230 for it must not be put in the hands of unworthy poets.
The great king Alexander had a taste
for Choerilus, whose misbegotten verses
were credited to him in the royal coinage.
But just as handling ink leaves stains or blots,
so writers tend to smudge resplendent deeds

The Hero William, and the Martyr Charles,
One knighted Blackmore, and one pension'd Quarles;
Which made old Ben, and surly Dennis swear,
'No Lord's anointed, but a Russian Bear.'

390 Not with such Majesty, such bold relief,
The forms august of King, or conqu'ring Chief,
E'er swell'd on Marble; as in Verse have shin'd
(In polish'd Verse) the Manners and the Mind.
Oh! could I mount on the Maeonian wing,
Your Arms, your Actions, your Repose to sing!
What seas you travers'd! and what fields you fought!
Your Country's Peace, how oft, how dearly bought!
How barb'rous rage subsided at your word,
And Nations wonder'd while they dropp'd the sword!

400 How, when you nodded, o'er the land and deep,
Peace stole her wing, and wrapt the world in sleep;
Till Earth's extremes your mediation own,
And Asia's Tyrants tremble at your Throne –
But Verse alas! your Majesty disdains;
And I'm not us'd to Panegyric strains:
The Zeal of Fools offends at any time,
But most of all, the Zeal of Fools in ryme.
Besides, a fate attends on all I write,
That when I aim at praise, they say I bite.

410 A vile Encomium doubly ridicules;
There's nothing blackens like the ink of fools;
If true, a woful likeness, and if lyes,
'Praise undeserv'd is scandal in disguise:'
Well may he blush, who gives it, or receives;
And when I flatter, let my dirty leaves
(Like Journals, Odes, and such forgotten things
As Eusden, Philips, Settle, writ of Kings)
Cloath spice, line trunks, or flutt'ring in a row,
Befringe the rails of Bedlam and Sohoe.   (pub. 1738)

        with dull poems. The very king who bought
        such laughable work at such an extravagant price
        decreed that no-one but Apelles paint,
        and no-one but Lysippus cast a likeness
240   of the mighty Alexander's face. But ask
        that fine and subtle judge of the visual arts
        to pronounce on books, the Muses' gift to men –
        you'd swear he sprang from the Boeotian fog.
        But your good judgement and your benefactions
        (a credit to the giver) are not disgraced
        by those poets you loved so well, Virgil and Varius:
        nor do bronze portrait-busts bring out more clearly
        the character and spirit of great men
        than the bard's work. And I should not prefer
250   my earthbound *causeries* to epic deeds,
        strange lands and rivers, fortresses set up
        on mountain-tops, exotic kingdoms, wars
        waged throughout the world under your standards,
        Janus, keeper of peace, locked in his temple,
        and Rome dreaded by Parthia in your reign,
        if my powers matched my wishes: but your greatness
        allows no minor poems, and my modesty
        dares not attempt a theme I could not sustain.
        A service pressed on those we admire ineptly
260   smothers them – most of all in the shape of verse;
        for men more readily memorize what makes them
        laugh than what they approve of and revere.
        I have no time for a favour that weighs me down,
        nor do I want myself exhibited
        as a waxen head or graced by shoddy verses;
        I'd blush at so gross a tribute, find myself
        cased with my author, coffined, carted down
        to the back-streets where they peddle balm and spice
        and everything that's draped in misused paper.   (pub. 1986)

PHILIP FRANCIS

Epistle I.5

For a closer translation, see the version by Colin Macleod (pp. 455–6).

If, dear Torquatus, you can kindly deign
To lie on Beds of simple Form, and plain,
Where Herbs alone shall be your frugal Feast,
At Evening I expect you for my Guest.
Nor old, I own, nor excellent, my Wine,
Of five Years Vintage, and a marshy Vine;
If you have better, bring th' enlivening Chear,
Or, from an humble Friend, this Summons bear.
    Bright shines my Hearth, my Furniture is clean,
With Joy my courtly Guest to entertain:
Then leave the Hope, that, wing'd with Folly flies;
Leave the mean Quarrels, that from Wealth arise;
Leave the litigious Bar, for Caesar's Birth
Proclaims the festal Hour of Ease and Mirth,
While social Converse, and sincere Delight,
Shall stretch beyond its Length the Summer's Night.
Say, what are Fortune's Gifts, if I'm denied
Their chearful Use? for nearly are allied
The Madman, and the fool, whose sordid Care
Makes himself poor, but to enrich his Heir.
Give me to drink, and, crown'd with Flowers despise
The grave Disgrace of being thought unwise.
    What cannot Wine perform? It brings to light
The secret Soul; it bids the Coward fight;
Gives Being to our Hopes, and from our Hearts
Drives the dull Sorrow, and inspires new Arts.
Whom hath not an inspiring Bumper taught
A Flow of Words, and Loftiness of Thought?

>   Even in th' oppressive Grasp of Poverty
> 30 It can enlarge, and bid the Wretch be free.
>   Chearful my usual Task I undertake,
>   (Nor a mean Figure in my Office make)
>   That no foul Linen wrinkle up the Nose;
>   That every Plate with bright Reflexion shows
>   My Guest his Face; that none when Life grows gay,
>   The social Hour of Confidence betray.
>   That all in equal Friendship may unite,
>   Your Butra and Septicius I'll invite,
>   And, if he's not engag'd to better Cheer,
> 40 Or a kind Girl, Sabinus shall be here.
>   Still there is Room, and yet the Summer's Heat
>   May prove offensive, if the Croud be great:
>   But write me word, how many you desire
>   Then instant from the busy World retire;
>   And while your tedious Clients fill the Hall,
>   Slip out at the Back-door, and bilk them all.   (pub. 1747)

Epistle I.20

For the final epistle of Book I Horace issues his tart 'Go litel bok'. Francis evades the *double entendre* of the second line: literally, the book is to go on sale, the ends of the papyrus roll smoothed with pumice. Secondary sense: offer yourself for sale depilated (like a male prostitute).

>   The Shops of Rome impatient to behold,
>   And, elegantly polish'd, to be sold,
>   You hate the tender Seal, and guardian Keys,
>   Which modest volumes love, and fondly praise,
>   The Public World, even sighing to be read, –
>   Unhappy Book! to other Manners bred.
>   Indulge the fond Desire, with which You burn,
>   Pursue thy Flight, yet think not to return.

But when insulted by the Critic's Scorn,
How often shall You cry, ah! me forlorn?
When he shall throw the tedious Volume by,
Nor longer view thee with a Lover's Eye.

If Rage pervert not my prophetic Truth,
Rome shall admire, while you can charm with Youth,
But soon as vulgar Hands thy Beauty soil,
The Moth shall batten on the silent Spoil;
Then fly to Afric, or be sent to Spain,
Our Colonies of Wits to entertain.
This shall thy fond Adviser laughing see,
As, when his Ass was obstinate like thee,
The Clown in Vengeance push'd him down the Hill:
For who would save an Ass against his Will?

At last thy stammering Age in Suburb-Schools
Shall toil in teaching Boys their Grammar-Rules:
But when in Evening mild the listening Tribe
Around thee throng, thy Master thus describe;
A Freed-man's Son, with moderate Fortune blest,
Who boldly spread his Wings beyond his Nest;
What from my Birth you take, to Virtue give,
And say, with Ease and Happiness I live,
With all that Rome in Peace and War calls great;
Of lowly Stature: fond of Summer's Heat:
Early turn'd gray: to Passion quickly rais'd,
Yet not ill-natur'd, and with Ease appeas'd.
Let them, who ask my Age, be frankly told,
That I was forty-four Decembers old,
When Lollius chose with Lepidus to share
The Powers and Honours of the Consul's Chair. (pub. 1747)

ANON.

Epistle I.10 An imitation

Included in William Duncombe's *The Works of Horace in English Verse. By Several Hands* (1757–9). For Horace's fable of the stag and the horse, thought to have a political application, the author substitutes an event from early English history: the 'British monarch' Vortigern called on the 'warlike Saxon' Hengist for help. In the fable the horse, regularly worsted by the stag, calls on a man to help him; the man does so, then becomes his master.

> Dellius, of rural Scenes a Lover grown,
> Salutes his Friend, a Lover of the Town:
> Except the Difference Town and Country make,
> Who think we disagree, perhaps mistake;
> (The Difference much the same as is between
> The Egg a Swan produces, and a Hen)
> Debating, scribbling, saunt'ring, sitting still,
> Studious of Ease, and Brothers of the Quill.
>   London your Choice, I know; but I approve
> The mossy Seat, the River and the Grove.
> If you should ask how I employ my Hour –
> Better than those in Place, or those in Power;
> Not plagu'd with Business, nor a Slave to Pelf,
> Lord of my Time, and Master of myself.
> What have your noisy Streets like this to give?
> Or what like this, Newcastle to receive?
> Cotta, disgrac'd, in Ariconian Vales,
> Likes, I am told, the Neighbourhood of Wales;
> Sick of Parade, Attendance and Resort,
> Flies, and exhales the Surfeit of a Court.
>   You want a Ground-plot for some new Design!
> Consult the Oracle at Nature's Shrine,

'Build in the Country,' says the Voice divine.
   Is there, where Winters purer Joys inspire,
Morn's wholesome Frost, and Evening's smokeless Fire?
Is there, where Summer's more refreshing Gales
Fan the scorch'd Hills, and chear the drooping Vales?
Where Discontent a rarer Guest is seen,
Or Sleep less broken by intruding Spleen?
30   What is that Marble Portal to this Bower,
Array'd in Green, or pearl'd by every Shower?
Or what the Stream which Pipes and Conduits yield,
To the bright Rill that trickles through my Field?
   Copying, ye own your Wants; the Case is clear;
In Town ye humbly mimic what is here.
Look at St James's or on Grosvenor-Square;
Behold our Walks, our Trees, and our Parterre!
Tell me, why Sheffield's House so pleasant stands?
Because a Length of Country it commands.
40   Nature, though of her Tone by Force bereft,
Returns elastic to the Point she left;
Spite of Distortion she appears the same,
And from the Bend recovers like the Palm.
   Not she, who, gull'd by Want of Taste, or Care,
Buys the resembling Delf for China Ware,
Nor they who to a City Vault resort,
And are, instead of Claret, dup'd with Port,
Will half so dearly the Deception rue,
As they who take false Blessings for the true.
50   Who launch too far on Fortune's peaceful Lake,
The Tempest of Adversity will shake.
'Tis hard to part with what allures the Eyes,
And the Hand pauses, ere it drops the Prize.
   Fly then betimes, with unambitious Wings,
To the still Vale, where Peace eternal springs,
Leave Anguish to the Great, and Cares to Kings!
   The British Monarch, by the Picts dismay'd,
Call'd in the warlike Saxon to his Aid.

His good Ally to Conquest led the Way,
60 But took the whole Dominion for his Pay:
The Stranger, wanton in his new Abode,
Soon on the Neck of Vassal Nobles trod,
And lifted high the Hand, and exercis'd the Rod.

    Thus, if my Friend should for Preferment trade,
And sell his Liberty, of Want afraid;
The meagre Monster is no more I own,
But a more lordly Tyrant mounts the Throne;
And who a Treasure by Dependence gains,
I wish him well and long to wear his Chains.
70 'Tis known that Shoes (just such is an Estate)
Pinch, or supplant, too little, or too great.

    If wise, you'll be content, though short of Wealth,
With the rich Gifts of Competence and Health:
Despise not then the Happiness they bring,
For virtuous Freedom is a sacred Thing.
And when you see me break the Rule laid down,
And on some Courtier fawning in the Town,
Give to your Indignation full Career,
Nor spare your Friend, but justly be severe.   (pub. 1759)

M. G. ('MONK') LEWIS
(1775–1818)

Born of wealthy parents, author of the Gothic shocker *The Monk* (1796), written in ten weeks, he claimed, while he was attaché to the British embassy at The Hague. Sat in the House of Commons for six years, acquainted with the royal family, Scott, Byron and Shelley. This imitation (for a closer version compare Francis, pp. 435–6) stands as the preface to his novel.

Epistle I.20 An imitation

Methinks, Oh! vain ill-judging Book,
I see thee cast a wishful look,
Where reputations won and lost are
In famous row called Paternoster.
Incensed to find your precious olio
Buried in unexplored port-folio,
You scorn the prudent lock and key,
And pant well bound and gilt to see
Your Volume in the window set
10 Of Stockdale, Hookham, or Debrett.

Go then, and pass that dangerous bourn
Whence never Book can back return:
And when you find, condemned, despised,
Neglected, blamed, and criticised,
Abuse from All who read you fall,
(If haply you be read at all)
Sorely will you your folly sigh at,
And wish for me, and home, and quiet.

Assuming now a conjuror's office, I
20 Thus on your future Fortune prophesy: –
Soon as your novelty is o'er,
And you are young and new no more,
In some dark dirty corner thrown,
Mouldy with damps, with cobwebs strown,
Your leaves shall be the Book-worm's prey;
Or sent to Chandler-Shop away,
And doomed to suffer public scandal,
Shall line the trunk, or wrap the candle!

But should you meet with approbation,
30 And some one find an inclination
To ask, by natural transition,
Respecting me and my condition;
That I am one, the enquirer teach,
Nor very poor, nor very rich;
Of passions strong, of hasty nature,
Of graceless form and dwarfish stature;
By few approved, and few approving;
Extreme in hating and in loving;

Abhorring all whom I dislike,
40 Adoring who my fancy strike;
In forming judgements never long,
And for the most part judging wrong;
In friendship firm, but still believing
Others are treacherous and deceiving,
And thinking in the present aera
That Friendship is a pure chimaera:
More passionate no creature living,
Proud, obstinate, and unforgiving,
But yet for those who kindness show,
50 Ready through fire and smoke to go.

Again, should it be asked your page,
'Pray, what may be the author's age?'
Your faults, no doubt, will make it clear,
I scarce have seen my twentieth year,
Which passed, kind Reader, on my word,
While England's Throne held George the Third.

Now then your venturous course pursue:
Go, my delight! Dear Book, adieu! (pub. 1796)

FRANCIS HOWES

Epistle I.2, lines 1–31

Writing to a young friend who is studying rhetoric, Horace – who in his first epistle had announced that he was giving up poetry in favour of philosophy – tells him how much there is to be learned from Homer, who, better than the philosopher, shows 'where moral fitness lies', or in Colin Macleod's more literal version, 'what's right or wrong, what helps or harms'.

> While in the schools at Rome, you, Lollius! plead,
> I at Praeneste with new rapture read
> The tale of Troy divine, whose facts declare
> Where moral fitness lies – expedience where,
> Better than all the logic of the sage,
> Than Crantor's precepts or Chrysippus' page.
> Ask you wherein our bard instructs so well?
> If time permit, give audience while I tell.
>   When he records the slow-consuming strife
> 10 That Greece encounter'd for a treacherous wife,
> His glowing pencil paints what mischief springs
> From the mad broils of nations and of kings.
> Antenor would the cause of war remove:
> Fond Paris deems the world well lost for love.
> Nestor in all the majesty of age
> Steps forth by sapient counsel to assuage
> The wrath that 'twixt the royal chieftains rose,
> Wrath better shown against their common foes; –
> In vain: – To pride and passion each holds true;
> 20 And while the monarchs rave, the people rue.
> By envy, faction, lust, and fraud they sin
> Alike without Troy's bulwarks and within.

What a firm soul and valorous heart avail
Mark in the hero of his second tale, –
Who, when the Trojan towers in dust were laid,
Saw various realms and well their manners weigh'd, –
And, toiling long his native shore to gain,
Stem'd countless hardships on the stormy main, –
Firm in adversity, in peril brave,
30 And buoyant upon Fortune's roughest wave.
You know the Sirens' song and Circe's draught,
Which had he with his crew unguarded quaff'd,
A harlot's slave he had been doom'd to pine
Sunk in the senseless hound or wallowing swine.
See pictur'd in the revelling suitor-train
The sensual, the voluptuous, and the vain!
Mark the spruce fribbles of Alcinous' court,
Soft sons of sloth dissolved in amorous sport,
Who snored till midnoon, and to melting airs
40 Lull'd in delicious trance life's anxious cares!
How many still with these poor idlers vie,
Born but to eat and drink and sleep and die! (pub. 1845)

JOHN CONINGTON

Epistle I.1

Having composed three books of odes, Horace is now to turn to a serious pursuit, to philosophy – philosophy in the spirit of Plato's question 'How should I live?' – that attends to the practical concerns of everyday life. Horace means what he says, but Pope's imitation provides a salutary hint that we should also attend to *how* he says it.

Theme of my earliest Muse in days long past,
Theme that shall be hereafter of my last,
Why summon back, Maecenas, to the list
Your worn-out swordsman, pensioned and dismissed?
My age, my mind, no longer are the same
As when I first was 'prenticed to the game.
Veianius fastens to Alcides' gate
His arms, then nestles in his snug estate:
Think you once more upon the arena's marge
10 He'd care to stand and supplicate discharge?
No: I've a Mentor who, not once nor twice,
Breathes in my well-rinsed ear his sound advice,
'Give rest in time to that old horse, for fear
At last he founder 'mid the general jeer.'
So now I bid my idle songs adieu,
And turn my thoughts to what is right and true;
I search and search, and when I find, I lay
The wisdom up against a rainy day.

But what's my sect? you ask me; I must be
20 A member sure of some fraternity:
Why no; I've taken no man's shilling; none
Of all your fathers owns me for his son;
Just where the weather drives me, I invite
Myself to take up quarters for the night.
Now, all alert, I cope with life's rough main,
A loyal follower in true virtue's train:
Anon, to Aristippus' camp I flit,
And say, the world's for me, not I for it.

Long as the night to him whose love is gone,
30 Long as the day to slaves that must work on,
Slow as the year to the impatient ward
Who finds a mother's tutelage too hard,
So long, so slow the moments that prevent
The execution of my high intent,
Of studying truths that rich and poor concern,
Which young and old are lost unless they learn.

Well, if I cannot be a student, yet
There's good in spelling at the alphabet.
Your eyes will never see like Lynceus'; still
40 You rub them with an ointment when they're ill:
You cannot hope for Glyco's stalwart frame,
Yet you'd avoid the gout that makes you lame.
Some point of moral progress each may gain,
Though to aspire beyond it should prove vain.

   Say, is your bosom fevered with the fire
Of sordid avarice or unchecked desire?
Know, there are spells will help you to allay
The pain, and put good part of it away.
You're bloated by ambition? take advice;
50 Yon book will ease you if you read it thrice.
Run through the list of faults; whate'er you be,
Coward, pickthank, spitfire, drunkard, debauchee,
Submit to culture patiently, you'll find
Her charms can humanize the rudest mind.

   To fly from vice is virtue: to be free
From foolishness is wisdom's first degree.
Think of some ill you feel a real disgrace,
The loss of money or the loss of place;
To keep yourself from these, how keen the strain!
60 How dire the sweat of body and of brain!
Through tropic heat, o'er rocks and seas you run
To furthest India, poverty to shun,
Yet scorn the sage who offers you release
From vagrant wishes that disturb your peace.
Take some provincial pugilist, who gains
A paltry cross-way prize for all his pains;
Place on his brow Olympia's chaplet, earned
Without a struggle, would the gift be spurned?

   Gold counts for more than silver, all men hold:
70 Why doubt that virtue counts for more than gold?
'Seek money first, good friends, and virtue next,'
Each Janus lectures on the well-worn text;

Lads learn it for their lessons; grey-haired men,
Like schoolboys, drawl the sing-song o'er again.
You lack, say, some six thousand of the rate
The law has settled as a knight's estate;
Though soul, tongue, morals, credit, all the while
Are yours, you reckon with the rank and file.
But mark those children at their play; they sing,
'Deal fairly, youngster, and we'll crown you king.'
Be this your wall of brass, your coat of mail,
A guileless heart, a cheek no crime turns pale.

   Which is the better teacher, tell me, pray,
The law of Roscius, or the children's lay
That crowns fair dealing, by Camillus trolled,
And manly Curius, in the days of old;
The voice that says, 'Make money, money, man;
Well, if so be, – if not, which way you can,'
That from a nearer distance you may gaze
At honest Pupius' all too moving plays;
Or that which bids you meet with dauntless brow,
The frowns of Fortune, ay, and shows you how?

   Suppose the world of Rome accosts me thus:
'You walk where we walk; why not think with us,
Be ours for better or for worse, pursue
The things we love, the things we hate eschew?'
I answer as sly Reynard answered, when
The ailing lion asked him to his den:
'I'm frightened at those footsteps: every track
Leads to your home, but ne'er a one leads back.'
Nay, you're a perfect Hydra: who shall choose
Which view to follow out of all your views?
Some farm the taxes; some delight to see
Their money grow by usury, like a tree;
Some bait a widow-trap with fruits and cakes,
And net old men, to stock their private lakes.
But grant that folks have different hobbies; say,
Does one man ride one hobby one whole day?

'Baiae's the place!' cries Croesus: all is haste;
110 The lake, the sea, soon feel their master's taste:
A new whim prompts: 'tis 'Pack your tools to-night!
Off for Teanum with the dawn of light!'
The nuptial bed is in his hall; he swears
None but a single life is free from cares:
Is he a bachelor? all human bliss,
He vows, is centred in a wedded kiss.
   How shall I hold this Proteus in my gripe?
How fix him down in one enduring type?
Turn to the poor: their megrims are as strange;
120 Bath, cockloft, barber, eating-house, they change;
They hire a boat; your born aristocrat
Is not more squeamish, tossing in his yacht.
   If, when we meet, I'm cropped in awkward style
By some uneven barber, then you smile;
You smile, if, as it haps, my gown's askew,
If my shirt's ragged while my tunic's new:
How, if my mind's inconsequent, rejects
What late it longed for, what it loathed affects,
Shifts every moment, with itself at strife,
130 And makes a chaos of an ordered life,
Builds castles up, then pulls them to the ground,
Keeps changing round for square and square for round?
You smile not; 'tis an every-day affair:
I need no doctor's, no, nor keeper's care:
Yet you're my patron, and would blush to fail
In taking notice of an ill-pared nail.
   So, to sum up: the sage is half divine,
Rich, free, great, handsome, king of kings, in fine;
A miracle of health from toe to crown,
140 Mind, heart, and head, save when his nose runs
   down.   (pub. 1870)

Epistle I.19

With acerb obliquity Horace defends his three books of odes and their creative use of Greek models against servile imitators and detractors.

If truth there be in old Cratinus' song,
No verse, you know, Maecenas, can live long
Writ by a water-drinker. Since the day
When Bacchus took us poets into pay
With fauns and satyrs, the celestial Nine
Have smelt each morning of last evening's wine.
The praises heaped by Homer on the bowl
At once convict him as a thirsty soul:
And father Ennius ne'er could be provoked
To sing of battles till his lips were soaked.
'Let temperate folk write verses in the hall
Where bonds change hands, abstainers not at all';
So ran my edict: now the clan drinks hard,
And vinous breath distinguishes a bard.
  What if a man appeared with gown cut short
Bare feet, grim visage, after Cato's sort?
Would you respect him, hail him from henceforth
The heir of Cato's mind, of Cato's worth?
The wretched Moor, who matched himself in wit
With keen Timagenes, in sunder split.
Faults are soon copied: should my colour fail,
Our bards drink cummin, hoping to look pale.
Mean, miserable apes! the coil you make
Oft gives my heart, and oft my sides, an ache.
  Erect and free I walk the virgin sod,
Too proud to tread the path by others trod.
The man who trusts himself, and dares step out,
Soon sets the fashion to the inferior rout.
'Tis I who first to Italy have shown
Iambics, quarried from the Parian stone;

EPISTLE I.19 · JOHN CONINGTON

Following Archilochus in rhythm and stave,
But not the words that dug Lycambes' grave.
Yet think not that I merit scantier bays,
Because in form I reproduce his lays:
Strong Sappho now and then adopts a tone
From that same lyre, to qualify her own;
So does Alcaeus, though in all beside,
Style, order, thought, the difference is wide;
'Gainst no false fair he turns his angry Muse,
40 Nor for her guilty father twists the noose.
Ay, and Alcaeus' name, before unheard,
My Latian harp has made a household word.
Well may the bard feel proud, whose pen supplies
Unhackneyed strains to gentle hands and eyes.

    Ask you what makes the uncourteous reader laud
My works at home, but run them down abroad?
I stoop not, I, to catch the rabble's votes
By cheap refreshments or by cast-off coats,
Nor haunt the benches where your pedants swarm,
50 Prepared by turns to listen and perform.
That's what this whimpering means. Suppose I say
'Your theatres have ne'er been in my way,
Nor I in theirs: large audiences require
Some heavier metal than my thin-drawn wire':
'You put me off,' he answers, 'with a sneer:
Your works are kept for Jove's imperial ear:
Yes, you're a paragon of bards, you think,
And no one else brews nectar fit to drink.'
What can I do? 'tis an unequal match;
60 For if my nose can sniff, his nails can scratch:
I say the place won't suit me, and cry shame;
'E'en fencers get a break 'twixt game and game.'
Games oft have ugly issue: they beget
Unhealthy competition, fume and fret:
And fume and fret engender in their turn
Battles that bleed, and enmities that burn.   (pub. 1870)

K. W. GRANSDEN

Epistle I.4

Appears here for the first time in print.

> What are you doing these days, friend?
> Am I to report that you're writing something new,
> Or just pottering quietly about,
> Living the good life of a sensible man.
> You've a soul as well a body, you're blessed
> With a decent physique, enough to live on,
> And you know how to enjoy yourself.
> What more could anyone wish for you?
> To think straight, say what you think,
> And count your blessings – health, reputation, charm –
> So in this world of delusion and angst and fear
> Live every day as if it were your last.
> Each hour you didn't count on counts as a bonus.
> And when you feel like a chat, come over and see me.

ROBERT PINSKY (1940–)

Author of several books of verse and a critical study of Landor's poetry (1968). This translation is from *An Explanation of America* (1979).

Epistle I.16 A free translation

'Dear Quinctius:
                 I'll tell you a little about
My farm – in case you ever happen to wonder
About the place: as, what I make in grain,
Or if I'm getting rich on olives, apples,
Timber or pasture.
                 There are hills, unbroken
Except for one soft valley, cut at an angle
That sweetens the climate, because it takes the sun
All morning on its right slope, until the left
Has its turn, warming as the sun drives past
All afternoon. You'd like it here: the plums
And low-bush berries are ripe; and where my cows
Fill up on acorns and ilex-berries a lush
Canopy of shade gives pleasure to their master.
The green is deep, so deep you'd say Tarentum
Had somehow nestled closer, to be near Rome.

There is a spring, fit for a famous river
(The Hebrus winds through Thrace no colder or purer),
Useful for healing stomach-aches and head-aches.
And here I keep myself, and the place keeps me –
A precious good, believe it, Quinctius –
In health and sweetness through September's heat.
You of course live in the way that is truly right,
If you've been careful to remain the man
That we all see in you. We here in Rome
Talk of you, always, as "happy" . . . there is the fear,
Of course, that one might listen too much to others,
Think what they see, and strive to be that thing,
And lose by slow degrees that inward man
Others first noticed – as though, if over and over
Everyone tells you you're in marvelous health,

You might towards dinner-time, when a latent fever
Falls on you, try for a long while to disguise it,
Until the trembling rattles your food-smeared hands.
It's foolishness to camouflage our sores.

Take "recognition" – what if someone writes
A speech about your service to your country,
Telling for your attentive ears the roll
Of all your victories by land or sea,
With choice quotations, dignified periods,
40   And skillful terms, all in the second person,
As in the citations for honorary degrees:
"*Only a mind beyond our human powers*
Could judge if your great love for Rome exceeds,
Or is exceeded by, Rome's need for you."

– You'd find it thrilling, but inappropriate
For anyone alive, except Augustus.

And yet if someone calls me "wise" or "flawless"
Must one protest? I like to be told I'm right,
And brilliant, as much as any other man.
50   The trouble is, the people who give out
The recognition, compliments, degrees
Can take them back tomorrow, if they choose;
The committee or electorate decide
You can't sit in the Senate, or have the Prize –
"Sorry, but isn't that ours, that you nearly took?"
What can I do, but shuffle sadly off?
If the same people scream that I'm a crook
Who'd strangle my father for money to buy a drink,
Should I turn white with pain and humiliation?
60   If prizes and insults from outside have much power
To hurt or give joy, something is sick inside.

Who is "the good man"?
                        Many people would answer,
"He is the man who never breaks the law
Or violates our codes. His judgment is sound.
He is the man whose word is as his bond.
If such a man agrees to be your witness,
Your case is won."
                        And yet this very man,
If you ask his family, or the people who know him,
Is like a rotten egg in its flawless shell.
70 And if a slave or prisoner should say
"I never steal; I never try to escape,"
My answer is, "You have your just rewards:
No beatings; no solitary; and your food."
"I have not killed." "You won't be crucified."
"But haven't I shown that I am good, and honest?"

To this, my country neighbor would shake his head
And sigh: "Ah no! The wolf himself is wary
Because he fears the pit, as hawks the snare
Or pike the hook. Some folk hate vice for love
80 Of the good: you're merely afraid of guards and crosses."

Apply that peasant wisdom to that "good man"
Of forum and tribunal, who in the temple
Calls loudly on "Father Janus" or "Apollo"
But in an undertone implores, "Laverna,
Goddess of thieves, O Fair One, grant me, please,
That I get away with it, let me pass as upright,
Cover my sins with darkness, my lies with clouds."

When a man stoops to pluck at the coin some boys
Of Rome have soldered to the street, I think
90 That just then he is no more free than any
Prisoner, or slave; it seems that someone who wants

Too much to get things is also someone who fears,
And living in that fear cannot be free.
A man has thrown away his weapons, has quit
The struggle for virtue, who is always busy
Filling his wants, getting things, making hay –
Weaponless and defenseless as a captive.

When you have got a captive, you never kill him
If you can sell him for a slave; this man
Truly will make a good slave: persevering,
Ambitious, eager to please – as ploughman, or shepherd,
Or trader plying your goods at sea all winter,
Or helping to carry fodder at the farm . . .
The truly good, and wise man has more courage;
And if need be, will find the freedom to say,
As in the *Bacchae* of Euripides:

*King Pentheus, Lord of Thebes, what will you force me
To suffer at your hands?*
                I will take your goods.

*You mean my cattle, furniture, cloth and plate?
Then you may have them.*
                *I will put you, chained,
Into my prison, under a cruel guard.*

*Then God himself, the moment that I choose,
Will set me free . . .*

I think that what this means is: "I will die."

Death is the chalk-line towards which all things race.'

(pub. 1979)

COLIN MACLEOD

For Macleod see the headnote to Pope's imitation of Epistle II.1 (p. 411).

Epistle I.5

If you can bear to lie on a plain couch
and dine off vegetables from modest plates,
I shall expect you, Torquatus, here at sundown.
There'll be wine racked in Taurus' second consulship
between Minturnae's marshes and Petrinum.
If you've better, send for it: if not, take orders.
My hearth has long been bright, my silver polished.
Leave those fluttering hopes and fights for wealth
and that poisoning case; tomorrow Caesar's birthday
affords us leave to sleep, so we can safely
spin out the summer night with friendly talk.
What good to me is wealth, if I cannot use it?
Thrift and austerity practised for an heir
are next to madness. I'll drink deep, strew flowers,
and even let it be thought I've lost my judgment.
Drink gets up to anything – takes off lids,
ratifies hopes, thrusts cowards into battle,
unburdens weary hearts, teaches fresh skills.
Whom have flowing cups not made fluent?
Whom have they not released from the pinch of need?
My orders are – and I'm competent and willing –
that no threadbare coverlet, no dirty napkin
crease up your nose; that no cup or plate
be less than a mirror to you; that no friend
publish abroad what's said; that all and each
mix and match. Butra, Septicius –
and if he's no better engagement, or girl he prefers,

Sabinus – are counted in. There's room for extras,
though tight-packed dinners feel the smell of goat.
30 Advise me on numbers; then leave by the back-door
and let down the dependants in your hall. (pub. 1986)

ARS POETICA (EPISTLE II.3)

A composite version of the poem in chronological order, translations and imitations by Ben Jonson, the Earl of Roscommon, John Oldham, Thomas Creech, Philip Francis, Francis Howes, Lord Byron (in *Hints from Horace*), John Conington, Roy Campbell, C. H. Sisson.

If to a Womans head a Painter would   BEN JONSON
Set a Horse-neck, and divers feathers fold
On every limbe, ta'en from a severall creature,
Presenting upwards, a faire female feature,
Which in some swarthie fish uncomely ends:
Admitted to the sight, although his friends,
Could you containe your laughter? Credit mee,
This peece, my Piso's, and that booke agree,
Whose shapes, like sick-mens dreames, are fain'd so vaine,
10 As neither head, nor foot, one forme retaine.
But equall power, to Painter, and to Poët,
Of daring all, hath still beene given; we know it:
And both doe crave, and give againe, this leave.
Yet, not as therefore wild, and tame should cleave
Together: not that we should Serpents see
With Doves; or Lambes, with Tygres coupled be.
    In grave beginnings, and great things profest,
Ye have oft-times, that may ore-shine the rest,
A Scarlet peece, or two, stitch'd in: when or
20 Diana's Grove, or Altar, with the bor-

Dring Circles of swift waters that intwine
The pleasant grounds, or when the River Rhine,
Or Rainbow is describ'd. But here was now
No place for these. And, Painter, hap'ly, thou
Know'st only well to paint a Cipresse tree.
What's this? if he whose money hireth thee
To paint him, hath by swimming, hopelesse, scap'd,
The whole fleet wreck'd? A great jarre to be shap'd,
Was meant at first. Why, forcing still about
30 Thy labouring wheele, comes scarce a Pitcher out?
In short; I bid, Let what thou work'st upon,
Be simple quite throughout, and wholly one.

(writ. 1604; rev.; pub. 1640)

Most Poets fall into the grossest faults,   EARL OF
Deluded by a seeming Excellence: ROSCOMMON,
By striving to be short, they grow Obscure,   LINES 24 FF.
And when they would write smoothly they want strength,
Their Spirits sink; while others that affect
A lofty Stile, swell to a Tympany;
Some timerous wretches start at every blast,
40 And fearing Tempests, dare not leave the Shore;
Others in love with wild variety,
Draw Boars in Waves, and Dolphins in a Wood;
Thus fear of Erring, Joyn'd with want of Skill,
Is a most certain way of Erring still.
The meanest Workman in the Aemilian Square,
May grave the Nails, or imitate the Hair,
But cannot finish what he hath begun;
What is there more ridiculous than he?
For one or two good features in a Face
50 Where all the rest are scandalously ill,
Make it but more remarkably deform'd.
Let Poets match their Subject to their strength,
And often try what weight they can support,
And what their Shoulders are too weak to bear,

After a serious and judicious choice,
Method and Eloquence will never fail;
As well the Force as Ornament of Verse,
Consists in choosing a fit time for things,
And knowing when a Muse should be indulg'd
60 In her full flight, and when she should be curb'd.
Words must be chosen, and be plac'd with skill,
You gain your point, if your industrious Art
Can make unusual words easie and plain,
But (if you write of things Abstruse or New)
Some of your own inventing may be us'd,
(So it be seldom and discreetly done)
But he that hopes to have new Words allow'd,
Must so derive them from the Graecian Spring,
As they may seem to flow without constraint;
70 Can an Impartial Reader discommend
In Varus, or in Virgil what he likes?
In Plautus or Coecilius? Why should I
Be envy'd for the little I Invent,
When Ennius and Cato's copious Style
Have so enrich'd, and so adorn'd our Tongue?
Men ever had, and ever will have leave,
To coin new words well suited to the age. (pub. 1684)

Words with the Leaves of Trees a sem-   JOHN OLDHAM,
    blance hold   LINES 60 FF.
In this respect, where every year the old
80 Fall off, and new ones in their places grow:
Death is the Fate of all things here below:
Nature her self by Art has changes felt,
The Tangier Mole (by our great Monarch built)
Like a vast Bulwark in the Ocean set,
From Pyrates and from Storms defends our Fleet:
Fens every day are drain'd, and men now Plow,
And Sow, and Reap, where they before might Row;

EPISTLE II.3 · ARS POETICA

  And Rivers have been taught by Middleton
  From their old course within new Banks to run,
90 And pay their useful Tribute to the Town.
  If Mans and Natures works submit to Fate,
  Much less must words expect a lasting date:
  Many which we approve for currant now,
  In the next Age out of request shall grow:
  And others which are now thrown out of doors,
  Shall be reviv'd, and come again in force,
  If custom please: from whence their vogue they draw,
  Which of our Speech is the sole Judg and Law.

   Homer first shew'd us in Heroick strains
100 To write of Wars, of Battles and Campaigns,
  Kings and great Leaders, mighty in Renown,
  And him we still for our chief Pattern own.

   Soft Elegy, design'd for grief and tears,
  Was first devis'd to grace some mournful Herse:
  Since to a brisker note 'tis taught to move,
  And cloaths our gayest Passions, Joy and Love.
  But, who was first Inventer of the kind,
  Criticks have sought, but never yet could find.

   Gods, Heroes, Warriors, and the lofty praise
110 Of peaceful Conquerors in Pisa's Race,
  The Mirth and Joys, which Love and Wine produce,
  With other wanton sallies of a Muse,
  The stately Ode does for its Subjects choose.

   Archilochus to vent his Gall and spite,
  In keen Iambicks first was known to write:
  Dramatick Authors us'd this sort of Verse
  On all the Greek and Roman Theaters,
  As for Discourse and Conversation fit,
  And aptst to drown the noises of the Pit.
120   If I discern not the true stile and air,
  Nor how to give the proper Character
  To every kind of work; how dare I claim,
  And challenge to my self a Poets Name?

And why had I with awkard modesty,
Rather than learn, always unskilful be?
Volpone and Morose will not admit
Of Catiline's high strains, nor is it fit
To make Sejanus on the Stage appear
In the low dress, which Comick persons wear.
130 What e're the Subject be, on which you write,
Give each thing its due place and time aright:
    Yet Comedy sometimes may raise her stile,
And angry Chremës is allow'd to swell,
And Tragedy alike sometimes has leave
To throw off Majesty, when 'tis to grieve:
Peleus and Telephus in misery,
Lay their big words, and blust'ring language by,
If they expect to make their Audience cry.
'Tis not enough to have your Plays succeed,
140 That they be elegant: they must not need
Those warm and moving touches which impart
A kind concernment to each Hearers heart,
And ravish it which way they please with art.
Where Joy and Sorrow put on good disguise,
Ours with the persons looks straight sympathize:
Would'st have me weep? thy self must first begin;
Then, Telephus, to pity I incline,
And think thy case, and all thy suff'rings mine;
But if thou'rt made to act thy part amiss,
150 I can't forbear to sleep, or laugh, or hiss.
Let words express the looks, which speakers wear;
Sad, fit a mournful and dejected air;
The passionate must huff, and storm, and rave;
The gay be pleasant, and the serious grave.
For Nature works and moulds our Frame within,
To take all manner of Impressions in:
Now makes us hot, and ready to take fire,
Now hope, now joy, now sorrow does inspire,
And all these passions in our face appear,

160 Of which the Tongue is sole interpreter:
But he whose words and Fortunes do not suit,
By Pit and Gall'ry both, is hooted out.   (pub. 1681)

> You must take care, and use quite different words, THOMAS CREECH,
> When Servants speak, or their commanding Lords, LINES 114 FF.
> When grave old Men, or head-strong Youths discourse,
> When stately Matrons, or a busy Nurse;
> A cheating Tradesman, or a labouring Clown,
> A Greek or Asian, bred at Court or Town.
>   Keep to old Tales, or if you must have new,
> 170 Feign things coherent, that may look like true:
> If you would draw Achilles in disgrace,
> Then draw Achilles, as Achilles was;
> Impatient, fierce, inexorable, proud,
> His Sword his Law, his own right hand his God:
> Medea must be furious, she must rave:
> Crafty Ixion a designing Knave;
> Io a wandring Cow, and Ino sad:
> And poor Orestes melancholy mad:
> But if you'll leave those Paths where most have gone,
> 180 And dare to make a Person of your own,
> Take care you still the same proportions strike,
> Let all the Parts agree, and be alike.
>   Unusual Subjects, Sir, 'tis hard to hit,
> It asks no common Pains, nor common Wit,
> Rather on Subjects known your Mind employ,
> And take from Homer some old tales of Troy,
> And bring those usual things again in view,
> Than venture on a Subject wholly new:
> Yet you may make these common Themes your own,
> 190 Unless you treat of things too fully known;
> Show the same humors, and that usual State,
> Or word for word too faithfully translate;

Or else your Pattern so confin'dly choose,
That you are still condemn'd to follow close,
Or break all decent measures to be loose.
　　First strain no higher, than your voice will hold,
Nor as that Cyclick writer did of old,
Begin my mighty Muse, and boldly dare,
I'll sing great Priam's Fate, and noble War.
200　What did He worth a Gape so large produce?
The travailing Mountain yields a silly Mouse,
Much better Homer, who doth all things well,
Muse, tell the Man, for you can surely tell,
Who, Troy once fall'n, to many Countries went,
And strictly view'd the Men, and Government.
As one that knows the Laws of writing right,
He makes Light follow Smoak, not Smoak the Light;
For streight, how fierce Charybdis rowls along!
How Scylla roars thro all his wondrous song!
210　Nor doth He, that He might seem deeply read,
Begin the fam'd Return of Diomed
From Meleager's death; nor dives as far,
As Leda's Eggs,
For the beginning of the Trojan War:
He always hastens on to the Events,
And still the middle of the Tale presents,
As 'twere the first, then draws the Reader on,
Till the whole Story is exactly known,
And what he can't improve he lets alone.
220　And so joins Lyes and Truth, that every part agrees,
And seem no Fiction, but a real Piece:
　　But Sir, observe; (shame waits on the neglect,)
This I, and all, as well as I, expect,
If you would have a judging Audience stay,
Be pleas'd, and clap, and sit out all the Play:
Observe what Humor in each Age appears,
Then draw your fit, and lively Characters,
And suit their changing Minds, and changing Years.

A Boy that just speaks plain, and goes alone,
230 Loves childish Play-mates, he is angry soon,
And pleas'd as soon: And both for nothing still,
Changing his Humor, various is his Will:
A Youth just loosned from his Tutor's care,
Leaves off his Books, and follows Hound and Hare;
The Horse is his delight, or Cards and Dice,
Rough to Reproof, and easy bent to Vice.
Inconstant, eager, haughty, fierce and proud;
A very slow provider for his good,
And prodigal of his Coin, and of his Blood.
240 The full grown Man doth aim at different ends,
He betters his Estate, and gets him Friends;
He courts gay Honor, and He fears to do
What he must alter on a second view.
An Old man's Character is hit with ease,
For he is pettish, and all one Disease:
Still covetous, and still he gripes for more,
And yet he fears to use his present Store:
Slow, long in Hope, still eager to live on,
And fond of no mans Judgment but his own:
250 On Youths gay frolicks peevishly severe,
And oh when He was young, what Times they were!
The Flow of Life brings in a wealthy Store,
The Ebb draws back, what e're was brought before,
And leaves a barren Sand, and naked Shore.
And therefore when you represent a Youth,
Lest you draw lines, that fit a Man of growth;
Observe the just decorum of the Stage,
And show those Humors still that suit the Age;
For otherwise 'twill seem as fond and wild,
260 As 'tis to clap a beard upon a Child.   (pub. 1684)

The Business of the Drama must appear PHILIP FRANCIS,
In Action or Description. What we hear, LINES 179 FF.
With weaker Passion will affect the Heart,
Than when the faithful Eye beholds the Part.
But let no Deed upon the Stage be brought,
Which better should behind the Scenes be wrought;
Nor force th' unwilling Audience to behold
What may with Grace and Eloquence be told.
Let not Medea, with unnatural Rage,
270 Slaughter her mangled Infants on the Stage:
Nor Atreus his detested Feast prepare,
Nor Cadmus roll a Snake, nor Progne wing the Air.
For while upon such monstrous Scenes we gaze,
They shock our Faith, our Indignation raise.

If you would have your Play deserve Success,
Give it five Acts complete; nor more, nor less:
Nor let a God in Person stand display'd,
Unless the labouring Plot deserve his Aid:
Nor a fourth Actor, on the crouded Scene,
280 A broken, tedious Dialogue maintain.
The Chorus must support an Actor's Part;
Defend the Virtuous, and advise with Art;
Govern the Choleric, the Proud appease,
And the short Feasts of frugal Tables praise;
Applaud the Justice of well-govern'd States,
And Peace triumphant with her open Gates.
Instructed Secrets let them ne'er betray,
But to the righteous Gods with Ardour pray,
That Fortune with returning Smiles may bless
290 Afflicted Worth, and impious Pride depress;
Yet let their Songs with apt Coherence join,
Promote the Plot, and aid the main Design.

Nor was the Flute at first with Silver bound,
Nor rival'd emulous the Trumpet's Sound:
Few were its Notes, its Form was simply plain,
Yet not unuseful was its feeble Strain

>   To aid the Chorus, and their Songs to raise,
>   Filling the little Theatre with Ease,
>   To which a thin and pious Audience came,
> 300 Of frugal Manners and unsullied Fame.
>   But when victorious Rome enlarg'd her State,
>   And broader Walls inclos'd th' imperial Seat,
>   Soon as with Wine grown dissolutely gay
>   Without Restraint she chear'd the festal Day,
>   Then Poesy in looser Numbers mov'd,
>   And music in licentious Tones improv'd;
>   Such ever is the Taste, when Clown and Wit,
>   Rustic and Critic, fill the crouded Pit.
>   He who before with modest Art had play'd,
> 310 Now call'd in wanton Movements to his Aid,
>   Fill'd with luxurious Tones the pleasing Strain,
>   And drew along the Stage a Length of train:
>   And thus the Lyre, once awfully severe,
>   Increas'd the Strings, and sweeter charm'd the Ear:
>   Thus Poetry precipitately flow'd,
>   And with unwonted Elocution glow'd;
>   Pour'd forth prophetic Truths in awful Strain;
>   Dark as the Language of the Delphic Fane.   (pub. 1747)

FRANCIS HOWES, LINES 220 FF.

>   He that in tragic lay late strain'd his throat
> 320 To win the paltry prize – a shaggy goat,
>   Soon bared upon the stage a sylvan crew
>   And brought the wanton Satyrs forth to view; –
>   The solemn tone not wholly laid aside,
>   To humour and burlesque his hand applied; –
>   And sought by grateful novelty of song
>   To rivet to their seats a boosy throng
>   From festive rites and revels just set free,
>   Ripe for loose pranks and full of tipsy glee.
>   Yet so to shift from grave to gay 'twere fit, –
> 330 So temper the light Satyrs' saucy wit,

That not each God, each Hero, that of late
Stalk'd forth in purple robes and royal state,
Anon should all his pomp of speech let down
To the low slang and gabble of a clown,
Or steering heaven-wards his flight too fast
Grasp empty clouds and soar into bombast.
The tragic muse, with bashfulness severe,
Disdaining the base gibe and trivial jeer,
Will, like a matron whom the priest perchance
340 Calls at some solemn festival to dance,
Amid the skittish Satyrs still be seen
Distinguish'd by her staid and sober mien.
Were I, my friends, to write Satyric plays,
Not wholly to low terms and homely phrase
Would I restrict my pen; nor so refuse
The richer colouring of the Tragic muse,
As that no difference should be mark'd between
What waggish Davus in the comic scene
Or Pythias prates, when in her knavery bold
350 She bubbles simple Simo of his gold, –
And what Silenus, when he steps abroad
The foster guardian of the nursling god.
Some well-known legend should support my theme;
This with such art I'd trace, that each should deem
He too could match the verse, – then task his brain,
And toiling long confess his efforts vain.
Such merit is to plan and structure due!
To vulgar themes such glory may accrue!
But let the Fauns still mindful what they are,
360 Fetch'd from the woods, by my advice beware
(As if at Rome they all their life had led,
Born in our streets and in our Forum bred)

---

350 *bubbles* swindles

They tattle in a languid love-sick style,
Or bolt unseemly jests and ribald vile.
For each that boasts birth, rank, and consequence
At such low trash is apt to take offence,
Nor all with patience hears or deigns to crown
That with the *nut-and-grey-pease* tribe goes down.

Two syllables, first short, then long, combine
To frame the light *Iambus*; whence the line,
Though to the ear six several beats it bears,
Was surnamed *Trimeter* and scann'd by pairs.
This measure, as its pristine form was cast,
Flow'd uniformly on from first to last.
But after no long time, to greet the ear
With more majestic grace and weight severe,
The foot, its birth-right waived, gen'rous and free,
Took in joint partnership the grave *Spondee*,
One special privilege reserving still –
That every even place itself should fill.
'Not so (says one) march the bold trimeters
Of Accius – Ennius; There it scarce occurs.'
Yet, maugre such high names, that author's page
Who thus with ponderous cadence loads the stage,
Speaks either gross neglect and slovenly haste,
Or ignorance of his art and want of taste.
Not every reader, it is true, has skill
To judge if verse be modulated ill;
And too indulgent Rome has fondly nursed
This laxness in her poets from the first.
But what of that? If readers will be fools,
Must I run riot and despise all rules,
Safe in that fault forsooth which, ev'n if seen
By all the world, long use perhaps shall screen?
Poor boast, to say, 'I have escaped from blame,
But after all to praise can urge no claim!'
Your standard then be Greece! Her models bright
By day peruse, and re-peruse by night!

Our forefathers, goodnatured easy folks,
400 Extoll'd the numbers and enjoy'd the jokes
Of Plautus, prompt both these and those to hear
With tolerant – not to say, with tasteless – ear:
At least if you and I with sense are blest
To tell a clownish from a courtly jest,
Or, by the finger's aid and ear's to-boot,
Can take just measure of a verse and foot.

   Thespis, we're told, the tragic song struck out,
And in rude waggons hawk'd his plays about;
His *corps dramatic*, every brow with lees
410 Of wine besmear'd, there sung and acted these.
Next Aeschylus brought on the trailing pall
And visor, rear'd a stage on platform small,
To strut in buskin'd pride his actors taught,
And gave big utterance to the manly thought.
The antique Comedy was next begun,
Nor light applause her frolic freedom won; –
But, into slanderous outrage waxing fast,
Call'd for the curb of law; – that law was past; –
And thus, its right of wronging quickly o'er,
420 Her chorus sank abash'd to rise no more.   (pub. 1845)

Whate'er their follies, and their faults beside,   LORD BYRON,
Our enterprising Bards pass nought untried,   LINES 285 FF.
Nor do they merit slight applause who choose
An English subject for an English Muse,
And leave to Minds which never dare invent,
French flippancy, and German sentiment.
Where is that living language which could claim
Poetic more, as Philosophic fame?
If all our Bards, more patient of delay,
430 Would stop like Pope – to polish by the way.

Lords of the quill! whose critical assaults
O'erthrow whole quartos, with their quires of faults,
Who soon detect, and mark where'er we fail,
And prove our Marble with too nice a nail,
Democritus himself was not so bad,
He only *thought* – but *you* would make us – mad!

But truth to say, most rhymers rarely guard
Against that ridicule they deem so hard.
In person negligent, they wear from sloth
440 Beards of a week, and nails of annual growth;
Reside in garrets, fly from those they meet,
And walk in Alleys, rather than the street.
With little rhyme, less reason, if you please,
The name of Poet may be got with ease,
So that not tuns of Helleboric juice
Shall ever turn your head to any use.
Write but like Wordsworth, – live beside a lake
And keep your bushy locks a year from Blake,
Then print your book, once more return to Town,
450 And boys shall hunt your Bardship up and down.

Am I not wise? if such some poet's plight
To purge in spring (like Bayes) before I write?
If this precaution softened not my Bile,
I know no scribbler with a madder style;
But since (perhaps my feelings are too nice)
I'll labour gratis as a Grinder's wheel,
And blunt myself, give edge to others' steel,
Nor write at all, unless to teach the Art
To those, rehearsing for the Poet's part,
460 From Horace, show the pleasing paths of song,
And from my own example – what is wrong.
Though modern practice sometimes differs quite,
'Tis just as well to think before you write,
Let every Book that suits your theme be read
So shall you trace it to the Fountain head.

He, who has learn'd the duty which he owes
To friends, and country – and to pardon foes,
Who models his deportment, as may best
Accord with Brother, Sire, or Stranger-guest,
470 Who takes our Laws, and Worship, as they are,
Nor roars reform for Senate, Church, and Bar,
In practice rather than loud precept wise,
Bids not his tongue, but heart – philosophize;
Such is the man, the poet should rehearse
As joint exemplar of his life and verse.

Sometimes a sprightly wit, and tale well told,
Without much grace, or weight, or art, will hold
A longer empire o'er the public mind,
Than sounding trifles, empty, though refined.

480 Unhappy Greece! thy Sons of ancient days
The Muse may celebrate with perfect praise,
Whose generous children narrow not their hearts
With Commerce, given alone to Arms, and Arts.
Our boys (save those whom public schools compel
To 'Long and Short' before they're taught to spell)
From frugal fathers soon imbibe by rote
'A penny saved, my Lad, 's a penny got.'
Babe of a city-birth! from sixpence take
The third – how much will the remainders make?
490 A groat – Ah bravo! Dick hath done the sum,
He'll swell my fifty thousand to a Plum!

They whose young souls receive this rust betimes
'Tis clear, are fit for any thing but rhymes,
And Locke will tell you that the Father's right,
Who hides all verses from his children's sight.

---

491 *Plum* £100,000

For Poets (says this Sage, and many more)
Make sad Mechanics with their Lyric lore,
And Delphi now, however rich of old,
Discovers little silver, and less gold,
500 Because Parnassus though a mount divine,
Is poor as Irus or – an Irish mine! (pub. 1821)

A bard will wish to profit or to please,   JOHN CONINGTON,
Or, as a *tertium quid*, do both of these.   LINES 333 FF.
Whene'er you lecture, be concise: the soul
Takes in short maxims, and retains them whole
But pour in water when the vessel's filled,
It simply dribbles over and is spilled.

 Keep near to truth in a fictitious piece,
Nor treat belief as matter of caprice.
510 If on a child you make a vampire sup,
It must not be alive when she's ripped up.
Dry seniors scout an uninstructive strain;
Young lordlings treat grave verse with tall disdain:
But he who, mixing grave and gay, can teach
And yet give pleasure, gains a vote from each:
His works enrich the vendor, cross the sea,
And hand the author down to late posterity.

 Some faults may claim forgiveness: for the lyre
Not always gives the note that we desire;
520 We ask a flat; a sharp is its reply;
And the best bow will sometimes shoot awry.
But when I meet with beauties thickly sown,
A blot or two I readily condone,
Such as may trickle from a careless pen,
Or pass unwatched: for authors are but men.
What then? the copyist who keeps stumbling still
At the same word had best lay down his quill:

---

501 *Irus* beggar in the *Odyssey*

> The harp-player, who for ever wounds the ear
> With the same discord, makes the audience jeer:
> So the poor dolt who's often in the wrong
> I rank with Choerilus, that dunce of song,
> Who, should he ever 'deviate into sense,'
> Moves but fresh laughter at his own expense:
> While e'en good Homer may deserve a tap,
> If, as he does, he drop his head and nap.
> Yet, when a work is long, 'twere somewhat hard
> To blame a drowsy moment in a bard.
>
>   Some poems, like some paintings, take the eye
> Best at a distance, some when looked at nigh.
> One loves the shade; one would be seen in light,
> And boldly challenges the keenest sight:
> One pleases straightway; one, when it has passed
> Ten times before the mind, will please at last.
>
>   Hope of the Pisos! trained by such a sire,
> And wise yourself, small schooling you require;
> Yet take this lesson home; some things admit
> A moderate point of merit, e'en in wit.
> There's yonder counsellor; he cannot reach
> Messalla's stately altitudes of speech,
> He cannot plumb Cascellius' depth of lore,
> Yet he's employed, and makes a decent score:
> But gods, and men, and booksellers agree
> To place their ban on middling poetry.
> At a great feast an ill-toned instrument,
> A sour conserve, or an unfragrant scent
> Offends the taste: 'tis reason that it should;
> We do without such things, or have them good:
> Just so with verse; you seek but to delight;
> If by an inch you fail, you fail outright.
>
>   He who knows naught of games abstains from all,
> Nor tries his hand at quoit, or hoop, or ball,
> Lest the thronged circle, witnessing the play,
> Should laugh outright, with none to say them nay:

He who knows nought of verses needs must try
To write them ne'ertheless. 'Why not?' men cry:
'Free, gently born, unblemished and correct,
His means a knight's, what more can folks expect?'
But you, my friend, at least have sense and grace;
You will not fly in Queen Minerva's face
In action or in word. Suppose some day
You should take courage and compose a lay
Entrust it first to Maecius's critic ears,
Your sire's and mine, and keep it back nine years.
What's kept at home you cancel by a stroke:
What's sent abroad you never can revoke. (pub. 1870)

When men lived in the wilds, Orpheus, the prophet, ROY CAMPBELL,
Saw their bloodthirsty life, and warned them off it, LINES 391 FF.
For doing which he won the mythic fame
Of making lions and fierce tigers tame:
And of Amphion's building Thebes they tell
Like tales. His lyre moved boulders with its spell,
And led them where he wanted them as well.
Of old it was thought wise to draw a line
'Twixt private things and public: to define
The sacred from the vulgar: to keep strict
The marriage law: loose love to interdict.
To build towns, and carve laws on slabs of wood
In those old times it was considered good.
And so on poets fame and glory fell,
And deified them, and their songs as well.
Then Homer won renown. Tyrtaeus drove
Men's souls, when in the Wars of Mars they strove.
Oracles spoke in song and showed the way
To better life. The poets in their day
Could sing preferment from the hearts of kings,
And after toil, in the Pierian springs,
Delight was found. So do not blush to follow
The lyre-skilled Muse and the divine Apollo.

Concerning a good poem, men enquire
Whether from art it stems, or native fire.
I find all effort vain which sets apart
Genius from toil, nature from conscious art.
For nature's talent needs the help of science
And vice versa – both in fond alliance.
He who would win the race before the rest
Must, even as a child, have stood the test
Of heat, cold, and fatigue. He must abstain
From Venus and from Bacchus. He who blows
The oboe at the Games learned what he knows
From a feared tutor by the dint of blows.
Not so verse-writers of the present day
'My verse is wonderful,' is what they say,
'He who comes last be damned. I've but one shame
And that's to be surpassed: but all the same
I never learned a thing about the game.'
Just like the public criers who collect
Crowds for some public sale which they expect,
The poet, if he owns a rich estate
Or leases property at a high rate,
Collects his flatterers, as meat does flies,
By flashing golden bribes before their eyes.
But if his power to such a pitch extends
That he to sumptuous feasts can treat his friends,
Or stand as surety for a poor man's debt,
Or rescue one whom law-suits have beset –
Confounding interests – he will never know
Whether his friends are hypocrites or no:
And you, yourself, if wishing to be pleasant,
You purpose giving anyone a present,
For heaven's sake, while he with joy is smitten,
Don't read him any verses you have written!
For he'll cry out 'Fine! Wondrous! Perfect! Splendid!'
And beating time until the verse is ended
Grow pale, and weep with dewy eyes distended.

475] EPISTLE II.3 · ARS POETICA

    As you may see in funeral processions,
    The hired mourners, more than the relations,
    Whose grief is real, howl, rave, and tear their locks,
    The flatterer, too, though in his heart he mocks,
    More than the true admirer shows delight,
640 Rejoices, and applauds with all his might.   (pub. 1960)

    A business man who is thinking of trusting another   C. H. SISSON, LINES 434 FF.
    May ply him with drinks in order to discover his mind:
    But alcohol is too weak in the case of poetry;
    It's truth-drugs you need for your friends, if you will write verse.
    But there is such a thing as the friend who notices what you write
    And may point out that this or that won't do,
    And when you've tried once or twice without success
    To improve what you wrote, invites you to tear it up;
    Yet if, after all, you decide to stick to your error,
650 Will waste no words on insisting on what he thinks
    But leave you the pleasure at least of self-admiration.
    The man who can actually tell when a verse is lifeless
    Will know when it doesn't sound right; he will point to stragglers,
    And equally put his pen through elaborations;
    He will even force you to give up your favourite obscurities,
    Tell you what isn't clear and what has got to be changed,
    Like Dr Johnson himself. There will be no nonsense
    About it not being worth causing trouble for trifles.
    Trifles like that amount in the end to disaster,
660 Derisory writing and the meaning misunderstood.

    Those who have any sense will get out of the way of the poet
    Who fancies himself inspired, as they would of a mad fanatic;
    They will fear his touch as they would the bubonic plague
    And leave him to talk with adolescent admirers.

He will explain his theories and offer samples
And wander off in a maze like a statistician.
If he is so blind that he walks slap into the traffic
And then yells out, let no one bother to help him!
To anyone offering to intervene and extract him
670 My comment would be: He probably wants to be run over;
What was it Mr Alvarez said about suicide?
Creative people must have their freedom, you know;
It isn't the first time, I'm sure it won't be the last;
His death, after all, might make him interesting.
It isn't clear why he writes, no doubt some early disorder
Has persisted in its irruption upon his reasonable mind.
What is clear is that unless he is under sedation
He will break out over the town like a bear
To the terror of ordinary people and intellectuals.
680 If he catches a victim, nothing will stop him reading
Nor will he stop when a glaze spreads over his listener's
    eye. (pub. 1975)

---

671 *Mr Alvarez* In A. Alvarez, *The Savage God: A Study of Suicide* (1973).

CODA

A Selection of Poems that would not
have been written but for Horace

GIANGIORGIO TRISSINO
(1478–1550)

Written in about 1519, this appears to be the first version of a Horatian ode in any language by a recognized poet. Trissino was a Vicentine patrician, author of *Sofonisba*, a tragedy complying with the precepts of Aristotle, and a twenty-seven-book epic in blank verse, *L'Italia liberata dai Goti*.

Ode III.9 An imitation

Amante e Donna

Amante.   Mentre che a voi non spiacqui,
        ne da' begl'occhi havea sì cruda guerra,
        a me medesmo piacqui,
        e'l più lieto vivea che fosse in terra.
Donna.   Mentre che al nostro amore
        ti vidi impallidir senz'altr'inganni,
        tal me ne sorse honore,
        che poteva durar dopo mill'anni.
Amante.   Amor con nuova fiamma
10   priva di quello ardente aspro martire
        così dolce m'infiamma,
        che lieve mi saria per lei morire.

Donna. Novellamente anch'io
son presa d'un amor leggiadro, in cui
è tutto il pensier mio,
tal ch'io non dotterei morir per lui.
Amante. Ditemi il ver, Madonna,
che fareste di me, quand'io volesse
lasciar quest'altra Donna,
e tutto in vostra libertà mi desse?
Donna. Se ben instabil sei,
e se questi ha bellezze alme e divine,
pur volentier vorrei
far teco la mia vita e la mia fine. (pub. 1529)

Lover. *While I did not displease you, nor those fine eyes made not so cruel war against me, I pleased myself, and no man lived on earth more joyfully than I.* – Lady. *While for our love I saw you turn pale with no false feigning, such honour befell me that I could have survived a thousand years.* – Lover. *Love with new fire free from that harsh and burning pain sets me aflame so sweetly that easy would it be to die for her.* – Lady. *Lately I too am captive to a charming love where all my thoughts are set, so that for him I would not fear to die.* – Lover. *Tell me true, my lady, what would you do with me were I to leave this other lady and freely give myself into your hands again?* – Lady. *Though you are fickle and he has heavenly beauty, yet willingly would I make my life with you and make my death.*

THOMAS CAMPION (1567–1620)

Poet and musician, an exquisite metrist described by C. S. Lewis as 'the seraphic doctor of English prosody'. Only the first stanza is from Horace (Ode I.22).

ODE I.22 · THOMAS CAMPION

The man of life upright,
    Whose guiltlesse hart is free
From all dishonest deedes,
    Or thought of vanitie,

The man whose silent dayes
    In harmeles joyes are spent,
Whome hopes cannot delude,
    Nor sorrow discontent,

That man needes neither towers
10   Nor armour for defence,
Nor secret vautes to flie
    From thunders violence.

Hee onely can behold
    With unafrighted eyes
The horrours of the deepe,
    And terrours of the Skies.

Thus, scorning all the cares
    That fate, or fortune brings,
He makes the heav'n his booke,
20   His wisedome heev'nly things,

Good thoughts his onely friendes,
    His wealth a well-spent age,
The earth his sober Inne,
    And quiet Pilgrimage.   (pub. 1601)

SIR HENRY WOTTON (1568–1639)

Educated at Winchester and at New College and The Queen's College, Oxford. Travelled extensively in Europe and under James I served in Venice as ambassador, a functionary he described as 'an honest man, sent to lie abroad for the good of his country'. Wrote a treatise on architecture and some pleasant lyrics.

The Character of a Happy Life

How happy is he born and taught,
That serveth not an others will?
Whose Armour is his honest thought:
And simple Truth his utmost Skill?

Whose Passions not his masters are,
Whose soul is still prepar'd for Death;
Untide unto the world, by care
Of Publick fame, or private breath.

Who envies none that Chance doth raise,
Nor Vice hath ever Understood;
How deepest wounds are given by praise,
Nor rules of State, but rules of good.

Who hath his life from rumors freed,
Whose Conscience is his strong retreat:
Whose state can neither flatterers feed,
Nor ruine make oppressors great.

Who God doth late and early pray,
More of his grace, then gifts to lend:
And entertaines the harmless day
With a Religious Book, or Friend.

This man is freed from servile bands
Of hope to rise, or feare to fall:
Lord of himselfe, though not of Lands,
And having nothing: yet hath all. (pub. 1614)

EDWARD, LORD HERBERT OF CHERBURY (1582–1648)

Attended University College, Oxford. Travelled widely, ambassador to France, 1619–24. Tried to stay neutral in the Civil War. Poet and philosopher (*De veritate*, a sceptical treatise on religion) rather than a philosophical poet; also historian and autobiographer.

To his Friend Ben. Johnson, of his Horace made English

'Twas not enough, Ben Johnson, to be thought
Of English Poets best, but to have brought
In greater state, to their acquaintance, one
So equal to himself and thee, that none
Might be thy second, while thy Glory is,
To be the Horace of our times and his. (pub. 1640)

THOMAS CAREW (1594/5–1640)

Attended Merton College, Oxford. On friendly terms with a number of the poets of the day, including Jonson; contributed to the poems written on the death of Donne.

The Spring

Carew begins by echoing Ode I.4, then his poem takes its own course: not the sudden intrusion of death into the season's juvenescence, but rather the season's failure to warm the cold heart of his mistress.

> Now that the winter's gone, the earth hath lost
> Her snow-white robes, and now no more the frost
> Candies the grasse, or castes an ycie creame
> Upon the silver Lake, or Chrystall streame:
> But the warme Sunne thawes the benummed Earth,
> And makes it tender, gives a sacred birth
> To the dead Swallow; wakes in hollow tree
> The drowzie Cuckow, and the Humble-Bee.
> Now doe a quire of chirping Minstrels bring
> In tryumph to the world, the youthfull Spring.
> The Vallies, hills, and woods, in rich araye,
> Welcome the comming of the long'd for May.
> Now all things smile; onely my Love doth lowre:
> Nor hath the scalding Noon-day-Sunne the power,
> To melt that marble yce, which still doth hold
> Her heart congeald, and makes her pittie cold.
> The Oxe which lately did for shelter flie
> Into the stall, doth now securely lie
> In open fields; and love no more is made
> By the fire side; but in the cooler shade
> Amyntas now doth with his Cloris sleepe
> Under a Sycamoure, and all things keepe
> Time with the season, only shee doth carry
> June in her eyes, in her heart January.

(pub. 1640)

CASIMIRE SARBIEWSKI (1595–1640) and G. HILS (*fl.* 1640)

Sarbiewski was a Polish Jesuit whose Christianized neo-Latin imitations of Horace won a wide European recognition and influenced a number of seventeenth-century English poets. His four books of odes and one of epodes were published in 1625 and 1628. About his translator G. Hils nothing seems to be known except the name and the publication date of his translations, 1640.

From 'A Palinode to the second Ode of the booke of Epodes of Q. H. Flaccus. The praise of a Religious Recreation. Ode 3. Lib. Epod.'

The central motif of Casimire's poem, Maren-Sofie Røstvig writes, 'is deeply connected with Hermetic lore. Mere rural retirement to a Sabine farm ... is insufficient as a basis for human happiness. Only he is truly happy who can penetrate the outer surface of things to reach the true core of things, which is God. The first step to the *unio mystica* has been achieved when the retired contemplator realises that the rural scene is pervaded by a ceaseless yearning for God, and that the "shining Deity" can be glimpsed in the shadow of the trees.' 'Casimire Sarbiewski and the English Ode', *Studies in Philology* (51), 1954, p. 445. Compare Vaughan's imitation (pp. 500–503).

31 ... Or when the Sun shines cleare, the aire serene,
    And Aprill Festivals begin,
His eyes, so us'd to Heaven, he downe doth throw,
    On a large prospect here below:
He viewes the fields, and wondring stands to see
    In's shade the shining Deitie.
See how (saies he) each herb with restlesse leaves
    To th' starres doth strive and upward heaves:

Remov'd from heaven they weep, the field appeares
40   All o're dissolv'd in pious teares:
The white-flowr'd Woodbine, and the blushing Rose
    Branch into th' aire with twining boughs;
The pale-fac'd Lilly on the bending stalke,
    To th' starres I know not what doth talke;
At night with fawning sighes they'expresse their fears
    And in the morning drop down teares.
Am I alone, wretch that I am, fast bound
    And held with heavy weight, to th' ground?
Thus spake he to the neigbouring trees, thus he
50   To th' Fountaines talk'd, and streames ran by,
And after, seekes the great Creator out
    By these faire traces of his foote ...   (pub. 1640)

Palinodia ad secundam libri Epodon Odam Q. Horatii Flacci. Laus Otii Religiosi. Ode 3. Lib. Epod.

31 ... Vel cum sereno fulserit dies Jove,
    Aprilibusque feriis,
Assueta caelo lumina, in terras vocat
    Lateque prospectum jacit,
Camposque lustrat, et relucentem sua
    Miratur in scena Deum.
En omnis inquit, herba non morantibus
    In astra luctatur comis:
Semota caelo lacrymantur, et piis
40   Liquuntur arva fletibus;
Ligustra canis, et rosa rubentibus
    Repunt in auras brachiis;
Astrisque panda nescio quid pallido
    Loquuntur ore lilia,
Et sero blandis ingemunt suspiriis,
    Et mane rorant lacrymis.

Egone solus, solus in terris piger
    Tenace figor pondere?
Sic et propinquas allocutus arbores,
50   Et multa coram fontibus
Rivisque fatus, quaerit Auctorem Deum
    Formosa per vestigia ...   (pub. 1625)

JOHN MILTON

Sonnet 20

The voice is Milton's, but the sonnet is studded with Horatian allusions. Line 1: cf. *O matre pulchra filia pulchrior*, Ode I. 16, line 1. Line 4: cf. *morantem saepe diem mero/fregi*, II.7, lines 6–7. Line 6: Favonius, the west wind, echoes the opening of Ode I.4. Line 9: *mundae ... cenae*, III.29, lines 14–15. Line 13: 'Spare' probably means 'spare the time'.

Lawrence of vertuous Father vertuous Son,
    Now that the Fields are dank, and ways are mire,
    Where shall we sometimes meet, and by the fire
    Help wast a sullen day; what may be won
From the hard Season gaining: time will run
    On smoother, till Favonius re-inspire
    The frozen earth; and cloth in fresh attire
    The Lillie and Rose, that neither sow'd nor spun.
What neat repast shall feast us, light and choice,
10   Of Attick tast, with Wine, whence we may rise
    To hear the Lute well toucht, or artfull voice
Warble immortal Notes and Tuskan Ayre?
    He who of those delights can judge, and spare
    To interpose them oft, is not unwise.   (pub. 1673)

Sonnet 21

Lines 7–8: cf. *Quid bellicosus Cantaber et Scythes . . . cogitet . . . remittas quaerere*, Ode II.11, lines 1–4.

    Cyriack, whose Grandsire on the Royal Bench
        Of Brittish Themis, with no mean applause
        Pronounc't and in his volumes taught our Lawes,
        Which others at their Barr so often wrench;
    To day deep thoughts resolve with me to drench
        In mirth, that after no repenting drawes;
        Let Euclid rest and Archimedes pause,
        And what the Swede intend, and what the French.
    To measure life, learn thou betimes, and know
10   Toward solid good what leads the nearest way;
        For other things mild Heav'n a time ordains,
    And disapproves that care, though wise in show,
        That with superfluous burden loads the day,
        And when God sends a cheerful hour, refrains.   (pub. 1673)

SIR RICHARD FANSHAWE

AN ODE upon occasion of His Majesties Proclamation in the yeare 1630. Commanding the Gentry to reside upon their Estates in the Country

Now warre is all the world about,
And every where Erynnis raignes,
Or else the Torch so late put out
        The stench remaines.

AN ODE · SIR RICHARD FANSHAWE

    Holland for many yeares hath beene
    Of Christian tragedies the stage,
    Yet seldome hath she play'd a Scene
            Of bloudyer rage.
    And France that was not long compos'd
    With civill Drummes againe resounds,
10   And ere the old are fully clos'd
            Receives new wounds.
    The great Gustavus in the west
    Plucks the Imperiall Eagles wing,
    Than whom the earth did ne're invest
            A fiercer King:
    Revenging lost Bohemia,
    And the proud wrongs which Tilly dud,
    And tempereth the German clay
20   With Spanish bloud.
    What should I tell of Polish Bands,
    And the blouds boyling in the North?
    Gainst whom the furied Russians
            Their Troops bring forth.
    Both confident: This in his purse,
    And needy valour set on worke;
    He in his Axe; which oft did worse
            Th' invading Turke.
    Who now sustaines a Persian storme:
30   There hell (that made it) suffers schisme.
    This warre (forsooth) was to reforme
            Mahumetisme.
    Onely the Island which wee sowe,
    (A world without the world) so farre
    From present wounds, it cannot showe
            An ancient skarre.

---

1 *warre* the Thirty Years War of 1618–48

White Peace (the beautiful'st of things)
Seemes here her everlasting rest
To fix, and spreads her downy wings
                Over the nest.
As when great Jove, usurping Reigne,
From the plagu'd world did her exile
And ty'd her with a golden chaine
                To one blest Isle:
Which in a sea of plenty swamme
And Turtles sang on ev'ry bowgh,
A safe retreat to all that came
                As ours is now.
Yet wee, as if some foe were here,
Leave the despised Fields to clownes,
And come to save our selves as 'twere
                In walled Townes.
Hither we bring Wives, Babes, rich clothes
And Gemms; Till now my Soveraigne
The growing evill doth oppose:
                Counting in vaine
His care preserves us from annoy
Of enemyes his Realmes to' invade,
Unlesse hee force us to enjoy
                The peace hee made.
To rowle themselves in envy'd leasure
He therefore sends the Landed Heyres,
Whilst hee proclaimes not his owne pleasure
                So much as theirs.
The sapp and bloud o' th' land, which fled
Into the roote, and choackt the heart,
Are bid their quickning pow'r to spread
                Through ev'ry part.

---

46 *Turtles* turtle-doves

AN ODE · SIR RICHARD FANSHAWE

O, 'twas an act, not for my muse
To celebrate, nor the dull Age,
Untill the country aire infuse
    A purer rage!
And if the Fields as thankfull prove
For benefits receiv'd, as seed,
They will, to quite so great a love,
    A Virgill breed;
A Tytirus, that shall not cease
Th' Augustus of our world to praise
In equall verse, author of peace
    And Halcyon dayes.
Nor let the Gentry grudge to goe
Into those places whence they grew,
But thinke them blest they may doe so:
    Who would pursue
The smoaky glory of the Towne,
That may goe till his native earth,
And by the shining fire sit downe
    Of his owne hearth,
Free from the griping Scriveners bands,
And the more byting Mercers books;
Free from the bayt of oyled hands
    And painted looks?
The country too ev'n chopps for raine:
You that exhale it by your power
Let the fat dropps fall downe againe
    In a full showre.
And you bright beautyes of the time,
That waste your selves here in a blaze,
Fixe to your Orbe and proper clime
    Your wandring rayes.

---

75 *quite* requite, pay back
90 *Mercers books* debts of gallants

Let no darke corner of the land
Be unimbellisht with one Gemme,
And those which here too thick doe stand
    Sprinkle on them.
Beleeve me Ladies you will finde
In that sweet life, more solid joyes,
More true contentment to the minde,
    Than all Town-toyes.
Nor Cupid there lesse bloud doth spill,
But heads his shafts with chaster love,
Not feathered with a Sparrowes quill
    But of a Dove.
There shall you heare the Nightingale
(The harmlesse Syren of the wood)
How prettily she tells a tale
    Of rape and blood.
The lyrricke Larke, with all beside
Of natures feathered quire: and all
The Common-wealth of Flowers in 'ts pride
    Behold you shall.
The Lillie (Queene), the (Royall) Rose,
The Gillyflowre (Prince of the bloud),
The (Courtyer) Tulip (gay in clothes),
    The (Regall) Budd,
The Vilet (purple Senatour),
How they doe mock the pompe of State,
And all that at the surly doore
    Of great ones waite.
Plant Trees you may, and see them shoote
Up with your Children, to be serv'd
To your cleane boards, and the fair'st Fruite
    To be preserv'd:
And learne to use their severall gummes,
"Tis innocence in the sweet blood
Of Cherryes, Apricocks and Plummes
    To be imbru'd.'

(pub. 1648)

RICHARD LOVELACE (1618–1658)

Heir to great estates in Kent, soldier, courtier, royalist, he died in poverty and received a pauper's funeral. Sometimes a more complex poet than the handful of fine lyrics for which he is remembered would suggest. Joanna Martindale describes this poem as 'a kind of meditation on *Odes* II.10, using each of Horace's stanzas as a starting point for further thoughts'. (*Horace Made New*, p. 69.)

Advice to my best Brother

  Frank, wil't live handsomely? trust not too far
Thy self to waving Seas, for what thy star
Calculated by sure event must be,
Look in the Glassy-epithite and see.

  Yet settle here your rest, and take your state,
And in calm Halcyon's nest ev'n build your Fate;
Prethee lye down securely, Frank, and keep
With as much no noyse the inconstant Deep
As its Inhabitants; nay stedfast stand,
10 As if discover'd were a New-found-land
Fit for Plantation here; dream, dream still,
Lull'd in Dione's cradle, dream, untill
Horrour awake your sense, and you now find
Your self a bubled pastime for the Wind,
And in loose Thetis blankets torn and tost;
Frank to undo thy self why art at cost?

---

4 *Glassy-epithite* crystal ball
12 *Dione* mother of sea-born Aphrodite

Nor be too confident, fix'd on the shore,
For even that too borrows from the store
Of her rich Neighbour, since now wisest know,
20 (And this to Galileo's judgement ow)
The palsie Earth it self is every jot
As frail, inconstant, waveing as that blot
We lay upon the Deep; That sometimes lies
Chang'd, you would think, with's botoms properties,
But this eternal strange Ixions wheel
Of giddy earth, ne'r whirling leaves to reel
Till all things are inverted, till they are
Turn'd to that Antick confus'd state they were.

Who loves the golden mean, doth safely want
30 A cobwebb'd Cot, and wrongs entail'd upon't;
He richly needs a Pallace for to breed
Vipers and Moths, that on their feeder feed;
The toy that we (too true) a Mistress call,
Whose Looking-glass and feather weighs up all;
And Cloaths which Larks would play with, in the Sun,
That mock him in the Night when's course is run.

To rear an edifice by Art so high
That envy should not reach it with her eye,
Nay with a thought come neer it, would'st thou know
40 How such a Structure should be raised? build low.
The blust'ring winds invisible rough stroak,
More often shakes the stubborn'st, prop'rest Oak,
And in proud Turrets we behold withal,
'Tis the Imperial top declines to fall.
Nor does Heav'ns lightning strike the humble Vales
But high aspiring Mounts batters and scales.

---

26 *ne'r whirling leaves to reel* whirling, never stops reeling
30 *wrongs entail'd* passed from heir to heir, rather than all on one
35 falconers dazzle a lark with scarlet cloth
44 *declines to fall* i.e. falls down

    A breast of proof defies all Shocks of Fate,
Fears in the best, hopes in the worser state;
Heaven forbid that, as of old, Time ever
50 Flourish'd in Spring, so contrary, now never:
That mighty breath which blew foul Winter hither,
Can eas'ly puffe it to a fairer weather.
Why dost despair then, Franck? Aeolus has
A Zephyrus as well as Boreas.

    'Tis a false Sequel, Soloecisme, 'gainst those
Precepts by fortune giv'n us, to suppose
That 'cause it is now ill, 't will ere be so;
Apollo doth not always bend his Bow;
But oft uncrowned of his Beams divine,
60 With his soft harp awakes the sleeping Nine.

    In strictest things magnanimous appear,
Greater in hope, howere thy fate, then fear:
Draw all your Sails in quickly, though no storm
Threaten your ruine with a sad alarm;
For tell me how they differ, tell me pray,
A cloudy tempest, and a too fair day.   (pub. 1659)

ANDREW MARVELL (1621–1678)

Attended Trinity College, Cambridge. At first sympathetic to the cause of Charles I, but came to accept and admire Cromwell. Colleague of Milton's in the Latin secretaryship to the Council of State, and is said to have protected him at the Restoration. Member for Hull from 1659 until his death.

An Horatian Ode upon Cromwel's Return from Ireland

Probably written in the summer of 1650, after Cromwell had returned from Ireland and before he set out on his Scottish campaign. The stanza form, admired for its equipollence to the weightier Horatian quatrain, had been used by Fanshawe (e.g. in his translation of Ode I.5, see pp. 89–90), but Marvell may not have been aware of this.

> The forward Youth that would appear
> Must now forsake his Muses dear,
>   Nor in the Shadows sing
>   His Numbers languishing.
> 'Tis time to leave the Books in dust,
> And oyl th' unused Armours rust:
>   Removing from the Wall
>   The Corslet of the Hall.
> So restless Cromwel could not cease
10 In the inglorious Arts of Peace,
>   But through adventrous War
>   Urged his active Star.
> And, like the three-fork'd Lightning, first
> Breaking the Clouds where it was nurst,
>   Did thorough his own Side
>   His fiery way divide.
> For 'tis all one to Courage high
> The Emulous or Enemy;
>   And with such to inclose
20 Is more then to oppose.
> Then burning through the Air he went,
> And Pallaces and Temples rent:
>   And Caesars head at last
>   Did through his Laurels blast.

AN HORATIAN ODE · ANDREW MARVELL

    'Tis Madness to resist or blame
    The force of angry Heavens flame:
        And, if we would speak true,
        Much to the Man is due.
    Who, from his private Gardens, where
30   He liv'd reserved and austere,
        As if his highest plot
        To plant the Bergamot,
    Could by industrious Valour climbe
    To ruine the great Work of Time,
        And cast the Kingdome old
        Into another Mold.
    Though Justice against Fate complain,
    And plead the antient Rights in vain:
        But those do hold or break
40   As Men are strong or weak.
    Nature that hateth emptiness,
    Allows of penetration less:
        And therefore must make room
        Where greater Spirits come.
    What Field of all the Civil Wars,
    Where his were not the deepest Scars?
        And Hampton shows what part
        He had of wiser Art.
    Where, twining subtile fears with hope,
50   He wove a Net of such a scope,
        That Charles himself might chase
        To Caresbrooks narrow case.
    That thence the Royal Actor born
    The Tragick Scaffold might adorn:
        While round the armed Bands
        Did clap their bloody hands.
    He nothing common did or mean
    Upon that memorable Scene:
        But with his keener Eye
60   The Axes edge did try:

Nor call'd the Gods with vulgar spight
To vindicate his helpless Right,
   But bow'd his comely Head,
   Down as upon a Bed.
This was that memorable Hour
Which first assur'd the forced Pow'r.
   So when they did design
   The Capitols first Line,
A bleeding Head where they begun,
70 Did fright the Architects to run;
   And yet in that the State
   Foresaw it's happy Fate.
And now the Irish are asham'd
To see themselves in one Year tam'd:
   So much one Man can do,
   That does both act and know.
They can affirm his Praises best,
And have, though overcome, confest
   How good he is, how just,
80   And fit for highest Trust:
Nor yet grown stiffer with Command,
But still in the Republick's hand:
   How fit he is to sway
   That can so well obey.
He to the Commons Feet presents
A Kingdome, for his first years rents:
   And, what he may, forbears
   His Fame to make it theirs:
And has his Sword and Spoyls ungirt,
90 To lay them at the Publick's skirt.
   So when the Falcon high
   Falls heavy from the Sky,
She, having kill'd, no more does search,
But on the next green Bow to pearch;

       Where, when he first does lure,
       The Falckner has her sure.
   What may not then our Isle presume
   While Victory his Crest does plume!
       What may not others fear
100   If thus he crown each Year!
   A Caesar he ere long to Gaul,
   To Italy an Hannibal,
       And to all States not free
       Shall Clymacterick be.
   The Pict no shelter now shall find
   Within his party-colour'd Mind;
       But from this Valour sad
       Shrink underneath the Plad:
   Happy if in the tufted brake
110 The English Hunter him mistake;
       Nor lay his Hounds in near
       The Caledonian Deer.
   But thou the Wars and Fortunes Son
   March indefatigably on;
       And for the last effect:
       Still keep thy Sword erect:
   Besides the force it has to fright
   The Spirits of the shady Night,
       The same Arts that did gain
120   A Pow'r must it maintain.   (pub. 1681)

HENRY VAUGHAN (1621/2–1695)

Of Welsh descent, probably educated at Jesus College, Oxford. Vaughan's claim to rank as one of our great religious poets rests on *Silex Scintillans* (1650 and 1655). His earlier work in fashionable modes he came to reject as 'idle verse'. His expansive imitation of

Casimire's third epode is not so much an 'answer' to Horace's poem as, to use Casimire's term, a palinode or recantation: like Vaughan, this Casimirian Horace is rejecting the mundane satisfactions of his original poetry.

The Praise of a Religious Life by Mathias Casimirus, in answer to that Ode of Horace, Beatus ille qui procul negotiis, &c.

Flaccus not so: That worldly He
Whom in the Countreys shade we see
Ploughing his own fields, seldome can
Be justly stil'd, the Blessed man.
   That title only fits a Saint,
Whose free thoughts far above restraint
And weighty Cares, can gladly part
With house and lands, and leave the smart
Litigious troubles, and lowd strife
10 Of this world for a better life.
He fears no Cold, nor heat to blast
His Corn, for his Accounts are cast,
He sues no man, nor stands in Awe
Of the devouring Courts of Law;
But all his time he spends in tears
For the Sins of his youthfull years,
Or having tasted those rich Joyes
Of a Conscience without noyse
Sits in some fair shade, and doth give
20 To his wild thoughts rules how to live.
   He in the Evening, when on high
The Stars shine in the silent skye
Beholds th' eternall flames with mirth,
And globes of light more large then Earth,
Then weeps for Joy, and through his tears
Looks on the fire-enamel'd Spheres,

Where with his Saviour he would be
Lifted above mortalitie.
Mean while the golden stars doe set,
And the slow-Pilgrim leave all wet
With his own tears, which flow so fast
They make his sleeps light, and soon past.
By this, the Sun o're night deceast
Breaks in fresh Blushes from the East,
When mindfull of his former falls
With strong Cries to his God he calls,
And with such deep-drawn sighes doth move
That he turns anger into love.

   In the Calme Spring, when the Earth bears,
And feeds on Aprils breath, and tears,
His Eyes accustom'd to the skyes
Find here fresh objects, and like spyes
Or busie Bees search the soft flowres
Contemplate the green fields, and Bowres,
Where he in Veyles, and shades doth see
The back Parts of the Deitye.
Then sadly sighing sayes, 'O how
These flowres With hasty, stretch'd heads grow
And strive for heav'n, but rooted here
Lament the distance with a teare!
The Honey-suckles Clad in white,
The Rose in Red point to the light,
And the Lillies hollow and bleak
Look, as if they would something speak,
They sigh at night to each soft gale,
And at the day-spring weep it all.
Shall I then only (wretched I!)
Opprest with Earth, on Earth still lye?'
Thus speaks he to the neighbour trees
And many sad Soliloquies
To Springs, and Fountaines doth impart,
Seeking God with a longing heart.

But if to ease his busie breast
He thinks of home, and taking rest,
A Rurall Cott, and Common fare
Are all his Cordials against Care.
There at the doore of his low Cell
Under some shade, or neer some Well
Where the Coole Poplar growes, his Plate
70 Of Common Earth, without more state
Expect their Lord. Salt in a shell,
Green Cheese, thin beere, Draughts that will tell
No Tales, a hospitable Cup,
With some fresh berries doe make up
His healthfull feast, nor doth he wish
For the fatt Carp, or a rare dish
Of Lucrine Oysters; The swift Quist
Or Pigeon sometimes (if he list)
With the slow Goose that loves the stream,
80 Fresh, various Sallads, and the Bean
By Curious Pallats never sought,
And to Close with, some Cheap unbought
Dish for digestion, are the most
And Choicest dainties he can boast.
    Thus feasted, to the flowrie Groves,
Or pleasant Rivers he removes,
Where neer some fair Oke hung with Mast
He shuns the Souths Infectious blast.
On shadie banks sometimes he lyes,
90 Sometimes the open Current tryes,
Where with his line and feather'd flye
He sports, and takes the Scaly frie.
Mean-while each hollow wood and hill
Doth ring with lowings long and shrill,

---

77 *Quist* ring dove   **87** *Mast* acorns

And shadie Lakes with Rivers deep,
Eccho the bleating of the Sheep.
The Black-bird with the pleasant Thrush
And Nightingale in ev'ry Bush
Choice Musick give, and Shepherds play
100 Unto their flocks some loving Lay;
The thirsty Reapers in thick throngs
Return home from the field with Songs,
And the Carts loden with ripe Corn
Come groning to the well-stor'd Barn.
    Nor passe wee by as the least good,
A peacefull, loving neighbourhood,
Whose honest Wit, and Chast discourse
Make none (by hearing it) the worse,
But Innocent and merry may
110 Help (without Sin) to spend the day.
Could now the Tyrant-usurer
Who plots to be a Purchaser
Of his poor neighbours seat, but taste
These true delights, o with what haste
And hatred of his wayes would he
Renounce his Jewish Crueltie,
And those Curs'd summes which poor men borrow
On use to day, remit to morrow!   (pub. 1651)

To my worthy friend Master T. Lewes

The poem starts as a variation on Ode I.9, then develops
independently.

Sees not my friend, what a deep snow
Candies our Countries wooddy brow?
The yeelding branch his load scarse bears
Opprest with snow, and frozen tears,
While the dumb rivers slowly float,
All bound up in an Icie Coat.

  Let us meet then! and while this world
 In wild Excentricks now is hurld,
 Keep wee, like nature, the same Key,
10 And walk in our forefathers way;
 Why any more cast wee an Eye
 On what may come, not what is nigh?
 Why vex our selves with feare, or hope
 And cares beyond our Horoscope?
 Who into future times would peere
 Looks oft beyond his terme set here,
 And cannot goe into those grounds
 But through a Church-yard which them bounds;
 Sorrows and sighes and searches spend
20 And draw our bottome to an end,
 But discreet Joyes lengthen the lease
 Without which life were a disease,
 And who this age a Mourner goes,
 Doth with his tears but feed his foes.   (pub. 1651)

ALLAN RAMSAY and WILLIAM HAMILTON OF GILBERTFIELD (1665?–1751)

An Exchange of Verse Epistles

Between June and December of 1719 Ramsay and Hamilton, an amateur poet best known (north of the border) for 'The Last Dying Words of Bonny Heck', exchanged a series of letters in the 'Standart Habbie' stanza (AAAbAb). Apart from an allusion to Ode IV.9 in

---

20 *bottome* skein of thread

one letter, there is nothing overtly Horatian here, but both men knew and translated Horace and this is the Horatian epistle adapted *ad usum Scotorum*. (Southrons stalled by the homely vernacular idiom will find that reading the lines aloud brings over the general sense if not always the exact meaning.)

Epistle I Gilbertfield, 26 June 1719

O fam'd and celebrated Allan!
Renowned Ramsay, canty Callan,
There's nowther Highlandman nor Lawlan,
    In Poetrie,
But may as soon ding down Tamtallan
    As match wi' thee.

For ten Times ten, and that's a hunder,
I ha'e been made to gaze and wonder,
When frae Parnassus thou didst thunder,
    Wi' Wit and Skill,
Wherefore I'll soberly knock under,
    And quat my Quill.

Of Poetry the hail Quintessence
Thou hast suck'd up, left nae Excrescence
To petty Poets, or sic Messens,
    Tho round thy Stool,
They may pick Crumbs, and lear some Lessons
    At Ramsay's School.

Tho Ben and Dryden of Renown
Were yet alive in London Town,
Like Kings contending for a Crown;

---

2 *canty Callan* merry fellow   **5** *ding* beat; *Tamtallan* fort on Firth of Forth
15 *Messens* lap-dogs

>   'Twad be a Pingle,
> Whilk o' you three wad gar Words sound
>   And best to gingle.
>
> Transform'd may I be to a Rat,
> Wer't in my Pow'r but I'd create
> Thee upo' sight the Laureat
>   Of this our Age,
> Since thou may'st fairly claim to that
>   As thy just Wage.
>
> Let modern Poets bear the Blame
> Gin they respect not Ramsay's Name,
> Wha soon can gar them greet for Shame,
>   To their great Loss;
> And send them a' right sneaking hame
>   Be Weeping-Cross.
>
> Wha bourds wi' thee had need be warry,
> And lear wi' Skill thy Thrust to parry,
> When thou consults thy Dictionary
>   Of ancient Words,
> Which come from thy Poetick Quarry,
>   As sharp as Swords.
>
> Now tho I should baith reel and rottle,
> And be as light as Aristotle,
> At Ed'nburgh we sall ha'e a Bottle
>   Of reaming Claret,
> Gin that my haff-pay Siller Shottle
>   Can safely spare it.

---

22 *Pingle* struggle   **24** *gingle* jingle, rhyme   **32** *Gin* if
33 *gar them greet* make them weep   **37** *bourds* jests   **46** *reaming* bubbling
47 *Shottle* drawer of a chest

At Crambo then we'll rack our Brain,
Drown ilk dull Care and aiking Pain,
Whilk aften does our Spirits drain
    Of true Content;
Wow, Wow! but we's be wonder fain,
    When thus acquaint.

Wi' Wine we'll gargarize our Craig,
Then enter in a lasting League,
Free of Ill Aspect or Intrigue,
    And gin you please it,
Like Princes when met at the Hague
    We'll solemnize it.

Accept of this and look upon it
With Favour, tho poor I have done it;
Sae I conclude and end my Sonnet,
    Who am most fully,
While I do wear a Hat or Bonnet,
    Yours – wanton Willy.

Postscript

By this my Postscript I incline
To let you ken my hail Design
Of sic a lang imperfect Line,
    Lyes in this Sentence,
To cultivate my dull Ingine
    By your Acquaintance.

---

49 *Crambo* rhyming game   **53** *fain* joyful   **55** *Craig* throat
5 *Ingine* wits

Your Answer therefore I expect,
And to your Friend you may direct,
At Gilbertfield do not neglect
      When ye have Leisure,
Which I'll embrace with great Respect
      And perfect Pleasure.

Answer I Edinburgh, 10 July 1719

Sonse fa me, witty, wanton Willy,
Gin blyth I was na as a Filly;
Not a fow Pint, nor short Hought Gilly,
      Or Wine that's better,
Cou'd please sae meikle, my dear Billy,
      As thy kind Letter . . .

Ha, heh! thought I, I canna say
But I may cock my Nose the Day,
When Hamilton the bauld and gay
      Lends me a Heezy,
In Verse that slides sae smooth away,
      Well tell'd and easy.

Sae roos'd by ane of well kend Mettle,
Nae sma did my Ambition pettle,
My canker'd Criticks it will nettle,
      And e'en sae be't:
This Month I'm sure I winna fettle,
      Sae proud I'm wi't.

---

1 *Sonse fa me* bless me   **2** *Gin* if   **3** *short Hought* short-legged; *Gilly* gill
16 *Lends me a Heezy* gives me a lift   **19** *roos'd* commended
20 *pettle* flatter   **23** *winna* will not

When I begoud first to cun Verse,
And cou'd your Ardry Whins rehearse,
Where Bonny Heck ran fast and fierce,
      It warm'd my Breast;
Then Emulation did me pierce,
        Whilk since ne'er ceast.

May I be licket wi' a Bittle,
Gin of your Numbers I think little;
Ye're never rugget, shan, nor kittle,
      But blyth and gabby,
And hit the Spirit to a Title,
      Of Standart Habby.

Ye'll quat your Quill! That were ill-willy,
Ye's sing some mair yet, nill ye will ye,
O'er meikle Haining wad but spill ye,
      And gar ye sour,
Then up and war them a' yet, Willy,
      'Tis in your Power.

To knit up dollars in a clout,
And then to card them round about,
Syne to tell up, they downa lout
      To lift the gear;
The Malison lights on that Rout,
      Is plain and clear.

---

25 *cun* study **26** *Ardry Whins* last words of Hamilton's poem 'Bonny Heck'
31 *licket wi' a Bittle* beaten with a wooden club
33 *shan* silly; *kittle* difficult **34** *gabby* fluent
35 *Title* tittle **39** *O'er meikle Haining* overmuch abstaining; *spill* spoil
40 *gar* make **41** *war* overcome **45** *lout* bend
47 *Malison* malediction

>   The Chiels of London, Cam, and Ox,
> 50 Ha'e rais'd up great Poetick Stocks
>   Of Rapes, of Buckets, Sarks and Locks,
>   While we neglect
>   To shaw their betters. This provokes
>   Me to reflect
>
>   On the lear'd Days of Gawn Dunkell,
>   Our Country then a Tale cou'd tell,
>   Europe had nane mair snack and snell
>   At Verse or Prose;
> 60 Our Kings were Poets too themsell,
>   Bauld and Jocose.
>
>   To Ed'nburgh, Sir, when e'er ye come,
>   I'll wait upon ye, there's my Thumb,
>   Were't frae the Gill-bells to the Drum,
>   And take a Bout,
>   And faith I hope we'll no sit dumb,
>   Nor yet cast out.

Epistle II Gilbertfield, 24 July 1719

> Dear Ramsay
>   When I receiv'd thy kind Epistle,
>   It made me dance, and sing, and whistle;
>   O sic a Fyke, and sic a Fistle
>   I had about it!
>   That e'er was Knight of the Scots Thistle
>   Sae fain, I doubted.

---

49 *Chiels* fellows   **55** *Gawn Dunkell* Gavin Douglas
57 *snack* clever; *snell* sharp
63 *Frae the Gill-bells to the Drum* from half an hour before noon to ten at night
66 *cast out* quarrel
3 *Fyke* excitement; *Fistle* commotion

The bonny Lines therein thou sent me,
How to the Nines they did content me;
Tho', Sir, sae high to compliment me,
          Ye might defer'd,
For had ye but haff well a kent me,
          Some less wad ser'd . . .

Answer II Edinburgh, 4 August 1719

Dear Hamilton ye'll turn me Dyver,
My Muse sae bonny ye descrive her,
Ye blaw her sae, I'm fear'd ye rive her,
          For wi' a Whid,
Gin ony higher up ye drive her,
          She'll rin red-wood.

Said I, – 'Whisht, quoth the vougy Jade,
William's a wise judicious Lad,
Has Havins mair than e'er ye had,
          Ill bred Bog-staker;
But me ye ne'er sae crouse had craw'd,
          Ye poor Scull-thacker . . .'

Quisquis vocabit nos Vain-glorious,
Shaw scanter Skill, than *malos mores*,
Multi et magni Men before us
          Did stamp and swagger,
Probatum est, exemplum Horace,
          Was a bauld Bragger.

---

1 *Dyver* bankrupt   **3** *blaw* inflate; *rive* destroy
4 *wi' a Whid* in a moment   **6** *rin red-wood* run distracted
7 *Whisht* silence; *vougy* proud; *Jade* i.e. the Muse   **9** *Havins* good breeding
10 *-staker* -stalker   **11** *But* but for, without; *crouse* happily; *craw'd* crowed
12 *-thacker* -thatcher

Then let the Doofarts fash'd wi' Spleen,
Cast up the wrang Side of their Een,
Pegh, fry and girn wi' Spite and Teen,
  And fa a flyting,
Laugh, for the lively Lads will screen
  Us frae Back-biting.

If that the Gypsies dinna spung us,
And foreign Whiskers ha'e na dung us;
Gin I can snifter thro' Mundungus,
  Wi' Boots and Belt on,
I hope to see you at St Mungo's
  Atween and Beltan.   (pub. 1721)

MATTHEW PRIOR (1664–1721)

Serving in his uncle's Rhenish Tavern, Prior was found by Charles Sackville, the Earl of Dorset, sitting behind the bar reading Horace. Dorset asked him to construe a few passages and then to turn an ode into English. The twelve-year-old boy did this so successfully that Dorset offered to pay his tuition fees at Westminster School, from which he passed to St John's College, Cambridge. Though he wrote a good deal of verse, most of his life was spent in the diplomatic service. This poem is a pendant to Ode III.9, the dialogue between 'Horace' and Lydia, here replaced by Prior and Cloe. The title refers to a previous poem, 'Answer to Cloe Jealous'.

---

61 *Doofarts* dull fellows; *fash'd* vexed
63 *Pegh* pant; *fry* be agitated; *girn* snarl; *Teen* rage
67 *Spung* rob   68 *dung* beaten
69 *snifter* sniff; *Mundungus* evil-smelling tobacco
71 *St Mungo's* i.e. Glasgow   72 *Atween and Beltan* before 1 or 3 May

A Better Answer

I
Dear Cloe, how blubber'd is that pretty Face?
   Thy Cheek all on Fire, and Thy Hair all uncurl'd:
Pr'ythee quit this Caprice; and (as Old Falstaf says)
   Let Us e'en talk a little like Folks of This World.

II
How can'st Thou presume, Thou hast leave to destroy
   The Beauties, which Venus but lent to Thy keeping?
Those Looks were design'd to inspire Love and Joy:
   More ord'nary Eyes may serve People for weeping.

III
To be vext at a Trifle or two that I writ,
   Your Judgment at once, and my Passion You wrong:
You take that for Fact, which will scarce be found Wit:
   Od's Life! must One swear to the Truth of a Song?

IV
What I speak, my fair Cloe, and what I write, shews
   The Diff'rence there is betwixt Nature and Art:
I court others in Verse; but I love Thee in Prose:
   And They have my Whimsies; but Thou hast my Heart.

V
The God of us Verse-men (You know Child) the Sun,
   How after his Journeys He sets up his Rest:
If at Morning o'er Earth 'tis his Fancy to run;
   At Night he reclines on his Thetis's Breast.

VI

So when I am weary'd with wand'ring all Day;
  To Thee my Delight in the Evening I come:
No Matter what Beauties I saw in my Way:
  They were but my Visits; but Thou art my Home.

VII

Then finish, Dear Cloe, this Pastoral War;
  And let us like Horace and Lydia agree:
For Thou art a Girl as much brighter than Her,
  As He was a Poet sublimer than Me. (pub. 1718)

ALEXANDER POPE

Epistle II To a Lady

'In writing of the characters of women,' Reuben Brower comments, 'Pope is philosophic in Horace's most characteristic manner, and the burden of the poem is thoroughly Horatian — an expression of mingled amusement and horror at the muddle most people make of their lives and of rare satisfaction in finding one life ... that seems to make sense. [The epistle] is Horatian too in Pope's refusal to be dazzled by social prestige or pretension to wisdom, and in his quiet testimony to deep but free and easy friendship. The epistle is also Horatian in its poetic art, in the placing of contrasting cases that culminate in a winning yet not over-serious portrait of an ideal, in establishing a tone of casual talk that can embrace literary parody and high allusion, and finally in the skilful handling of transitions, which for Pope as for Horace is not only a technique of style, but a technique of moving freely among moral and emotional possibilities.' (*Alexander Pope: The Poetry of Allusion* (1959), p. 281.)

EPISTLE II TO A LADY · ALEXANDER POPE

Of the Characters of women

Nothing so true as what you once let fall,
'Most Women have no Characters at all'.
Matter too soft a lasting mark to bear,
And best distinguish'd by black, brown, or fair.

How many pictures of one Nymph we view,
All how unlike each other, all how true!
Arcadia's Countess, here, in ermin'd pride,
Is there, Pastora by a fountain side:
Here Fannia, leering on her own good man,
10 Is there, a naked Leda with a Swan.
Let then the Fair one beautifully cry,
In Magdalen's loose hair and lifted eye,
Or drest in smiles of sweet Cecilia shine,
With simp'ring Angels, Palms, and Harps divine;
Whether the Charmer sinner it, or saint it,
If Folly grows romantic, I must paint it.

Come then, the colours and the ground prepare!
Dip in the Rainbow, trick her off in Air,
Chuse a firm Cloud, before it fall, and in it
20 Catch, ere she change, the Cynthia of this minute.

Rufa, whose eye quick-glancing o'er the Park,
Attracts each light gay meteor of a Spark,
Agrees as ill with Rufa studying Locke,
As Sappho's diamonds with her dirty smock,
Or Sappho at her toilet's greazy task,
With Sappho fragrant at an ev'ning Mask:
So morning Insects that in muck begun,
Shine, buzz, and fly-blow in the setting-sun.

How soft is Silia! fearful to offend,
30 The Frail one's advocate, the Weak one's friend:
To her, Calista prov'd her conduct nice,
And good Simplicius asks of her advice.
Sudden, she storms! she raves! You tip the wink,
But spare your censure; Silia does not drink.

All eyes may see from what the change arose,
All eyes may see – a Pimple on her nose.
    Papillia, wedded to her doating spark,
Sighs for the shades – 'How charming is a Park!'
A Park is purchas'd, but the Fair he sees
40 All bath'd in tears – 'Oh odious, odious Trees!'
    Ladies, like variegated Tulips, show,
'Tis to their Changes that their charms we owe;
Their happy Spots the nice admirer take,
Fine by defect, and delicately weak.
'Twas thus Calypso once each heart alarm'd,
Aw'd without Virtue, without Beauty charm'd;
Her Tongue bewitch'd as odly as her Eyes,
Less Wit than Mimic, more a Wit than wise:
Strange graces still, and stranger flights she had,
50 Was just not ugly, and was just not mad;
Yet ne'er so sure our passion to create,
As when she touch'd the brink of all we hate.
    Narcissa's nature, tolerably mild,
To make a wash, would hardly stew a child,
Has ev'n been prov'd to grant a Lover's pray'r,
And paid a Tradesman once to make him stare,
Gave alms at Easter, in a Christian trim,
And made a Widow happy, for a whim.
Why then declare Good-nature is her scorn,
60 When 'tis by that alone she can be born?
Why pique all mortals, yet affect a name?
A fool to Pleasure, and a slave to Fame:
Now deep in Taylor and the Book of Martyrs,
Now drinking citron with his Grace and Chartres.
Now Conscience chills her, and now Passion burns;
And Atheism and Religion take their turns;
A very Heathen in the carnal part,
Yet still a sad, good Christian at her heart.
    See Sin in State, majestically drunk,
70 Proud as a Peeress, prouder as a Punk;

EPISTLE II TO A LADY · ALEXANDER POPE

Chaste to her Husband, frank to all beside,
A teeming Mistress, but a barren Bride.
What then? let Blood and Body bear the fault,
Her Head's untouch'd, that noble Seat of Thought:
Such this day's doctrine – in another fit
She sins with Poets thro' pure Love of Wit.
What has not fir'd her bosom or her brain?
Caesar and Tall-boy, Charles and Charlema'ne.
As Helluo, late Dictator of the Feast,
80   The Nose of Hautgout, and the Tip of Taste,
Critick'd your wine, and analyz'd your meat,
Yet on plain Pudding deign'd at-home to eat;
So Philomedé, lect'ring all mankind
On the soft Passion, and the Taste refin'd,
Th' Address, the Delicacy – stoops at once,
And makes her hearty meal upon a Dunce.

    Flavia's a Wit, has too much sense to Pray,
To Toast our wants and wishes, is her way;
Nor asks of God, but of her Stars to give
90   The mighty blessing, 'while we live, to live.'
Then all for Death, that Opiate of the soul!
Lucretia's dagger, Rosamonda's bowl.
Say, what can cause such impotence of mind?
A Spark too fickle, or a Spouse too kind.
Wise Wretch! with Pleasures too refin'd to please,
With too much Spirit to be e'er at ease,
With too much Quickness ever to be taught,
With too much Thinking to have common Thought:
Who purchase Pain with all that Joy can give,
100 And die of nothing but a Rage to live.

    Turn then from Wits; and look on Simo's Mate,
No Ass so meek, no Ass so obstinate:
Or her, that owns her Faults, but never mends,
Because she's honest, and the best of Friends:
Or her, whose life the Church and Scandal share,
For ever in a Passion, or a Pray'r:

Or her, who laughs at Hell, but (like her Grace)
Cries, 'Ah! how charming if there's no such place!'
Or who in sweet vicissitude appears
Of Mirth and Opium, Ratafie and Tears,
The daily Anodyne, and nightly Draught,
To kill those foes to Fair ones, Time and Thought.
Woman and Fool are two hard things to hit,
For true No-meaning puzzles more than Wit.

But what are these to great Atossa's mind?
Scarce once herself, by turns all Womankind!
Who, with herself, or others, from her birth
Finds all her life one warfare upon earth:
Shines, in exposing Knaves, and painting Fools,
Yet is, whate'er she hates and ridicules.
No Thought advances, but her Eddy Brain
Whisks it about, and down it goes again.
Full sixty years the World has been her Trade,
The wisest Fool much Time has ever made.
From loveless youth to unrespected age,
No Passion gratify'd except her Rage.
So much the Fury still out-ran the Wit,
The Pleasure miss'd her, and the Scandal hit.
Who breaks with her, provokes Revenge from Hell,
But he's a bolder man who dares be well:
Her ev'ry turn with Violence pursu'd,
Nor more a storm her Hate than Gratitude.
To that each Passion turns, or soon or late;
Love, if it makes her yield, must make her hate:
Superiors? death! and Equals? what a curse!
But an Inferior not dependant? worse.
Offend her, and she knows not to forgive;
Oblige her, and she'll hate you while you live:
But die, and she'll adore you – Then the Bust
And Temple rise – then fall again to dust.
Last night, her Lord was all that's good and great,
A Knave this morning, and his Will a Cheat.

EPISTLE II TO A LADY · ALEXANDER POPE

    Strange! by the Means defeated of the Ends,
By Spirit robb'd of Pow'r, by Warmth of Friends,
By Wealth of Follow'rs! without one distress
Sick of herself thro' very selfishness!
Atossa, curs'd with ev'ry granted pray'r,
Childless with all her Children, wants an Heir.
To Heirs unknown descends th' unguarded store
Or wanders, Heav'n-directed, to the Poor.
    Pictures like these, dear Madam, to design,
Asks no firm hand, and no unerring line;
Some wand'ring touch, or some reflected light,
Some flying stroke alone can hit 'em right:
For how should equal Colours do the knack?
Chameleons who can paint in white and black?
    'Yet Cloe sure was form'd without a spot –'
Nature in her then err'd not, but forgot.
'With ev'ry pleasing, ev'ry prudent part,
Say, what can Cloe want?' – she wants a Heart.
She speaks, behaves, and acts just as she ought;
But never, never, reach'd one gen'rous Thought.
Virtue she finds too painful an endeavour,
Content to dwell in Decencies for ever.
So very reasonable, so unmov'd,
As never yet to love, or to be lov'd.
She, while her Lover pants upon her breast,
Can mark the figures on an Indian chest;
And when she sees her Friend in deep despair,
Observes how much a Chintz exceeds Mohair.
Forbid it Heav'n, a Favour or a Debt
She e'er should cancel – but she may forget.
Safe is your Secret still in Cloe's ear;
But none of Cloe's shall you ever hear.
Of all her Dears she never slander'd one,
But cares not if a thousand are undone.
Would Cloe know if you're alive or dead?
She bids her Footman put it in her head.

Cloe is prudent – would you too be wise?
Then never break your heart when Cloe dies.
    One certain Portrait may (I grant) be seen,
Which Heav'n has varnish'd out, and made a Queen:
The same for ever! and describ'd by all
With Truth and Goodness, as with Crown and Ball:
Poets heap Virtues, Painters Gems at will,
And show their zeal, and hide their want of skill.
'Tis well – but, Artists! who can paint or write,
To draw the Naked is your true delight:
That Robe of Quality so struts and swells,
None see what Parts of Nature it conceals.
Th' exactest traits of Body or of Mind,
We owe to models of an humble kind.
If Queensberry to strip there's no compelling,
'Tis from a Handmaid we must take a Helen.
From Peer or Bishop 'tis no easy thing
To draw the man who loves his God, or King:
Alas! I copy (or my draught would fail)
From honest Mah'met, or plain Parson Hale.
    But grant, in Public Men sometimes are shown,
A Woman's seen in Private life alone:
Our bolder Talents in full light display'd,
Your Virtues open fairest in the shade.
Bred to disguise, in Public 'tis you hide;
There, none distinguish 'twixt your Shame or Pride,
Weakness or Delicacy; all so nice,
That each may seem a Virtue, or a Vice.
    In Men, we various Ruling Passions find,
In Women, two almost divide the kind;
Those, only fix'd, they first or last obey,
The Love of Pleasure, and the Love of Sway.
That, Nature gives; and where the lesson taught
Is but to please, can Pleasure seem a fault?
Experience, this; by Man's oppression curst,
They seek the second not to lose the first.

Men, some to Bus'ness, some to Pleasure take;
But ev'ry Woman is at heart a Rake:
Men, some to Quiet, some to public Strife;
But ev'ry Lady would be Queen for life.
  Yet mark the fate of a whole Sex of Queens!
Pow'r all their end, but Beauty all the means.
In Youth they conquer, with so wild a rage,
As leaves them scarce a Subject in their Age:
For foreign glory, foreign joy, they roam;
No thought of Peace or Happiness at home.
But Wisdom's Triumph is well-tim'd Retreat,
As hard a science to the Fair as Great!
Beauties, like Tyrants, old and friendless grown,
Yet hate to rest, and dread to be alone,
Worn out in public, weary ev'ry eye,
Nor leave one sigh behind them when they die.
  Pleasures the sex, as children Birds, pursue,
Still out of reach, yet never out of view,
Sure, if they catch, to spoil the Toy at most,
To covet flying, and regret when lost:
At last, to follies Youth could scarce defend,
'Tis half their Age's prudence to pretend;
Asham'd to own they gave delight before,
Reduc'd to feign it, when they give no more:
As Hags hold Sabbaths, less for joy than spight,
So these their merry, miserable Night;
Still round and round the Ghosts of Beauty glide,
And haunt the places where their Honour dy'd.
  See how the World its Veterans rewards!
A Youth of frolicks, an old Age of Cards,
Fair to no purpose, artful to no end,
Young without Lovers, old without a Friend,
A Fop their Passion, but their Prize a Sot,
Alive, ridiculous, and dead, forgot!
  Ah Friend! to dazzle let the Vain design,
To raise the Thought and touch the Heart, be thine!

That Charm shall grow, while what fatigues the Ring
Flaunts and goes down, an unregarded thing.
So when the Sun's broad beam has tir'd the sight,
All mild ascends the Moon's more sober light,
Serene in Virgin Modesty she shines,
And unobserv'd the glaring Orb declines.

    Oh! blest with Temper, whose unclouded ray
Can make to morrow chearful as to day;
She, who can love a Sister's charms, or hear
260 Sighs for a Daughter with unwounded ear;
She, who ne'er answers till a Husband cools,
Or, if she rules him, never shows she rules;
Charms by accepting, by submitting sways,
Yet has her humour most, when she obeys;
Lets Fops or Fortune fly which way they will;
Disdains all loss of Tickets, or Codille;
Spleen, Vapours, or Small-pox, above them all,
And Mistress of herself, tho' China fall.

    And yet, believe me, good as well as ill,
270 Woman's at best a Contradiction still.
Heav'n, when it strives to polish all it can
Its last best work, but forms a softer Man;
Picks from each sex, to make its Fav'rite blest,
Your love of Pleasure, our desire of Rest,
Blends, in exception to all gen'ral rules,
Your Taste of Follies, with our Scorn of Fools,
Reserve with Frankness, Art with Truth ally'd,
Courage with Softness, Modesty with Pride,
Fix'd Principles, with Fancy ever new;
280 Shakes all together, and produces – You.

    Be this a Woman's Fame: with this unblest,
Toasts live a scorn, and Queens may die a jest.
This Phoebus promis'd (I forget the year)
When those blue eyes first open'd on the sphere;
Ascendant Phoebus watch'd that hour with care,
Averted half your Parents simple Pray'r,

>   And gave you Beauty, but deny'd the Pelf
>   Which buys your sex a Tyrant o'er itself.
>   The gen'rous God, who Wit and Gold refines,
> 290 And ripens Spirits as he ripens Mines,
>   Kept Dross for Duchesses, the world shall know it,
>   To you gave Sense, Good-humour, and a Poet.   (pub. 1735)

From Epistle I   To Richard Temple, Viscount Cobham, *lines 252–61*

One of Pope's 'virtuoso performances in fragmentary dialogue, the Horatian art that [he] has now made completely his own'. (Reuben Brower, *Alexander Pope: The Poetry of Allusion*, p. 262.)

> 252   The Courtier smooth, who forty years had shin'd
>   An humble servant to all human kind,
>   Just brought out this, when scarce his tongue could stir,
>   'If – where I'm going – I could serve you, Sir?'
>   'I give and I devise, (old Euclio said,
>   And sigh'd) My lands and tenements to Ned.'
>   Your money, Sir? 'My money, Sir, what all?
>   Why, – if I must – (then wept) I give it Paul.'
> 260   The Manor, Sir? – 'The Manor! hold,' he cry'd,
>   'Not that, – I cannot part with that' – and dy'd.   (pub. 1734)

GEORGE BERKELEY (1685–1753)

Bishop of Cloyne, on friendly terms with leading literary figures in England, the philosopher wrote this poem – one that Horace might have written had he heard of the founding of America – while on a three-year visit to the New World. He probably had in mind the latter part of Epode 16, lines 41ff.

Verses . . . on the Prospect of Planting Arts and Learning in America

The Muse, disgusted at an Age and Clime,
    Barren of every glorious Theme,
In distant Lands now waits a better Time,
    Producing Subjects worthy Fame:

In happy Climes, where from the genial Sun
    And virgin Earth such Scenes ensue,
The Force of Art by Nature seems outdone,
    And fancied Beauties by the true:

In happy Climes the Seat of Innocence,
10   Where Nature guides and Virtue rules,
Where Men shall not impose for Truth and Sense,
    The Pedantry of Courts and Schools:

There shall be sung another golden Age,
    The rise of Empire and of Arts,
The Good and Great inspiring epic Rage,
    The wisest Heads and noblest Hearts.

Not such as Europe breeds in her decay;
    Such as she bred when fresh and young,
When heav'nly Flame did animate her Clay,
20   By future Poets shall be sung.

Westward the Course of Empire takes its Way;
    The four first Acts already past,
A fifth shall close the Drama with the Day;
    Time's noblest Offspring is the last.   (writ. 1716; pub. 1752)

CHRISTOPHER PITT

Invitation . . . to a Friend at Court

An original poem, no less Horatian in manner than the imitations Pitt and others were writing, that reflects the scientific interests of the day. See Introduction, pp. 20–21. In the third of his papers on the *Pleasures of the imagination* (1712) Addison wrote: 'We are not a little pleased to find every green Leaf swarm with Millions of Animals, that at their largest Growth are not Visible to the naked Eye ... But when we survey the whole Earth at once, and the several Planets that lie within its Neighbourhood, we are filled with a pleasing Astonishment, to see so many Worlds hanging one above another, and sliding round their Axles in such an amazing Pomp and Solemnity. If, after this, we contemplate the wide Fields of Aether, that reach in height as far from Saturn to the fixt Stars, and run abroad almost to an Infinitude, our Imagination finds its Capacity filled with so immense a Prospect, and puts itself upon the Stretch to comprehend it.'

> If you can leave for books the crouded court,
> And generous Bourdeaux for a glass of Port,
> To these sweet solitudes without delay
> Break from the world's impertinence away.
>   Soon as the sun the face of nature gilds,
> For health and pleasure will we range the fields;
> O'er her gay scenes and op'ning beauties run,
> While all the vast creation is our own.
> But when his golden globe with faded light
> 10 Yields to the solemn empire of the night;
> And in her sober majesty the moon
> With milder glories mounts her silver throne;
> Amidst ten thousand orbs with splendour crown'd,
> That pour their tributary beams around;

Thro' the long levell'd tube our strengthen'd sight
Shall mark distinct the spangles of the night;
From world to world shall dart the boundless eye,
And stretch from star to star, from sky to sky.
    The buzzing insect families appear,
When suns unbind the rigour of the year;
Quick glance the myriads round the ev'ning bow'r,
Hosts of a day, or nations of an hour.
Astonish'd we shall see th' unfolding race,
Stretch'd out in bulk, within the polish'd glass;
Thro' whose small convex a new world we spy,
Ne'er seen before, but by a Seraph's eye!
So long in darkness shut from human kind
Lay half God's wonders to a point confin'd!
But in one peopled drop we now survey
In pride of pow'r some little monster play;
O'er tribes invisible he reigns alone,
And struts a tyrant of a world his own.
    Now will we study Homer's awful page,
Now warm our souls with Pindar's noble rage:
To English lays shall Flaccus' lyre be strung,
And lofty Virgil speak the British tongue.
Immortal Virgil! at thy sacred name
I tremble now, and now I pant for fame;
With eager hopes this moment I aspire
To catch or emulate thy glorious fire;
The next pursue the rash attempt no more,
But drop the quill, bow, wonder, and adore;
By thy strong genius overcome and aw'd!
That fire from heav'n! that spirit of a God!
Pleas'd and transported with thy name I tend
Beyond my theme, forgetful of my friend;
And from my first design by rapture led,
Neglect the living poet for the dead.

(1750)

WILLIAM COWPER

An Epistle to Joseph Hill, Esq.

Dear Joseph – five and twenty years ago –
Alas, how time escapes! – 'tis even so –
With frequent intercourse, and always sweet,
And always friendly, we were wont to cheat
A tedious hour – and now we never meet!
As some grave gentleman in Terence says,
('Twas therefore much the same in ancient days)
Good lack, we know not what to-morrow brings –
Strange fluctuation of all human things!
10 True. Changes will befall, and friends may part,
But distance only cannot change the heart:
And were I call'd to prove th' assertion true,
One proof should serve – a reference to you.

Whence comes it then, that in the wane of life,
Though nothing have occurr'd to kindle strife,
We find the friends we fancied we had won,
Though num'rous once, reduc'd to few or none?
Can gold grow worthless that has stood the touch?
No – gold they seem'd, but they were never such.

20 Horatio's servant once, with bow and cringe,
Swinging the parlour-door upon its hinge,
Dreading a negative, and overaw'd
Lest he should trespass, begg'd to go abroad.
Go, fellow! – whither? – turning short about –
Nay – stay at home – you're always going out.
'Tis but a step, sir, just at the street's end. –
For what? – An please you, sir, to see a friend.
A friend! Horatio cry'd, and seem'd to start –
Yea, marry shalt thou, and with all my heart. –

    And fetch my cloak: for, though the night be raw,
I'll see him too – the first I ever saw.
    I knew the man, and knew his nature mild,
And was his plaything often when a child;
But somewhat at that moment pinch'd him close,
Else he was seldom bitter or morose.
Perhaps, his confidence just then betray'd,
His grief might prompt him with the speech he made;
Perhaps 'twas mere good-humour gave it birth,
The harmless play of pleasantry and mirth.
Howe'er it was, his language, in my mind,
Bespoke at least a man that knew mankind.
    But, not to moralize too much, and strain
To prove an evil of which all complain,
(I hate long arguments, verbosely spun)
One story more, dear Hill, and I have done.
Once on a time an emp'ror, a wise man –
No matter where, in China or Japan –
Decreed that whosoever should offend
Against the well-known duties of a friend,
Convicted once, should ever after wear
But half a coat, and show his bosom bare.
The punishment importing this, no doubt,
That all was naught within, and all found out.
    Oh, happy Britain! we have not to fear
Such hard and arbitrary measure here;
Else, could a law like that which I relate
Once have the sanction of our triple state,
Some few that I have known in days of old,
Would run most dreadful risk of catching cold;
While you, my friend, whatever wind should blow,
Might traverse England safely to and fro,
An honest man, close-button'd to the chin,
Broad-cloth without, and a warm heart within.   (pub. 1785)

WILLIAM WORDSWORTH

To M. H.

Fifth in the group of 'Poems on the Naming of Places.' For a possible relation to Horace's ode on the Bandusian Spring (translated by Wordsworth in his later teens) see Introduction, pp. 37–8.

    Our walk was far among the antient trees:
There was no road nor any wood-man's path,
But the thick umbrage, checking the wild growth
Of weed and sapling, on the soft green turf
Beneath the branches of itself had made
A track which brought us to a slip of lawn
And a small bed of water in the woods.
All round this pool both flocks and herds might drink
On its firm margin, even as from a well
10 Or some stone-bason which the Herdsman's hand
Had shaped for their refreshment, nor did sun
Or wind from any quarter ever come
But as a blessing to this calm recess,
This glade of water and this one green field.
The spot was made by Nature for herself:
The travellers know it not, and 'twill remain
Unknown to them; but it is beautiful
And if a man should plant his cottage near,
Should sleep beneath the shelter of its trees,
20 And blend its waters with his daily meal,
He would so love it that in his death-hour
Its image would survive among his thoughts,
And therefore, my sweet Mary, this still nook
With all its beeches we have named from You.   (pub. 1800)

ALFRED TENNYSON

To the Rev. F. D. Maurice

An invitation poem in the tradition of Horace's Epistle I.5 and Jonson's 'Inviting a Friend to Supper'. The stanza is one that Tennyson had used already in 'The Daisy', and was designed to represent 'in some measure the grandest of metres, the Horatian Alcaic'. Here he changes the metre of the last line (/∪∪/∪∪/∪/), bringing it closer to the Latin model: –∪∪–∪∪–∪–∪̣. Maurice had been forced to resign his professorship at King's College, London, on account of his liberal views on eternal punishment.

> Come, when no graver cares employ,
> Godfather, come and see your boy:
>   Your presence will be sun in winter,
> Making the little one leap for joy.
>
> For, being of that honest few,
> Who give the Fiend himself his due,
>   Should eighty-thousand college-councils
> Thunder 'Anathema,' friend, at you;
>
> Should all our churchmen foam in spite
> At you, so careful of the right,
>   Yet one lay-hearth would give you welcome
> (Take it and come) to the Isle of Wight;
>
> Where, far from noise and smoke of town,
> I watch the twilight falling brown
>   All round a careless-ordered garden
> Close to the ridge of a noble down.

You'll have no scandal while you dine,
But honest talk and wholesome wine,
   And only hear the magpie gossip
20 Garrulous under a roof of pine:

For groves of pine on either hand,
To break the blast of winter, stand;
   And further on, the hoary Channel
Tumbles a billow on chalk and sand;

Where, if below the milky steep
Some ship of battle slowly creep,
   And on through zones of light and shadow
Glimmer away to the lonely deep,

We might discuss the Northern sin
30 Which made a selfish war begin;
   Dispute the claims, arrange the chances;
Emperor, Ottoman, which shall win:

Or whether war's avenging rod
Shall lash all Europe into blood;
   Till you should turn to dearer matters,
Dear to the man that is dear to God;

How best to help the slender store,
How mend the dwellings, of the poor;
   How gain in life, as life advances,
40 Valour and charity more and more.

Come, Maurice, come: the lawn as yet
Is hoar with rime, or spongy-wet;
   But when the wreath of March has blossomed,
Crocus, anemone, violet,

Or later, pay one visit here,
For those are few we hold as dear;
  Nor pay but one, but come for many,
Many and many a happy year. (pub. 1855)

CONSTANTINE CAVAFY
(1863–1933)

Horace in Athens

In this early 'repudiated' poem, Cavafy makes an imaginative guess at a Horace not to be found in the *Odes*, the Roman undergraduate with enough money in his pocket to cut a stylish figure in the exciting world of Athens, and indulge in the romantic affairs that must lie somewhere behind the love poems of Horace's maturity.

Who enters Leah's chamber, what young man
nearing her double bed of wealth and elegance
offers the hetaera a spray of jasmine
now, the gleam of brilliant gems on his hands?

His tunic's made of finely-woven white silk
bordered with a red, oriental pattern;
but even though his speech is pure Attic,
still the slightest accent of native Latin

taints his flawless Greek with a trace of the Tiber.
10 Yet so quietly the Athenian listens
to this Horace, her eloquent new lover,

you might think a breeze had parted silk curtains
and new worlds of beauty were dawning on her,
so intently she listens to the great Italian. (1897)

(TRANS. GEORGE KALOGERIS)

RUDYARD KIPLING

'Horace, Bk V, Ode 3'

This 'translation' (it is not a translation though it distantly recalls Ode I.1) is the first of Kipling's odes from 'Book V', a book so far unknown to classical scholarship. It follows 'Regulus' (in *A Diversity of Creatures*, 1917), a story about a Latin lesson in which the boys are taken through the Regulus Ode, III.5, and made to translate it. Next door a chemistry lesson is taking place, known then to schoolboys as 'Stinks'.

A Translation

There are whose study is of smells,
    And to attentive schools rehearse
How something mixed with something else
    Makes something worse.

Some cultivate in broths impure
    The clients of our body – these,
Increasing without Venus, cure,
    Or cause, disease.

Others the heated wheel extol,
10   And all its offspring, whose concern
Is how to make it farthest roll
    And fastest turn.

Me, much incurious if the hour
    Present, or to be paid for, brings
Me to Brundusium by the power
    Of wheels or wings;

Me, in whose breast no flame hath burned
   Life-long, save that by Pindar lit,
Such lore leaves cold. I am not turned
20   Aside to it

More than when, sunk in thought profound
   Of what the unaltering Gods require,
My steward (friend but slave) brings round
   Logs for my fire.   (pub. 1917)

'Horace, Ode 17, Bk V'

In the story which this poem introduces, 'The United Idolaters' (*Debits and Credits*, 1926), Kipling returns to the jape-ridden world of *Stalky & Co.*, written twenty-five years earlier.

To the Companions

How comes it that, at even-tide,
   When level beams should show most truth,
Man, failing, takes unfailing pride
   In memories of his frolic youth?

Venus and Liber fill their hour;
   The games engage, the law-courts prove;
Till hardened life breeds love of power
   Or Avarice, Age's final love.

Yet at the end, these comfort not –
10   Nor any triumph Fate decrees –
Compared with glorious, unforgot-
      ten innocent enormities

---

5 *Liber* Bacchus

Of frontless days before the beard,
    When, instant on the casual jest,
The God Himself of Mirth appeared
    And snatched us to His heaving breast.

And we – not caring who He was
    But certain He would come again –
Accepted all He brought to pass
    As Gods accept the lives of men . . .

Then He withdrew from sight and speech,
    Nor left a shrine. How comes it now
While Charon's keel grates on the beach,
    He calls so clear: 'Rememberest thou?'   (pub. 1926)

'Horace, Ode 31, Bk V'

The poem follows 'The Eye of Allah' (also in *Debits and Credits*), standing to it in an oblique relation somewhat resembling that of choral ode to scene in Greek tragedy. The story treats of a scientific discovery made before its time and hence threatening the order of its time, the later Middle Ages. The poem looks wonderingly at an event, the birth of Christ, that will threaten the order of the Roman state and perhaps, or perhaps not, restore 'the lost shades that were our loves'. (Maecenas died in 8 BC, Horace some two months later. Virgil died eleven years before.)

The Last Ode (Nov. 27, BC 8)

As watchers couched beneath a Bantine oak,
    Hearing the dawn-wind stir,
Know that the present strength of night is broke
    Though no dawn threaten her
Till dawn's appointed hour – so Virgil died,
Aware of change at hand, and prophesied

> Change upon all the Eternal Gods had made
>   And on the Gods alike –
> Fated as dawn but, as the dawn, delayed
10   Till the just hour should strike –
>
> A Star new-risen above the living and dead;
>   And the lost shades that were our loves restored
> As lovers, and for ever. So he said;
>   Having received the word . . .
>
> Maecenas waits me on the Esquiline:
>   Thither to-night go I. . . .
> And shall this dawn restore us, Virgil mine,
>   To dawn? Beneath what sky?   (pub. 1926)

ROBERT FROST (1874–1963)

This poem was read before the Phi Beta Kappa Society at Harvard in June 1941. For Frost's relation to Horace one may consult Reuben Brower, *The Poetry of Robert Frost* (1963), chapter 3.

The Lesson for Today

> If this uncertain age in which we dwell
> Were really as dark as I hear sages tell,
> And I convinced that they were really sages,
> I should not curse myself with it to hell,
> But leaving not the chair I long have sat in,
> I should betake me back ten thousand pages
> To the world's undebatably dark ages,
> And getting up my medieval Latin,

THE LESSON FOR TODAY · ROBERT FROST

    Seek converse common cause and brotherhood
10 (By all that's liberal – I should, I should)
    With poets who could calmly take the fate
    Of being born at once too early and late,
    And for these reasons kept from being great.
    Yet singing but Dione in the wood
    And *ver aspergit terram floribus*
    They slowly led old Latin verse to rhyme
    And to forget the ancient lengths of time,
    And so began the modern world for us.

      I'd say, O Master of the Palace School,
20 You were not Charles' nor anybody's fool:
    Tell me as pedagogue to pedagogue,
    You did not know that since King Charles did rule
    You had no chance but to be minor, did you?
    Your light was spent perhaps as in a fog
    That at once kept you burning low and hid you.
    The age may very well have been to blame
    For your not having won to Virgil's fame.
    But no one ever heard you make the claim.
    You would not think you knew enough to judge
30 The age when full upon you. That's my point.
    We have today and I could call their name
    Who know exactly what is out of joint
    To make their verse and their excuses lame.
    They've tried to grasp with too much social fact
    Too large a situation. You and I
    Would be afraid if we should comprehend
    And get outside of too much bad statistics
    Our muscles never could again contract:
    We never could recover human shape,
40 But must live lives out mentally agape,
    Or die of philosophical distention.
    That's how we feel – and we're no special mystics.

We can't appraise the time in which we act.
But for the folly of it, let's pretend
We know enough to know it for adverse.
One more millennium's about to end.
Let's celebrate the event, my distant friend,
In publicly disputing which is worse,
The present age or your age. You and I
As schoolmen of repute should qualify
To wage a fine scholastical contention
As to whose age deserves the lower mark,
Or should I say the higher one, for dark.
I can just hear the way you make it go:
There's always something to be sorry for,
A sordid peace or an outrageous war.
Yes, yes, of course. We have the same convention.
The groundwork of all faith is human woe.
It was well worth preliminary mention.
There's nothing but injustice to be had,
No choice is left a poet, you might add,
But how to take the curse, tragic or comic.
It was well worth preliminary mention.
But let's go on to where our cases part,
If part they do. Let me propose a start.
(We're rivals in the badness of our case,
Remember, and must keep a solemn face.)
Space ails us moderns: we are sick with space.
Its contemplation makes us out as small
As a brief epidemic of microbes
That in a good glass may be seen to crawl
The patina of this the least of globes.
But have we there the advantage after all?
You were belittled into vilest worms
God hardly tolerated with his feet;
Which comes to the same thing in different terms.
We both are the belittled human race,
One as compared with God and one with space.

> I had thought ours the more profound disgrace;
> But doubtless this was only my conceit.
> The cloister and the observatory saint
> Take comfort in about the same complaint.
> So science and religion really meet.
>
>   I can just hear you call your Palace class:
> Come learn the Latin Eheu for alas.
> You may not want to use it and you may.
> O paladins, the lesson for today
> Is how to be unhappy yet polite.
> And at the summons Roland, Olivier,
> And every sheepish paladin and peer,
> Being already more than proved in fight,
> Sits down in school to try if he can write
> Like Horace in the true Horatian vein,
> Yet like a Christian disciplined to bend
> His mind to thinking always of the end.
> Memento mori and obey the Lord.
> Art and religion love the somber chord.
> Earth's a hard place in which to save the soul,
> And could it be brought under state control,
> So automatically we all were saved,
> Its separateness from Heaven could be waived;
> It might as well at once be kingdom-come.
> (Perhaps it will be next millennium.)
>
>   But these are universals, not confined
> To any one time, place, or human kind.
> We're either nothing or a God's regret.
> As ever when philosophers are met,
> No matter where they stoutly mean to get,
> Nor what particulars they reason from,
> They are philosophers, and from old habit
> They end up in the universal Whole
> As unoriginal as any rabbit.

One age is like another for the soul.
I'm telling you. You haven't said a thing,
Unless I put it in your mouth to say.
I'm having the whole argument my way —
But in your favor — please to tell your King —
In having granted you all ages shine
With equal darkness, yours as dark as mine.
120 I'm liberal. You, you aristocrat,
Won't know exactly what I mean by that.
I mean so altruistically moral
I never take my own side in a quarrel.
I'd lay my hand on his hand on his staff,
Lean back and have my confidential laugh,
And tell him I had read his Epitaph.

It sent me to the graves the other day.
The only other there was far away
Across the landscape with a watering pot
130 At his devotions in a special plot.
And he was there resuscitating flowers
(Make no mistake about its being bones);
But I was only there to read the stones
To see what on the whole they had to say
About how long a man may think to live,
Which is becoming my concern of late.
And very wide the choice they seemed to give;
The ages ranging all the way from hours
To months and years and many many years.
140 One man had lived one hundred years and eight.
But though we all may be inclined to wait
And follow some development of state,
Or see what comes of science and invention,
There is a limit to our time extension.
We all are doomed to broken-off careers,
And so's the nation, so's the total race.
The earth itself is liable to the fate

Of meaninglessly being broken off.
(And hence so many literary tears
150 At which my inclination is to scoff.)
I may have wept that any should have died
Or missed their chance, or not have been their best,
Or been their riches, fame, or love denied;
On me as much as any is the jest.
I take my incompleteness with the rest.
God bless himself can no one else be blessed.

   I hold your doctrine of Memento Mori.
And were an epitaph to be my story
I'd have a short one ready for my own.
160 I would have written of me on my stone:
I had a lover's quarrel with the world.   (pub. 1942)

RICARDO REIS (FERNANDO PESSOA) (1888–1935)

Pessoa's contribution to Modernism brought Portuguese poetry to a position in European literature it had not enjoyed since Camoëns. *Odes de Ricardo Reis*, one of Pessoa's heteronyms, a poet of a neo-Horatian cast, appeared in 1946.

To be great

To be great, be whole; neither exclude
    Or exaggerate a single thing.
Be complete, in every instance. Put all you are
    In the smallest action.
Thus in each lake the moon intact
    Shines, so high it lives.

Para ser grande, sê inteiro: nada
    Teu exagera ou exclui.
Sê todo em cada coisa. Põe quanto és
    No mínimo que fazes.
Assim em cada lago a lua toda
    Brilha, porque alta vive.   (pub. 1933)

Already on my head

Already on my head starts to gray
The hair of the young man I lost.
    My eyes are getting dim.
My mouth no longer deserves a single kiss.
If you still love me — I beg you, don't
For love's sake; you would betray me
    With myself.

Já sobre a fronte vã se me acinzenta
O cabelo do jovem que perdi.
    Meus olhos brilham menos.
Já não tem jus a beijos minha boca.
Se me ainda amas, por amor não ames:
    Traíras-me comigo.   (pub. 1928)
                                        (Trans. ALBERTO DE LACERDA)

DONALD DAVIE (1922–1995)

Poet and critic, educated at St Catharine's College, Cambridge, held academic posts in England, Ireland, and America. His *Collected Poems* was published in 1990. For the image of the railway tunnel he was probably indebted to a discussion of Ode I.9 by J. V. Cunningham in *Collected Essays* (1976), p. 419. The final stanza refers to the long coal strike led by Arthur Scargill in 1984–5.

Wombwell on Strike

Horace of course is not
a temporizer, but
his sudden and smooth transitions
        (as, into a railway tunnel,
           then out, to a different landscape)

it must be admitted elide,
and necessarily, what
happens up there on the hill
        or hill-ridge that the tunnel
        of syntax so featly slides under.

I have been reminded of this
when, gratefully leaving my native
haunts, the push-and-pull diesel
        clatters into a tunnel
        under a wooded escarpment:

Wentworth Woodhouse, mounded
or else in high shaws drifted
over the miners' tramways.
        Horace's streaming style
        exhorts me never to pause;

'Press on,' he says, and indeed his
suavities never entirely
exclude the note of alarm:
        'Leave the unlikely meaning
        to eddy, or you are in trouble.'

---

16 *Wentworth Woodhouse* great house in the West Riding

Wombwell – 'womb well': it is
foolish and barbarous wordplay,
though happily I was
        born of this tormented
        womb, the taut West Riding.

Yours was solid advice,
Horace, and centuries have
endorsed it; but over this tunnel
        large policemen grapple
        the large men my sons have become. (1990)

LIST OF EDITIONS

References are to modern critical editions, where possible. Some titles have been abbreviated. In all cases, texts have been slightly modernized. Some quotations and i/j and v/u have been made to conform to modern usage; we have removed italics from most texts published before the nineteenth century and have corrected obvious typographical errors.

John Quincy Adams. *Poems of Religion and Society*, William H. Graham, 1848.
Joseph Addison. *Miscellaneous Works*, ed. A. C. Guthkelch, G. Bell, 1914.
Anonymous, in the *Works of Horace in English Verse. By Several Hands. Collected and Published by Mr. Duncombe*, London, 1759.
Anonymous, formerly ascribed to Ben Jonson. *Ben Jonson*, ed. C. H. Herford, Percy and Evelyn Simpson, Oxford, Clarendon Press, 1925–52.
Anonymous, in *Tottel's Miscellany*, revised edition, ed. Hyder Edward Rollins, Harvard University Press, 1965.
Anonymous, in Henry Wotton, *Reliquiae Wottonianae*, London, editions in 1651, 1654 and 1672.
John Ashmore. *Certain Selected Odes of Horace*, London, 1621.
Francis Atterbury. In Philip Francis, *Poetical Translation of the Works of Horace*.
Sir John Beaumont. *Shorter Poems*, ed. Roger D. Sell, Åbo, Åbo Akademi, 1974.
Aphra Behn. *Works*, ed. Janet Todd, Ohio State University Press, 1992.

Richard Bentley. In James Henry Monk, *Life of Richard Bentley*, second edition, London, 1833.

George Berkeley. *Works*, ed. A. A. Luce and T. E. Jessop, Thomas Nelson, 1948–57.

Samuel Boyse. *Translations and Poems Written on Several Occasions*, Edinburgh, 1738.

Patrick Branwell Brontë. *Poems*, ed. Victor A. Neufeldt, Garland, 1990.

Tom Brown. *A Collection of Miscellany Poems, Letters, &c.*, second edition, London, 1700. Ode I.27 first published in *Gentleman's Journal*, 10 March 1962.

Edward Bulwer-Lytton, Lord Lytton. *Odes and Epodes of Horace*, Blackwood, 1869. First published in *Blackwood's Magazine*, April 1868.

Basil Bunting. *Collected Poems*, new edition, Oxford University Press, 1978.

George Gordon, Lord Byron. *Complete Poetical Works*, ed. Jerome J. McGann, Oxford, 1980–93.

C. S. Calverley. *Complete Works*, G. Bell, 1901.

Roy Campbell. *Collected Works*, ed. Peter Alexander, Michael Chapman and Marcia Leveson, A. D. Donker, 1985–88.

Thomas Campion. *Works*, ed. Walter R. Davis, Doubleday, 1967.

Thomas Carew. *Poems*, ed. Rhodes Dunlap, Oxford, Clarendon Press, 1949.

Arthur Hugh Clough. *Poems*, ed. F. L. Mulhauser, second edition, translations edited by Jane Turner, Oxford, Clarendon Press, 1974.

William Congreve. In *Examen Poeticum: Being the Third Part of Miscellany Poems*, London, 1693.

John Conington. *Odes and Carmen Saeculare*, Ball and Daldy, 1863. *Satires, Epistles and Art of Poetry*, Ball and Daldy, 1870.

Abraham Cowley. *Poems*, ed. A. R. Waller, Cambridge, The University Press, 1905. *Essays, Plays and Sundry Verses*, ed. A. R. Waller, Cambridge, The University Press, 1906. *Works*, ed. Thomas O. Calhoun, Laurence Heyworth, Allan Pritchard, University of Delaware Press, 1989–.

William Cowper. *Poetical Works*, ed. H. S. Milford, fourth edition, with corrections and additions by Norma Russell, Oxford University Press, 1967. *Poems*, ed. John D. Baird and Charles Ryskamp, Oxford, Clarendon Press, 1980–.

Richard Crashaw. *Poems*, second edition, ed. L. C. Martin, Oxford, Clarendon Press, 1957.

Thomas Creech. *The Odes, Satyrs, and Epistles of Horace*, second edition, London, 1688. First edition, 1684.

J. V. Cunningham, *Collected Poems and Epigrams*, Swallow Press, 1971.

Donald Davie. *Collected Poems*, Carcanet, 1990.

Sir Stephen E. de Vere. *Translations from Horace*, third edition, enlarged, Walter Scott, 1888.

Wentworth Dillon, Earl of Roscommon. In *Miscellany Poems*, London, 1684. The imitation of Odes I.22 appears in *The Odes and Satires of Horace That have been done into English by the Most Eminent Hands*, London, 1715, but is not printed in the 1717 *Poems* (or in the 1749 *Poetical Works*). His 1684 translation of Horace's *Ars Poetica* was reprinted in 1971 by the Scolar Press.

Austin Dobson. *Complete Poetical Works*, Oxford University Press, 1923.

John Dryden. *Works*, University of California Press, 1956–.

Richard Duke. In *Miscellany Poems*, London, 1684.

William Dunkin. In Philip Francis, *Poetical Translation of the Works of Horace*.

Sir Richard Fanshawe. In *Poems of Horace*, ed. A. Brome, 1666. Reprinted by AMS Press, 1978. *Shorter Poems and Translations*, ed. N. W. Bawcutt, Liverpool University Press, 1964.

Robert Fergusson, *Poems*, ed. Matthew P. McDiarmid, Edinburgh, 1954. Scottish Text Society, third series, 21 and 24.

David Ferry. *Strangers*, University of Chicago Press, 1983. Recent translations of Horace by David Ferry have appeared in *Arion*, the *Boston Review*, *Pequod*, *Raritan* and the *Southern Humanities Review*.

Philip Francis. *Poetical Translation of the Works of Horace*, London. Nine editions between 1746 and 1791. (First edition: *Odes, Epodes, and Carmen Saeculare of Horace*, 1743–46.)

Robert Frost. *Poetry of Robert Frost*, ed. Edward Connery Lathem, Holt, Rinehart and Winston, 1969.

W. E. Gladstone. *Translations by Lord Lyttelton and the Right Hon. W. E. Gladstone*, second edition, Bernard Quaritch, 1863.

Oliver Goldsmith. *Collected Works*, ed. Arthur Friedman, Oxford, Clarendon Press, 1966.

Friedrich von Hardenberg [Novalis]. *Schriften*, ed. Paul Kluckhohn and Richard Samuel, Kohlhammer, Stuttgart, 1960.

Sir Thomas Hawkins. Odes I.11 in *Poems of Horace*, ed. A. Brome, 1666. Reprinted by AMS Press, 1978. Odes II.3 in Thomas Hawkins, *Odes of Horace*, London, 1631.

Anthony Hecht. *The Venetian Vespers*, Atheneum, 1979.

Edward, Lord Herbert of Cherbury. *The Poems English and Latin*, ed. G. C. Moore Smith, Oxford, Clarendon Press, 1923.

John Herington. In *Arion*, volume 9, numbers 2–3, Summer/Autumn 1970.

Robert Herrick. *Poetical Works*, ed. L. C. Martin, Oxford, Clarendon Press, 1956.

John Cam Hobhouse, Lord Broughton. In *Imitations and Translations*, Garland, 1977. Reprint of the 1809 volume.

Gerard Manley Hopkins. *Poetical Works*, ed. Norman H. Mackenzie, Oxford, Clarendon Press, 1990.

A. E. Housman. *Collected Poems and Selected Prose*, ed. Christopher Ricks, Penguin, 1988.

George Howard, Viscount Morpeth (later sixth Earl of Carlisle). In *Poetry of the Anti-Jacobin*, ed. L. Rice-Oxley, Basil Blackwell, 1924.

Henry Howard, Earl of Surrey. *Poems*, ed. Emrys Jones. Oxford, Clarendon Press, 1964.

Francis Howes. *Epodes, Satires, and Epistles of Horace*, W. Pickering, 1845.

Leigh Hunt. *Poetical Works*, ed. H. S. Milford, Oxford University Press, 1923.

Samuel Johnson. *Works*, Yale University Press, 1958–.

Ben Jonson. *Ben Jonson*, ed. C. H. Herford, Percy and Evelyn Simpson, Oxford, Clarendon Press, 1925–52.

Rudyard Kipling. *Early Verse*, ed. Andrew Rutherford, Oxford,

Clarendon Press, 1986. *Verse*, definitive edition, Anchor Press, 1940.

M. G. Lewis. *The Monk*. ed. Howard Anderson, Oxford University Press, 1973.

Richard Lovelace. *Poems*, ed. C. H. Wilkinson, Oxford, Clarendon Press, 1930.

Robert Lowell. *Near the Ocean*, Farrar, Straus and Giroux, 1967.

Lord Lytton. See Edward Bulwer-Lytton.

Colin Macleod. *Horace, the Epistles*, Rome, Edizioni dell'Ateneo, 1986.

Andrew Marvell. *Poems and Letters*, ed. H. M. Margoliouth, third edition, revised by Pierre Legouis with E. E. Duncan-Jones, Oxford, Clarendon Press, 1971.

James Michie. *The Odes of Horace*, Penguin, 1967. First published by Orion Press in 1963.

John Milton. *Works*, Columbia University Press, 1931-8. *Complete Prose Works*, Yale University Press, 1953-82.

Lady Mary Wortley Montagu. *Essays and Poems and Simplicity*, ed. Robert Halsband and Isobel Grundy, Oxford, Clarendon Press, 1977.

Thomas Moore. *Poetical Works*, ed. A. D. Godley, Oxford University Press, 1915.

Novalis. See Friedrich von Hardenberg.

George Ogle. *Of Legacy-Hunting*, London, 1737.

John Oldham. *Poems*, ed. Harold F. Brooks, with Raman Selden, Oxford, Clarendon Press, 1987.

William Oldisworth. *The Odes, Epodes, and Carmen Saeculare of Horace in English verse*, second edition, London, 1719. First edition 1712-13.

Thomas Otway. *Works*, ed. J. C. Ghosh, Oxford, Clarendon Press, 1932.

Robert Pinsky. *An Explanation of America*, Princeton University Press, 1979.

Christopher Pitt. *Poems and Translations*, London, 1727. *The Student*, vol. 1, 1750.

Alexander Pope. *Imitations of Horace*, ed. John Butt, second edition, Yale University Press, 1961. *Epistles to Several Persons*, ed. F. W. Bateson, second edition, Yale University Press, 1961.

Walter Pope? In *Poems of Horace*, ed. A. Brome, 1666. Reprinted by AMS Press, 1978.

Richard Porson. *Morning Chronicle*, 25 June 1794.

Ezra Pound. *Translations*, enlarged edition, New Directions, 1963.

Matthew Prior. *Literary Works*, ed. H. Bunker Wright and Monroe K. Spears, second edition, Oxford University Press, 1971.

Alexander Pushkin. In *Three Russian Poets*, translated by Vladimir Nabokov, New Directions, 1944.

Allan Ramsay. *Works*, ed. Burns Martin and John W. Oliver, Edinburgh, 1951–74. Scottish Text Society, third series, 19–20, 29; fourth series, 6–8.

Earl of Rochester. See John Wilmot.

Earl of Roscommon. See Wentworth Dillon.

Susanna Rowson. *Miscellaneous Poems*, Gilbert and Dean, 1804.

Casimire Sarbiewski. *The Odes of Casimire Translated by G. H.*, London, 1646. Reprinted by the Augustan Reprint Society, 1953.

Sir Charles Sedley. *Poetical and Dramatic Works*, ed. V. de Sola Pinto, Constable, 1928.

Sir Edward Sherburne. *Poems and Translations*, ed. F. J. Beeck, Van Gorcum, 1961.

Sir Philip Sidney. *Poems*, ed. W. A. Ringler, Oxford, Clarendon Press, 1962.

C. H. Sisson. *In the Trojan Ditch*, Carcanet, 1974. *The Poetic Art*, Carcanet, 1975. The second epode is printed in *Horace Made New*, ed. Charles Martindale and David Hopkins, Cambridge University Press, 1993.

Christopher Smart. *Christopher Smart's Verse Translation of Horace's Odes*, ed. Arthur Sherbo, Victoria, B.C., English Literary Studies, University of Victoria, 1979. *Poetical Works*, ed. Karina Wilkinson and Marcus Walsh, Oxford, Clarendon Press, 1980–.

James and Horatio Smith. *Horace in London*, Gale and Fenner, 1813.

William Somerville. *An Imitation of the Ninth Ode of the Fourth Book of Horace*, London, 1715.

George Stepney. In *Odes and Satires of Horace That have been done into English by the most Eminent Hands*, London, 1715.

Earl of Surrey. See Henry Howard.

Jonathan Swift. *Poems*, ed. Harold Williams, second edition, Oxford, Clarendon Press, 1958. *Poetical Works*, ed. Herbert Davis, Oxford University Press, 1967.

Alfred Tennyson. *Poems*, ed. Christopher Ricks, second edition, University of Califonia Press, 1987.

James Thomson. *Liberty*, ed. James Sambrook, Oxford, Clarendon Press, 1986.

Thomas Tickell. *Die Gedichte Thomas Tickells*, ed. Helgard Stöver-Leidig, Frankfurt am Main, Peter Lang, 1981.

Giovan Giorgio Trissino. *Rime 1529*, ed. Amedeo Quondam, Vicenza, Neri Pozza, 1981.

Henry Vaughan. *Works*, ed. L. C. Martin, second edition, Oxford, Clarendon Press, 1957.

Thomas Warton. Odes III.13 printed in Joseph Warton's *Odes on Various Subjects*, London, 1746. *Poetical Works*, ed. Richard Mant, Oxford, University Press, 1802. Reprinted by Gregg, 1969.

G. M. and G. F. Whicher. *On the Tibur Road*, Princeton University Press, 1912.

John Wilmot, Earl of Rochester. *Poems*, ed. Keith Walker, Basil Blackwell, 1984.

William Wordsworth. *An Evening Walk*, ed. James Averill, Cornell University Press, 1984. *Lyrical Ballads and Other Poems*, ed. James Butler and Karen Green, Cornell University Press, 1992.

Henry Wotton. *Reliquiae Wottonianae*, London, editions in 1651, 1654 and 1672. 'The Character of a Happy Life' was first published in the fifth edition of Sir Thomas Overbury's *A Wife now the Widdow of Sir T. Overburye*, 1614. See *Poems by Sir Henry Wotton, Sir Walter Raleigh, and others*, ed. Rev. John Hannah, London, W. Pickering, 1845.

Thomas Yalden. In *The Annual Miscellany for the Year 1694 being the Fourth Part of Miscellany Poems*, London, 1694.

Young Gentlemen of Mr Rule's Academy at Islington. *Poetical Blossoms by the Young Gentlemen of Mr Rule's Academy*, 1766.

TABLE OF HORACE IN TRANSLATION

Odes

Book I
1. Allan Ramsay (p. 154), Anthony Hecht (p. 263), David Ferry (p. 266)
3. John Dryden (p. 107), Christopher Smart (p. 193), Arthur Hugh Clough (p. 234)
4. Allan Ramsay (p. 157), Lady Mary Wortley Montagu (p. 165), David Ferry (p. 267)
5. John Milton (p. 88), Sir Richard Fanshawe (p. 89), Abraham Cowley (p. 99), Aphra Behn (p. 120), Allan Ramsay (p. 158), Lady Mary Wortley Montagu (p. 167), Christopher Smart (p. 194)
8. Christopher Smart (p. 195)
9. Sir Edward Sherburne (p. 97), John Dryden (p. 109), William Cowper (p. 203), James and Horatio Smith (p. 217), Alfred Tennyson (p. 227), C. S. Calverley (p. 240), J. V. Cunningham (p. 256)
10. David Ferry (p. 268)
11. Sir Thomas Hawkins (p. 87), Robert Fergusson (p. 207), C. S. Calverley (p. 241), Ezra Pound (p. 252), John Herington (p. 265), David Ferry (p. 269)
14. W. E. Gladstone (p. 228)
15. Thomas Tickell (p. 162), David Ferry (p. 270)
16. Patrick Branwell Brontë (p. 232)
17. Thomas Creech (p. 129)
19. William Congreve (p. 144)
20. James Michie (p. 284)

21. Patrick Branwell Brontë (p. 233)
22. Earl of Roscommon (pp. 114, 115), Christopher Pitt (p. 168), Samuel Johnson (p. 188), John Quincy Adams (p. 212), Thomas Moore (p. 219)
23. Austin Dobson (p. 243)
24. C. S. Calverley (p. 241)
25. The Young Gentlemen of Mr Rule's Academy (p. 211)
27. Sir Richard Fanshawe (p. 90), Dr P. [Walter Pope?] (p. 93), Tom Brown (p. 139), Richard Porson (p. 208), G. M. and G. F. Whicher (p. 250)
28. Thomas Creech (p. 131)
31. John Oldham (p. 123), Ezra Pound (p. 253)
34. K. W. Gransden (p. 282)
35. George Howard, Viscount Morpeth (later sixth Earl of Carlisle) (p. 215)
37. Charles Tomlinson (p. 293)
38. Samuel Boyse (p. 171), William Cowper (p. 203), Gerard M. Hopkins (p. 246).

Book II
3. Anon. early 17th c. (p. 77), Sir Thomas Hawkins (p. 87), Philip Francis (p. 172), David Ferry (p. 272)
4. Richard Duke (p. 128), Christopher Smart (pp. 190, 196)
6. John Cam Hobhouse (p. 222)
7. Robert Lowell (p. 262), David Ferry (p. 273)
8. Sir Charles Sedley (p. 119)
9. John Conington (p. 237)
10. Earl of Surrey (p. 67), Anon. 16th c. (pp. 68, 69), Sir Philip Sidney (p. 73), William Cowper (p. 204)
11. Tom Brown (p. 141), John Conington (p. 238), James Michie (p. 284)
12. Leigh Hunt (p. 221)
13. Richard Crashaw (p. 95)
14. Robert Herrick (p. 82), John Oldham (p. 124), Christopher Smart (p. 197), Lord Lytton (p. 226), Basil Bunting (p. 255), C. H. Sisson (p. 257)

15. Oliver Goldsmith (p. 202), C. H. Sisson (p. 258), James Michie (p. 285)
16. John Ashmore (p. 85), Thomas Otway (p. 121), William Cowper (p. 205), Sir Stephen de Vere (p. 230)
17. Susanna Rowson (p. 210)
18. Christopher Smart (p. 198)
20. Charles Tomlinson (p. 294)

Book III

1. Sir Richard Fanshawe (p. 91), Abraham Cowley (p. 100), Gerard M. Hopkins (p. 246)
2. Richard Bentley (p. 136), Jonathan Swift (p. 142)
3. Joseph Addison (p. 145), Lord Byron (p. 223)
4. Arthur Hugh Clough (p. 237), James Michie (p. 286)
5. James Thomson (p. 170), Philip Francis (p. 173), David Ferry (p. 274)
6. Earl of Roscommon (p. 116), William Oldisworth (p. 151), David Ferry (p. 276)
7. George Stepney (p. 137), Arthur Hugh Clough (p. 236), Austin Dobson (p. 243)
9. Giangiorgio Trissino (Coda, p. 479), Anon. early 17th c. (p. 74), Ben Jonson (p. 75), Robert Herrick (p. 81), John Oldham (p. 127), Rudyard Kipling (p. 251)
10. James Michie (p. 289)
12. John Conington (p. 239)
13. Thomas Warton (p. 200), William Wordsworth (p. 214), Christopher Middleton (p. 283)
15. William Dunkin (p. 187)
16. Abraham Cowley (p. 102)
18. Thomas Creech (p. 132), Thomas Warton (p. 201)
22. David Ferry (p. 278)
23. Thomas Creech (p. 133)
25. Philip Francis (p. 175), Novalis (Introduction, pp. 35–7)
26. William Dunkin (p. 187)
29. Sir John Beaumont, (p. 78) John Dryden (p. 110), Philip Francis (p. 176)

30. William Oldisworth (p. 153), Christopher Smart (p. 192), Alexander Pushkin/Vladimir Nabokov (p. 224), W. E. Gladstone (p. 229), Ezra Pound (p. 254)

Book IV
1. Ben Jonson (p. 76), Alexander Pope (p. 159)
2. Abraham Cowley (p. 104), Philip Francis (p. 179)
3. Francis Atterbury (p. 134), David Ferry (p. 279)
5. Philip Francis (p. 181)
7. Anon. 16th c. (p. 71), Sir Richard Fanshawe (p. 92), Samuel Johnson (p. 189), A. E. Housman (p. 248)
9. William Somerville (p. 150), Alexander Pope (p. 161), Philip Francis (p. 183)
10. Sir Edward Sherburne (p. 98), Philip Francis (p. 186)
11. David Ferry (p. 280)
13. Christopher Smart (p. 199), David Ferry (p. 281)

Carmen Saeculare

C. H. Sisson (p. 259), James Michie (p. 290)

Epodes

2. Ben Jonson (p. 299), Sir John Beaumont (p. 301), Sir Richard Fanshawe (p. 303), John Dryden (p. 307), C. H. Sisson (p. 312)
13. Thomas Creech (p. 306)
15. Thomas Yalden (p. 310)

Satires

Book I
1. Abraham Cowley (p. 326), Francis Howes (p. 368)
4. Francis Howes (p. 373)
5. William Cowper (p. 363)

6. Philip Francis (p. 359)
9. John Oldham (p. 336), Francis Howes (p. 380)
10. Earl of Rochester (p. 333), Francis Howes (p. 384)

Book II
1. Ben Jonson (p. 317), Alexander Pope (p. 349)
2. Thomas Creech (p. 342)
3. Francis Howes (p. 388)
5. George Ogle (p. 354)
6. Sir John Beaumont (p. 321), Abraham Cowley (p. 329), Jonathan Swift and Alexander Pope (p. 342)

Epistles

Book I
1. Alexander Pope (p. 399), John Conington (p. 443)
2. Francis Howes (p. 442)
4. K. W. Gransden (p. 450)
5. Philip Francis (p. 434), Colin Macleod (p. 455)
6. Thomas Creech (p. 396), Alexander Pope (p. 404)
10. Abraham Cowley (p. 393), Anon., 18th c. (p. 437)
16. John Milton (p. 393), Robert Pinsky (p. 451)
19. John Conington (p. 448)
20. Philip Francis (p. 435), M. G. Lewis (p. 440)

Book II
1. Alexander Pope, Colin Macleod *en face* (p. 410)
3. (*Ars Poetica*) A composite version by Ben Jonson, Earl of Roscommon, John Oldham, Thomas Creech, Philip Francis, Francis Howes, Lord Byron, John Conington, Roy Campbell and C. H. Sisson (p. 456)

INDEX OF TRANSLATORS

Adams, John Quincy: Ode I.22, 212–14
Addison, Joseph: Ode III.3, 145–9
Anon.: Epistle I.10, 437–9; Ode II.3, 77–8; Ode II.10, 68–9, 69–71; Ode III.9, 74–5; Ode IV.7, 71–2
Ashmore, John: Ode II.16, 85–6
Atterbury, Francis: Ode IV.3, 134–5

Beaumont, Sir John: Epode 2, 301–3; Ode III.29, 78–80; Satire II.6, 321–6
Behn, Aphra: Ode I.5, 120–21
Bentley, Richard: Ode III.2, 136–7
Berkeley, George: 'Verses ... on the Prospect of Planting Arts and Learning in America', 524
Boyse, Samuel: Ode I.38, 171
Brontë, Patrick Branwell: Ode I.16, 232–3; Ode I.21, 233
Brown, Tom: Ode I.27, 139–40; Ode II.11, 141–2
Bulwer-Lytton, Edward George Earle Lytton, Baron Lytton: Ode II.14, 226–7
Bunting, Basil: Ode II.14, 255
Byron, George Gordon Noel, Baron: *Ars Poetica* (composite translation), 468–71; Ode III.3, 223–4

Calverley, C.S.: Ode I.9, 240; Ode I.11, 241; Ode I.24, 241–2
Campbell, Roy: *Ars Poetica* (composite translation), 473–5
Campion, Thomas: 'The man of life upright' 481
Carew, Thomas: 'The Spring', 484
Cavafy, Constantine: 'Horace in Athens', 532
Cherbury, Edward, Lord Herbert of: *see* Herbert of Cherbury, Edward Herbert, Lord
Clough, Arthur Hugh; Ode I.3, 234–5; Ode III.4, 237; Ode III.7, 236
Congreve, William: Ode I.19, 144
Conington, John: *Ars Poetica* (composite translation), 471–3; Epistle I.1, 443–7; Epistle I.19, 448–9; Ode II.9, 238–9; Ode II.11, 238–9; Ode III.12, 239
Cowley, Abraham: Epistle I.10, 393–6; Ode I.5, 99–100; Ode III.1, 100–102; Ode III.16, 102–4; Ode IV.2, 104–6; Satire I.1, 326–9; Satire II.6, 329–32
Cowper William: 'An Epistle to Joseph Hill, Esq.', 527–8; Ode I.9, 203; Ode I.38, 203; Ode II.10, 204–5, Ode II.16, 205–7; Satire I.5, 363–7
Crashaw, Richard: Ode II.13, 95–6

Creech, Thomas: *Ars Poetica* (composite translation), 461–3; Epistle I.6, 396–8; Epode 13, 306–7; Ode I.17, 129–31; Ode I.28, 131–2; Ode III.18, 132–3; Ode III.23, 133–4; Satire II.2, 340–42

Cunningham, J.V.: Ode I.9, 256–7

Davie, Donald: 'Wombwell on Strike', 543–4

de Vere, Sir Stephen: Ode II.16, 230–32

Dillon, Wentworth, Earl of Roscommon: *Ars Poetica* (composite translation), 457–8; Ode I.22, 114–15, 115–16; Ode III.6, 116–18

Dobson, Austin: Ode I.23, 243; Ode III.7, 243–5

Dryden, John: Epode 2, 307–10; Ode I.3, 107–8; Ode I.9, 109–10; Ode III.29, 110–14

Duke, Richard: Ode II.4, 128–9

Dunkin, William: Ode III.15, 187; Ode III.26, 187–8

Fanshawe, Sir Richard: Epode 2, 303–5; Ode I.5, 89–90; Ode I.27, 90–91, Ode III.1, 91–2; Ode IV.7, 92–3; 'An Ode upon occasion of His Majesties Proclamation . . .', 488–92

Fergusson, Robert: Ode I.11, 207–8

Ferry, David: Ode I.1, 266–7; Ode I.4, 267–8; Ode I.10, 268–9; Ode I.11, 269–70; Ode I.15, 270–71; Ode II.3, 272–3; Ode II.7, 273–4; Ode III.5, 274–6; Ode III.6, 276–8; Ode III.22, 278; Ode IV.3, 279–80; Ode IV.11, 280–81; Ode IV.13, 281–2

Francis, Philip: *Ars Poetica* (composite translation), 464–5; Epistle I.5, 434–5; Epistle I.20, 435–6; Ode II.3, 172–3; Ode III.5, 173–5; Ode III.25, 175–6; Ode III.29, 176–9; Ode IV.2, 179–81; Ode IV.5, 181–3; Ode IV.9, 183–6; Ode IV.10, 186; Satire I.6, 359–63

Frost, Robert: 'The Lesson for Today', 536–41

Gladstone, W.E.: Ode I.14, 228–9; Ode III.30, 229–30

Goldsmith, Oliver: Ode II.15, 202

Gransden, K.W.: Epistle I.4, 450; Ode I.34, 282

Hamilton, William, of Gilbertfield: *see under* Ramsay, Allan

Hardenberg, Friedrich von [Novalis]: Ode III.25, 36

Hawkins, Sir Thomas: Ode I.11, 87; Ode II.3, 87–8

Hecht, Anthony: Ode I.1, 263–4

Herbert of Cherbury, Edward Herbert, Lord: 'To his friend Ben. Johnson . . .', 483

Herington, John: Ode I.11, 265

Herrick, Robert: Ode II.14, 82–4; Ode III.9, 81–2

Hils, G.: *see* Sarbiewski, Casimire

Hobhouse, John Cam, Baron Broughton: Ode II.6, 222–3

Hopkins, Gerard M.: Ode I.38, 246; Ode III.1, 246–8

Housman, A.E.: Ode IV.7, 248–9

Howard, George, Viscount Morpeth: Ode I.35, 215–17

Howard, Henry, Earl of Surrey: Ode II.10, 67–8

INDEX OF TRANSLATORS

Howes, Francis: *Ars Poetica* (composite translation), 465–8; Epistle I.2, 442–3; Satire I.1, 368–73; Satire I.4, 373–80; Satire I.9, 381–4; Satire I.10, 384–8; Satire II.3, 388–9
Hunt, Leigh: Ode II.12, 221–2

Johnson, Samuel: Ode I.22, 188–9; Ode IV.7, 189–90
Jonson, Ben: *Ars Poetica* (composite translation), 456–7; Epode 2, 299–301; Ode III.9, 75–6; Ode IV.1, 76–7; Satire II.1, 317–21

Kipling, Rudyard: 'Horace, Bk V, Ode 3', 533–4; 'Horace, Ode 17, Bk V, 534–5; 'Horace, Ode 31, Bk V', 535–6; Ode III.9, 251–2

Lewis, M.G. ('Monk'): Epistle I.20, 440–41
Lovelace, Richard: 'Advice to my best Brother', 493–5
Lowell, Robert: Ode II.7, 262–3

Macleod, Colin: Epistle I.5, 455–6; Epistle II.1, 411–33 (rectos)
Marvell, Andrew: 'An Horatian Ode upon Cromwel's Return from Ireland', 496–9
Michie, James: *Carmen Saeculare*, 290–93; Ode I.20, 284; Ode II.11, 284–5; Ode II.15, 285–6; Ode III.4, 286–9; Ode III.10, 289–90
Middleton, Christopher: Ode III.13, 283
Milton, John: Epistle I.16, 393; Ode I.5, 88–9; 'Sonnet 20', 487; 'Sonnet 21', 488

Montagu, Lady Mary Wortley: Ode I.4, 165–6; Ode I.5, 166–7
Moore, Thomas: Ode I.22, 219–20
Morpeth, George Howard, Viscount: *see* Howard, George, Viscount Morpeth

Nabokov, Vladimir: *see* Pushkin, Alexander
Novalis: *see* Hardenberg, Friedrich von

Ogle, George: Satire II.5, 354–9
Oldham, John: *Ars Poetica* (composite translation), 458–61; Ode I.31, 123–4; Ode II.14, 124–6; Ode III.9, 127–8; Satire I.9, 337–40
Oldisworth, William: Ode III.6, 151–3; Ode III.30, 153
Otway, Thomas: Ode II.16, 121–3

P., Dr: Ode I.27, 93–4
Pessoa, Fernando: *see* Reis, Ricardo
Pinsky, Robert: Epistle I.16, 451–4
Pitt, Christopher: 'Invitation . . . to a Friend at Court', 525–6; Ode I.22, 168–70
Pope, Alexander: 'Epistle I To Richard Temple . . .', 523; Epistle I.1, 399–404; Epistle I.6, 404–8; 'Epistle II to a Lady', 514–23; Epistle II.1, 410–32 (versos); Ode IV.1, 159–60; Ode IV.9, 161; Satire II.1, 349–53; *see also under* Swift, Jonathan
Porson, Richard: Ode I.27, 208–9
Pound, Ezra: Ode I.11, 252–3; Ode I.31, 253; Ode III.30, 254
Prior, Matthew: 'A Better Answer', 513–14

INDEX OF TRANSLATORS

Pushkin, Alexander: (and Vladimir Nabokov) Ode III.30, 224–5

Ramsay, Allan: Ode I.1, 154–6; Ode I.4, 157–9; Ode I.5, 158; (and William Hamilton of Gilbertfield) 'An Exchange of Verse Epistles', 504–12
Reis, Ricardo (Fernando Pessoa): 'Already on my head', 542; 'To be great', 541–2
Rochester, John Wilmot, Earl of: see Wilmot, John, Earl of Rochester
Roscommon, Wentworth Dillon, Earl of: see Dillon, Wentworth, Earl of Roscommon
Rowson, Susanna: Ode II.17, 210–11

Sarbiewski, Casimire: (and G. Hils) 'A Palinode to the second Ode . . .', 485–6; see also under Vaughan, Henry
Sedley, Sir Charles: Ode II.8, 119–20
Sherburne, Sir Edward: Ode I.9, 97–8, Ode IV.10, 98
Sidney, Sir Philip: Ode II.10, 72–3
Sisson, C.H.: *Ars Poetica* (composite translation), 475–6; *Carmen Saeculare*, 259–62; Epode 2, 312–14; Ode II.14, 257–8; Ode II.15, 258–9
Smart, Christopher: Ode I.3, 193–4; Ode I.5, 194–5; Ode I.8, 195–6; Ode II.4, 190–92, 196–7; Ode II.14, 197–8; Ode II.18, 198–9; Ode III.30, 192–3; Ode IV.13, 199–200

Smith, James and Horatio: Ode I.9, 217–18
Somerville, William: Ode IV.9, 150
Stepney, George: Ode III.7, 137–9
Surrey, Henry Howard, Earl of: see Howard, Henry, Earl of Surrey
Swift, Jonathan: Ode III.2, 142; (and Alexander Pope) Satire II.6, 342–8

Tennyson, Alfred Lord: Ode I.9, 227–8; 'To the Rev. F. D. Maurice', 530–32
Thomson, James: Ode III.5, 170
Tickell, Thomas: Ode I.15, 162–5
Tomlinson, Charles: Ode I.37, 293–4; Ode II.20, 294–5
Trissino, Giangiorgio: Ode III.9, 479–80

Vaughan, Henry: 'The Praise of a Religious Life . . .', 500–503; 'To my worthy friend Master T. Lewes', 503–4

Warton, Thomas: Ode III.13, 200–201; Ode III.18, 201
Whicher, G.M. and G.F.: Ode I.27, 250
Wilmot, John, Earl of Rochester: Satire I.10, 333–6
Wordsworth, William: Ode III.13, 214–15; 'To M.H.', 529
Wotton, Sir Henry: 'The Character of a Happy Life', 482–3

Yalden, Thomas: Epode 15, 310–12
Young Gentlemen of Mr Rule's Academy at Islington: Ode I.25, 211–12